SUZANNE BROCKMANN

TALL, DARK AND FEARLESS

H
HQN™

ISBN-13: 978-0-373-77517-0

TALL, DARK AND FEARLESS

Copyright © 2010 by Harlequin Books S.A.

Recycling programs
for this product may
not exist in your area.

The publisher acknowledges the copyright holder
of the individual works as follows:

FRISCO'S KID
Copyright © 1996 by Suzanne Brockmann

EVERYDAY, AVERAGE JONES
Copyright © 1998 by Suzanne Brockmann

This edition published by arrangement with Harlequin Books S.A.

For questions and comments about the quality of this book
please contact us at Customer_eCare@Harlequin.ca.

® and TM are trademarks of the publisher. Trademarks indicated with
® are registered in the United States Patent and Trademark Office, the
Canadian Trade Marks Office and in other countries.

www.HQNBooks.com

Printed in U.S.A.

CONTENTS

FRISCO'S KID

For my cousin, Elise Kramer,
who played with and loved my mother,
then me and now my children, too,
as if we were her own kids.

With all my love, Elise, this one's for you.

CHAPTER ONE

FRISCO'S KNEE WAS on fire.

He had to lean heavily on his cane to get from the shower to the room he shared with three other vets, and still his leg hurt like hell with every step he took.

But pain was no big deal. Pain had been part of Navy Lt. Alan "Frisco" Francisco's everyday life since his leg had damn near been blown off more than five years ago during a covert rescue operation. The pain he could handle.

It was this cane that he couldn't stand.

It was the fact that his knee wouldn't—couldn't— support his full weight or fully extend that made him crazy.

It was a warm California day, so he pulled on a pair of shorts, well aware that they wouldn't hide the raw, ugly scars on his knee.

His latest surgery had been attempted only a few months ago. They'd cut him open all over again, trying, like Humpty Dumpty, to put all the pieces back together. After the required hospital stay, he'd been sent here, to this physical therapy center, to build up strength in his leg, and to see if the operation had worked—to see if he had more flexibility in his injured joint.

But his doctor had been no more successful than the legendary King's horses and King's men. The operation hadn't improved Frisco's knee. His doctor couldn't put Frisco together again.

There was a knock on the door, and it opened a crack.

"Yo, Frisco, you in here?"

It was Lt. Joe Catalanotto, the commander of SEAL Team Ten's Alpha Squad—the squad to which, an aeon of pain and frustration and crushed hopes ago, Frisco had once belonged.

"Where else would I be?" Frisco said.

He saw Joe react to his bitter words, saw the bigger man's jaw tighten as he came into the room, closing the door behind him. He could see the look in Joe's dark eyes—a look of wary reserve. Frisco had always been the optimist of Alpha Squad. His attitude had always been upbeat and friendly. Wherever they went, Frisco had been out in the street, making friends with the locals. He'd been the first one smiling, the man who'd make jokes before a high-altitude parachute jump, relieving the tension, making everyone laugh.

But Frisco wasn't laughing now. He'd stopped laughing five years ago, when the doctors had walked into his hospital room and told him his leg would never be the same. He'd never walk again.

At first he'd approached it with the same upbeat, optimistic attitude he'd always had. *He'd* never walk again? Wanna make a bet? He was going to do more than walk again. He was going to bring himself back to active duty as a SEAL. He was going to run and jump and dive. No question.

It had taken years of intense focus, operations and physical therapy. He'd been bounced back and forth from hospitals to physical therapy centers to hospitals and back again. He'd fought long and hard, and he *could* walk again.

But he couldn't run. He could do little more than limp along with his cane—and his doctors warned him against doing too much of that. His knee couldn't support his weight, they told him. The pain that he stoically ignored was a warning signal. If he wasn't careful, he'd lose what little use he did have of his leg.

And that wasn't good enough.

Because until he could run, he couldn't be a SEAL again.

Five years of disappointment and frustration and failure had worn at Frisco's optimism and upbeat attitude. Five years of itching to return to the excitement of his life as a Navy SEAL; of being placed into temporary retirement with no real, honest hope of being put back into active duty; of watching as Alpha Squad replaced him—*replaced* him; of shuffling along when he *burned* to run. All those years had worn him down. He wasn't upbeat anymore. He was depressed. And frustrated. And angry as hell.

Joe Catalanotto didn't bother to answer Frisco's question. His hawklike gaze took in Frisco's well-muscled body, lingering for a moment on the scars on his leg. "You look good," Joe said. "You're keeping in shape. That's good. That's real good."

"Is this a social call?" Frisco asked bluntly.

"Partly," Joe said. His rugged face relaxed into a smile. "I've got some good news I wanted to share with you."

Good news. Damn, when was the last time Frisco had gotten *good* news?

One of Frisco's roommates, stretched out on his bed, glanced up from the book he was reading.

Joe didn't seem to mind. His smile just got broader.

"Ronnie's pregnant," he said. "We're going to have a kid."

"No way." Frisco couldn't help smiling. It felt odd, unnatural. It had been too long since he'd used those muscles in his face. Five years ago, he'd have been pounding Joe on the back, cracking ribald jokes about masculinity and procreation and laughing like a damn fool. But now the best he could muster up was a smile. He held out his hand and clasped Joe's in a handshake of congratulations. "I'll be damned. Who would've ever thought *you'd* become a family man? Are you terrified?"

Joe grinned. "I'm actually okay about it. Ronnie's the one who's scared to death. She's reading every book she can get her hands on about pregnancy and babies. I think the books are scaring her even more."

"God, a *kid,*" Frisco said again. "You going to call him Joe Cat, Junior?"

"I want a girl," Joe admitted. His smile softened. "A redhead, like her mother."

"So what's the other part?" Frisco asked. At Joe's blank look, he added, "You said this was partly a social call. That means it's also partly something else. Why else are you here?"

"Oh. Yeah. Steve Horowitz called me and asked me to come sit in while he talked to you."

Frisco slipped on a T-shirt, instantly wary. Steve Horowitz was his doctor. Why would his doctor want *Joe* around when he talked to Frisco? "What about?"

Joe wouldn't say, but his smile faded. "There's an officer's lounge at the end of the hall," he said. "Steve said he'd meet us there."

A talk in the officer's lounge. This was even more serious than Frisco had guessed. "All right," he said evenly. It was pointless to pressure Joe. Frisco knew his former commander wouldn't tell him a thing until Steve showed up.

"How's the knee?" Joe asked as they headed down the corridor. He purposely kept his pace slow and easy so that Frisco could keep up.

Frisco felt a familiar surge of frustration. He hated the fact that he couldn't move quickly. Damn, he used to break the sprint records during physical training.

"It's feeling better today," he lied. Every step he took hurt like hell. The really stupid thing was that Joe knew damn well how much pain he was in.

He pushed open the door to the officer's lounge. It was a pleasant enough room, with big, overstuffed furniture and a huge picture window overlooking the gardens. The carpet was a slightly lighter shade of blue than the sky, and the green of the furniture upholstery matched the abundant life growing outside the window. The colors surprised him. Most of the time Frisco had spent in here was late at night, when he couldn't sleep. In the shadowy darkness, the walls and furniture had looked gray.

Steven Horowitz came into the room, a step behind them. "Good," he said in his brisk, efficient manner. "Good, you're here." He nodded to Joe. "Thank you, Lieutenant, for coming by. I know your schedule's heavy, too."

"Not too heavy for this, Captain," Joe said evenly.

"What exactly is 'this'?" Frisco asked. He hadn't felt this uneasy since he'd last gone out on a sneak-and-peek—an information-gathering expedition behind enemy lines.

The doctor gestured to the couch. "Why don't we sit down?"

"I'll stand, thanks." Frisco had sat long enough during those first few years after he'd been injured. He'd spent far too much time in a wheelchair. If he had his choice, he'd never sit again.

Joe made himself comfortable on the couch, his long legs sprawled out in front of him. The doctor perched on the edge of an armchair, his body language announcing that he wasn't intending to stay long.

"You're not going to be happy about this," Horowitz said bluntly to Frisco, "but yesterday I signed papers releasing you from this facility."

Frisco couldn't believe what he was hearing. "You did *what?*"

"You're out of here," the doctor said, not unkindly. "As of fourteen hundred hours today."

Frisco looked from the doctor to Joe and back. Joe's eyes were dark with unhappiness, but he didn't contradict the doctor's words. "But my physical therapy sessions—"

"Have ended," Horowitz said. "You've regained sufficient use of your knee and—"

"Sufficient for *what?*" Frisco asked, outraged. "For hobbling around? That's not good enough, dammit! I need to be able to run. I need to be able to—"

Joe sat up. "Steve told me he's been watching your chart for weeks," the commander of Alpha Squad told Frisco quietly. "Apparently, there's been no improvement—"

"So I'm in a temporary slump. It happens in this kind of—"

"Your therapist has expressed concern that you're overdoing it." Horowitz interrupted him. "You're pushing yourself too hard."

"Cut the crap." Frisco's knuckles were white as he gripped his cane. "My time is up. That's what this is about, isn't it?" He looked back at Joe. "Someone upstairs decided that I've had my share of the benefits. Someone upstairs wants my bed emptied, so that it can be filled by some other poor son of a bitch who has no real hope of a full recovery, right?"

"Yeah, they want your bed," Joe said, nodding. "That's certainly part of it. There's limited bed space in every VA facility. You know that."

"Your progress has begun to decline," the doctor added. "I've told you this before, but you haven't seemed to catch on. Pain is a signal from your body to your brain telling you that something is wrong. When your knee hurts, that does *not* mean push harder. It means back off. Sit down. Give yourself a break. If you keep abusing yourself this way, Lieutenant, you'll be back in a wheelchair by August."

"I'll *never* be back in a wheelchair. Sir." Frisco said the word *sir,* but his tone and attitude said an entirely different, far-less-flattering word.

"If you don't want to spend the rest of your life sitting down, then you better stop punishing a severely injured joint," Dr. Horowitz snapped. He sighed, taking a deep breath and lowering his voice again. "Look, Alan, I don't want to fight with you. Why can't you just be grateful for the fact that you can stand? You can *walk*. Sure, it's with a cane, but—"

"I'm going to run," Frisco said. "I'm not going to give up until I can run."

"You can't run," Steven Horowitz said bluntly. "Your knee won't support your weight—it won't even properly extend. The best you'll manage is an awkward hop."

"Then I need another operation."

"What you need is to get on with your life."

"My life requires an ability to run," Frisco said hotly. "I don't know too many active-duty SEALs hobbling around with a cane. Do you?"

Dr. Horowitz shook his head, looking to Joe for help. But Joe didn't say a word.

"You've been in and out of hospitals and PT centers for five years," the doctor told Frisco. "You're not a kid in your twenties anymore, Alan. The truth is, the SEALs don't need you. They've got kids coming up from BUD/S training who could run circles around you even if you *could* run. Do you really think the top brass are going to want some old guy with a bum knee to come back?"

Frisco carefully kept his face expressionless. "Thanks a lot, man," he said tightly as he gazed sightlessly out of the window. "I appreciate your vote of confidence."

Joe shifted in his seat. "What Steve's saying is harsh—and not entirely true," he said. "Us 'old guys' in our thirties have experience that the new kids lack, and that usually makes us better SEALs. But he's right about something—you *have* been out of the picture for half a decade. You've got more to overcome than the physical challenge—as if that weren't enough. You've got to catch up with the technology, relearn changed policies…"

"Give yourself a break," Dr. Horowitz urged again.

Frisco turned his head and looked directly at the doctor. "No," he said. He looked at Joe, too. "No breaks. Not until I can walk without this cane. Not until I can run a six-minute mile again."

The doctor rolled his eyes in exasperation, standing up and starting for the door. "A six-minute mile? Forget it. It's *not* going to happen."

Frisco looked out the window again. "Captain, you also said I'd never walk again."

Horowitz turned back. "This is *different*, Lieutenant. The truth—whether you believe it or not—is that the kind of physical exertion you've been up to is now doing your knee more damage than good."

Frisco didn't turn around. He stood silently, watching bright pink flowers move gently in the breeze.

"There are other things you can do as a SEAL," the doctor said more gently. "There are office jobs—"

Frisco spun around, his temper exploding. "I'm an expert in ten different fields of warfare, and you want me to be some kind of damn pencil pusher?"

"Alan—"

Joe stood up. "You've at least got to take some time and think about your options," he said. "Don't say no until you think it through."

Frisco gazed at Joe in barely disguised horror. Five years ago they'd joked about getting injured and being sucked into the administrative staff. It was a fate worse than death, or so they'd agreed. "You want me to think about jockeying a desk?" he said.

"You could teach."

Frisco shook his head in disbelief. "That's just perfect, man. Can't you just see me writing on a blackboard…?" He shook his head in disgust. "I would've expected *you* of all people to understand why I could never do that."

"You'd still be a SEAL," Joe persisted. "It's that or accept your retirement as permanent. *Some*one's got to teach these new kids how to survive. Why can't you do it?"

"Because I've been in the middle of action," Frisco nearly shouted. "I know what it's like. I want to go back there, I want to *be* there. I want to be *doing,* not…teaching. *Damn!*"

"The Navy doesn't want to lose you," Joe said, his voice low and intense. "It's been five years, and there's *still* been nobody in the units who can touch you when it comes to strategic warfare. Sure, you can quit. You can spend the rest of your life trying to get back what you once had. You can lock yourself away and feel sorry for yourself. Or you can help pass your knowledge on to the next generation of SEALs."

"Quit?" Frisco said. He laughed, but there was no humor in it at all. "I can't quit—because I've already been kicked out. Right, Captain Horowitz? As of fourteen hundred hours, I'm outta here."

There was silence then—silence that settled around them all, heavy and still and thick.

"I'm sorry," the doctor finally said. "I've got to do what is best for you and for this facility. We need to use your bed for someone who really could use it. You need to give your knee a rest before you damage it further. The obvious solution was to send you home. Someday you'll thank me for this." The door clicked as it closed behind him.

Frisco looked at Joe. "You can tell the Navy that I'm not going to accept anything short of active duty," he said bluntly. "I'm not going to teach."

There was compassion and regret in the bigger man's dark eyes. "I'm sorry," Joe said quietly.

Frisco glared up at the clock that was set into the wall. It was nearly noon. Two more hours, and he'd have to pack up his things and leave. Two more hours, and he wouldn't be a Navy SEAL, temporarily off the active duty list, recovering from a serious injury. In two hours he'd be *former* Navy SEAL Lt. Alan Francisco. In two hours, he'd be a civilian, with nowhere to go, nothing to do.

Anger hit him hard in the gut. Five years ago, it was a sensation he'd rarely felt. He'd been calm, he'd been cool. But nowadays, he rarely felt anything besides anger.

But wait. He *did* have somewhere to go. The anger eased up a bit. Frisco had kept up the payments on his little condo in San Felipe, the low-rent town outside of the naval base. But…once he arrived in San Felipe, then what? He would, indeed, have nothing to do.

Nothing to do was worse than nowhere to go. What *was* he going to do? Sit around all day, watching TV and collecting disability checks? The anger was back, this time lodging in his throat, choking him.

"I can't afford to continue the kind of physical therapy I've been doing here at the hospital," Frisco said, trying to keep his desperation from sounding in his voice.

"Maybe you should listen to Steve," Joe said, "and give your leg a rest."

Easy for Joe to say. Joe was going to stand up and walk out of this hospital without a cane, without a limp, without his entire life shattered. Joe was going to go back to the home he shared with his beautiful wife—who was pregnant with their first child. He was going to have dinner with Veronica, and later he'd probably make love to her and fall asleep with her in his arms. And in the morning, Joe was going to get up, go for a run, shower, shave and get dressed, and go into work as the commanding officer of SEAL Team Ten's Alpha Squad.

Joe had everything.

Frisco had an empty condo in a bad part of town.

"Congratulations about the baby, man," Frisco said, trying as hard as he could to actually mean it. Then he limped out of the room.

CHAPTER TWO

THERE WAS A LIGHT on in condo 2C.

Mia Summerton stopped in the parking lot, her arms straining from the weight of her grocery bags, and looked up at the window of the second-floor condo that was next to her own. Apartment 2C had remained empty and dark for so many years, Mia had started to believe that its owner would never come home.

But that owner—whoever he was—was home tonight.

Mia knew that the owner of 2C was, indeed, a "he." She got a better grip on the handles of her cloth bags and started for the outside cement stairs that led up to the second story and her own condo. His name was Lt. Alan Francisco, U.S.N., Ret. She'd seen his name in the condo association owner's directory, and on the scattered pieces of junk mail that made it past the post office's forwarding system.

As far as Mia could figure out, her closest neighbor was a retired naval officer. With no more than his name and rank to go on, she had left the rest to her imagination. He was probably an older man, maybe even elderly. He had possibly served during the Second World War. Or perhaps he'd seen action in Korea or Vietnam.

Whatever the case, Mia was eager to meet him. Next September, her tenth graders were going to be studying American history, from the stock market crash through to the end of the Vietnam conflict. With any luck, Lt. Alan

Francisco, U.S.N., Ret., would be willing to come in and talk to her class, tell his story, bring the war he'd served in down to a personal level.

And that was the problem with studying war. Until it could be understood on a personal level, it couldn't be understood at all.

Mia unlocked her own condo and carried her groceries inside, closing the door behind her with her foot. She quickly put the food away and stored her cloth grocery bags in the tiny broom closet. She glanced at herself in the mirror and adjusted and straightened the high ponytail that held her long, dark hair off her neck.

Then she went back outside, onto the open-air corridor that connected all of the second-floor units in the complex.

The figures on the door, 2C, were slightly rusted, but they still managed to reflect the floodlights from the courtyard, even through the screen. Not allowing herself time to feel nervous or shy, Mia pressed the doorbell.

She heard the buzzer inside of the apartment. The living room curtains were open and the light was on inside, so she peeked in.

Architecturally, it was the mirror image of her own unit. A small living room connected to a tiny dining area, which turned a corner and connected to a galley kitchen. Another short hallway led back from the living room to two small bedrooms and a bath. It was exactly the same as her place, except the layout of the rooms faced the opposite direction.

His furniture was an exact opposite of Mia's, too. Mia had decorated her living room with bamboo and airy, light colors. Lieutenant Francisco's was filled with faintly shabby-looking mismatched pieces of dark furniture. His couch was a dark green plaid, and the slipcovers were fraying badly. His carpeting was the same forest green that Mia's had been when she'd first moved in, three years ago. She'd replaced hers immediately.

Mia rang the bell again. Still no answer. She opened the screen and knocked loudly on the door, thinking if Lieutenant Francisco *was* an elderly man, he might be hard of hearing....

"Looking for someone in particular?"

Mia spun around, startled, and the screen door banged shut, but there was no one behind her.

"I'm down here."

The voice carried up from the courtyard, and sure enough, there was a man standing in the shadows. Mia moved to the railing.

"I'm looking for Lieutenant Francisco," she said.

He stepped forward, into the light. "Well, aren't you lucky? You found him."

Mia was staring. She knew she was staring, but she couldn't help herself.

Lt. Alan Francisco, U.S.N., Ret., was no elderly, little man. He was only slightly older than she was—in his early thirties at the most. He was young and tall and built like a tank. The sleeveless shirt he was wearing revealed muscular shoulders and arms, and did very little to cover his powerful-looking chest.

His hair was dark blond and cut short, in an almost boxlike military style. His jaw was square, too, his features rugged and harshly, commandingly handsome. Mia couldn't see what color his eyes were—only that they were intense, and that he examined her as carefully as she studied him.

He took another step forward, and Mia realized he limped and leaned heavily on a cane.

"Did you want something besides a look at me?" he asked.

His legs were still in the shadows, but his arms were in the light. And he had tattoos. One on each arm. An anchor on one arm, and something that looked like it might be a mermaid on the other. Mia pulled her gaze back to his face.

"I, um…" she said. "I just…wanted to say…hi. I'm Mia Summerton. We're next-door neighbors," she added lamely. Wow, she sounded like one of her teenage students—tongue-tied and shy.

It was more than his rugged good looks that was making her sound like a space cadet. It was because Lt. Alan Francisco was a career military man. Despite his lack of uniform, he was standing there in front of her, shoulders back, head held high—the Navy version of G.I. Joe. He was a warrior not by draft but by choice. He'd chosen to enlist. He'd chosen to perpetuate everything Mia's antiwar parents had taught her to believe was wrong.

He was still watching her as closely as she'd looked at him. "You were curious," he said. His voice was deep and accentless. He didn't speak particularly loudly, but his words carried up to her quite clearly.

Mia forced a smile. "Of course."

"Don't worry," he said. He didn't smile back. In fact, he hadn't smiled once since she'd turned to look over the railing at him. "I'm not loud. I don't throw wild parties. I won't disturb you. I'll stay out of your way and I hope you'll have the courtesy to do the same."

He nodded at her, just once, and Mia realized that she'd been dismissed. With a single nod, he'd just dismissed her as if she were one of his enlisted troops.

As Mia watched, the former Navy lieutenant headed

toward the stairs. He used his cane, supporting much of his weight with it. And every step he took looked to be filled with pain. Was he honestly going to climb those stairs…?

But of course he was. This condo complex wasn't equipped with elevators or escalators or anything that would provide second-floor accessibility to the physically challenged. And this man was clearly challenged.

But Lieutenant Francisco pulled himself up, one painful step at a time. He used the cast-iron railing and his upper-body strength to support his bad leg, virtually hopping up the stairs. Still, Mia could tell that each jarring movement caused him no little amount of pain. When he got to the top, he was breathing hard, and there was a sheen of sweat on his face.

Mia spoke from her heart as usual, not stopping to think first. "There's a condo for sale on the ground floor," she said. "Maybe the association office can arrange for you to exchange your unit for the…one on the…"

The look he gave her was withering. "You still here?" His voice was rough and his words rude. But as he looked up again, as for one brief moment he glanced into her eyes, Mia could see myriad emotions in his gaze. Anger. Despair. Shame. An incredible amount of shame.

Mia's heart was in her throat. "I'm sorry," she said, her gaze dropping almost involuntarily to his injured leg. "I didn't mean to—"

He moved directly underneath one of the corridor lights, and held up his right leg slightly. "Pretty, huh?" he said.

His knee was a virtual railroad switching track of scars. The joint itself looked swollen and sore. Mia swallowed. "What—" she said, then cleared her throat. "What… happened…?"

His eyes were an odd shade of blue, she realized, gazing up into the swirl of color. They were dark blue, almost black. And they were surrounded by the longest, thickest eyelashes she'd ever seen on a man.

Up close, even despite the shine of perspiration on his face, Mia had to believe that Lt. Alan Francisco was the single most attractive man she had ever seen in her entire twenty-seven years.

His hair was dark blond. Not average, dirty blond, but rather a shiny mixture of light brown with streaks and flashes of gold and even hints of red that gleamed in the light. His nose was big, but not too big for his face, and slightly crooked. His mouth was wide. Mia longed to see him smile. What a smile this man would have, with a generous mouth like that. There were laugh lines at the corners of his mouth and his eyes, but they were taut now with pain and anger.

"I was wounded," he said brusquely. "During a military op."

He had been drinking. He was close enough for Mia to smell whiskey on his breath. She moved back a step. "Military...op?"

"Operation," he said.

"That must have been...awful," she said. "But...I wasn't aware that the United States has been involved in any naval battles recently. I mean, someone like, oh, say...the *President* would let us all know if we were at war, wouldn't he?"

"I was wounded during a search-and-rescue counterterrorist operation in downtown Baghdad," Francisco said.

"Isn't Baghdad a little bit inland for a sailor?"

"I'm a Navy SEAL," he said. Then his lips twisted into a grim version of a smile. "*Was* a Navy SEAL," he corrected himself.

Frisco realized that she didn't know what he meant. She was looking up at him with puzzlement in her odd-colored eyes. They were a light shade of brown and green—hazel, he thought it was called—with a dark brown ring encircling the edges of her irises. Her eyes had a slightly exotic tilt to them, as if somewhere, perhaps back in her grandparents' generation, there was Asian or Polynesian blood. Hawaiian. That was it. She looked faintly Hawaiian. Her cheekbones were wide and high, adding to the exotic effect. Her nose was small and delicate, as were her graceful-looking lips. Her skin was smooth and clear and a delicious shade of tan. Her long, straight black hair was up in a ponytail, a light fringe of bangs softening her face. Her hair was so long that if she wore it down it would hang all the way to her hips.

His next-door neighbor was strikingly beautiful.

She was nearly an entire twelve inches shorter than he was, with a slender build. She was wearing a loose-fitting T-shirt and a pair of baggy shorts. Her shapely legs were that same light shade of brown and her feet were bare. Her figure was slight, almost boyish. Almost. Her breasts may have been small, but they swelled slightly beneath the cotton of her shirt in a way that was decidedly feminine.

At first glance, from the way she dressed and from her clean, fresh beauty, Frisco had thought she was a kid, a teenager. But up close, he could see faint lines of life on her face, along with a confidence and wisdom that no mere teenager could possibly exude. Despite her youthful appearance, this Mia Summerton was probably closer to his own age.

"Navy SEALs," he explained, still gazing into her remarkable hazel eyes, "are the U.S. military's most elite special operations group. We operate on sea, in the air and on land. SEa, Air, Land. SEAL."

"I get it," she said with a smile. "Very cute."

Her smile was crooked and made her look just a little bit goofy. Surely she knew that her smile marred her perfect beauty, but that didn't keep her from smiling. In fact, Frisco was willing to bet that, goofy or not, a smile was this woman's default expression. Still, her smile was uncertain, as if she wasn't quite sure he deserved to be smiled at. She was ill at ease—whether that was caused by his injury or his imposing height, he didn't know. She *was* wary of him, however.

"'Cute' isn't a word used often to describe a special operations unit."

"Special operations," Mia repeated. "Is that kind of like the Green Berets or the Commandos?"

"Kind of," Frisco told her, watching her eyes as he spoke. "Only, smarter and stronger and tougher. SEALs are qualified experts in a number of fields. We're all sharpshooters, we're all demolitions experts—both underwater and on land—we can fly or drive or sail any jet or plane or tank or boat. We all have expert status in using the latest military technology."

"It sounds to me as if you're an expert at making war." Mia's goofy smile had faded, taking with it much of the warmth in her eyes. "A professional soldier."

Frisco nodded. "Yeah, that's right." She didn't like soldiers. *That* was her deal. It was funny. Some women went for military men in a very major way. At the same time, others went out of their way to keep their distance. This Mia Summerton clearly fell into the second category.

"What do you do when there's no war to fight? Start one of your own?"

Her words were purposely antagonistic, and Frisco

felt himself bristle. He didn't have to defend himself or his former profession to this girl, no matter how pretty she was. He'd run into plenty of her type before. It was politically correct these days to be a pacifist, to support demilitarization, to support limiting funds for defense—without knowing the least little thing about the current world situation.

Not that Frisco had anything against pacifists. He truly believed in the power of negotiation and peace talks. But he followed the old adage: walk softly and carry a big stick. And the Navy SEALS were the biggest, toughest stick America could hope to carry.

And as for war, they were currently fighting a great big one—an ongoing war against terrorism.

"I don't need your crap." Frisco turned away as he used his cane to limp toward the door of his condo.

"Oh, my opinion is crap?" She moved in front of him, blocking his way. Her eyes flashed with green fire.

"What I *do* need is another drink," Frisco announced. "Badly. So if you don't mind moving out of my way…?"

Mia crossed her arms and didn't budge. "I'm sorry," she said. "I confess that my question *may* have sounded a bit hostile, but I don't believe that it was *crap*."

Frisco gazed at her steadily. "I'm not in the mood for an argument," he said. "You want to come in and have a drink—please. Be my guest. I'll even find an extra glass. You want to spend the night—even better. It's been a long time since I've shared my bed. But I have no intention of standing here arguing with you."

Mia flushed, but her gaze didn't drop. She didn't look away. "Intimidation is a powerful weapon, isn't it?" she said. "But I know what you're doing, so it won't work. I'm not intimidated, Lieutenant."

He stepped forward, moving well into her personal space, backing her up against the closed door. "How about now?" he asked. "Now are you intimidated?"

She wasn't. He could see it in her eyes. She *was* angrier, though.

"How typical," she said. "When psychological attack doesn't work, resort to the threat of physical violence." She smiled at him sweetly. "I'm calling your bluff, G.I. Joe. What are you going to do now?"

Frisco gazed down into Mia's oval-shaped face, out of ideas, although he'd never admit that to her. She was *supposed* to have turned and run away by now. But she hadn't. Instead, she was still here, glaring up at him, her nose mere inches from his own.

She smelled amazingly good. She was wearing perfume—something light and delicate, with the faintest hint of exotic spices.

Something had stirred within him when she'd first given him one of her funny smiles. It stirred again and he recognized the sensation. Desire. Man, it had been a long time....

"What if I'm not bluffing?" Frisco said, his voice no more than a whisper. He was standing close enough for his breath to move several wisps of her hair. "What if I really do want you to come inside? Spend the night?"

He saw a flash of uncertainty in her eyes. And then she stepped out of his way, moving deftly around his cane. "Sorry, *I'm* not in the mood for casual sex with a jerk," she retorted.

Frisco unlocked his door. He should have kissed her. She'd damn near dared him to. But it had seemed wrong. Kissing her would have been going too far. But, Lord, he'd wanted to....

He turned to look back at her before he went inside. "If you change your mind, just let me know."

Mia laughed and disappeared into her own apartment.

CHAPTER THREE

"YEAH?" FRISCO RASPED into the telephone. His mouth was dry and his head was pounding as if he'd been hit by a sledgehammer. His alarm clock read 9:36, and there was sunlight streaming in underneath the bedroom curtains. It was bright, cutting like a laser beam into his brain. He closed his eyes.

"Alan, is that you?"

Sharon. It was his sister, Sharon.

Frisco rolled over, searching for something, *any*thing with which to wet his impossibly dry mouth. There was a whiskey bottle on the bedside table with about a half an inch of amber liquid still inside. He reached for it, but stopped. No way was he going to take a slug of that. Hell, that was what his old man used to do. He'd start the day off with a shot—and end it sprawled, drunk, on the living room couch.

"I need your help," Sharon said. "I need a favor. The VA hospital said you were released and I just couldn't believe how lucky my timing was."

"How big a favor?" Frisco mumbled. She was asking for money. It wasn't the first time, and it wouldn't be the last. His older sister Sharon was as big a drunk as their father had been. She couldn't hold a job, couldn't pay her rent, couldn't support her five-year-old daughter, Natasha.

Frisco shook his head. He'd been there when Tasha

was born, brought into the world, the offspring of an
unknown father and an irresponsible mother. As much
as Frisco loved his sister, he knew damn well that Sharon
was irresponsible. She floated through life, drifting from
job to job, from town to town, from man to man. Having
a baby daughter hadn't rooted Sharon in any one place.

Five years ago, back when Natasha was born, back
before his leg had damn near been blown off, Frisco had
been an optimist. But even he hadn't been able to imagine much happiness in the baby's future. Unless Sharon
owned up to the fact that she had a drinking problem,
unless she got help, sought counseling and finally settled
down, he'd known that little Natasha's life would be filled
with chaos and disruption and endless change.

He'd been right about that.

For the past five years, Frisco had sent his sister money
every month, hoping to hell that she used it to pay her
rent, hoping Natasha had a roof over her head and food
to fill her stomach.

Sharon had visited him only occasionally while he
was in the VA hospital. She only came when she needed
money, and she never brought Natasha with her—the one
person in the world Frisco would truly have wanted to
see.

"This one's a major favor," Sharon said. Her voice
broke. "Look, I'm a couple of blocks away. I'm gonna
come over, okay? Meet me in the courtyard in about three
minutes. I broke my foot, and I'm on crutches. I can't
handle the stairs."

She hung up before giving Frisco a chance to answer.
Sharon broke her foot. Perfect. Why was it that people
with hard luck just kept getting more and more of the
same? Frisco rolled over, dropped the receiver back

onto the phone, grabbed his cane and staggered into the bathroom.

Three minutes. It wasn't enough time to shower, but man, he needed a shower badly. Frisco turned on the cold water in the bathroom sink and then put his head under the faucet, both drinking and letting the water flow over his face.

Damn, he hadn't meant to kill that entire bottle of whiskey last night. During the more than five years he'd been in and out of the hospital and housed in rehabilitation centers, he'd never had more than an occasional drink or two. Even before his injury, he was careful not to drink too much. Some of the guys went out at night and slammed home quantities of beer and whiskey—enough to float a ship. But Frisco rarely did. He didn't want to be like his father and his sister, and he knew enough about it to know that alcoholism could be hereditary.

And last night? He'd meant to have one more drink. That was all. Just one more to round down the edges. One more to soften the harsh slap of his release from the therapy center. But one drink had turned into two.

Then he'd started thinking about Mia Summerton, separated from him by only one very thin wall, and two had become three. He could hear the sound of her stereo. She was listening to Bonnie Raitt. Every so often, Mia would sing along, her voice a clear soprano over Bonnie's smoky alto. And after three drinks, Frisco had lost count.

He kept hearing Mia's laughter, echoing in his head, the way she'd laughed at him right before she'd gone into her own condo. It had been laughter loaded with meaning. It had been "a cold day in hell" kind of laughter, as in, it would be a cold day in hell before she'd even deign to so much as *think* about him again.

That was good. That was exactly what he wanted. Wasn't it?

Yes. Frisco splashed more water on his face, trying to convince himself that that was true. He didn't want some neighbor lady hanging around, giving him those goddamned pitying looks as he hobbled up and down the stairs. He didn't need suggestions about moving to a lousy ground-floor condo as if he were some kind of cripple. He didn't need self-righteous soapbox speeches about how war is not healthy for children and other living things. If anyone should know *that,* he sure as hell should.

He'd been in places where bombs were falling. And, yes, the bombs had military targets. But that didn't mean if a bomb accidentally went off track, it would fail to explode. Even if it hit a house or a church or a school, it was gonna go off. Bombs had no conscience, no remorse. They fell. They exploded. They destroyed and killed. And no matter how hard the people who aimed those bombs tried, civilians ended up dead.

But if a team of SEALs was sent in before air strikes became necessary, those SEALs could conceivably achieve more with fewer casualties. A seven-man team of SEALs such as the Alpha Squad could go in and totally foul up the enemy's communication system. Or they could kidnap the enemy's military leader, ensuring chaos and possibly reopening negotiations and peace talks.

But more often than not, because the top brass failed to realize the SEALs' full potential, they weren't utilized until it was too late.

And then people died. Children died.

Frisco brushed his teeth, then drank more water. He dried his face and limped back into his bedroom. He searched for his sunglasses to no avail, uncovered his

SUZANNE BROCKMANN 35

checkbook, pulled on a clean T-shirt and, wincing at the bright sunlight, he headed outside.

THE WOMAN IN the courtyard burst into tears.

Startled, Mia looked up from her garden. She'd seen this woman walk in—a battered, worn-out-looking blonde on crutches, awkwardly carrying a suitcase, followed by a very little, very frightened red-haired girl.

Mia followed the weeping woman's gaze and saw Lieutenant Francisco painfully making his way down the stairs. Wow, he looked awful. His skin had a grayish cast, and he was squinting as if the brilliant blue California sky and bright sunshine were the devil's evil doing. He hadn't shaved, and the stubble on his face made him look as if he'd just been rolled from a park bench. His T-shirt looked clean, but his shorts were the same ones he'd had on last night. Clearly he'd slept in them.

He'd obviously had "another" drink last night, and quite probably more than that afterward.

Fabulous. Mia forced her attention back to the flowers she was weeding. She had been convinced beyond a shadow of a doubt that Lt. Alan Francisco was *not* the kind of man she even wanted to have for a friend. He was rude and unhappy and quite possibly dangerous. And now she knew that he drank way too much, too.

No, she was going to ignore condo 2C from now on. She would pretend that the owner was still out of town.

The blond woman dropped her crutches and wrapped her arms around Francisco's neck. "I'm sorry," she kept saying, "I'm sorry."

The SEAL led the blonde to the bench directly across from Mia's garden plot. His voice carried clearly across the courtyard—she couldn't help but overhear, even though she tried desperately to mind her own business.

"Start at the beginning," he said, holding the woman's hands. "Sharon, tell me what happened. From the beginning."

"I totaled my car," the blonde—Sharon—said, and began to cry again.

"When?" Francisco asked patiently.

"Day before yesterday."

"That was when you broke your foot?"

She nodded. Yes.

"Was anyone else hurt?"

Her voice shook. "The other driver is still in the hospital. If he dies, I'll be up on charges of vehicular manslaughter."

Francisco swore. "Shar, if he dies, he'll be dead. That's a little bit worse than where you'll be, don't you think?"

Blond head bowed, Sharon nodded.

"You were DUI." It wasn't a question, but she nodded again. DUI—driving under the influence. Driving drunk.

A shadow fell across her flowers, and Mia looked up to see the little red-haired girl standing beside her.

"Hi," Mia said.

The girl was around five. Kindergarten age. She had amazing strawberry-blond hair that curled in a wild mass around her round face. Her face was covered with freckles, and her eyes were the same pure shade of dark blue as Alan Francisco's.

This had to be his daughter. Mia's gaze traveled back to the blonde. That meant Sharon was his...wife? Ex-wife? Girlfriend?

It didn't matter. What did she care if Alan Francisco had a *dozen* wives?

The red-haired girl spoke. "I have a garden at home. Back in the old country."

"Which old country is that?" Mia asked with a smile. Kindergarten-age children were so wonderful.

"Russia," the little girl said, all seriousness. "My real father is a Russian prince."

Her *real* father, hmm? Mia couldn't blame the little girl for making up a fictional family. With a mother up on DUI charges, and a father who was only a step or two behind...Mia could see the benefits of having a pretend world to escape to, filled with palaces and princes and beautiful gardens.

"Do you want to help me weed?" Mia asked.

The little girl glanced over at her mother.

"The bottom line is that I have no more options," Sharon was tearfully telling Alan Francisco. "If I voluntarily enter the detox program, I'll win points with the judge who tries my case. But I need to find someplace for Natasha to stay."

"No way," the Navy lieutenant said, shaking his head. "I'm sorry. There's no way in hell I can take her."

"Alan, please, you've got to help me out here!"

His voice got louder. "What do I know about taking care of a kid?"

"She's quiet," Sharon pleaded. "She won't get in the way."

"I don't want her." Francisco had lowered his voice, but it still carried clearly over to Mia. And to the little girl—to Natasha.

Mia's heart broke for the child. What an awful thing to overhear: Her own father didn't want her.

"I'm a teacher," Mia said to the girl, hoping she wouldn't hear the rest of her parents' tense conversation. "I teach older children—high school kids."

Natasha nodded, her face a picture of concentration as

she imitated Mia and gently pulled weeds from the soft earth of the garden.

"I'm supposed to go into detox in an hour," Sharon said. "If you don't take her, she'll be a ward of the state— she'll be put into foster care, Alan."

"There's a man who works for my father the prince," Natasha told Mia, as if she, too, were trying desperately not to listen to the other conversation, "who only plants flowers. That's all he does all day. Red flowers like these. And yellow flowers."

On the other side of the courtyard, Mia could hear Alan Francisco cursing. His voice was low, and she couldn't quite make out the words, but it was clear he was calling upon his full sailor's salty vocabulary. He wasn't angry at Sharon—his words weren't directed at her, but rather at the cloudless California sky above them.

"My very favorites are the blue flowers," Mia told Natasha. "They're called morning glories. You have to wake up very early in the morning to see them. They close up tightly during the day."

Natasha nodded, still so serious. "Because the bright sun gives them a headache."

"Natasha!"

The little girl looked up at the sound of her mother's voice. Mia looked up, too—directly into Alan Francisco's dark blue eyes. She quickly lowered her gaze, afraid he'd correctly read the accusations she knew were there. How could he ignore his own child? What kind of man could admit that he didn't want his daughter around?

"You're going to be staying here, with Alan, for a while," Sharon said, smiling tremulously at her daughter.

He'd given in. The former special operations lieutenant had given in. Mia didn't know whether to be glad for the little girl, or concerned. This child needed more than this man could give her. Mia risked another look up, and found his disturbingly blue eyes still watching her.

"Won't that be fun?" Sharon hopefully asked Natasha.

The little girl considered the question thoughtfully. "No," she finally said.

Alan Francisco laughed. Mia hadn't thought him capable, but he actually smiled and snorted with laughter, covering it quickly with a cough. When he looked up again, he wasn't smiling, but she could swear she saw amusement in his eyes.

"I want to go with you," Natasha told her mother, a trace of panic in her voice. "Why can't I go with you?"

Sharon's lip trembled, as if she were the child. "Because you can't," she said ineffectively. "Not this time."

The little girl's gaze shifted to Alan and then quickly back to Sharon. "Do we know him?" she asked.

"Yes," Sharon told her. "Of course we know him. He's your uncle Alan. You remember Alan. He's in the Navy...?"

But the little girl shook her head.

"I'm your mom's brother," Alan said to the little girl.

Her brother. Alan was Sharon's brother. Not her husband. Mia didn't want to feel anything at that news. She refused to feel relieved. She refused to feel, period. She weeded her garden, pretending she couldn't hear any of the words being spoken.

Natasha gazed at her mother. "Will you come back?" she asked in a very small voice.

Mia closed her eyes. But she did feel. She felt for this little girl; she felt her fear and pain. Her heart ached for the mother, too, God help her. And she felt for blue-eyed

Alan Francisco. But what she felt for him, she couldn't begin to define.

"I always do," Sharon said, dissolving once more into tears as she enveloped the little girl in a hug. "Don't I?" But then she quickly set Natasha aside. "I've got to go. Be good. I love you." She turned to Alan. "The address of the detox center is in the suitcase."

Alan nodded, and with a creak of her crutches, Sharon hurried away.

Natasha stared expressionlessly after her mother, watching until the woman disappeared from view. Then, with only a very slight tightening of her lips, she turned to look at Alan.

Mia looked at him, too, but this time his gaze never left the little girl. All of the amusement was gone from his eyes, leaving only sadness and compassion.

All of his anger had vanished. All of the rage that seemed to burn endlessly within him was temporarily doused. His blue eyes were no longer icy—instead they seemed almost warm. His chiseled features looked softer, too, as he tried to smile at Natasha. He may not have wanted her—he'd said as much—but now that she was here, it seemed as if he were going to do his best to make things easier for her.

Mia looked up to see that the little girl's eyes had filled with tears. She was trying awfully hard not to cry, but one tear finally escaped, rolling down her face. She wiped at it fiercely, fighting the flood.

"I know you don't remember me," Alan said to Natasha, his voice impossibly gentle. "But we met five years ago. On January 4."

Natasha all but stopped breathing. "That's my birthday," she said, gazing across the courtyard at him.

Alan's forced smile became genuine. "I know," he said.

"I was driving your mom to the hospital and…" He broke off, looking closely at her. "You want a hug?" he asked. "Because I could really use a hug right now, and I'd sure appreciate it if you could give me one."

Natasha considered his words, then nodded. She slowly crossed to him.

"You better hold your breath, though," Alan told her ruefully. "I think I smell bad."

She nodded again, then carefully climbed onto his lap. Mia tried not to watch, but it was nearly impossible not to look at the big man, with his arms wrapped so tentatively around the little girl, as if he were afraid she might break. But when Natasha's arms went up and locked securely around his neck, Alan closed his eyes, holding the little girl more tightly.

Mia had thought his request for a hug had been purely for Natasha's sake, but now she had to wonder. With all of his anger and his bitterness over his injured leg, it was possible Alan Francisco hadn't let anyone close enough to give him the warmth and comfort of a hug in quite some time. And everyone needed warmth and comfort—even big, tough professional soldiers.

Mia looked away, trying to concentrate on weeding her last row of flowers. But she couldn't help but over- hear Natasha say, "You don't smell bad. You smell like Mommy—when she wakes up."

Alan didn't look happy with that comparison. "Terrific," he murmured.

"She's grouchy in the morning," Natasha said. "Are you grouchy in the morning, too?"

"These days I'm afraid I'm grouchy all the time," he admitted.

Natasha was quiet for a moment, considering that.

"Then I'll keep the TV turned down really quiet so it doesn't bother you."

Alan laughed again, just a brief exhale of air. Still, it drew Mia's eyes to his face. When he smiled, he transformed. When he smiled, despite the pallor of his skin and his heavy stubble and his uncombed hair, he became breathtakingly handsome.

"That's probably a good idea," he said.

Natasha didn't get off his lap. "I don't remember meeting you before," she said.

"You wouldn't," Alan said. He shifted painfully. Even Natasha's slight weight was too much for his injured knee, and he moved her so that she was sitting on his good leg. "When we first met, you were still inside your mom's belly. You decided that you wanted to be born, and you didn't want to wait. You decided you wanted to come into the world in the front seat of my truck."

"Really?" Natasha was fascinated.

Alan nodded. "Really. You came out before the ambulance could get there. You were in such a hurry, I had to catch you and hold on to you to keep you from running a lap around the block."

"Babies can't run," the little girl scoffed.

"Maybe not *regular* babies," Alan said. "But you came out doing the tango, smoking a cigar and hollering at everybody. Oh, baby, were you loud."

Natasha giggled. "Really?"

"Really," Alan said. "Not the tango and the cigar, but the loud. Come on," he added, lifting her off his lap. "Grab your suitcase and I'll give you the nickel tour of my condo. You can do…something…while I take a shower. Man, do I need a shower."

Natasha tried to pick up her suitcase, but it was too heavy for her. She tried dragging it after her uncle, but she was never going to get it up the stairs. When Alan turned back to see her struggle, he stopped.

"I better get that," he said. But even as he spoke, a change came over his face. The anger was back. Anger and frustration.

Mia was only one thought behind him, and she realized almost instantly that Alan Francisco was not going to be able to carry Natasha's suitcase up the stairs. With one hand on his cane, and the other pulling himself up on the cast-iron railing, it wasn't going to happen.

She stood up, brushing the dirt from her hands. However she did this, it was going to be humiliating for him. And, as with all painful things, it was probably best to do it quickly—to get it over with.

"I'll get that," she said cheerfully, taking the suitcase out of Natasha's hand. Mia didn't wait for Alan to speak or react. She swept up the stairs, taking them two at a time, and set the suitcase down outside the door to 2C.

"Beautiful morning, isn't it?" she called out as she went into her own apartment and grabbed her watering can.

She was outside again in an instant, and as she started down the stairs, she saw that Alan hadn't moved. Only the expression on his face had changed. His eyes were even darker and angrier and his face was positively stormy. His mouth was tight. All signs of his earlier smile were gone.

"I didn't ask for your help," he said in a low, dangerous voice.

"I know," Mia said honestly, stopping several steps from the bottom so she could look at him, eye to eye. "I figured you wouldn't ask. And if *I* asked, I knew you would get all mad and you wouldn't let me help. This way, you can get as mad as you want, but the suitcase is already upstairs." She smiled at him. "So go on. Get mad. Knock yourself out."

As Mia turned and headed back to her garden, she could feel Alan's eyes boring into her back. His expression hadn't changed—he *was* mad. Mad at her, mad at the world.

She knew she shouldn't have helped him. She should have simply let him deal with his problems, let him work things out. She knew she shouldn't get entangled with someone who was obviously in need.

But Mia couldn't forget the smile that had transformed Alan into a real human being instead of this rocky pillar of anger that he seemed to be most of the time. She couldn't forget the gentle way he'd talked to the little girl, trying his best to set her at ease. And she couldn't forget the look on his face when little Natasha had given him a hug.

Mia couldn't forget—even though she knew that she'd be better off if she could.

CHAPTER FOUR

FRISCO STARTED TO open the bathroom door, but on second thought stopped and wrapped his towel around his waist first.

He could hear the sound of the television in the living room as he leaned heavily on his cane and went into his bedroom, shutting the door behind him.

A kid. What the hell was he going to do with a kid for the next six weeks?

He tossed his cane on the unmade bed and rubbed his wet hair with his towel. Of course, it wasn't as if his work schedule were overcrowded. He'd surely be able to squeeze Natasha in somewhere between "Good Morning, America" and the "Late Show with David Letterman."

Still, little kids required certain specific attention—like food at regular intervals, baths every now and then, a good night's sleep that didn't start at four in the morning and stretch all the way out past noon. Frisco could barely even provide those things for himself, let alone someone else.

Hopping on his good leg, he dug through his still-packed duffel bag, searching for clean underwear. Nothing.

It had been years since he'd had to cook for himself. His kitchen skills were more geared toward knowing which cleaning solutions made the best flammable substances when combined with other household products.

He moved to his dresser, and found only a pair of silk boxers that a lady friend had bought him a lifetime ago. He pulled on his bathing suit instead.

There was nothing to eat in his refrigerator besides a lemon and a six-pack of Mexican beer. His kitchen cabinets contained only shakers of moisture-solidified salt and pepper and an ancient bottle of tabasco sauce.

The second bedroom in his condo was nearly as bare as his cabinets. It had no furniture, only several rows of boxes neatly stacked along one wall. Tasha was going to have to crash on the couch until Frisco could get her a bed and whatever other kind of furniture a five-year-old girl needed.

Frisco pulled on a fresh T-shirt, throwing the clothes he'd been wearing onto the enormous and ever-expanding pile of dirty laundry in the corner of the room…some of it dating from the last time he'd been here, over five years ago. Even the cleaning lady who'd come in yesterday afternoon hadn't dared to touch it.

They'd kicked him out of the physical therapy center before laundry day. He'd arrived here yesterday with two bags of gear and an enormous duffel bag filled with dirty laundry. Somehow he was going to have to figure out a way to get his dirty clothes down to the laundry room on the first floor—and his clean clothes back up again.

But the first thing he had to do was make sure his collection of weapons were all safely locked up. Frisco didn't know much about five-year-olds, but he was certain of one thing—they didn't mix well with firearms.

He quickly combed his hair and, reaching for the smooth wood of his cane, he headed toward the sound of the TV. After he secured his private arsenal, he and Tasha would hobble on down to the grocery store on the corner and pick up some chow for lunch and…

On the television screen, a row of topless dancers gyrated. Frisco lunged for the off switch. Hell! His cable must've come with some kind of men's channel—the Playboy Channel or something similar. He honestly hadn't known.

"Whoa, Tash. I've got to program that off the remote control," he said, turning to the couch to face her.

Except she wasn't sitting on the couch.

His living room was small, and one quick look assured him that she wasn't even in the room. Hell, that was a relief. He limped toward the kitchen. She wasn't there, either, and his relief turned to apprehension.

"Natasha...?" Frisco moved as quickly as he could down the tiny hallway toward the bedrooms and bathroom. He looked, and then he looked again, even glancing underneath his bed and in both closets.

The kid was gone.

His knee twinged as he used a skittering sort of hop and skip to propel himself back into the living room and out the screen door.

She wasn't on the second-floor landing, or anywhere in immediate view in the condo courtyard. Frisco could see Mia Summerton still working, crouched down among the explosion of flowers that were her garden, a rather silly-looking floppy straw hat covering the top of her head.

"Hey!"

She looked up, startled and uncertain as to where his voice had come from.

"Up here."

She was too far away for him to see exactly which shade of green or brown her eyes were right now. They were wide though. Her surprise quickly changed to wariness.

He could see a dark vee of perspiration along the collar

and down the front of her T-shirt. Her face glistened in the morning heat, and she reached up and wiped her forehead with the back of one arm. It left a smudge of dirt behind.

"Have you seen Natasha—you know, the little girl with red hair? Did she come down this way?"

Mia rinsed her hands in a bucket of water and stood up. "No—and I've been out here since you went upstairs."

Frisco swore and started down past his condo door, toward the stairs at the other side of the complex.

"What happened?" Mia came up the stairs and caught up with him easily.

"I got out of the shower and she was gone," he told her curtly, trying to move as quickly as he could. Damn, he didn't want to deal with this. The morning sun had moved high into the sky and the brightness still made his head throb—as did every jarring step he took. It was true that living with him wasn't going to be any kind of party, but the kid didn't have to run away, for God's sake.

But then he saw it.

Sparkling and deceptively pure looking, the alluring blue Pacific Ocean glimmered and danced, beckoning in the distance. The beach was several blocks away. Maybe the kid was like him and had saltwater running through her veins. Maybe she caught one look at the water and headed for the beach. Maybe she wasn't running away. Maybe she was just exploring. Or maybe she was pushing the edge of the obedience envelope, testing him to see just what she could get away with.

"Do you think she went far? Do you want me to get my car?" Mia asked.

Frisco turned to look at her and realized she was keeping pace with him. He didn't want her help, but dammit, he needed it. If he was going to find Tasha quickly, four eyes were definitely better than two. And a car was far better than a bum knee and a cane when it came to getting someplace fast.

"Yeah, get your car," he said gruffly. "I want to check down at the beach."

Mia nodded once then ran ahead. She'd pulled her car up at the stairs that led to the parking lot before he'd even arrived at the bottom of them. She reached across the seat, unlocking the passenger's side door of her little subcompact.

Frisco knew he wasn't going to fit inside. He got in anyway, forcing his right knee to bend more than it comfortably could. Pain and its accompanying nausea washed over him, and he swore sharply—a repetitive, staccato chant, a profane mantra designed to bring him back from the edge.

He looked up to find Mia watching him, her face carefully expressionless.

"Drive," he told her, his voice sounding harsh to his own ears. "Come on—I don't even know if this kid can swim."

She put the car into first gear and it lurched forward. She took the route the child might well have taken if she was, indeed, heading for the beach. Frisco scanned the crowded sidewalks. What exactly had the kid been wearing? Some kind of white shirt with a pattern on it… balloons? Or maybe flowers? And a bright-colored pair of shorts. Or was she wearing a skirt? Was it green or blue? He couldn't remember, so he watched for her flaming red hair instead.

"Any sign of her?" Mia asked. "Do you want me to slow down?"

"No," Frisco said. "Let's get down to the water and

make sure she's not there first. We can work our way back more slowly."

"Aye, aye, sir." Mia stepped on the gas, risking a glance at Alan Francisco. He didn't seem to notice her military-style affirmative. He was gripping the handle up above the passenger window so tightly that his knuckles were white. The muscles in his jaw were just as tight, and he kept watching out the window, searching for any sign of his tiny niece in the summertime crowd.

He'd shaved, she noticed, glancing at him again. He looked slightly less dangerous without the stubble—but only slightly.

He'd hurt his knee getting into her car, and Mia knew from the paleness of his face underneath his tan that it hurt him still. But he didn't complain. Other than his initial explosion of profanity, he hadn't said a word about it. Finding his niece took priority over his pain. Obviously it took priority, since finding Natasha was important enough for him to call a temporary truce with Mia and accept her offer of help.

She was signaling to make the left into the beach parking lot when the man finally spoke.

"There she is! With some kid. At two o'clock—"

"Where?" Mia slowed, uncertain.

"Just stop the car!"

Francisco opened the door, and Mia slammed on the brakes, afraid he would jump out while the car was still moving. And then she saw Natasha. The little girl was at the edge of the parking lot, sitting on the top of a picnic table, paying solemn attention to a tall African-American teenage boy who was standing in front of her. Something about the way he wore his low-riding, baggy jeans was familiar. The kid turned, and Mia saw his face.

"That's Thomas King," she said. "That boy who's with Natasha—I know him."

But Francisco was already out of the car, moving as fast as he could with his limp and his cane toward the little girl.

There was nowhere to park. Mia watched through the windshield as the former Navy lieutenant descended upon his niece, pulling her none-too-gently from the table and setting her down on the ground behind him. She couldn't hear what he was saying, but she could tell that it wasn't a friendly greeting. She saw Thomas bristle and turn belligerently toward Francisco, and she threw on her hazard lights and left the car right where it was in the middle of the lot as she jumped out and ran toward them.

She arrived just in time to hear Thomas say, "You raise one hand to that girl and I'll clean the street with your face."

Alan Francisco's blue eyes had looked deadly and cold when Mia first ran up, but now they changed. Something shifted. "What are you talking about? I'm not going to *hit* her." He sounded incredulous, as if such a thing would never have occurred to him.

"Then why are you shouting at her as if you are?" Thomas King was nearly Francisco's height, but the former SEAL had at least fifty pounds of muscle over him. Still, the teenager stood his ground, his dark eyes flashing and narrowed, his lips tight.

"I'm not—"

"Yes, you are," Thomas persisted. He mimicked the older man. "'What the hell are you doing here? Who the hell gave you permission to leave...' I thought you were going to slam her—and *she* did, too."

Frisco turned to look at Natasha. She had scurried

underneath the picnic table, and she looked back at him, her eyes wide. "Tash, you didn't think…"

But she had thought that. He could see it in her eyes, in the way she was cowering. Man, he felt sick.

He crouched down next to the table as best he could. "Natasha, did your mom hit you when she was angry?" He couldn't believe softhearted Sharon would hurt a defenseless child, but liquor did funny things to even the gentlest of souls.

The little girl shook her head no. "Mommy didn't," she told him softly, "but Dwayne did once and I got a bloody lip. Mommy cried, and then we moved out."

Thank God Sharon had had that much sense. Damn Dwayne to hell, whoever he was. What kind of monster would strike a five-year-old child?

What kind of monster would scare her to death by shouting at her the way he just had?

Frisco sat down heavily on the picnic table bench, glancing up at Mia. Her eyes were soft, as if she could somehow read his mind.

"Tash, I'm sorry," he said, rubbing his aching, bleary eyes. "I didn't mean to scare you."

"This some kind of *friend* of yours?" the black kid said to Mia, his tone implying she might want to be more selective in her choice of friends in the future.

"He's in 2C," Mia told the boy. "The mystery neighbor—Lieutenant Alan Francisco." She directed her next words to Frisco. "This is Thomas King. He's a former student of mine. He lives in 1N with his sister and her kids."

A former…student? That meant that Mia Summerton was a teacher. Damn, if he had had teachers who looked like her, he might've actually gone to high school.

She was watching him now with wariness in her eyes,

as if he were a bomb on a trick timer, ready to blow at any given moment.

"Lieutenant," Thomas repeated. "Are you the badge?"

"No, I'm not a cop," Frisco said, tearing his eyes away from Mia to glance at the kid. "I'm in the Navy...." He caught himself, and shook his head, closing his eyes briefly. "I *was* in the Navy."

Thomas had purposely crossed his arms and tucked both hands underneath them to make sure Frisco knew he had no intention of shaking hands.

"The lieutenant was a SEAL," Mia told Thomas. "That's a branch of special operations—"

"I *know* what a SEAL is," the kid interrupted. He turned to run a bored, cynical eye over Frisco. "One of those crazy freaks that ride the surf and crash their little rubber boats into the rocks down by the hotel in Coronado. Did *you* ever do that?"

Mia was watching him again, too. Damn but she was pretty. And every time she looked at him, every time their eyes met, Frisco felt a very solid slap of mutual sexual awareness. It was almost funny. With the possible exception of her exotic fashion-model face and trim, athletic body, everything about the woman irritated him. He didn't want a nosy neighbor poking around in his life. He didn't need a helpful do-gooder getting in his face and reminding him hourly of his limitations. He had no use for a disgustingly cheerful, flower-planting, antimilitary, unintimidatable, fresh-faced girl-next-door type.

But every single time he looked into her hazel eyes, he felt an undeniable surge of physical attraction. Intellectually, he may have wanted little more than to hide from her, but physically... Well, his body apparently had quite a different agenda. One that included moonlight gleaming on smooth, golden tanned skin, long dark hair trailing across his face, across his chest and lower.

Frisco managed a half smile, wondering if she could read his mind now. He couldn't look away from her, even to answer Thomas's question. "It's called rock portage," he said, "and, yeah. I did that during training."

She didn't blush. She didn't look away from him. She just steadily returned his gaze, slightly lifting one exotic eyebrow. Frisco had the sense that she did, indeed, know exactly what he was thinking. *Cold day in hell.* She hadn't said those exact words last night, but they echoed in his mind as clearly as if she had.

It was just as well. He was having a pure, raw-sex reaction to her, but she wasn't the pure, raw type. He couldn't picture her climbing into his bed and then slipping away before dawn, no words spoken, only intense pleasure shared. No, once she got into his bed, she would never get out. She had "girlfriend" written all over her, and that was the last thing he needed. She would fill his apartment with flowers from her garden and endless conversation and little notes with smiley faces on them. She'd demand tender kisses and a clean bathroom and heart-to-heart revelations and a genuine interest in her life.

How could he begin to be interested in *her* life, when he couldn't even muster up the slightest enthusiasm for his own?

But he was getting *way* ahead of himself here. He was assuming that he'd have no trouble getting her into his bed in the first place. That might've been true five years ago, but he wasn't exactly any kind of prize anymore. There was no way a girl like Mia would want to be saddled with a man who could barely even walk.

Cold day in hell. Frisco looked out at the blinding

blueness of the ocean, feeling his eyes burn from the glare.

"What's a SEAL doing with a kid who can't swim?" Thomas asked. Most of the anger had left the teenager's eyes, leaving behind a cynical disdain and a seemingly ancient weariness that made him look far older than his years. He had scars on his face, one bisecting one of his eyebrows, the other marking one of his high, pronounced cheekbones. That, combined with the fact that his nose had been broken more than once, gave him a battle-worn look that erased even more of his youth. But except for a few minor slang expressions, Thomas didn't speak the language of the street. He had no discernible accent of any kind, and Frisco wondered if the kid had worked as hard to delete that particular tie with his past and his parents as he himself had.

"Natasha is the lieutenant's niece," Mia explained. "She's going to stay with him for a few weeks. She just arrived today."

"From Mars, right?" Thomas looked under the table and made a face at Natasha.

She giggled. "Thomas thinks I'm from Mars 'cause I didn't know what that water was." Natasha slithered on her belly out from underneath the table. The sand stuck to her clothes, and Frisco realized that she was wet.

"A little Martian girl is the only kind of girl I can think of who hasn't seen the ocean before," Thomas said. "She didn't even seem to know kids shouldn't go into the water alone."

Mia watched myriad emotions cross Alan Francisco's face. The lifeguard's flag was out today, signaling a strong undertow and dangerous currents. She saw him look at Thomas and register the fact that the teenager's jeans were wet up to his knees.

"You went in after her," he said, his low voice deceptively even.

Thomas was as nonchalant. "I've got a five-year-old niece, too."

Francisco pulled himself painfully up with his cane. He held out his hand to Thomas. "Thanks, man. I'm sorry about before. I'm...new at this kid thing."

Mia held her breath. She knew Thomas well, and if he'd decided that Alan Francisco was the enemy, he'd never shake his hand.

But Thomas hesitated only briefly before he clasped the older man's hand.

Again, a flurry of emotions flickered in Francisco's eyes, and again he tried to hide it all. Relief. Gratitude. Sorrow. Always sorrow and always shame. But it was all gone almost before it was even there. When Alan Francisco tried to hide his emotions, he succeeded, tucking them neatly behind the ever-present anger that simmered inside of him.

He managed to use that anger to hide everything quite nicely—everything except the seven-thousand-degree nuclear-powered sexual attraction he felt for her. That he put on display, complete with neon signs and million-dollar-a-minute advertising.

Good grief, last night when he'd made that crack about wanting her to share his bed, she'd thought he'd been simply trying to scare her off.

She had been dead wrong. The way he'd looked at her just minutes ago had nearly singed her eyebrows off.

And the *truly* stupid thing was that the thought of having a physical relationship with this man didn't send her running for her apartment and the heavy-duty dead bolt that she'd had installed on her door. She couldn't figure out why. Lt. Alan Francisco was a real-life version of G.I. Joe, he was probably a male chauvinist, he drank so much that he still looked like hell at noon on a weekday *and* he carried a seemingly permanent chip on his shoulder. Yet for some bizarre reason, Mia had no trouble imagining herself pulling him by the hand into her bedroom and melting together with him on her bed.

It had nothing to do with his craggy-featured, handsome face and enticingly hard-muscled body. Well, yes, okay, so she wasn't being completely honest with herself. It had at least a *little* bit to do with that. It was true—the fact that the man looked as if he should have his own three-month segment in a hunk-of-the-month calendar was not something she'd failed to notice. And notice, and notice and notice.

But try as she might, it was the softness in his eyes when he spoke to Natasha and his crooked, painful attempts to smile at the little girl that she found hard to resist. She was a sucker for kindness, and she suspected that beneath this man's outer crust of anger and bitterness, and despite his sometimes crude language and rough behavior, there lurked the kindest of souls.

"Here's the deal about the beach," Alan Francisco was saying to his niece. "You never come down here without a grown-up, and you never, *ever* go into the water alone."

"That's what Thomas said," Tasha told him. "He said I might've drownded."

"Thomas is right," Francisco told her.

"What's drownded?"

"Drowned," he corrected her. "You ever try to breathe underwater?"

Tash shook her head no, and her red curls bounced.

"Well, don't try it. People can't breathe underwater. Only fish can. And you don't look like a fish to me."

The little girl giggled, but persisted. "What's drownded?"

Mia crossed her arms, wondering if Francisco would try to sidestep the issue again, or if he would take the plunge and discuss the topic of death with Natasha.

"Well," he said slowly, "if someone goes into the water, and they can't swim, or they hurt themselves, or the waves are too high, then the water might go over their head. Then they can't breathe. Normally, when the water goes over your head it's no big deal. You hold your breath. And then you just swim to the surface and stick your nose and mouth out and take a breath of air. But like I said, maybe this person doesn't know how to swim, or maybe their leg got a cramp, or the water's too rough, so they can't get up to the air. And if there's no air for them to breathe... well, they'll die. They'll drown. People need to breathe air to live."

Natasha gazed unblinkingly at her uncle, her head tilted slightly to one side. "I don't know how to swim," she finally said.

"Then I'll teach you," Francisco said unhesitatingly. "Everyone should know how to swim. But even when you *do* know how to swim, you still don't swim alone. That way, if you *do* get hurt, you got a friend who can save you from drowning. Even in the SEALs we didn't swim alone. We had something called swim buddies—a friend who looked out for you, and you'd look out for him, too. You and me, Tash, for the next few weeks, we're going to be swim buddies, okay?"

"I'm outta here, Ms. S. I don't want to be late for work."

Mia turned to Thomas, glad he'd broken into her reverie. She'd been standing there like an idiot, gazing at

Alan Francisco, enthralled by his conversation with his niece. "Be careful," she told him.

"Always am."

Natasha crouched down in the sand and began pushing an old Popsicle stick around as if it were a car. Thomas bent over and ruffled her hair. "See you later, Martian girl." He nodded to Francisco. "Lieutenant."

The SEAL pulled himself up and off the bench. "Call me Frisco. And thanks again, man."

Thomas nodded once more and then was gone.

"He works part-time as a security guard at the university," Mia told Francisco. "That way he can audit college courses in his spare time—spare time that doesn't exist because he also works a full day as a landscaper's assistant over in Coronado."

He was looking at her again, his steel blue eyes shuttered and unreadable this time. He hadn't told *her* she could call him Frisco. Maybe it was a guy thing. Maybe SEALs weren't allowed to let women call them by their nicknames. Or maybe it was more personal than that. Maybe Alan Francisco didn't want her as a friend. He'd certainly implied as much last night.

Mia looked back at her car, still sitting in the middle of the parking lot. "Well," she said, feeling strangely awkward. She had no problem holding her own with this man when he came on too strong or acted rudely. But when he simply stared at her like this, with no expression besides the faintest glimmer of his ever-present anger on his face, she felt off balance and ill at ease, like a schoolgirl with an unrequited crush. "I'm glad we found—*you* found Natasha…" She glanced back at her car again, more to escape his scrutiny than to reassure herself it was still there. "Can I give you a lift back to the condo?"

Frisco shook his head. "No, thanks."

"I could adjust the seat, see if I could make it more comfortable for you to—"

"No, we've got some shopping to do."

"But Natasha's all wet."

"She'll dry. Besides, I could use the exercise."

Exercise? Was he kidding? "What you could use is a week or two off your feet, in bed."

Just like that, he seemed to come alive, his mouth twisting into a sardonic half smile. His eyes sparked with heat and he lowered his voice, leaning forward to speak directly into her ear. "Are you volunteering to keep me there? I knew sooner or later you'd change your mind."

He knew nothing of the sort. He'd only said that to rattle and irritate her. Mia refused to let him see just how irritated his comment had made her. Instead, she stepped even closer, looking up at him, letting her gaze linger on his mouth before meeting his eyes, meaning to make him wonder, and to make him squirm before she launched her attack.

But she launched nothing as she looked into his eyes. His knowing smile had faded, leaving behind only heat. It magnified, doubling again and again, increasing logarithmically as their gazes locked, burning her down to her very soul. She knew that he could see more than just a mere reflection of his desire in her eyes, and she knew without a doubt that she'd given too much away. This fire that burned between them was not his alone.

The sun was beating down on them and her mouth felt parched. She tried to swallow, tried to moisten her dry lips, tried to walk away. But she couldn't move.

He reached out slowly. She could see it coming—he was going to touch her, pull her close against the hard muscles of his chest and cover her mouth with his own in a heated, heart-stopping, nuclear meltdown of a kiss.

But he touched her only lightly, tracing the path of a bead of sweat that had trailed down past her ear, down her neck and across her collarbone before it disappeared beneath the collar of her T-shirt. He touched her gently, only with one finger, but in many ways it was far more sensual, far more intimate than even a kiss.

The world seemed to spin and Mia almost reached for him. But sanity kicked in, thank God, and instead she backed away.

"When I change my mind," she said, her voice barely louder than a whisper, "it'll be a cold day in July."

She turned on legs that were actually trembling—*trembling*—and headed toward her car. He made no move to follow, but as she got inside and drove away, she could see him in the rearview mirror, still watching her.

Had she convinced him? She doubted it. She wasn't sure she'd even managed to convince herself.

CHAPTER FIVE

"OKAY, TASH," FRISCO called down from the second-floor landing where he'd finally finished lashing the framework to the railing. "Ready for a test run?"

She nodded, and he let out the crank and lowered the rope down to her.

The realization had come to him while they were grocery shopping. He wasn't going to be able to carry the bags of food he bought up the stairs to his second-floor condominium. And Tasha, as helpful as she tried to be when she wasn't wandering off, couldn't possibly haul all the food they needed up a steep flight of stairs. She could maybe handle one or two lightweight bags, but certainly no more than that.

But Frisco had been an expert in unconventional warfare for the past ten years. He could come up with alternative, creative solutions to damn near any situation—including this one. Of course, this wasn't war, which made it that much easier. Whatever he came up with, he wasn't going to have to pull it off while underneath a rain of enemy bullets.

It hadn't taken him long to come up with a solution. He and Tasha had stopped at the local home building supply store and bought themselves the fixings for a rope-and-pulley system. Frisco could've easily handled just a rope to pull things up to the second-floor landing, but with a crank and some pulleys, Natasha would be able to use it, too.

The plastic bags filled with the groceries they'd bought were on the ground, directly underneath the rope to which he'd attached a hook.

"Hook the rope to one of the bags," Frisco commanded his niece, leaning over the railing. "Right through the handles—that's right."

Mia Summerton was watching him.

He'd been hyperaware of her from the moment he and Tash had climbed out of the taxi with all of their groceries. She'd been back in her garden again, doing God knows what and watching him out of the corner of her eye.

She'd watched as he'd transferred the frozen food and perishables into a backpack he'd bought and carried them inside. She'd watched as he'd done the same with the building supplies and set them out on the second-floor landing. She'd watched as he awkwardly lowered himself down to sit on the stairs with his tool kit and began to work.

She'd watched, but she'd been careful never to let him catch her watching.

Just the same, he felt her eyes following him. And he could damn near smell her awareness.

Man, whatever it was that they'd experienced back on the beach... He shook his head in disbelief. Whatever it was, he wanted some more. A whole lot of more. She'd looked at him, and he'd been caught in an amazing vortex of animal magnetism. He hadn't been able to resist touching her, hadn't been able to stop thinking about exactly where that droplet of perspiration had gone after it had disappeared from view beneath her shirt. It hadn't taken much imagination to picture it traveling slowly between her breasts, all the way down to her softly indented belly button.

He'd wanted to dive in after it.

It had been damn near enough to make him wonder if he'd seriously underrated smiley-face-endowed notes.

But he'd seen the shock in Mia's eyes. She hadn't expected the attraction that had surged between them. She didn't want it, didn't want him. Certainly not for a single, mind-blowing sexual encounter, and *definitely* not for anything longer term. That was no big surprise.

"I can't get it," Natasha called up to him, her face scrunched with worry.

Mia had kept to herself ever since they'd arrived home. Her offers to help had been noticeably absent. But now she stood up, apparently unable to ignore the note of anxiety in Tasha's voice.

"May I help you with that, Natasha?" She spoke directly to the little girl. She didn't even bother to look up at Frisco.

Frisco wiped the sweat from his face as he watched Tasha step back and Mia attach the hook to the plastic handles of the grocery bags. It had to be close to ninety degrees in the shade, but when Mia finally did glance up at him there was a definite wintry chill in the air.

She was trying her damnedest to act as if she had not even the slightest interest in him. Yet she'd spent the past hour and a half watching him. Why?

Maybe whatever this was that constantly drew his eyes in her direction, whatever this was that had made him hit his thumb with his hammer more times than he could count, whatever this was that made every muscle in his body tighten in anticipation when he so much as *thought* about her, whatever this uncontrollable sensation was— maybe she felt it, too.

It was lust and desire, amplified a thousandfold, mutated into something far more powerful.

He didn't want her. He didn't want the trouble, didn't want the hassle, didn't want the grief. And yet, at the same time, he wanted her desperately. He wanted her more than he'd ever wanted any woman before.

If he'd been the type to get frightened, he would've been terrified.

"We better stand back," Mia warned Tasha as Frisco began turning the crank.

It went up easily enough, the bag bulging and straining underneath the weight. But then, as if in slow motion, the bottom of the plastic bag gave out, and its contents went plummeting to the ground.

Frisco swore loudly as a six-pack shattered into pieces of brown glass, the beer mixing unappetizingly with cranberry juice from a broken half-gallon container, four flattened tomatoes and an avocado that never again would see the light of day. The loaf of Italian bread that had also been in the bag had, thankfully, bounced free and clear of the disaster.

Mia looked down at the wreckage, and then up at Alan Francisco. He'd cut short his litany of curses and stood silently, his mouth tight and his eyes filled with far more despair than the situation warranted.

But she knew he was seeing more than a mess on the courtyard sidewalk as he looked over the railing. She knew he was seeing his life, shattered as absolutely as those beer bottles.

Still he took a deep breath, and forced himself to smile down into Natasha's wide eyes.

"We're on the right track here," he said, lowering the rope again. "We're definitely very close to outrageous success." Using his cane, he started down the stairs. "How about we try double bagging? Or a paper bag inside of the plastic one?"

"How about cloth bags?" Mia suggested.

"Back away, Tash—that's broken glass," Alan called warningly. "Yeah, cloth bags would work, but I don't have any."

Alan, Mia thought. When had he become Alan instead of Francisco? Was it when he looked down at his niece and made himself smile despite his pain, or was it earlier, at the beach parking lot, when he'd nearly lit Mia on fire with a single look?

Mia ran up the stairs past him, suddenly extremely aware that he'd taken off his shirt nearly an hour ago. His smooth tanned skin and hard muscles had been hard to ignore even from a distance. Up close it was impossible for Mia not to stare.

He wore only a loose-fitting, bright-colored bathing suit, and it rode low on his lean hips. His stomach was a washboard of muscles, and his skin gleamed with sweat. And that other tattoo on his biceps was a sea serpent, not a mermaid, as she'd first thought.

"I've got some bags," Mia called out, escaping into the coolness of her apartment, stopping for a moment to take a long, shaky breath. What was it about this man that made her heart beat double time? He was intriguing; she couldn't deny that. And he exuded a wildness, a barely tamed sexuality that constantly managed to captivate her. But so what? He was sexy. He was gorgeous. He was working hard to overcome a raftload of serious problems, making him seem tragic and fascinating. But these were not the criteria she usually used to decide whether or not to enter into a sexual relationship with a man.

The fact was that she *wasn't* going to sleep with him,

she told herself firmly. Definitely probably not. She rolled her eyes in self-disgust. Definitely *probably...?*

It had to be the full moon making her feel this way. Or—as her mother might say—maybe her astrological planets were lined up in some strange configuration, making her feel restless and reckless. Or maybe as she neared thirty, her body was changing, releasing hormones in quantities that she could no longer simply ignore.

Whatever the reason—mystical or scientific—the fact remained that she would *not* have sex with a stranger. Whatever happened between them, it wasn't going to happen until she'd had a chance to get to know this man. And once she got to know him and his vast collection of both physical and psychological problems, she had a feeling that staying away from him wasn't going to be so very difficult.

She took her cloth grocery bags from the closet and went back outside. Alan was crouched awkwardly down on the sidewalk, attempting to clean up the mess.

"Alan, wait. Don't try to pick up the broken glass," she called down to him. "I've got work gloves and a shovel you can use to clean it up." She didn't dare offer to do the work for him. She knew he would refuse. "I'll get 'em. Here—catch."

She threw the bags over the railing, and he caught them with little effort as she turned to go back inside.

Frisco looked at the printed message on the outside of the bags Mia had tossed him and rolled his eyes. Of course it had to be something political. Shaking his head, he sat down on the grass and began transferring the un-demolished remainder of the groceries into the cloth bags.

"'Wouldn't it be nice if we fully funded education, and the government had to hold a bake sale to buy a bomber?'" he quoted from the bags when Mia came back down the stairs.

She was holding a plastic trash bag, a pair of work gloves and what looked rather suspiciously like a pooper-scooper. She gave him a crooked smile. "Yeah," she said. "I thought you would like that."

"I'd be glad to get into a knock-down, drag-out argument about the average civilian's ignorance regarding military spending some other time," he told her. "But right now I'm not really in the mood."

"How about if I pretend you didn't just call me ignorant, and *you* pretend I don't think you're some kind of rigid, militaristic, dumb-as-a-stone professional soldier?" she said much too sweetly.

Frisco had to laugh. It was a deep laugh, a belly laugh, and he couldn't remember the last time he'd done that. He was still smiling when he looked up at her. "That sounds fair," he said. "And who knows—maybe we're both wrong."

Mia smiled back at him, but it was tentative and wary.

"I didn't get to thank you for helping me this morning," he said. "I'm sorry if I was…"

Mia gazed at him, waiting for him to finish his sentence. Unfriendly? Worried? Upset? Angry? Inappropriate? Too sexy for words? She wondered exactly what he was apologizing for.

"Rude," he finally finished. He glanced over at Natasha. She was lying on her back in the shade of a palm tree, staring up at the sky through both her spread fingers and the fronds, singing some unintelligible and probably improvised song. "I'm in way over my head here," he admitted with another crooked smile. "I don't

know the first thing about taking care of a kid, and…"
He shrugged. "Even if I did, these days I'm not exactly in the right place psychologically, you know?"

"You're doing great."

The look he shot her was loaded with amusement and disbelief. "She was under my care for not even thirty minutes and I managed to lose her." He shifted his weight, trying to get more comfortable, wincing slightly at the pain in his leg. "While we were walking home, I talked to her about setting up some rules and regs—basic stuff, like she has to tell me if she's going outside the condo, and she's got to play inside the courtyard. She looked at me like I was speaking French." He paused, glancing back at the little girl again. "As far as I can tell, Sharon had absolutely no rules. She let the kid go where she pleased, when she pleased. I'm not sure anything I said sunk in."

He pulled himself up with his cane, and carried one of the filled cloth bags toward the hook and rope, sidestepping the puddle of broken glass, sodden cardboard and cranberry juiced-beer.

"You've got to give her time, Alan," Mia said. "You've got to remember that living here without her mom around has to be as new and as strange to her as it is to you."

He turned to look back at her as he attached the hook to the cloth handles. "You know," he said, "generally people don't call me Alan. I'm Frisco. I've been Frisco for years." He started up the stairs. "I mean, Sharon—my sister—she calls me Alan, but everyone else calls me Frisco, from my swim buddy to my CO…."

Frisco looked down at Mia. She was standing in the courtyard, watching him and not trying to hide it this time. Her gardening clothes were almost as filthy as his, and several strands of her long, dark hair had escaped from her ponytail. How come he felt like a sweat-sodden reject from hell, while she managed to look impossibly beautiful?

"CO?" she repeated.

"Commanding Officer," he explained, turning the crank. The bag went up, and this time it made it all the way to the second floor.

Mia applauded and Natasha came over to do several clumsy forward rolls in the grass in celebration.

Frisco reached over the railing and pulled the bag up and onto the landing next to him.

"Lower the rope. I'll hook up the next one," Mia said.

It went up just as easily.

"Come on, Tash. Come upstairs and help me put away these supplies," Frisco called, and the little girl came barreling up the stairs. He turned back to look down at Mia. "I'll be down in a minute to clean up that mess."

"Alan, you know, I don't have anything better to do and I can—"

"Frisco," he interrupted her. "Not Alan. And *I'm* cleaning it up, not you."

"Do you mind if I call you Alan? I mean, after all, it is your *name*—"

"Yeah, I mind. It's not my name. Frisco's my name. Frisco is who I became when I joined the SEALs." His voice got softer. "Alan is nobody."

FRISCO WOKE TO the sound of a blood-chilling scream.

He was rolling out of bed, onto the floor, reaching, searching for his weapon, even before he was fully awake. But he had no firearm hidden underneath his pillow or down alongside his bed—he'd locked them all up in a trunk in his closet. He wasn't in the jungle on some dangerous mission, catching a combat nap. He was in his bedroom, in San Felipe, California, and the noise that had kicked him out of bed came from the powerful vocal cords of his five-year-old niece, who was supposed to be sound asleep on the couch in the living room.

Frisco stumbled to the wall and flipped on the light. Reaching this time for his cane, he opened his bedroom door and staggered down the hallway toward the living room.

He could see Natasha in the dim light that streamed down the hallway from his bedroom. She was crying, sitting up in a tangle of sheets on the couch, sweat matting her hair.

"Hey," Frisco said. "What the h…uh… What's going on, Tash?"

The kid didn't answer. She just kept on crying.

Frisco sat down next to her, but all she did was cry.

"You want a hug or something?" he asked, and she shook her head no and kept on crying.

"Um," Frisco said, uncertain of what to do, or what to say.

There was a tap on the door.

"You want to get that?" Frisco asked Natasha.

She didn't respond.

"I guess I'll get it then," he said, unlocking the bolt and opening the heavy wooden door.

Mia stood on the other side of the screen. She was wearing a white bathrobe and her hair was down loose around her shoulders. "Is everything all right?"

"No, I'm not murdering or torturing my niece," Frisco said flatly and closed the door. But he opened it again right away and pushed open the screen. "You wouldn't happen to know where Tash's On/Off switch is, would you?"

"It's dark in here," Mia said, stepping inside. "Maybe you should turn on all the lights so that she can see where she is."

Frisco turned on the bright overhead light—and realized he was standing in front of his neighbor and his niece in nothing but the new, tight-fitting, utilitarian white briefs he'd bought during yesterday's second trip to the grocery store. Good thing he'd bought them, or he quite possibly would have been standing there buck naked.

Whether it was the sudden light or the sight of him in his underwear, Frisco didn't know, but Natasha stopped crying, just like that. She still sniffled, and tears still flooded her eyes, but her sirenlike wail was silenced.

Mia was clearly thrown by the sight of him—and determined to act as if visiting with a neighbor who was in his underwear was the most normal thing in the world. She sat down on the couch next to Tasha and gave her a hug. Frisco excused himself and headed down the hall toward his bedroom and a pair of shorts.

It wasn't really that big a deal—Lucky O'Donlon, Frisco's swim buddy and best friend in the SEAL unit, had bought Frisco a tan-through French bathing suit from the Riviera that covered far less of him than these briefs. Of course, the minuscule suit wasn't something he'd ever be caught dead in....

He threw on his shorts and came back out into the living room.

"It must've been a pretty bad nightmare," he heard Mia saying to Tasha.

"I fell into a big, dark hole," Tash said in a tiny voice in between a very major case of hiccups. "And I was screaming and screaming and *screaming,* and I could see Mommy way, way up at the top, but she didn't hear me. She had on her mad face, and she just walked away.

And then water went up and over my head, and I knew I was gonna drown."

Frisco swore silently. He wasn't sure he could relieve Natasha's fears of abandonment, but he would do his best to make sure she didn't fear the ocean. He sat down next to her on the couch and she climbed into his lap. His heart lurched as she locked her little arms around his neck.

"Tomorrow morning we'll start your swimming lessons, okay?" he said gruffly, trying to keep the emotion that had suddenly clogged his throat from sounding in his voice.

Natasha nodded. "When I woke up, it was so dark. And someone turned off the TV."

"I turned it off when I went to bed," Frisco told her.

She lifted her head and gazed up at him. The tip of her nose was pink and her face was streaked and still wet from her tears. "Mommy always sleeps with it on. So she won't feel lonely."

Mia was looking at him over the top of Tasha's red curls. She was holding her tongue, but it was clear that she had something to say.

"Why don't you make a quick trip to the head?" he said to Tasha.

She nodded and climbed off his lap. "The head is the bathroom on a boat," she told Mia, wiping her runny nose on her hand. "Before bedtime, me and Frisco pretended we were on a pirate boat. He was the cap'n."

Mia tried to hide her smile. So *that* was the cause of the odd sounds she'd heard from Frisco's apartment at around eight o'clock.

"We also played Russian Princess," the little girl added.

Frisco actually blushed—his rugged cheekbones were tinged with a delicate shade of pink. "It's after 0200,

Tash. Get moving. And wash your face and blow your nose while you're in there."

"Yo ho ho and a bottle of rum," Mia said to him as the little girl disappeared down the hallway.

The pink tinge didn't disappear, but Frisco met her gaze steadily. "I'm doomed, aren't I?" he said, resignation in his voice. "You're going to tease me about this until the end of time."

Mia grinned. "I *do* feel as if I've been armed with a powerful weapon," she admitted, adding, "Your Majesty. Oh, or did you let Natasha take a turn and be the princess?"

"Very funny."

"What I would give to have been a fly on the wall…."

"She's five years old," he tried to explain, running his hand through his disheveled blond hair. "I don't have a single toy in the house. Or any books besides the ones I'm reading—which are definitely inappropriate. I don't even have paper and pencils to draw with—"

She'd gone too far with her teasing. "You don't have to explain. Actually, I think it's incredibly sweet. It's just… surprising. You don't really strike me as the make-believe type."

Frisco leaned forward.

"Look, Tash is gonna come back out soon. If there's something you want to tell me without her overhearing, you better say it now."

Mia was surprised again. He hadn't struck her as being extremely perceptive. In fact, he always seemed to be a touch self-absorbed and tightly wrapped up in his anger. But he was right. There *was* something that she wanted to ask him about the little girl.

"I was just wondering," she said, "if you've talked to Natasha about exactly where her mother is right now."

He shook his head.

"Maybe you should."

He shifted his position, obviously uncomfortable. "How do you talk about things like addiction and alcoholism to a five-year-old?"

"She probably knows more about it than you'd believe," Mia said quietly.

"Yeah, I guess she would," he said.

"It might make her feel a little bit less as if she's been deserted."

He looked up at her, meeting her eyes. Even now, in this moment of quiet, serious conversation, when Mia's eyes met his, there was a powerful burst of heat.

His gaze slipped down to the open neckline of her bathrobe, and she could see him looking at the tiny piece of her nightgown that was exposed. It was white, with a narrow white eyelet ruffle.

He wanted to see the rest of it—she knew that from the hunger in his eyes. Would he be disappointed if he knew that her nightgown was simple and functional? It was plain, not sexy, made from lightweight cotton.

He looked into her eyes again. No, he wouldn't be disappointed, because if they ever were in a position in which he would see her in her nightgown, she would only be wearing it for all of three seconds before he removed it and it landed in a pile on the floor.

The bathroom door opened, and Frisco finally looked away as their pint-size chaperon came back into the living room.

"I'd better go." Mia stood up. "I'll just let myself out."

"I'm hungry," the little girl said.

Frisco pulled himself to his feet. "Well, let's go into the kitchen and see what we can find to eat." He turned to look back at Mia. "I'm sorry we woke you."

"It's all right." Mia turned toward the door.

"Hey, Tash," she heard Frisco say as she let herself out through the screen door, "did your mom talk to you at all about where she was going?"

Mia shut the door behind her and went back into her own apartment.

She took off her robe and got into bed, but sleep was elusive. She couldn't stop thinking about Alan Francisco.

It was funny—the fact that Mia had found out he'd been kind enough to play silly make-believe games with his niece made him blush, yet he'd answered the door dressed only in his underwear with nary a smidgen of embarrassment.

Of course, with a body like his, what was there to be embarrassed about?

Still, the briefs he'd been wearing were brief indeed. The snug-fitting white cotton left very little to the imagination. And Mia had a *very* vivid imagination.

She opened her eyes, willing that same imagination not to get too carried away. Talk about make-believe games. She could make believe that she honestly wasn't bothered by the fact that Alan had spent most of his adult life as a professional soldier, and *Alan* could make believe that he wasn't weighed down by his physical challenge, that he was psychologically healthy, that he wasn't battling depression and resorting to alcohol to numb his unhappiness.

Mia rolled over onto her stomach and switched on the lamp on her bedside table. She was wide-awake, so she would read. It was better than lying in the dark dreaming about things that would never happen.

FRISCO COVERED THE sleeping child with a light blanket. The television provided a flickering light and the soft murmur of voices. Tasha hadn't fallen asleep until he'd turned it on, and he knew better now than to turn it off.

He went into the kitchen and poured himself a few fingers of whiskey and took a swallow, welcoming the burn and the sensation of numbness that followed. Man, he needed that. Talking to Natasha about Sharon's required visit to the detox center had *not* been fun. But it had been necessary. Mia had been right.

Tash had had no clue where her mother had gone. She'd thought, in fact, that Sharon had gone to jail. The kid had heard bits and pieces of conversations about the car accident her mother had been involved in, and thought Sharon had been arrested for running someone over.

Frisco had explained how the driver of the car Sharon had struck was badly hurt and in the hospital, but not dead. He didn't go into detail about what would happen if the man were to die—she didn't need to hear that. But he did try to explain what a detox center was, and why Sharon couldn't leave the facility to visit Natasha, and why Tash couldn't go there to visit her.

The kid had looked skeptical when Frisco told her that when Sharon came out of detox, she wouldn't drink anymore. Frisco shook his head. A five-year-old cynic. What was the world coming to?

He took both his glass and the bottle back through the living room and outside onto the dimly lit landing. The sterile environment of air-conditioned sameness in his condo always got to him, particularly at this time of night.

He took a deep breath of the humid, salty air, filling his lungs with the warm scent of the sea.

He sat down on the steps and took another sip of the whiskey. He willed it to make him relax, to put him to sleep, to carry him past these darkest, longest hours of the early morning. He silently cursed the fact that here it was, nearly 0300 again, and here he was, wide awake. He'd been so certain when he'd climbed into bed tonight that his exhaustion would carry him through and keep him sound asleep until the morning. He hadn't counted on Tasha's 0200 reveille. He drained his glass and poured himself another drink.

Mia's door barely made a sound as it opened, but he heard it in the quiet. Still, he didn't move as she came outside, and he didn't speak until she stood at the railing, looking down at him.

"How long ago did your dog die?" he asked, keeping his voice low so as not to wake the other condo residents.

She stood very, very still for several long seconds. Finally she laughed softly and sat down next to him on the stairs. "About eight months ago," she told him, her voice velvety in the darkness. "How did you know I had a dog?"

"Good guess," he murmured.

"No, really... Tell me."

"The pooper-scooper you lent me to clean up the mess in the courtyard was a major hint," he said. "And your car had—how do I put this delicately?—a certain canine perfume."

"Her name was Zu. She was about a million years old in dog years. I got her when I was eight."

"*Z-o-o?*" Frisco asked.

"Z-u," she said. "It was short for Zu-zu. I named her after a little girl in a movie—"

"It's a Wonderful Life," he said.

Mia gazed at him, surprised again. "You've seen it?"

He shrugged. "Hasn't everybody?"

"Probably. But most people don't remember the name of George Bailey's youngest daughter."

"It's a personal favorite." He gave her a sidelong glance. "Amazing that I should like it, huh? All of the war scenes in it are incidental."

"I didn't say that…."

"But you were thinking it." Frisco took a sip of his drink. It was whiskey. Mia could smell the pungent scent from where she was sitting. "Sorry about your dog."

"Thanks," Mia said. She wrapped her arms around her knees. "I still miss her."

"Too soon to get another, huh?" he said.

She nodded.

"What breed was she? No, let me guess." He shifted slightly to face her. She could feel him studying her in the darkness, as if what he could see would help him figure out the answer.

She kept her eyes averted, suddenly afraid to look him in the eye. Why had she come out here? She didn't usually make a habit of inviting disaster, and sitting in the dark a mere foot away from this man was asking for trouble.

"Part lab, part spaniel," Frisco finally said, and she did look up.

"You're half-right—although cocker spaniel was the only part I could ever identify. Although sometimes I thought I saw a bit of golden retriever." She paused. "How did you know she was a mix?"

He lowered his eyebrows in a look of mock incredulousness. "Like you'd ever get a dog from anywhere but the pound…? And probably from death row at the pound, too, right?"

She had to smile. "Okay, obviously you've figured me out completely. There's no longer any mystery in our relationship—"

"Not quite. There's one last thing I need you to clear up for me."

He was smiling at her in the darkness, flirting with her, indulging in lighthearted banter. Mia would have been amazed, had she not learned by now that Alan Francisco was full of surprises.

"What are you doing still awake?" he asked.

"I could ask the same of you," she countered.

"I'm recovering from my talk with Tasha." He looked down into his glass, the light mood instantly broken. "I'm not sure I helped any. She's pretty jaded when it comes to her mom." He laughed, but there was no humor in it. "She has every right to be."

Mia looked over toward Frisco's condo. She could see the flicker of the television through a gap in the curtains. "She's not still up, is she?"

He sighed, shaking his head no. "She needs the TV on to sleep. I wish *I* could find a solution to not sleeping that's as easy."

Mia looked down at the drink in his hand. "That's probably not it."

Frisco didn't say anything—he just looked at her. To Mia's credit, she didn't say another word. She didn't preach, didn't chastise, didn't lecture.

But after several long moments when he didn't respond, she stood up.

"Good night," she said.

He didn't want her to leave. Oddly enough, the night

wasn't so damned oppressive when she was around. But he didn't know what to say to make her stay. He could've told her that he wasn't like Sharon, that he could stop drinking when and if he wanted to, but that would have sounded exactly like a problem drinker's claim.

He could've told her he was strong enough to stop—he just wasn't strong enough right now to face the fact that the Navy had quit on him.

Instead, he said nothing, and she quietly went inside, locking her door behind her.

And he poured himself another drink.

CHAPTER SIX

MIA'S LEGS BURNED as she rounded the corner onto Harris Avenue. She was nearly there, down to the last quarter mile of her run, so she put on a burst of speed.

There was construction going on just about a block and a half from the condo complex. Someone was building another fast-food restaurant—just what this neighborhood needed, she thought.

They'd poured the concrete for the foundation, and the project was at a temporary standstill while the mixture hardened. The lot was deserted. Several A&B Construction Co. trucks were parked at haphazard angles among huge hills of displaced dirt and broken asphalt.

A little girl sat digging on top of one of those hills, her face and clothing streaked with dirt, her red hair gleaming in the sunlight.

Mia skidded to a stop.

Sure enough, it was Natasha. She was oblivious to everything around her, digging happily in the sun-hardened dirt, singing a little song.

Mia tried to catch her breath as she ducked underneath the limp yellow ribbon that was supposed to warn trespassers off the construction sight.

"Natasha?"

The little girl looked down at her and smiled. "Hi, Mia."

"Honey, does your uncle know where you are?"

"He's asleep," Tasha said, returning to her digging. She'd found a plastic spoon and a discarded paper cup and was filling it with dirt and stirring the dirt as if it were coffee. She had mud covering close to every inch of her exposed skin—which was probably good since the morning sun was hot enough to give her a bad sunburn. "It's still early. He won't be up 'til later."

Mia glanced at her watch. "Tash, it's nearly ten. He's got to be awake by now. He's probably going crazy, looking for you. Don't you remember what he told you—about not leaving the courtyard, and not even going out of the condo without telling him?"

Tasha glanced up at her. "How can I tell him when he's asleep?" she said matter of factly. "Mommy always slept until after lunchtime."

Mia held out her hands to help Tasha down from the dirt pile. "Come on. I'll walk you home. We can check to see if Frisco's still asleep."

The little girl stood up and Mia swung her down to the ground.

"You *are* dirty, aren't you?" she continued as they began walking toward the condo complex. "I think a bath is in your immediate future."

Tasha looked at her arms and legs. "I already had a bath—a mud bath. Princesses always have mud baths, and they never have more than one bath a day."

"Oh?" Mia said. "I thought princesses always had bubble baths right after their mud baths."

Tasha considered that thoughtfully. "I never had a bubble bath."

"It's very luxurious," Mia told her. What a sight they must've made walking down the street—a mud-encrusted child and an adult literally dripping with perspiration. "The bubbles go right up to your chin."

Natasha's eyes were very wide. "Really?"

"Yeah, and I just happen to have some bubble-bath soap," Mia told her. "You can try it out when we get home—unless you're absolutely certain you don't want a second bath today…?"

"No, princesses can only have one *mud* bath a day," Tasha told her in complete seriousness. "It's okay if they have a mud bath *and* a bubble bath."

"Good." Mia smiled as they entered the condo courtyard.

The complex was still pretty quiet. Most of the residents had left for work hours ago. Still, it was summer vacation for the few kids who lived in the building. Mia could hear the distant strains of television sets and stereo systems. Tasha followed her up the stairs to unit 2C.

The door was ajar and Mia knocked on the screen. "Hello?" she called, but there was no answer. She leaned on the bell. Still nothing.

Mia looked at the mud caked on Natasha's body and clothes. "You better wait out here," she told the little girl.

Tasha nodded.

"*Right* here," Mia said in her best teacher's voice, pointing to the little spot of concrete directly in front of Frisco's door. "Sit. And don't go *any*where, do you understand, miss?"

Tasha nodded again and sat down.

Feeling very much like a trespasser, Mia opened the screen door and went inside. With the curtains closed, the living room was dim. The television was on, but the volume was set to a low, barely discernible murmur. The air was cool, almost cold, as if the air conditioner had been working overtime to compensate for the slightly opened door. Mia turned off the TV as she went past.

"Hello?" Mia called again. "Lieutenant Francisco…?"

The condo was as silent as a tomb.

"He's gonna be grumpy if you wake him up," Tasha said, up on her knees with her nose pressed against the screen.

"I'll take my chances," Mia said, starting down the hall toward the bedrooms.

She *was* tiptoeing, though. When she reached the end of the hall, she glanced quickly into the bathroom and the smaller of the two bedrooms. Both were empty. The larger bedroom's door was half-closed, and she crept closer. Taking a deep breath, she pushed it open as she knocked.

The double bed was empty.

In the dimness, she could see that the sheets were twisted into a knot. The blanket had been kicked onto the floor, and the pillows were rumpled, but Alan Francisco was not still lying there.

There was not much furniture in the room—just the bed, a bedside table and a dresser. The setup was Spartan. The top of his dresser held only a small pile of loose change. There were no personal items, no knickknacks, no souvenirs. The sheets on the bed were plain white, the blanket a light beige. The closet door hung open, as did one of the drawers in the modest-size dresser. Several duffel bags sagged nearby on the floor. The whole place had a rather apathetic feel, as if the person living here didn't care enough to unpack, or to hang pictures on the wall and make the place his own.

There was nothing that gave any sense of personality to the resident of the room, with the exception of an enormous pile of dirty laundry that seemed to glower from one dark corner. That and a nearly empty bottle of whiskey standing on Frisco's bedside table were the only telling things. And the bottle, at least, certainly told quite a bit. It was similar to the bottle he'd had outside last night—except *that* bottle had been nearly full.

No wonder Tasha hadn't been able to wake him.

But eventually he *had* awakened and found the little girl gone. He was probably out searching for her right now, worried nearly out of his mind.

The best thing *they* could do was stay put. Eventually, Frisco would come back to see if Natasha had returned.

But the thought of hanging out in Frisco's condo wasn't extremely appealing. His belongings may have been impersonal to the point of distastefulness, but she felt as if by being there, she was invading his privacy.

Mia turned to leave when a gleam of reflected light from the closet caught her eye. She switched on the overhead light.

It was amazing. She'd never seen anything like it in her entire life. A naval uniform hung in the closet, bright white and crisply pressed. And on the upper left side of the jacket, were row after row after row after row of colorful medals. And above it—the cause of that reflected light—was a pin in the shape of an eagle, wings outspread, both a gun and a trident clasped in its fierce talons.

Mia couldn't imagine the things Frisco had done to get all of those medals. But because there were so many of them, there was one thing that she suddenly did see quite clearly. Alan Francisco had a dedication to his job unlike anyone she'd ever met. These medals told her that as absolutely as if they could talk. If he had had one or two medals—sure, that would have told her he was a brave and capable soldier. But there had to be more than ten of these colorful bars pinned to his uniform. She counted them quickly with her finger. Ten...*eleven*. Eleven medals surely meant that Frisco had gone above and beyond the call of duty time after time.

She turned, and in the new light of her discovery, his bedroom had an entirely different look to it. Instead of being the room of a someone who didn't care enough to add any personal touches, it became the room of a man who'd never taken the time to have a life outside of his dangerous career.

Even the whiskey bottle looked different. It looked far more sad and desperate than ever before.

And the room *wasn't* entirely devoid of personal items. There was a book on the floor next to the bed. It was a collection of short stories by J. D. Salinger. *Salinger.* Who would've thought...?

"Mia?"

Natasha was calling her from the living room door.

Mia turned off the light on her way out of Frisco's room. "I'm here, hon, but your uncle's not," she said, coming into the living room.

"He's not?" Tasha scrambled to her feet to get out of the way of the opening screen door.

"What do you say we go next door and see about that bubble-bath soap of mine?" Mia continued, shutting the heavy wooden door to unit 2C tightly behind her. "I'll write a note for your uncle so that he knows you're at my place when he gets back."

She'd call Thomas, too. If he was home, he might be willing to go out looking for the Navy lieutenant, to tell him Natasha was safe.

"Let's go right into the bathroom," Mia told Tasha as she opened her screen door and unlocked the dead bolt to her condo. "We'll pop you directly into the tub, okay?"

Natasha hung back, her eyes very wide in her mud-streaked face. "Is Frisco gonna be mad at me?"

Mia gazed at the little girl. "Would you blame him very much if he was?"

Tasha's face fell as she shook her head, her lips stretching into that unmistakable shape children's mouths made when they were about to cry. "He was asleep."

"Just because he's sleeping doesn't mean you can break his rules," Mia told her.

"I was gonna come home before he woke up...."

Aha. Mia suddenly understood. Natasha's mother had frequently slept off her alcoholic binges until well past noon, unknowing and perhaps even uncaring of her daughter's private explorations. It was tantamount to neglect, and obviously Tasha expected the same treatment from Frisco.

Something was going to have to change.

"If I were you," Mia advised her, "I'd be good and ready to say I'm sorry the moment Frisco gets home."

FRISCO SAW THE note on his door from down in the courtyard. It was a pink piece of paper taped to the outside of the screen, and it lifted in the first stirrings of a late-morning breeze. He hurried up the stairs, ignoring the pain in his knee, and pulled the note from the door.

"Found Natasha," it said in clean, bold printing. Thank *God.* He closed his eyes briefly, grateful beyond belief. He'd searched the beach for nearly an hour, terrified his niece had broken his rule and gone down to the ocean again. Hell, if she would break his rule about leaving the condo, she could just as well have broken his rule about never swimming alone.

He'd run into a lifeguard who'd told him he'd heard a rumor that a kid's body had washed up on the beach early in the morning. Frisco's heart had damn near stopped beating. He'd waited for nearly forty-five minutes at a pay phone, trying to get through to the shore patrol, trying to find out if the rumor was true.

It turned out that the body that had washed up in the surf had been that of a baby seal. And with that relief had come the knowledge that he'd wasted precious time. And the search had started again.

Frisco opened his eyes and found he had crumpled the pink paper. He smoothed it out to read the rest. "Found Natasha. We're at my place. Mia."

Mia Summerton. Saving the day again.

Leaning on his cane, he went toward Mia's door, catching his reflection in his living room window. His hair was standing straight up, and he looked as if he were hiding from the sunlight behind his dark sunglasses. His T-shirt looked slept in, and his shorts *were* slept in. He looked like hell and he *felt* worse. His head had been pounding from the moment he'd stumbled out into the living room and found that Natasha was gone again. No, strike that. His head had been pounding from the moment he'd opened his eyes. It had risen to a nearly unbearable level when he'd discovered Tash was AWOL. It was still just shy of intolerable.

He rang the doorbell anyway, well aware that in addition to the not-so-pretty picture he made, he didn't smell too damn good, either. His shirt reeked of a distillery. He hadn't been too picky when he snatched it off the floor of his room this morning on his way out the door to search for Tash. Just his luck, he'd grabbed the one he'd used to mop up a spilled glass of whiskey last night.

The door swung open, and Mia Summerton stood there, looking like something out of a sailor's fantasy. She was wearing running shorts that redefined the word *short,* and a midriff-baring athletic top that redefined the word *lust.* Her hair was back in a single braid, and still damp from perspiration.

"She's here, she's safe," Mia said in way of greeting. "She's in the tub, getting cleaned up."

"Where did you find her?" His throat felt dry and his voice came out raspy and harsh.

Mia looked back into her condo unit and raised her voice. "How you doing in there, Tasha?"

"Fine," came a cheery reply.

She opened the screen door and stepped outside. "Harris Avenue," she told Frisco. "She was over on Harris Avenue, playing in the dirt at that construction site—"

"*Dammit!* What the *hell* does she think she's doing? She's five years old! She shouldn't be walking around by herself or—God!—playing on a *construction* site!" Frisco ran one hand down his face, fighting to control his flare of anger. "I know that yelling at the kid's not going to help…." He forced himself to lower his voice, to take a deep breath and try to release all of the frustration and anger and worry of the past several hours. "I don't know what to do," he admitted. "She blatantly disobeyed my orders."

"That's not the way she sees it," Mia told him.

"The rule was for her to tell me when she went outside. The rule was to stay in the courtyard."

"In her opinion, all bets are off if Mom—or Uncle Frisco—can't drag themselves out of bed in the morning." Mia fixed him with her level gaze. Her eyes were more green than brown in the bright morning sun. "She told me she thought she'd be back before you even woke up."

"A rule is a rule," Frisco started.

"Yeah, and *her* rule," Mia interrupted, "is that if you climb into a bottle, she's on her own."

Frisco's headache intensified. He looked away, unable to meet her gaze. It wasn't that she was looking at him accusingly. There was nothing even remotely accusative in her eyes. In fact, her eyes were remarkably gentle, softening the harshness of her words.

"I'm sorry," she murmured. "That was uncalled for."

He shook his head, uncertain as to whether he was agreeing with her or disagreeing with her.

"Why don't you come inside?" Mia said, holding open the screen door for him.

Mia's condo might as well have been from a different planet than his. It was spacious and open, with unspotted, light brown carpeting and white painted bamboo-framed furniture. The walls were freshly painted and clean, and potted plants were everywhere, their vines lacing across the ceiling on a system of hooks. Music played softly on the stereo. Frisco recognized the smoky Texas-blues-influenced vocals of Lee Roy Parnell.

Pictures hung on the wall—gorgeous blue and green watercolors of the ocean, and funky, quirkily colorful figures of people walking along the beach.

"My mother's an artist," Mia said, following his gaze. "Most of this is her work."

Another picture was that of the beach before a storm. It conveyed all of the dangerous power of the wind and the water, the ominous, darkening sky, the rising surf, the palm trees whipped and tossed—nature at her most deadly.

"She's good," Frisco said.

Mia smiled. "I know." She raised her voice. "How's it going in bubbleland, Natasha?"

"Okay."

"While she was out playing in the dirt, she gave herself a Russian princess mud bath." With a wry smile, she led Frisco into the tiny kitchen. It was exactly like his—and nothing like his. Magnets of all shapes and sizes covered the refrigerator, holding up photos of smiling people, and notes and coupons and theater schedules. Fresh fruit hung in wire baskets that were suspended from hooks on the ceiling. A coffee mug in the shape of a cow wearing a graduate's cap sat on the counter next to the telephone, holding pencils and pens. The entire room was filled with little bits and pieces of Mia. "I managed to convince her that true royalty always followed a mud bath with a bubble bath."

"Bless you," Frisco said. "And thank you for bringing her home."

"It was lucky I ran that way." Mia opened the refrigerator door. "I usually take a longer route, but I was feeling the heat this morning." She looked up at Frisco. "Ice tea, lemonade or soda?"

"Something with caffeine, please," Frisco told her.

"Hmm," Mia said, reaching into the back of the fridge and pulling out a can of cola. She handed it to him. "And would you like that with two aspirin or three?"

Frisco smiled. It was crooked but it was a smile. "Three. Thanks."

She motioned to the small table that was in the dining area at the end of the kitchen, and Frisco lowered himself into one of a pair of chairs. She had a napkin holder in the shape of a pig and tiny airplanes for salt and pepper shakers. There were plants everywhere in here, too, and a fragile wind chime directly over his head, in front of a window that looked out over the parking lot. He reached up and brushed the wind chime with one finger. It sounded as delicate and ghostly as it looked.

The doors to her kitchen cabinets had recently been replaced with light, blond wood. The gleaming white countertop looked new, too. But he only spared it half a glance, instead watching Mia as she stood on tiptoes to reach up into one of the cabinets for her bottle of aspirin. She was a blinding mixture of muscles and curves. He couldn't look away, even when she turned around. Great, just what she needed. Some loser leering at her in her own kitchen. He could see her apprehension and discomfort in her eyes.

She set the bottle of aspirin down in front of him on the table and disappeared, murmuring some excuse about checking on Natasha.

Frisco pressed the cold soda can against his forehead. When Mia returned, she was wearing a T-shirt over her running gear. It helped, but not a lot.

He cleared his throat. A million years ago, he had been so good at small talk. "So…how far do you run?" Cripes, he sounded like some kind of idiot.

"Usually three miles," she answered, opening the refrigerator again and taking out a pitcher of ice tea. She poured herself a glass. "But today I only went about two and a half."

"You gotta be careful when it's hot like this." Man, could he sound any more lame? *Lame?* Yeah, that was the perfect word to describe him, in more ways than one.

She nodded, turning to look at him as she leaned back against the kitchen counter and took a sip of her tea.

"So…your mother's an artist."

Mia smiled. Damn, she had a beautiful smile. Had he really thought that it was goofy-looking just two days ago?

"Yeah," she said. "She has a studio near Malibu. That's where I grew up."

Frisco nodded. This was where he was supposed to counter by telling her where he came from. "I grew up right here in San Felipe, the armpit of California."

Her smile deepened. "Armpits have their purpose—not that I agree with you and think that San Felipe is one."

"You're entitled to your opinion," he said with a shrug. "To me, San Felipe will always be an armpit."

"So sell your condo and move to Hawaii."

"Is that where your family's from?" he asked.

She looked down into her glass. "To tell you the truth, I'm not really sure. I think I must have some Hawaiian or Polynesian blood, but I'm not certain."

"Your parents don't know?"

"I was adopted from an overseas agency. The records were extremely sketchy." She looked up at him. "I went through a phase, you know, when I tried to find my birth parents."

"Birth parents aren't always worth finding. I would've been better off without knowing mine."

"I'm sorry," Mia said quietly. "There was a time when I might've said that you can't possibly mean that, or that that couldn't possibly be true. But I've been teaching at an urban high school for over five years, and I'm well aware that most people didn't have the kind of child-hood or the kind of parents that I did." Her eyes were a beautiful mixture of brown and green and compassion. "I don't know what you might have gone through, but...I *am* sorry."

"I've heard that teaching high school is a pretty dangerous job these days, what with guns and drugs and violence," Frisco said, trying desperately to bring the conversation out of this dark and ultrapersonal area. "Did they give you any special kind of commando training when you took the job?"

Mia laughed. "No, we're on our own. Thrown to the wolves naked, so to speak. Some of the teachers have compensated by becoming real drill sergeants. I've found that positive reinforcement works far better than punishment." She took another sip of her ice tea, gazing at him speculatively over the top of her glass. "In fact, you might want to consider that when you're dealing with Natasha."

Frisco shook his head. "What? Give her a cookie for running away? I don't think so."

"But what kind of punishment will possibly get through to her?" Mia persisted. "Think about it. The poor kid's already been given the ultimate punishment for a five-year-old—her mommy's gone. There's probably nothing else that you can take away from her that will matter. You can yell at her and make her cry. You can even frighten her and make her afraid of you, and maybe even give her worse nightmares. But if you reward her when she *does* follow your rules, if you make a really big deal about it and make her feel as if she's worth a million bucks, well, she'll catch on much more quickly."

He ran his fingers through his hair. "But I can't just ignore what she did this morning."

"It's difficult," Mia admitted. "You have to achieve a balance between letting a child know her behavior is unacceptable, and not wanting to reward the child's bad behavior by giving her too much attention. Kids who crave attention often misbehave. It's the easiest way to get a parent or teacher to notice them."

Frisco pushed his mouth up into another smile. "I know some so-called grown-ups who operate on the same principle."

Mia gazed at the man sitting at her kitchen table. It was amazing. He looked as if he'd been rolled from a park bench, yet she still found him attractive. What would he look like, she wondered, shiny clean and dressed in that uniform she'd found in his closet?

He'd probably look like someone she'd go out of her way to avoid. She'd never been impressed by men in uniform. It wasn't likely that she'd be impressed now.

Still, all those medals...

Mia set her empty glass down and pushed herself off the counter. "I'll get Tasha out of the tub," she told Frisco. "You probably have things to do—she told me you promised to take her shopping for furniture for her bedroom."

"Yeah." Frisco nodded and pulled himself clumsily to his feet. "Thanks again for bringing her home."

Mia smiled and slipped down the hall toward the bathroom. Considering their rocky start, they'd actually achieved quite a nice, neighborly relationship.

Nice and neighborly—that's exactly where they were going to leave it, too. Despite the fact that this man had the ability to make her blood heat with a single look, despite the fact that she genuinely liked him more and more each time they met, she *was* going to be careful to keep her distance.

Because the more Mia found out about her neighbor, the more she was convinced that they were absolute polar opposites.

CHAPTER SEVEN

IT WAS PINK. It was definitely, undeniably pink. Its back was reminiscent of a scallop shell, and its arms were scrolled. Its cushions were decorated with shiny silver buttons that absolutely, positively could not have been comfortable to sit upon.

It was far too fancy to be called a couch or even a sofa. It was advertised as a "settee."

For Natasha, it was love at first sight.

Fortunately for Frisco, she didn't spot it until they were on their way *out* of the furniture store.

She sat down on it and went into Russian princess mode. Frisco was so tired, and his knee and head ached so badly, he sat down, too.

"Kneel in front of the Russian princess," Tash commanded him sternly.

Frisco put his head back and closed his eyes. "Not a chance, babe," he mumbled.

After Tash's bath at Mia's place, he'd taken her home, then they'd both suited up and headed to the beach for the kid's first swimming lesson. The current had still been quite strong, and he'd kept his fingers solidly locked on Tash's bathing suit the entire time.

The kid was fearless. Considering that she hadn't even seen the ocean before yesterday, she was entirely enthusiastic about the water. At the end of the week, she'd be well on her way to swimming like a fish.

Frisco shook his head. How on earth had Sharon's kid managed to live to the ripe old age of five without having even *seen* the ocean? Historically, the Franciscos were coastline people. His old man had worked on a fishing boat for years. Vacations were spent at the water. Frisco and his two older brothers had loved the beach. But not Sharon, he remembered suddenly. Sharon had damn near drowned when she was hardly any older than Natasha was now. As an adult, Sharon moved inland, spending much of her time in Las Vegas and Reno. Tash had been born in Tucson, Arizona. Not much beachfront property there.

After the swimming lesson and a forty-five-minute lecture on why Tash had to follow Frisco's rules, they'd dragged themselves home, had lunch, changed and gone shopping for furniture for Frisco's second bedroom.

They'd found this particular store in the Yellow Pages. It was right around the corner, and—the advertisement boasted—it had free, same-day delivery. Frisco had picked out a simple mattress, box spring and metal-framed bed, and Tash had chosen a pint-size bright yellow chest of drawers. Together, they'd found a small desk and chair and a petite bookshelf.

"Can we get this, Frisco?" Tash now asked hopefully.

He snorted as he opened his eyes. "A *pink* couch? Man, are you kidding?"

As usual, she answered his rhetorical question as if he'd asked it seriously. "No."

"Where the hell would we put it?" He glanced at the price tag. It was supposedly on sale, marked down to a mere small fortune.

"We could put it where that other icky one is."

"Great. Just what that condo needs." Shaking his head,

Frisco pulled himself to his feet. "Come on. If we don't hurry, the delivery truck is going to beat us home. We don't want them to deliver your new furniture to some other kid."

That got Tasha moving, but not without one final love-lorn glance at the pink sofa.

They were only two blocks from home, but Frisco flagged down a cab. The sun was merciless, and his knee was damn near making him scream with pain. His head wasn't feeling too great, either.

There was no sign of Mia out in her garden in the condo courtyard. Her door was tightly shut, and Frisco found himself wondering where she had gone.

Bad mistake, he told himself. She had been making it clear that she didn't want to be anything more than a neighbor. She didn't want the likes of him sniffing around her door.

Mia actually thought he was a drunk, like his old man and his sister. It was entirely possible that if he wasn't careful, she would be proven right.

No more, he vowed, pulling himself up the stairs. To-night, if insomnia struck, he'd tough it out. He'd face the demons who were at their ugliest in the wee hours of the morning by spitting in their faces. If he awoke in the middle of the night, he'd spend the time working out, doing exercises that would strengthen his leg and support his injured knee.

He unlocked the door to his condo and Tasha went inside first, dashing through the living room and down the hall to the bedrooms.

Frisco followed more slowly, each painful step making him grit his teeth. He needed to sit down and get his weight off his knee, elevate the damn thing and ice the hell out of it.

Tasha was in her bedroom, lying down on the wall-to-wall carpeting. She was flat on her back on the floor, staring up at the ceiling.

As Frisco stood in the doorway and watched, she scrambled to her feet and then lay down on the floor in another part of the room.

"What are you doing?" he asked as she did the exact same thing yet a third time.

"I'm picking where to put the bed," Tash told him from her position on the floor.

Frisco couldn't hide his smile. "Good idea," he said. "Why don't you work on that for a while? I'm gonna chill for a few minutes before the delivery truck comes, okay?"

"'Kay."

He headed back into the kitchen and grabbed an ice pack from the freezer. He moved into the living room and sat on his old plaid couch, swinging his injured leg up and onto the cushions. The ice felt good, and he put his head back and closed his eyes.

He had to figure out a way to move those boxes out of Tash's room. There were a half a dozen of them, and they were all too ungainly for him to carry with only one arm. But he could drag 'em, though. That would work. He could use a blanket or sheet, and wrestle the boxes on top of it, one at a time. With the box firmly trapped in the sheet like a fish in a fishing net, he could pull the sheet, sliding the box along the rug out of Tash's room and into his own and…

Frisco held his breath. He'd sensed more than heard the movement of Tasha crossing the living room floor, but now he heard the telltale squeak of the front door being opened.

He opened his eyes and sat up, but she was already out the door.

"Natasha! *Damn* it!"

His cane had slipped underneath the couch and he scrambled for it, grabbing it and moving quickly to the door.

"Tash!"

He supported himself on the railing near his rope and pulley setup. Natasha looked up at him from the courtyard, eyes wide.

"Where the *hell* are you going?" he growled.

"To see if Thomas is home."

She didn't get it. Frisco could tell just from looking at the little girl that she honestly didn't understand why he was upset with her.

He took a deep breath and forced his racing pulse to slow. "You forgot to tell me where you were going."

"You were asleep."

"No, I wasn't. And even if I was, that doesn't mean you can just break the rules."

She was silent, gazing up at him.

Frisco went down the stairs. "Come here." He gestured with his head toward one of the courtyard benches. He sat down and she sat next to him. Her feet didn't touch the ground, and she swung them back and forth. "Do you know what a rule is?" he asked.

Tasha chewed on her lower lip. She shook her head.

"Take a guess," Frisco told her. "What's a rule?"

"Something you want me to do that I don't want to do?" she asked.

It took all that he had in him not to laugh. "It's more than that," he said. "It's something that you *have* to do, whether or not you want to. And it's always the same, whether I'm asleep or awake."

She didn't get it. He could see her confusion and disbelief written clearly on her face.

He ran one hand down his face, trying to clear his cobweb-encrusted mind. He was tired. He couldn't think how to explain to Natasha that she *had* to follow his rules all of the time. He couldn't figure out how to get through to her.

"Hi, guys."

Frisco looked up to see Mia Summerton walking toward them. She was wearing a summery, sleeveless, flower-print dress with a long, sweeping skirt that reached almost all the way to the ground. She had sandals on her feet and a large-brimmed straw hat on her head and a friendly smile on her pretty face. She looked cool and fresh, like a long-awaited evening breeze in the suffocating late-afternoon heat.

Where had she been, all dressed up like that? On a lunch date with some boyfriend? Or maybe she wasn't coming, maybe she was going. Maybe she was waiting for her dinner date to arrive. Lucky bastard. Frisco scowled, letting himself hate the guy, allowing himself that small luxury.

"There's a furniture truck unloading in the driveway," Mia said, ignoring his dark look. In fact, she was ignoring him completely. She spoke directly to Tash. "Does that pretty yellow dresser belong to you, by any chance?"

Natasha jumped up, their conversation all but forgotten. "Me," she said, dashing toward the parking lot. "It belongs to me!"

"Don't run too far ahead," Frisco called out warningly, pulling himself to his feet. He tightened his mouth as he put his weight on his knee, resisting the urge to wince, not wanting to show Mia how much he was hurting. "And do not step off that sidewalk."

But Mia somehow knew. "Are you all right?" she asked him, no longer ignoring him, her eyes filled with concern. She followed him after Natasha, back toward the parking lot.

"I'm fine," he said brusquely.

"Have you been chasing around after her all day?"

"I'm fine," he repeated.

"You're allowed to be tired," she said with a musical laugh. "I babysat a friend's four-year-old last week, and I practically had to be carried out on a stretcher afterward."

Frisco glanced at her. She gazed back at him innocently. She was giving him an out, pretending that the lines of pain and fatigue on his face were due to the fact that he wasn't used to keeping up with the high energy of a young child, rather than the result of his old injury.

"Yeah, right."

Mia knew better than to show her disappointment at Frisco's terse reply. She wanted to be this man's friend, and she'd assumed they'd continue to build a friendship on the shaky foundation they'd recently established. But whatever understanding they'd reached this morning seemed to have been forgotten. The old, angry, tight-lipped Frisco had returned with a vengeance.

Unless…

It was possible his knee was hurting worse than she thought.

A delivery man approached. "You Alan Francisco?" he asked, not waiting for a reply before he held out his clipboard. "Sign at the X."

Frisco signed. "It's going up to Unit 2C. It's right at the top of the stairs—"

"Sorry, pal, this is as far as I go." The man didn't sound

even remotely apologetic. "My instructions are to get it off the truck. You've got to take it from here."

"You're kidding." Frisco's voice was flat, unbelieving. The furniture was standing there on the asphalt, next to the delivery vehicle.

The man closed the sliding back door of his truck with a crash. "Read the small print on your receipt. It's free delivery—and you got exactly what you paid for."

How was Frisco supposed to get all this up a flight of stairs? Mia saw the frustration and anger in his eyes and in the tight set of his mouth.

The man climbed into the cab and closed the door behind him.

"I bought this stuff from your store because you advertise a free delivery," Frisco said roughly. "If you're not going to deliver it, you can damn well load it up and take it back."

"First of all, it's not *my* store," the man told him, starting the engine with a roar and grinding the gears as he put it into first, "and secondly, you already signed for it."

It was all Frisco could do to keep himself from pulling himself up on the running board and slamming his fist into the man's surly face. But Tash and Mia were watching him. So he did nothing. He stood there like a damned idiot as the truck pulled away.

He stared after it, feeling helpless and impotent and frustrated beyond belief.

And then Mia touched his arm. Her fingers felt cool against his hot skin. Her touch was hesitant and light, but she didn't pull away even when he turned to glare down at her.

"I sent Tasha to see if Thomas is home," she said quietly. "We'll get this upstairs."

"I hate this," he said. The words were out of his mouth

before he could stop them. They were dripping with de-spair and shame. He hadn't meant to say it aloud, to reveal so much of himself to her. It wasn't a complaint, or even self-pity. It was a fact. He hated his limitations.

Her brown-green eyes grew warmer, more liquid. She slid her hand all the way down to his, and intertwined their fingers. "I know," she said huskily. "I'm so sorry."

He turned to look at her then, to *really* look at her. "You don't even like me," he said. "How can you stand to be so nice?"

"I *do* like you," she said, trying to step back, away from the intensity of his gaze. But he wouldn't let go of her hand. "I want to be your friend."

Friend. She tugged again, and this time he released her. She wanted to be his friend. He wanted so much more....

"Yo, Frisco!"

Frisco turned. The voice was as familiar to him as breathing. It was Lucky O'Donlon. He'd parked his mo-torcycle in one of the visitor's spaces, and now sauntered toward them. He was wearing his blue dress uniform and looked to be one hundred percent spit and polish. Frisco knew better.

"Hey, guy, having a tag sale or something?" Lucky's wide smile and warm blue eyes traveled lazily over the furniture, Frisco's damned cane, and Mia. He took an especially long time taking in Mia. "You gonna introduce me to your friend?"

"Do I have a choice?"

Lucky held out his hand to Mia. "I'm Lt. Luke O'Donlon, U.S. Navy SEALs. And you are...?"

Mia smiled. Of course she would smile. No one could resist Lucky. "Mia Summerton. I'm Frisco's neighbor."

"I'm his swim buddy."

"*Former* swim buddy."

Lucky shook his head. "No such thing." He looped his arm around Frisco's neck and smiled at Mia. "We went through BUD/S together. That makes you swim buddies for life."

"BUD/S is basic training for SEALs," Frisco translated for her, pushing Lucky away from him. "Where are you going, dressed like that?"

"Some kind of semiformal affair at the OC. A shindig for some top brass pencil pusher who's being promoted." He grinned at Frisco, but his gaze kept returning to Mia. "I thought maybe you'd want to come along."

Frisco snorted. "Dream on, man. I hated those parties when I was required to go."

"Please?" Lucky begged. "I need someone to keep me company or I'll spend all night dancing with the admiral's wife, trying to keep her from grabbing my butt." He smiled at Mia and winked.

"Even if I wanted to," Frisco told him, "which I *don't,* I couldn't. I'm taking care of my sister's kid for the next six weeks." He gestured to the furniture. "This is supposed to be for her bedroom."

"The kid's either fond of the outdoors, or you got yourself some kind of snafu here."

"Number two," Frisco said.

"Yo, neighbor babe," Lucky said, picking up one end of the mattress. "You look healthy. Grab the other end."

"Her name is Mia," Frisco said.

"Excuse me," Lucky said. "Mia babe, grab the other end."

Mia was laughing, thank God. As Frisco watched, she and Lucky carried the mattress into the courtyard. He could hear Mia's laughter long after they moved out of sight.

As Frisco picked up the lightweight bookcase and carried it slowly toward the courtyard, he could also hear Tasha's excited chirping, and Thomas King's rich voice coming toward him.

"Hey, Navy." Thomas nodded a greeting as he passed. He knew better than to offer to take the bookcase from Frisco on his way out to the parking lot.

"Thanks for helping out, man," Frisco said to him.

"No problem," the teenager replied.

No problem. It was possible that this whole deal wasn't a problem for anybody—except Frisco.

He set the bookcase down at the bottom of the stairs, and looked up to see Lucky come out of his condo, with Tasha in his arms. He was tickling the little girl, and she was giggling. Mia was right behind them, and she was laughing, too.

He'd never seen Mia look so beautiful or relaxed. Lucky leaned toward her and said something into her ear, and she laughed again. She started down the stairs, and Lucky watched her go, his eyes following the movement of her hips.

Frisco had to look away. He couldn't blame Lucky. At one time, the two of them had been so much alike. They still were alike in so many ways. It didn't surprise him that his best friend would be attracted to Mia, too.

It took all of ten minutes to transport Tasha's furniture into her bedroom and to move the boxes that were in there into Frisco's room.

Thomas headed off to work, and Mia made her excuses and disappeared into her condo—after smiling at the big deal Lucky made out of shaking her hand once again.

"She, uh, said you guys were just friends, huh?" Lucky said much too casually as Frisco walked him to his bike.

Frisco was silent, wondering what he could possibly say to that statement. If he agreed, then Lucky would be dropping by all the time, asking Mia out, working his famous O'Donlon charm and persistence until she gave in. And she would give in. No one could resist Lucky. And then Frisco would have to watch as his best friend dated and probably seduced this woman that he wanted so badly.

It was true. He wanted Mia. And dammit, he was going to do everything in his power to get her.

"She's wrong," he told Lucky. "We're more than friends. She just doesn't know it yet."

If Lucky was disappointed, he hid it well. And it didn't take long for his disappointment to turn into genuine pleasure. "This is great. This means you're coming back," he said.

"To the SEALs?" Frisco shook his head. "Man, haven't you heard, I'm—"

"No," Lucky interrupted. "I meant to the world of the living."

Frisco gazed at his friend. He didn't understand. He was alive. He'd had five years of pain and frustration to prove that.

"Call me sometime," Lucky said, strapping on his motorcycle helmet. "I miss you, man."

FRISCO AWOKE TO the sound of an electronic buzzer. It was loud as hell and it was right in his ear and…

He sat up, wide-awake.

It was the sound of the booby trap he'd rigged to the front door last night before he went to bed. Tasha was AWOL again, dammit.

He pulled on a pair of shorts as he rolled out of bed, and grabbed his cane from the floor.

Oh, Lord, he was tired. He may have gone to bed last night, but he hadn't gone to sleep. It couldn't have been more than two hours ago that he'd finally closed his eyes. But he'd done it. He'd stared down the night without even a sip of whiskey to help him along.

He may have been exhausted, but he wasn't hung over.

And that was damn good, because if he had been, the sound of this blasted buzzer would have taken the top of his head clear off.

He quickly disconnected it. It was a simple system, designed for the circuit to break if the door was open. If the circuit was broken, the buzzer would sound.

He pulled the door the rest of the way open and…

Tasha, with Mia directly behind her, stood on the other side of the screen door.

Tash was still wearing her pajamas. Mia was wearing her bathing suit underneath a pair of shorts and a T-shirt. Frisco could see the brightly colored strap that tied up and around her neck.

"Good morning," she said.

Frisco glared at Tash. "Where the h—"

Mia cut him off. "Tasha was coming over to visit me," she told Frisco, "but she remembered that she was supposed to tell you first where she was going." She looked down at the little girl. "Right, Tash?"

Tasha nodded.

Tasha remembered? Mia remembered was more like it.

Mia mouthed "Positive reinforcement" over Tasha's head.

Frisco swallowed his frustration. All right. If Mia thought he could get through to Tasha this way, he'd give it a shot. Somehow he mustered up far more enthusiasm than he felt. "Excellent job remembering," he said to the little girl, opening the screen door and letting both Tasha and Mia inside.

He forced himself to smile, and Natasha visibly brightened. Jeez, maybe there *was* something to this.

He scooped the little girl into his arms and awkwardly spun her around until she began to giggle, then collapsed with her onto the couch. "In fact," he continued, "you are so *amazingly* excellent, I think you should probably get a medal. Don't you?"

She nodded, her eyes wide. "What's a medal?"

"It's a very special pin that you get for doing something really great—like remembering my rules," Frisco told her. He dumped her off his lap and onto the soft cushions of the couch. "Wait right here—I'll get it."

Mia was standing near the door, and as she watched, Frisco pushed himself off the couch and headed down the hall to his bedroom.

"Getting a medal is a really big deal." Frisco raised his voice so they could hear him in the living room. "It requires a very special ceremony."

Tasha was bouncing up and down on the couch, barely able to contain her excitement. Mia had to smile. It seemed that Frisco understood the concept of positive reinforcement.

"Here we go," he said, coming back into the living room. He caught Mia's eye and smiled. He looked like hell this morning. He looked more exhausted than she'd ever seen him. He'd clearly been sound asleep mere moments ago. But somehow he seemed more vibrant, his eyes more clear. And the smile that he'd sent her was remarkably sweet, almost shy.

Mia's heart was in her throat as she watched him with his little niece.

"For the remarkable remembering of my rules and regs, including rule number one—'Tell Frisco where you're going before you leave the condo,'" he intoned, "I award Natasha Francisco this medal of honor."

He pinned one of the colorful bars Mia had seen attached to his dress uniform onto Tasha's pajama shirt.

"Now I salute you and you salute me," he whispered to the little girl after he attached the pin.

He stood at sharp attention, and snapped a salute. Tasha imitated him remarkably well.

"The only time SEALs ever salute is when someone gets a medal," Frisco said with another glance in Mia's direction. He pulled Tasha back to the couch with him. "Here's the deal," he told her. "In order to keep this medal, you have to remember my rules all day today. Do you remember the rules?"

"Tell you when I want to go outside…."

"Even when I'm asleep. You have to wake me up, okay? And what else?"

"Stay here…."

"In the courtyard, right. And…?"

"No swimming without my buddy."

"Absolutely, incredibly correct. Gimme a high five."

Natasha giggled, slapping hands with her uncle.

"Here's the rest of the deal," he said. "Are you listening, Tash?"

She nodded.

"When you get enough of these medals, you know what happens?"

Tasha shook her head no.

"We trade this thing in," Frisco told her, smacking the back of the couch they were sitting on with one hand, "for a certain pink sofa."

Mia thought it was entirely possible that the little girl was going to explode with pleasure.

"You're going to have to work really hard to follow the rules," Frisco was telling her. "You've got to remember that the reason I want you to obey these rules is because I want you to be safe, and it really gets me upset when I don't know for certain that you're safe. You have to think about that and remember that, because I know you don't want to make me feel upset, right?"

Tasha nodded. "Do you have to follow *my* rules?"

Frisco was surprised, but he hid it well. "What are *your* rules?"

"No more bad words," the little girl said without hesitation.

Frisco glanced up at Mia again, chagrin in his eyes. "Okay," he said, looking back at Tasha. "That's a tough one, but I'll try."

"More playing with Mia," Tasha suggested.

He laughed nervously. "I'm not sure we can make that a rule, Tash. I mean, things that concern you and me are fine, but…"

"I'd love to play with you," Mia murmured.

Frisco glanced up at her. She couldn't possibly have meant that the way it sounded. No, she was talking to Natasha. Still… He let his imagination run with the scenario. It was a very, *very* good one.

"But we don't have to make a rule about it," Mia added.

"Can you come to the beach with us for my swimming lesson?" Tasha asked her.

Mia hesitated, looking cautiously across the room at Frisco. "I don't want to get in the way."

"You've already got your bathing suit on," he pointed out.

She seemed surprised that he'd noticed. "Well, yes, but…"

"Were you planning to go to a different beach?"

"No… I just don't want to…you know…" She shrugged and smiled apologetically, nervously. "Interfere."

"It wouldn't be interfering," Frisco told her. Man, he felt as nervous as she sounded. When had this gotten so hard? He used to be so good at this sort of thing. "Tasha wants you to come with us." Perfect. Now he sounded as if he wanted her to come along as a playmate for his niece. That wasn't it at all. "And I…I do, too," he added.

Jeez, his heart was in his mouth. He swallowed, trying to make it go back where it belonged as Mia just gazed at him.

"Well, okay," she finally said. "In that case, I'd love to come. If you want, I could pack a picnic lunch…?"

"Yeah!" Tasha squealed, hopping around the room. "A picnic! A picnic!"

Frisco felt himself smile. A picnic on the beach with Mia. He couldn't remember the last time he'd felt such anticipation. And his anticipation was for more than his wanting to see what her bathing suit looked like, although he was feeling plenty of that, too. "I guess that's a yes. But it shouldn't be just up to you to bring the food."

"I'll make sandwiches," Mia told him, opening the door. "You guys bring something to drink. Soda. Or beer if you want it."

"No beer," Frisco said.

She paused, looking back at him, her hand on the handle of the screen door.

"It's another one of the rules I'm going to be following from now on," he said quietly. Natasha had stopped dancing around the room. She was listening, her eyes wide. "No more drinking. Not even beer."

Mia stepped away from the door, her eyes nearly as wide as Tasha's. "Um, Tash, why don't you go put on your bathing suit?"

Silently Tasha vanished down the hallway.

Frisco shook his head. "It's not that big a deal."

Mia clearly thought otherwise. She stepped closer to him, lowering her voice for privacy from Tasha's sensitive ears. "You know, there are support groups all over town. You can find a meeting at virtually any time of day—"

Did she honestly think his drinking was *that* serious a problem? "Look, I can handle this," he said gruffly. "I went overboard for a couple of days, but that's all it was. I didn't drink at all while I was in the hospital—right up 'til two days ago. These past few days—you haven't exactly been seeing me at my best."

"I'm sorry," she murmured. "I didn't mean to imply…"

"It's no big deal."

She touched his arm, her fingers gentle and cool and so soft against his skin. "Yes, it is," she told him. "To Natasha, it's a *very* big deal."

"I'm not doing it for Tash," he said quietly, looking down at her delicate hand resting on the corded muscles of his forearm, wishing she would leave it there, but knowing she was going to pull away. "I'm doing it for myself."

CHAPTER EIGHT

"Is THOMAS REALLY a king?"

Mia looked up from the sand castle she was helping Tasha build. The little girl was making dribble turrets on the side of the large mound using wet sand and water from a plastic pail that Mia had found in her closet. She had remarkable dexterity for a five-year-old, and managed to make most of her dribbles quite tall and spiky.

"Thomas's last name is King," Mia answered. "But here in the United States, we don't have kings and queens."

"Is he a king somewhere else? Like I'm a princess in Russia?"

"Well," Mia said diplomatically, "you might want to check with Thomas, but I think King is just his last name."

"He looks like a king." Natasha giggled. "He thinks I'm from Mars. I'm gonna marry him."

"Marry who?" Frisco asked, sitting down in the sand next to them.

He'd just come out of the ocean, and water beaded on his eyelashes and dripped from his hair. He looked more relaxed and at ease than Mia had ever seen him.

"Thomas," Tasha told him, completely serious.

"Thomas." Frisco considered that thoughtfully. "I like him," he said. "But you're a little young to be getting married, don't you think?"

"Not now, silly," she said with exasperation. "When I'm a grown-up, of course."

Frisco tried to hide his smile. "Of course," he said.

"You can't marry my mom 'cause you're her brother, right?" she asked.

"That's right," Frisco told her. He leaned back in the sand on his elbows. Mia tried not to stare at the way the muscles in his arms flexed as they supported his weight. She tried to pull her gaze away from his broad shoulders and powerful chest and smooth, tanned skin. This wasn't the first time she'd seen him without a shirt, after all. She should be getting used to this....

"Too bad," Tash said with a sigh. "Mommy's always looking for someone to marry, and I like you."

Frisco's voice was husky. "Thanks, Tash. I like you, too."

"I didn't like Dwayne," the little girl said. "He scared me, but Mommy liked living in his house."

"Maybe when your mom comes back, the two of you could live a few doors down from me," Frisco said.

"You could marry Mia," Tasha suggested. "And move in with her. And we could live in your place."

Mia glanced up. Frisco met her eyes, clearly embarrassed. "Maybe Mia doesn't want to get married," he said.

"Do you?" the little girl asked, looking up from her handiwork to gaze at Mia with those pure blue eyes that were so like Frisco's.

"Well," she said carefully. "Someday I'd like to get married and have a family, but—"

"She does," Tasha informed her uncle. "She's pretty and she makes good sandwiches. You should ask her to marry you." She stood up and, taking her bucket, went down to the edge of the water, where she began to chase waves up the sand.

"I'm sorry about that," Frisco said with a nervous laugh. "She's...you know, *five*. She's heavily into happily ever after."

"It's all right," Mia said with a smile. "And don't worry. I won't hold you to any promises that Tasha makes on your behalf." She brushed the sand from her knees and moved back onto the beach blanket she'd spread out.

Frisco moved to join her. "That's good to know." He turned to look at Mia, his warm gaze skimming up her legs, lingering on her red two-piece bathing suit and the enormous amount of skin it exposed, before settling on her face. "She's right, though. You *are* pretty, and you make damn good sandwiches."

Mia's pulse was racing. When had it started to matter so much whether or not this man thought that she was pretty? When had the urge disappeared—the urge to cover herself up with a bulky T-shirt every time he looked at her with that heat in his eyes? When had her heart started to leap at his crooked, funny smiles? When had he crossed that boundary that defined him as more than a mere friend?

It had started days ago, with that very first hug he had given Natasha in the courtyard. He was so gentle with the child, so patient. Mia's attraction to him had been there from the start, yet now that she had come to know more of him, it was multilayered, existing on more complicated levels than just basic, raw sexual magnetism.

It was crazy. Mia knew it was crazy. This was not a man with whom she could picture herself spending the rest of her life. He'd been trained as a killer—a professional soldier. And if that wasn't enough, he had barrels of anger and frustration and pain to work through before he could be considered psychologically and emotionally healthy. And if *that* wasn't enough, there was the fact of his drinking.

Yes, he'd vowed to stop, but Mia's experience as a high school teacher had made her an expert on the disease of alcoholism. The best way to fight it was not to face it alone, but to seek help. He seemed hell-bent on handling it himself, and more often than not, such a course would end in failure.

No, if she were smart, she'd pack up her beach bag right now and get the heck out of there.

Instead, she put more sunblock on her face. "I went into your kitchen to help Natasha load the cooler with soda," she said. "And I noticed you had only one thing stuck onto your refrigerator. A list."

He glanced at her, his expression one of wariness. "Yeah?"

"I wasn't sure," she said, "but…it looked like it might've been a list of things that you have difficulty doing with your injured knee."

The list had included things like run, jump, skydive, bike, and climb stairs.

He gazed out at the ocean, squinting slightly in the brightness. "That's right."

"You forgot to include that you're no longer able to play on the Olympic basketball team, so I added that to the bottom," she said, her tongue firmly in her cheek.

He let loose a short burst of air that might've been called a laugh if he'd been smiling. "Very funny. If you'd looked carefully, you'd have noticed that the word *walk* was at the top. I crossed it off when I could walk. I intend to do the same with the rest of those things on that list."

His eyes were the same fierce shade of blue as the sky.

Mia rolled onto her stomach and propped her chin up in her hands. "Tell me about this amazing pink couch," she said. "What's that all about?"

This time Frisco *did* laugh, and the lines around his eyes crinkled with genuine amusement. He stretched out next to her on the blanket, making sure he could still see Tasha from where they lay. "Oh, that," he said. "It's gonna look great in my living room, don't you think? Dirt brown and ugly green go real well with pink and silver."

Mia smiled. "You'll have to redecorate. Maybe a white carpet and lots of Art Deco type mirrors on the walls would work."

"And it would be so me," he said, deadpan.

"Seriously, though," Mia said. "If anything will give Tasha incentive to follow your rules, that will. She's only mentioned it five thousand times today already."

"Tell me the truth," Frisco said, supporting his head with one hand as he gazed at her. "Did I go too far? Did I cross the line from positive reinforcement into sheer bribery?"

Mia shook her head, caught in the intense blue of his eyes. "You're giving her the opportunity to earn something that she truly wants, along with learning an important lesson about following rules. That's not bribery."

"I feel like I'm taking the point and heading into totally uncharted territory," Frisco admitted.

Mia didn't understand. "Taking the point...?"

"If you take the point, if you're the pointman," he explained, "that means you lead the squad. You're the first guy out there—the first guy either to locate or step on any booby traps or land mines. It's a pretty intense job."

"At least you know that Natasha's not suddenly going to explode."

Frisco smiled. "Are you sure about that?"

With amusement dancing in his eyes, a smile softening his face and the ocean breeze gently ruffling his hair,
Frisco looked like the kind of man Mia would go far out
of her way to meet. He looked charming and friendly and
pleasant and sinfully handsome.

"You're doing a wonderful job with Tasha," she told
him. "You're being remarkably consistent in dealing with
her. I know how hard it is not to lose your temper when
she disobeys you—I've seen you swallow it, and I know
that's not easy. And giving her that medal—that was brilliant." She sat up, reaching for the T-shirt Tasha had been
wearing over her bathing suit. "Look." She held it up so
he could see. "She's so proud of that medal, she asked
me to pin it onto this shirt for her so she could wear it to
the beach. If you keep this up, it's only a matter of time
before she'll remember to follow your rules."

Frisco had rolled over onto his back and was shielding
his eyes from the glare of the sun with one hand as he
looked up at her. He sat up now, in one smooth effortless
motion, glancing back at Natasha, checking briefly to be
sure the little girl was safe.

She was crouched in the sand halfway between the
blanket and the water, starting a new dribble castle.

"I'm doing a wonderful job and I'm brilliant?" he said
with a half smile. "Sounds like you're giving *me* a little
positive reinforcement here."

Natasha's T-shirt was damp and Mia spread it out on
top of the cooler to dry in the sun. "Well…maybe," she
admitted with a sheepish smile.

He touched her gently under her chin, pulling her head
up so that she was forced to look at him.

His smile had faded, and the amusement in his eyes
was gone, replaced by something else entirely, something
hot and dangerous and impossible to turn away from.

"I like my positive reinforcement delivered a little differently," he told her, his voice no more than a husky whisper.

His gaze flickered down to her mouth, then up again to meet her eyes, and Mia knew that he was going to kiss her. He leaned forward slowly, giving her plenty of time to back away. But she didn't move. She couldn't move. Or maybe she just plain didn't want to move.

She felt him sigh as his lips met hers. His mouth was warm and sweet, and he kissed her so softly. He touched her lips gently with his tongue, waiting until she granted him access before he deepened the kiss. And even then, even as she opened herself to him, he kissed her breathtakingly tenderly.

It was the sweetest kiss she'd ever shared.

He pulled back to look into her eyes, and she could feel her heart pounding. But then he smiled, one of his beautiful, heart-stoppingly perfect crooked smiles, as if he'd just found gold at the end of a rainbow. And this time she reached for him, wrapping her arms up around his neck, pressing herself against him, stabbing her fingers up into the incredible softness of his hair as she kissed him again.

This time it was pure fire. This time he touched her with more than just his lips, pulling her even harder against his chest, running his hands along the bare skin of her back, through her hair, down her arms as he met her tongue in a kiss of wild, bone-melting intensity.

"Frisco! Frisco! The ice-cream truck is here! Can I get an ice cream?"

Mia pushed Frisco away from her even as he released her. He was breathing as hard as she was, and he looked thoroughly shaken. But Natasha was oblivious to everything but the ice-cream truck that had pulled into the beach parking lot.

"Please, please, please, please, please," she was saying, running in circles around and around the beach blanket.

Frisco looked up toward the end of the beach, where the ice-cream truck was parked, and then back at Mia. He looked as shocked and as stunned as she felt. "Uh," he said. He leaned toward her and spoke quickly, in a low voice. "Can you take her? I can't."

"Of course." She quickly pulled on her T-shirt. God, her hands were shaking. She glanced up at him. "Is your knee all right?"

He dug a five-dollar bill out of his wallet and handed it to her with a weak grin. "Actually, it has nothing to do with my knee."

Suddenly Mia understood. She felt her cheeks heat with a blush. "Come on, Tasha," she said, pulling her hair out from the collar of her T-shirt as she led the little girl up the beach.

What had she just done?

She'd just experienced both the sweetest and the most arousing kisses of her entire life—with a man she'd vowed to stay away from. Mia stood in line with Tasha at the ice-cream truck, trying to figure out her next move.

Getting involved with Frisco was entirely out of the question. But, oh, those kisses… Mia closed her eyes. Mistake, she told herself over and over. She'd already made the mistake—to continue in this direction would be sheer foolishness. So okay. He was an amazing mixture of sweetness and sexiness. But he was a man who needed saving, and she knew better than to think she could save him. To become involved would only pull her under, too.

Only he could save himself from his unhappiness and despair, and only time would tell if he'd succeed.

She'd have to be honest with him. She'd have to make sure he understood.

In a fog, she ordered Tasha's ice cream and two ice bars for herself and Frisco. The trek back to the blanket seemed endlessly long. The sand seemed hotter than before and her feet burned. Tasha went back to her sand castle, ice cream dripping down her chin.

Frisco was sitting on the edge of the blanket, soaking wet, as if he'd thrown himself into the ocean to cool down. That was good. Mia wanted him cooled down, didn't she?

She handed him the ice pop and tried to smile as she sat down. "I figured we could all use something to cool us off, but you beat me to it."

Frisco looked at Mia, sitting as far from him as she possibly could on the beach blanket, and then down at the ice bar in his hands. "I kind of liked the heat we were generating," he said quietly.

Mia shook her head, unable even to look him in the eye. "I have to be honest. I hardly even know you and…"

He stayed silent, just waiting for her to go on.

"I don't think we should… I mean, I think it would be a mistake to…" She was blushing again.

"Okay." Frisco nodded. "That's okay. I…I understand." He couldn't blame her. How could he blame her? She wasn't the type who went for short-term ecstasy. If she played the game, it would be for keeps, and face it, he wasn't a keeper. He was not the kind of man Mia would want to be saddled with for the rest of her life. She was so full of life, and he was forced to move so slowly. She was so complete; he was less than whole.

"I should probably get home," she said, starting to gather up her things.

"We'll walk you back," he said quietly.

"Oh, no—you don't have to."

"Yeah, we do, okay?"

She glanced up at him, and something she saw in his eyes or on his face made her know not to argue. "All right."

Frisco stood up, reaching for his cane. "Come on, Tash, let's go into the water one last time and wash that ice cream off your face."

He tossed the unopened ice pop into a garbage can as he walked Natasha down to the ocean. He stared out at the water and tried his damnedest not to think about Mia as Tasha rinsed the last of her ice cream from her face and hands. But he couldn't do it. He could still taste her, still feel her in his arms, still smell her spicy perfume.

And for those moments that he'd kissed her, for those incredible few minutes that she'd been in his arms, for the first time since the last dose of heavy-duty pain medication had worn off five years ago, he'd actually forgotten about his injured knee.

NATASHA DIDN'T SEEM to notice the awkward silence. She chattered on, to Mia, to Frisco, to no one in particular. She sang snatches of songs and chanted bits of rhymes.

Mia felt miserable. Rejection was never fun, from either the giving or the receiving end. She knew she'd hurt Frisco by backing away. But her worst mistake had been to let him kiss her in the first place.

She wished she'd insisted that they take her car to the beach, rather than walk. Frisco was a master at hiding his pain, but she could tell from the subtle changes in the way he held himself and the way he breathed that he was hurting.

Mia closed her eyes briefly, trying not to care, but she couldn't. She *did* care. She cared far too much.

"I'm sorry," she murmured to Frisco as Natasha skipped ahead of them, hopping over the cracks in the sidewalk.

He turned and looked at her with those piercing blue eyes that seemed to see right through to her very soul. "You really are, aren't you?"

She nodded.

"I'm sorry, too," he said quietly.

"Frisco!" Natasha launched herself at him, nearly knocking him over.

"Whoa!" he said, catching her in his left arm while he used his right to balance both of their weight with his cane. "What's wrong, Tash?"

The little girl had both of her arms wrapped tightly around his waist, and she was hiding her face in his T-shirt.

"Tash, what's going on?" Frisco asked again, but she didn't move. Short of yanking the child away from himself, he couldn't get her to release him.

Mia crouched down next to the little girl. "Natasha, did something scare you?"

She nodded yes.

Mia pushed Tasha's red curls back from her face. "Honey, what scared you?"

Tasha lifted her head, looking at Mia with tear-filled eyes. "Dwayne," she whispered. "I saw Dwayne."

Mia looked up at Frisco, frowning her confusion. "Who…?"

"One of Sharon's old boyfriends." He pulled Natasha up

and into his arms. "Tash, you probably just saw someone who reminded you of him."

Natasha shook her head emphatically as Mia stood up. "I saw Dwayne," she said again, tears overflowing onto her cheeks and great gulping sobs making her nearly impossible to understand. "I saw him."

"What would he be doing here in San Felipe?" Frisco asked the little girl.

"He'd be looking for Sharon Francisco," a low voice drawled. "That's what he'd be doing here."

Natasha was suddenly, instantly silent.

Mia gazed at the man standing directly in front of them. He was a big man, taller and wider even than Frisco, but softer and heavily overweight. He was wearing a dark business suit that had to have been hand tailored to fit his girth, and lizard-skin boots that were buffed to a gleaming shine. His shirt was dark gray—a slightly lighter shade of the same black of his suit, and his tie was a color that fell somewhere between the two. His hair was thick and dark, and it tumbled forward into his eyes in a style reminiscent of Elvis Presley. His face was fifty pounds too heavy to be called handsome, with a distinctive hawklike nose and deep-set eyes that were now lost among the puffiness of his excess flesh.

In one big, beefy hand, he held a switchblade knife that he opened and closed, opened and closed, with a rhythmic hiss of metal on metal.

"My sister's not here," Frisco said evenly.

Mia felt him touch her shoulder, and she turned toward him. His eyes never left Dwayne and the knife in the man's right hand as he handed her Natasha. "Get behind me," he murmured. "And start backing away."

"I can see that your sister's not here," the heavy man had a thick New Orleans accent. The gentlemanly old

South politeness of his speech somehow made him seem all the more frightening. "But since you have the pleasure of her daughter's company, I must assume you know of her whereabouts."

"Why don't you leave me your phone number," Frisco suggested, "and I'll have her call you."

Dwayne flicked his knife open again, and this time he didn't close it. "I'm afraid that's unacceptable. You see, she owes me a great deal of money." He smiled. "Of course, I could always take the child as collateral…."

Frisco could still sense Mia's presence behind him. He heard her sharp intake of breath. "Mia, take Tash into the deli on the corner and call the police," he told her without turning around.

He felt her hesitation and anxiety, felt the coolness of her fingers as she touched his arm. "Alan…"

"Do it," he said sharply.

Mia began backing away. Her heart was pounding as she watched Frisco smile pleasantly at Dwayne, always keeping his eyes on that knife. "You know I'd die before I'd let you even touch the girl," the former SEAL said matter-of-factly. Mia knew that what he said was true. She prayed it wouldn't come to that.

"Why don't you just tell me where Sharon is?" Dwayne asked. "I'm not interested in beating the hell out of a poor, pathetic cripple, but I will if I have to."

"The same way you had to hit a five-year-old?" Frisco countered. Everything about him—his stance, his face, the look in his eyes, the tone of his voice—was deadly. Despite the cane in his hand, despite his injured knee, he looked anything but poor and pathetic.

But Dwayne had a knife, and Frisco only had his cane—which he needed to use to support himself.

Dwayne lunged at Frisco, and Mia turned and ran for the deli.

Frisco saw Mia's sudden movement from the corner of his eye. Thank God. It would be ten times easier to fight this enormous son of a bitch knowing that Mia and Tash were safe and out of the way.

Dwayne lunged with the knife again, and Frisco side-stepped him, gritting his teeth against the sudden screaming pain as his knee was forced to twist and turn in ways that it no longer could. He used his cane and struck the heavyset man on the wrist, sending the sharp-bladed knife skittering into the street.

He realized far too late that he had played right into Dwayne's hand. With his cane up and in the air, he couldn't use it to support himself. And Dwayne came at him again, spinning and turning with the graceful agility of a much smaller, lighter man. Frisco watched, almost in slow motion, as his opponent aimed a powerful karate kick directly at his injured knee.

He saw it coming, but as if he, too, were caught in slow motion, he couldn't move out of the way.

And then there was only pain. Sheer, blinding, excruciating pain. Frisco felt a hoarse cry rip from his throat as he went down, hard, onto the sidewalk. He fought the darkness that threatened to close in on him as he felt Dwayne's foot connect violently with his side, this time damn near launching him into the air.

Somehow he held on to the heavy man's leg. Somehow he brought his own legs up and around, twisting and kicking and tripping, until Dwayne, too, fell onto the ground.

There were no rules. One of Dwayne's elbows landed squarely in Frisco's face, and he felt his nose gush with blood. He struggled to keep the bigger man's weight off of him, trying to keep Dwayne pinned as he hit him in the face again and again.

Another, smaller man would've been knocked out, but Dwayne was like one of those pop-up punching bag dolls. He just kept coming. The son of a bitch went for his knee again. There was no way he could miss, and again pain ripped into Frisco like a freight train. He grabbed hold of Dwayne's head and slammed it back against the sidewalk.

There were sirens in the distance—Frisco heard them through waves of nausea and dizziness. The police were coming.

Dwayne should have been out for the count, but he scrambled up and onto his feet.

"You tell Sharon I want that money back," he said through bruised and bleeding lips before he limped away.

Frisco tried to go after him, but his knee crumbled beneath his weight, sending another wave of searing pain blasting through him. He felt himself retch and he pressed his cheek against the sidewalk to make the world stop spinning.

A crowd had gathered, he suddenly realized. Someone pushed through the mob, running toward him. He tensed, moving quickly into a defensive position.

"Yo, Lieutenant! Whoa, back off, Navy, it's me, *Thomas.*"

It was. It was Thomas. The kid crouched down next to Frisco on the sidewalk.

"Who ran *you* over with a truck? My God…" Thomas stood up again, looking into the crowd. "Hey, someone call an ambulance for my friend! *Now!*"

Frisco reached for Thomas.

"Yeah, I'm here, man. I'm here, Frisco. I saw this big

guy running away—he looked only a little bit better than you do," Thomas told him. "What happened? You make some kind of uncalled-for fat joke?"

"Mia," Frisco rasped. "She's got Natasha…at the deli. Stay with them…make sure they're okay."

"You're the one who looks like you need help—"

"I'm *fine*," Frisco ground out between clenched teeth. "If you won't go to them, I will." He searched for his cane. Where the hell was his cane? It was in the street. He crawled toward it, dragging his injured leg.

"God," Thomas said. His eyes were wide in amazement that Frisco could even move. For once he actually looked only eighteen years old. "You stay here, I'll go find them. If it's that important to you…"

"Run," Frisco told him.

Thomas ran.

CHAPTER NINE

THE HOSPITAL EMERGENCY room was crowded. Mia was ignored by the nurses at the front desk, so she finally gave up and simply walked into the back. She was stepped around, pushed past and nearly knocked over as she searched for Frisco.

"Excuse me, I'm looking for—"

"Not now, dear," a nurse told her, briskly moving down the hallway.

Mia heard him before she saw him. His voice was low, and his language was abominable. It was definitely Alan Francisco.

She followed the sound of his voice into a big room that held six beds, all filled. He was sitting up, his right leg stretched out in front of him, his injured knee swollen and bruised. His T-shirt was covered with blood, he had a cut on his cheekbone directly underneath his right eye and his elbows and other knee looked abraded and raw.

A doctor was examining his knee. "That hurt, too?" he asked, glancing up at Frisco.

Yes, was the gist of the reply, minus all of the colorful superlatives. A new sheen of sweat had broken out on Frisco's face, and he wiped at his upper lip with the back of one hand as he braced himself for the rest of the examination.

"I thought you promised Tasha no more bad words."

Startled, he looked up, and directly into her eyes. "What are you doing here? Where's Tash?"

Mia had surprised him. And not pleasantly, either. She could see myriad emotions flicker across hisface. Embarrassment. Shame. Humiliation. She knew he didn't want her to see him like this, looking beaten and bloodied.

"She's with Thomas," Mia told him. "I thought you might want..." What? She thought he might want a hand to hold? No, she already knew him well enough to know he wouldn't need or want that. She shook her head. She'd come here purely for herself. "*I* wanted to make sure you were all right."

"I'm fine."

"You don't look fine."

"Depends on your definition of the word," he said. "In my book, it means I'm not dead."

"Excuse me, miss, but is Mr. Francisco a friend of yours?" It was the doctor. "Perhaps you'll be able to convince him to take the pain medication we've offered him."

Mia shook her head. "No, I don't think I'll be able to do that. He's extremely stubborn—and it's Lieutenant, not Mister. If he's decided that he doesn't want it—"

"Yes, he *has* decided he doesn't want it," Frisco interjected. "And he also *hates* being talked about as if he weren't in the room, so do you mind...?"

"The medication would make him rest much more comfortably—"

"Look, all I want you to do is X-ray my damn knee and make sure it's not broken. Do you think *maybe* you can do that?"

"He's a lieutenant in which organization?" the doctor asked Mia.

"Please ask him directly," she said. "Surely you can respect him and not talk over his head this way."

"I'm with the Navy SEALs—*was* with the SEALs," Frisco said.

The doctor snapped closed Frisco's patient clipboard. "Perfect. I should have known. Nurse!" he shouted, already striding away. "Send this man to X-ray, and then arrange a transfer over to the VA facility up by the naval base...."

Frisco was watching Mia, and when she turned to look at him, he gave her a half smile. "Thanks for trying."

"Why don't you take the pain medicine?" she asked.

"Because I don't want to be stoned and drooling when Dwayne comes back for round two."

Mia couldn't breathe. "Comes back?" she repeated. "Why? Who was he anyway? And what did he want?"

Frisco shifted his weight, unable to keep from wincing. "Apparently my darling sister owes him some money."

"How much money?"

"I don't know, but I'm going to find out." He shook his head. "I'm gonna pay Sharon a little visit in the morning—to hell with the detox center's rules."

"When I saw that knife he was holding..." Mia's voice shook and she stopped. She closed her eyes, willing back the sudden rush of tears. She couldn't remember the last time she'd been that scared. "I didn't want to leave you there alone."

She opened her eyes to find him watching her, the expression on his face unreadable. "Didn't you think I could take that guy and win?" he asked softly.

She didn't need to answer him—she knew he could read her reply in her eyes. She knew how painful it was for him to walk, even with a cane. She knew his limitations. How could he have taken on a man as big as Dwayne—a man who had a knife, as well—and not been hurt? And he *had* been hurt. Badly, it looked like.

He laughed bitterly, looking away from her. "No wonder you damn near ran away from me on the beach. You don't think I'm much of a man, do you?"

Mia was shocked. "That's not true! That's not why—"

"Time to go down to X-ray," a nurse announced, pushing a wheelchair up to Frisco's bed.

Frisco didn't wait for the nurse to help him. He lifted himself off the bed and lowered himself into the chair. He jostled his knee, and it had to have hurt like hell, but he didn't say a word. When he looked up at Mia, though, she could see all of his pain in his eyes. "Just go home," he said quietly.

"They're backed up down there—this could take a while, a few hours even," the nurse informed Mia as she began pushing Frisco out of the room. "You can't come with him, so you'll just be sitting out in the waiting room. If you want to leave, he could call you when he's done."

"No, thank you," Mia said. She turned to Frisco. "Alan, you are *so* wrong about—"

"Just go home," he said again.

"No," she said. "No, I'm going to wait for you."

"Don't," he said. He glanced up at her just before the nurse pushed him out the door. "And don't call me Alan."

FRISCO RODE IN the wheelchair back to the E.R. lobby with his eyes closed. His X-rays had taken a few aeons longer than forever, and he had to believe Mia had given up on him and gone home.

It was nearly eight o'clock at night. He was still supposed to meet with the doctor to talk about what his

X-rays had shown. But he'd seen the film and already knew what the doctor was going to say. His knee wasn't broken. It was bruised and inflamed. There may have been ligament damage, but it was hard to tell—his injury and all of his subsequent surgeries had left things looking pretty severely scrambled.

The doctor was going to recommend shipping him over to the VA hospital for further consultation and possible treatment.

But that was going to have to wait. He had Natasha at home to take care of, and some lunatic named Dwayne to deal with.

"Where are you taking him?" It was Mia's musical voice. She was still here, waiting for him, just as she'd said. Frisco didn't know whether to feel relieved or disappointed. He kept his eyes closed, and tried not to care too much either way.

"The doctor has to take a look at the X-rays," the nurse told her. "We're overcrowded tonight. Depending on how things go, it could be another five minutes or two hours."

"May I sit with him?" Mia asked.

"Sure," the nurse said. "He can wait out here as well as anyplace else."

Frisco felt his wheelchair moved awkwardly into position, heard the nurse walk away. Then he felt Mia's cool fingers touch his forehead, pushing his hair back and off his face.

"I know you're not really asleep," she said.

Her hand felt so good in his hair. Too good. Frisco reached up and caught her wrist as he opened his eyes, pushing her away from him. "That's right," he said. "I'm just shutting everything out."

She was gazing at him with eyes that were a perfect

mixture of green and brown. "Well, before you shut me out again, I want you to know—I don't judge whether or not someone is a *man* based on his ability to beat an opponent into a bloody pulp. And I wasn't running away from *you* on the beach today."

Frisco shut his eyes again. "Look, you don't have to explain why you don't want to sleep with me. If you don't, then you don't. That's all I need to know."

"I was running away from myself," she said very softly, a catch in her voice.

Frisco opened his eyes. She was looking at him with tears in her beautiful eyes and his heart lurched. "Mia, don't, really...it's all right." It wasn't, but he would have said or done anything to keep her from crying.

"No, it's not," she said. "I really want to be your friend, but I don't know if I can. I've been sitting here for the past few hours, just thinking about it, and..." She shook her head and a tear escaped down her cheek.

Frisco was lost. His chest felt so tight, he could barely breathe, and he knew the awful truth. He was glad Mia had waited for him. He was glad she'd come to the hospital. Yeah, he'd also been mortified that she'd seen him like this, but at the same time, her presence had made him feel good. For the first time in forever he didn't feel so damned alone.

But now he'd somehow made her cry. He reached for her, cupping her face with his hand and brushing away that tear with his thumb. "It's not that big a deal," he whispered.

"No?" she said, looking up at him. She closed her eyes and pressed her cheek more fully into the palm of his hand. She turned her head slightly and brushed his fingers with her lips. When she opened her eyes again, he could see a fire burning, white-hot and molten. All sweetness, all girlish innocence was gone from her face. She was all woman, pure female desire as she gazed back at him.

His mouth went totally, instantly dry.

"You touch me, even just like this, and I feel it," she said huskily. "This chemistry—it's impossible to ignore."

She was right, and he couldn't help himself. He pushed his hand up and into the softness of her long, dark hair. She closed her eyes again at the sensation, and he felt his heart begin to pound.

"I know you feel it, too," she whispered.

Frisco nodded. Yes. He traced the soft curve of her ear, then let his hand slide down her neck. Her skin was so smooth, like satin beneath his fingers.

But then she reached for his hand, intertwining their fingers, squeezing his hand, breaking the spell. "But for me, that's not enough," she told him. "I need more than sexual chemistry. I need…love."

Silence. Big, giant silence. Frisco could hear his heart beating and the rush of his blood through his veins. He could hear the sounds of other people in the waiting room—hushed conversations, a child's quiet crying. He could hear a distant television, the clatter of an empty gurney being wheeled too quickly down the hall.

"I can't give you that," he told her.

"I know," she said softly. "And that's why I ran away." She smiled at him, so sweetly, so sadly. The seductive temptress was gone, leaving behind this nice girl who wanted more than he could give her, who knew enough not even to ask.

Or maybe she knew enough not to *want* to ask. He was no prize. He wasn't even whole.

She released his hand, and he immediately missed the warmth of her touch.

"I see they finally got you cleaned up," she said.

"I did it myself," he told her, amazed they could sit here talking like this after what she'd just revealed. "I went into the bathroom near the X-ray department and washed up."

"What happens next?" Mia asked.

What had she just revealed? Nothing, really, when it came down to it. She'd admitted that the attraction between them was powerful. She'd told him that she was looking for more than sex, that she wanted a relationship based on love. But she hadn't said that she wanted *him* to love her.

Maybe she was glossing over the truth. Maybe she'd simply omitted the part about how, even if he *was* capable of giving her what she wanted, she had no real interest in any kind of a relationship with some crippled has-been.

"The doctor will look at my X-rays and he'll tell me that nothing's broken," Frisco told her. "Nothing he can see, anyway."

How much of that fight had she seen? he wondered. Had she seen Dwayne drop him with a single well-placed blow to his knee? Had she seen him hit the sidewalk like a stone? Had she seen Dwayne kick him while he was down there, face against the concrete like some pathetic hound dog too dumb to get out of the way?

And look at him now, back in a wheelchair. He'd sworn he'd never sit in one of these damned things again, yet here he was.

"Dammit, Lieutenant, when I sent you home to rest, I meant you should *rest,* not start a new career as a street fighter." Captain Steven Horowitz was wearing his white dress uniform and he gleamed in the grimy E.R. waiting room. What the hell was *he* doing here?

"Dr. Wright called and said he had a former patient

of mine in his emergency room, waiting to get his knee X-rayed. He said this patient's knee was swollen and damaged from a previous injury, and on top of that, it looked as if it had recently been hit with a sledgehammer. Although apparently this patient claimed there were no sledgehammers involved in the fight he'd been in," Horowitz said, arms folded across his chest. "The *fight* he'd been in. And I asked myself, now, which of my former knee-injury patients would be *stupid* enough to put himself into a threatening situation like a *fight* that might irrevocably damage his injured knee? I came up with Alan Francisco before Wright even mentioned your name."

"Nice to see you, too, Steve," Frisco said, wearily running his hand through his hair, pushing it off his face. He could feel Mia watching him, watching the Navy captain.

"What were you thinking?"

"Allow me to introduce Mia Summerton," Frisco said. "Mia, I know you're going to be disappointed, but as much as Steve looks like it, he *isn't* the White Power Ranger. He's really only just a Navy doctor. His name's Horowitz. He answers to Captain, Doctor, Steve and sometimes even God."

Steven Horowitz was several years older than Frisco, but he had an earnestness about him that made him seem quite a bit younger. Frisco watched him do a double take as he looked at Mia, with her long, dark hair, her beautiful face, her pretty flowered sundress that revealed her smooth, tanned shoulders and her slender, graceful arms. He watched Steve look back at his own bloody T-shirt and battered face. He knew what the doctor was thinking— what was *she* doing with him?

Nothing. She was doing nothing. She'd made that more than clear.

Horowitz turned back to Frisco. "I looked at the X-rays—I think you may have been lucky, but I won't be able to know for certain until the swelling goes down." He pulled a chair over, and looked at the former SEAL's knee, probing it lightly with gentle fingers.

Frisco felt himself start to sweat. From the corner of his eye, he saw Mia lean forward, as if she were going to reach for his hand. But he closed his eyes, refusing to look at her, refusing to need her.

She took his hand anyway, holding it tightly until Steve was through. By then, Frisco was drenched with sweat again, and he knew his face must've looked gray or maybe even green. He let go of her hand abruptly, suddenly aware that he was damn near mashing her fingers.

"All right," Steve finally said with a sigh. "Here's what I want you to do. I want you to go home, and I want you to stay off your feet for the next two weeks." He took his prescription pad from his leather bag. "I'll give you something to make you sleep—"

"And I won't take it," Frisco said. "I have a…situation to deal with."

"What kind of situation?"

Frisco shook his head. "It's a family matter. My sister's in some kind of trouble. All you need to know is that I'm not taking anything that's going to make me sleep. I won't object to a local painkiller, though."

Steven Horowitz laughed in disgust. "If I give you that, your knee won't hurt. And if your knee doesn't hurt, you're going to be up running laps, doing God knows what kind of damage. No. No way."

Frisco leaned forward, lowering his voice, wishing Mia weren't listening, hating himself for having to admit his weaknesses. "Steve, you know I wouldn't ask for it if I weren't in serious pain. I *need* it, man. I can't risk taking the stuff that will knock me out."

The doctor's eyes were a flat, pale blue, but for a brief moment, Frisco saw a flare of warmth and compassion behind the customary chill. Steve shook his head. "I'm going to regret doing this. I *know* I'm going to regret doing this." He scribbled something on his pad. "I'm going to give you something to bring down the swelling, too. Go easy with it." He glared at Frisco. "In return, you have to *promise* me you won't get out of this wheelchair for two weeks."

Frisco shook his head. "I can't promise that," he said. "In fact, I'd rather die than stay in this chair for a minute longer than I have to."

Dr. Horowitz turned to Mia. "His knee has already been permanently damaged. It's something of a miracle that he can even walk at all. There's nothing he can do to make his knee any better, but he *could* make things worse. Will you please try to make him understand—"

"We're just friends," she interrupted. "I can't make him do anything."

"Crutches," Frisco said. "I'll use crutches, but no chair, all right?"

He didn't look at Mia. But he couldn't stop thinking about the way her eyes had looked filled with tears, and the way that had made him feel. She was wrong. She was dead wrong. She didn't know it, but she had the power to damn well make him do anything.

Maybe even fall in love with her.

MIA PULLED THE car up near the emergency room entrance. She could see Frisco through the windows of the brightly lit lobby, talking to the doctor. The doctor handed Frisco a bag, and then the two men shook hands. The doctor vanished quickly down the hallway, while Frisco moved slowly on his crutches toward the automatic door.

It slid open with a whoosh, and then he was outside, looking around.

Mia opened the car door and stood up. "Over here." She saw his surprise. This wasn't her car. This thing was about twice the size of her little subcompact—he wouldn't have any trouble fitting inside it. "I traded cars with a friend for a few days," she explained.

He didn't say a word. He just put the bag the doctor had given him into the middle of the wide bench seat and slid his crutches into the back. He climbed in carefully, lowering himself down and using both hands to lift his injured leg into the car.

She got in next to him, started the powerful engine and pulled out of the driveway. She glanced at Frisco. "How's your knee doing?"

"Fine," he said tersely.

"Do you really think Dwayne's going to come back?"

"Yep."

Mia waited for him to elucidate, but he didn't continue. He obviously wasn't in a talkative mood. Not that he ever was, of course. But somehow the fairly easygoing candidness of their previous few conversations had vanished.

She knew his knee was anything but fine. She knew it hurt him badly—and that the fact that he'd been unable to defeat his attacker hurt him even more.

She knew that his injured knee and his inability to walk without a cane made him feel like less of a man. It was idiotic. A man was made up of so much more than a pair of strong legs and an athletic body.

It was idiotic, but she understood. Suddenly she understood that the list she'd seen on Frisco's refrigerator of all the things he couldn't do wasn't simply pessimistic whining, as she'd first thought. It was a recipe. It was specific directions for a magical spell that would make Frisco a man again.

Jump, run, skydive, swim, stretch, bend, extend…

Until he could do all those things and more, he wasn't going to feel like a man.

Until he could do all those things again… But he wasn't going to. That Navy doctor had said he wasn't going to get any better. This was it. Frisco had come as far as he could—and the fact that he could walk at all was something of a miracle at that.

Mia pulled the car into the condominium parking lot and parked. Frisco didn't wait for her to help him out of the car. Of course not. Real men didn't need help.

Her heart ached for him as she watched him pull out his crutches from the backseat. He grimly positioned them under his arms, and carrying the bag that the doctor had given him, swung toward the courtyard.

She followed more slowly.

Jump, run, skydive, swim, stretch, bend, extend…

It wasn't going to happen. Dr. Horowitz knew it. Mia knew it. And she suspected that deep inside, Frisco knew it, too.

She followed him into the courtyard and could barely stand to watch as he pulled himself painfully up the stairs.

He was wrong. He was wrong about it all. Moving onto the ground floor wouldn't make him less of a man. Admitting that he had physical limitations—that there were things he could no longer do—that wouldn't make him less of a man, either.

But relentlessly questing after the impossible, making goals that were unattainable, setting himself up only for failure—that would wear him down and burn him out. It would take away the last of his warmth and spark, leaving him bitter and angry and cold and incomplete. Leaving him less of a man.

CHAPTER TEN

FRISCO SAT IN the living room, cleaning his handgun.

When Sharon's charming ex-boyfriend Dwayne had pulled out his knife this afternoon, Frisco had felt, for the first time in a while, the noticeable lack of a sidearm.

Of course, carrying a weapon meant concealing that weapon. Although he was fully licensed to carry whatever he damn well pleased, he couldn't exactly wear a weapon in a belt holster, like a cop or an old West gunslinger. And wearing a shoulder holster meant he'd have to wear a jacket over it, at least out in public. And—it was a chain reaction—if he wore a jacket, he'd have to wear long pants. Even *he* couldn't wear a jacket with shorts.

Of course, he could always do what Blue McCoy did. Blue was the Alpha Squad's XO—Executive Officer and second in command of the SEAL unit. Blue rarely wore anything other than cutoffs and an old worn-out, loose olive-drab fatigue shirt with the sleeves removed. And he always wore one of the weapons he carried in a shoulder holster underneath his shirt, the smooth leather directly against his skin.

Frisco's knee twinged, and he glanced at the clock. It was nearly 0300. Three o'clock in the morning.

Steve Horowitz had given him a number of little vials filled with a potent local pain reliever similar to novocaine. It wasn't yet time for another injection, but it was getting close. Frisco had given himself an injection at close to nine o'clock, after Mia had driven him home from the hospital.

Mia...

Frisco shook his head, determined to think about anything but Mia, separated from him by only a few thin walls, her hair spread across her pillow, wearing only a tantalizingly thin cotton nightgown. Her beautiful soft lips parted slightly in sleep....

Yeah, he was a master at self-torture. He'd been sitting here, awake for hours, spending most of his time remembering—hell, *reliving*—the way Mia had kissed him at the beach. Dear, sweet God, what a kiss that had been.

It wasn't likely he was going to get a chance to kiss her like that again. She'd made it clear that she wouldn't welcome a repeat performance. If he knew what was best, he'd stay far, far away from Mia Summerton. That wasn't going to be hard to do. From now on, she was going to be avoiding him, too.

A loud thump from the bedroom made him sit up. What the hell was that?

Frisco grabbed his crutches and his handgun and moved as quickly as he could down the hall to Tasha's room.

He'd bought a cheap portable TV. It was quite possibly the most expensive night-light and white noise machine in the world. Its bluish light flickered, illuminating the small room.

Natasha was sitting on the floor, next to her bed, sleepily rubbing her eyes and her head. She was whimpering, but only very softly. Her voice almost didn't carry above the soft murmurings of the television.

"Poor Tash, did you fall out of bed?" Frisco asked her, moving awkwardly through the narrow doorway and into the room. He slipped the safety onto his weapon and slid it into the pocket of his shorts. "Come on, climb back up. I'll tuck you in again."

But when Tasha stood up, she staggered, almost as if she'd had too much to drink, and sat back down on her rear end. As Frisco watched, she crumpled, pressing her forehead against the wall-to-wall carpeting.

Frisco leaned his crutches against the bed and bent down to pick her up. "Tash, it's three in the morning. Don't play silly games."

Lord, the kid was on fire. Frisco felt her forehead, her cheek, her neck, double-checking, praying that he was wrong, praying that she was simply sweaty from a nightmare. But with each touch, he knew. Natasha had a raging fever.

He lifted her and put her in her bed.

How could this have happened? She'd been fine all day today. She'd had her swimming lesson with her usual enthusiasm. She'd gone back into the water over and over again with her usual energy. True, she'd been asleep when he'd returned from the hospital, but he'd chalked that up to exhaustion after the excitement of the day—watching Uncle Frisco get the living daylights kicked out of him by old, ugly Dwayne had surely been tiring for the kid.

Her eyes were half-closed and she pressed her head against her pillow as if it hurt, still making that odd, whimpering sound.

Frisco was scared to death. He tried to judge how high her fever was by the touch of his hand, and she seemed impossibly, dangerously hot.

"Tasha, talk to me," he said, sitting next to her on the bed. "Tell me what's wrong. Tell me your symptoms."

Cripes, listen to him. *Tell me your symptoms.* She was five years old, she didn't know what the hell a symptom was. And from the looks of things, she didn't even know she was here, couldn't hear him, couldn't see him.

He had medical training, but most of it was first-aid. He could handle gunshot wounds, knife wounds, burns and lacerations. But sick kids with sky-high fevers...

He had to get Natasha to the hospital.

He could call a cab, but man, he wouldn't be able to get Tasha down the stairs. He could barely make it himself with his crutches. He certainly couldn't do it carrying the girl, could he? It would be far too dangerous to try. What if he dropped her?

"I'll be right back, Tash," he told her, grabbing his crutches and heading out toward the kitchen telephone, where he kept his phone book.

He flipped the book open, searching for the phone number for the local cab company. He quickly dialed. It rang at least ten times before someone picked up.

"Yellow Cab."

"Yeah," Frisco said. "I need a cab right away. 1210 Midfield Street, unit 2C. It's the condo complex on the corner of Midfield and Harris?"

"Destination?"

"City Hospital. Look I need the driver to come to the door. I got a little girl with a fever, and I'll need help carrying her down—"

"Sorry, sir. Our drivers do not leave their vehicles. He'll wait for you in the parking lot."

"Didn't you hear what I just said? This is an emergency. I have to get this kid to the hospital." Frisco ran his hand through his hair, trying to curb his anger and frustration. "I can't get her down the stairs by myself. I'm..." He nearly choked on the words. "I'm physically disabled."

"I'm sorry, sir. The rule is for our drivers' safety.

However, the cab you requested will arrive in approximately ninety minutes."

"Ninety minutes? I can't wait *ninety* minutes!"

"Shall I cancel your request for a cab?"

"Yes." Cursing loudly, Frisco slammed down the phone.

He picked it up again and quickly dialed 911. It seemed to take forever before the line was picked up.

"What is the nature of your emergency?"

"I have a five-year-old with a very high fever."

"Is the child breathing?"

"Yes—"

"Is the child bleeding?"

"No, I said she's got a fever—"

"I'm sorry, sir. We have quite a number of priority calls and a limited number of ambulances. You'll get her to the hospital faster if you drive her yourself."

Frisco fought the urge to curse. "I don't have a car."

"Well, I can put you on the list, but since your situation isn't life or death per se, you risk being continuously bumped down as new calls come in," the woman told him. "Things usually slow down by dawn."

Dawn. "Forget it," Frisco said, hanging up none too gently.

Now what?

Mia. He was going to have to ask Mia for help.

He moved as quickly as he could back down the hall to Tasha's room. Her eyes were closed, but she was moving fitfully. She was still as hot to the touch. Maybe even hotter.

"Hang on, kid," Frisco said. "Hang on, princess. I'll be back in a sec."

He was starting to be able to move pretty nimbly with

the crutches. He made it into the living room and out of the front door before he'd even had time to think.

But as he rang Mia's bell again and again, as he opened up the screen and hammered on the heavy wooden door, as he waited for her to respond, he couldn't help but wonder.

What the hell was he doing? He'd just spent the past six hours resolving to stay away from this woman. She didn't want him—she'd made that more than clear. So here he was, pounding on her door in the middle of the night, ready to humiliate himself even further by having to ask for help carrying a featherweight forty-pound little girl down the stairs.

The light went on inside Mia's apartment. She opened the door before she'd even finished putting on her bathrobe.

"Alan, what's wrong?"

"I need your help." She would never know how much it cost him to utter those words. It was only for Natasha that he would ask for help. If it had been himself in there, burning up with fever, he wouldn't've asked. He would have rather died. "Tasha's sick. She's got a really high fever—I want to take her over to the hospital."

"All right," Mia said without hesitation. "Let me throw on a pair of shorts and some sneakers and I'll pull the car around to the outside stairs."

She moved to go back toward her bedroom and her clothes, but he stopped her.

"Wait."

Mia turned back to the door. Frisco was standing on the other side of the screen, crutches under his arms. He was staring away from her, down at the carpeting. When he looked up, all of his customary crystal anger was gone from his eyes, leaving only a deeply burning shame. He could barely hold her gaze. He looked away, but then he forced himself to look up again, this time steadily meeting her eyes.

"I can't carry her down the stairs."

Mia's heart was in her throat. She knew what it had taken for him to say those words, and she so desperately didn't want to say the wrong thing in response. She didn't want to make light of it, but at the same time, she didn't want to embarrass him further by giving it too much weight.

"Of course not," she said quietly. "That would be dangerous to try on crutches. I'll get the car, then I'll come back up for Natasha."

He nodded once and disappeared.

She'd said the right thing, but there was no time to sag with relief. Mia dashed into her bedroom to change her clothes.

"AN *EAR* INFECTION?" Frisco repeated, staring at the emergency room doctor.

This doctor was an intern, still in his twenties, but he had a bedside manner reminiscent of an old-fashioned, elderly country doctor, complete with twinkling blue eyes and a warm smile.

"I already started her on an antibiotic, and I gave her something to bring down that fever," he said, looking from Frisco to Mia, "along with a decongestant. That'll keep her knocked out for a while. Don't be surprised if she sleeps later than usual in the morning."

"That's it?" Frisco asked. "It's just an ear infection?" He looked down at Tasha, who was sound asleep, curled up in the hospital bed. She looked impossibly small and incredibly fragile, her hair golden red against the white sheets.

"She may continue to experience the dizziness you described for a day or two," the doctor told them. "Keep her in bed if you can, and make sure she finishes the *entire* bottle of antibiotic. Oh, and ear plugs next time she goes swimming, all right?"

Frisco nodded. "You sure you don't want to keep her here for a while?"

"I think she'll be more comfortable at home," the young doctor said. "Besides, her fever's already gone down. Call me if she doesn't continue to improve."

An ear infection. Not encephalitis. Not appendicitis. Not scarlet fever or pneumonia. It still hadn't fully sunk in. Tash was going to be all right. An ear infection wasn't life threatening. The kid wasn't going to die. Frisco still couldn't quite believe it. He couldn't quite shake the tight feeling in his chest—the incredible fear, the sense of total and complete helplessness.

He felt Mia touch his arm. "Let's get her home," she said quietly.

"Yeah," he said, looking around, trying to collect himself, wondering when the relief was going to set in and push away this odd sensation of tightness and fear. "I've had enough of this place for one day."

The ride home was shorter than he remembered. He watched as Mia carried Tash back up the stairs and into his condo. She gently placed the still sleeping child into bed, and covered her with a sheet and a light blanket. He watched, trying not to think about the fact that she was taking care of Tasha because he couldn't.

"You ought to try to get some sleep, too," Mia told him, whispering as they went back down the hallway to the living room. "It's nearly dawn."

Frisco nodded.

Mia's face was in the shadows as she stood at the doorway, looking back at him. "Are you all right?"

No. He wasn't all right. He nodded. "Yeah."

"Good night, then." She opened the screen door.

"Mia…"

She stopped, turning back to face him. She didn't say a word, she just waited for him to speak.

"Thank you." His voice was husky, and to his horror he suddenly had tears in his eyes. But it was dark in the predawn, and there was no way she could have noticed.

"You're welcome," she said quietly and closed the door behind her.

She disappeared, but the tears that flooded his eyes didn't do the same. Frisco couldn't stop them from overflowing and running down his face. A sob escaped him, shaking him, and like ice breaking up on a river, another followed, faster and harder until, God, he was crying like a baby.

He'd honestly thought Tasha was going to die.

He had been totally terrified. Him, Frisco, terrified. He'd gone on rescue missions and information-gathering expeditions deep into hostile territory where he could've been killed simply for being American. He'd sat in cafés and had lunch, surrounded by the very people who wouldn't have hesitated to slit his throat had they known his true identity. He'd infiltrated a terrorist fortress and snatched back a cache of stolen nuclear weapons. He'd looked death—his own death—in the eye on more than one occasion. He'd been plenty scared all those times; only a fool wouldn't have been. That fear had been sharp edged, keeping him alert and in control. But it was nothing compared to the sheer, helpless terror he'd felt tonight.

Frisco stumbled back into the sanctuary of his bedroom, unable to stanch the flow of his tears. He didn't

want to cry, dammit. Tasha was safe. She was okay. He
should have enough control over his emotions to keep the
intensity of his relief from wiping him out this way.

He clenched his teeth and fought it. And lost.

Yeah, Tasha was safe. For now. But what if he hadn't
been able to get her to the hospital? It had been good that
he'd brought her in when he did, the doctor had said. Her
fever had been on the verge of becoming dangerously
high.

What if Mia hadn't been home? What if he hadn't
been able to get Tash down the stairs? Or what if during
the time he spent figuring out how to get Tash to the
hospital, her fever *had* risen dangerously high? What if
his inability to do something so simple as carry a child
down a set of stairs had jeopardized her life? What if she
had died, because he lived on the second floor? What if
she had died, because he was too damn proud to admit
the truth—that he was physically disabled.

He'd said the words tonight when he spoke to the cab
dispatcher. *I'm physically disabled.* He wasn't a SEAL
anymore. He was a crippled man with a cane—crutches
now—who might've let a kid die because of his damned
pride.

Frisco sat down on his bed and let himself cry.

MIA SET HER purse down on her kitchen table with an
odd-sounding thunk. She lifted it up and set it down
again. Thunk.

What was in there?

She remembered even before she opened the zipper.

Natasha's medicine. Frisco had picked up Tasha's
antibiotic directly from the hospital's twenty-four-hour
pharmacy.

Mia took it out of her purse and stared at it. Tash wasn't

due for another dose of the liquid until a little before noon, unless she woke up earlier.

She'd better take it over now, rather than wait.

She left her apartment and went over to Frisco's. All of his windows were dark. Damn. She opened the screen door, wincing as it screeched, and tried the door knob.

It was unlocked.

Slowly, stealthily, she let herself in. She would tiptoe into the kitchen, put the medicine in the fridge and…

What was that…? Mia froze.

It was a strange sound, a soft sound, and Mia stood very, very still, hardly daring to breathe as she listened for it again.

There it was. It was the sound of ragged breathing, of nearly silent crying. Had Tasha awoken? Was Frisco already so soundly asleep that he didn't hear her?

Quietly Mia crept down the hall toward Tasha's bedroom and peeked in.

The little girl was fast asleep, breathing slowly and evenly.

Mia heard the sound again, and she turned and saw Frisco in the dim light that filtered in through his bedroom blinds.

He was sitting on his bed, doubled over as if in pain, his elbows resting on his legs, one hand covering his face; a picture of despair.

The noise she had heard—it was Frisco. Alan Francisco was weeping.

Mia was shocked. Never, *ever* in a million years had she expected him to cry. She would have thought him incapable, unable to release his emotions in such a visible, expressive way. She would have expected him to internalize everything, or deny his feelings.

But he was crying.

Her heart broke for him, and silently she backed away, instinctively knowing that he would feel ashamed and humiliated if he knew she had witnessed his emotional breakdown. She crept all the way back into his living room and out of his apartment, holding her breath as she shut the door tightly behind her.

Now what?

She couldn't just go back into her own condominium, knowing that he was alone with all of his pain and fears. Besides, she was still holding Tasha's medicine.

Taking a deep breath, knowing full well that even if Frisco *did* come to the door, he might very well simply take the medicine and shut her out, she rang the bell.

She knew he heard it, but no lights went on, nothing stirred. She opened the screen and knocked on the door, pushing it open a few inches. "Alan?"

"Yeah," his voice said raspily. "I'm in the bathroom. Hang on, I'll be right out."

Mia came inside again, and closed the door behind her. She stood there, leaning against it, wondering if she should turn on the lights.

She heard the water running in the bathroom sink and could picture Frisco splashing his face with icy water, praying that she wouldn't be able to tell that he'd been crying. She left the lights off.

And he made no move to turn them on when he finally appeared at the end of the darkened hallway. He didn't say anything; he just stood there.

"I, um…I had Tasha's medicine in my purse," Mia said. "I thought it would be smart to bring it over now instead of…in the morning…."

"You want a cup of tea?"

His quiet question took her entirely by surprise. Of all the things she'd imagined he'd say to her, inviting her to stay for a cup of tea was not one of them. "Yes," she said. "I would."

His crutches creaked as he went into the kitchen. Mia followed more hesitantly.

He didn't turn on the overhead lamp. He didn't need to. Light streamed in through the kitchen window from the brightly lit parking lot. It was silvery and it made shadows on the walls, but it was enough to see by.

As Frisco filled a kettle with water from the faucet, Mia opened the refrigerator door and put Tasha's medicine inside. As she closed the door, she saw that list that he kept there on the fridge, the list of all the things he could no longer do—the list of things that kept him, in his eyes, from being a man.

"I know it was hard for you to come and ask me for help tonight," she said softly.

Using only his right crutch for support, he carried the kettle to the stove and set it down. He didn't say a word until after he'd turned the burner on. Then he turned to face her. "Yeah," he said. "It was."

"I'm glad you did, though. I'm glad I could help."

"I actually…" He cleared his throat and started again. "I actually thought she was going to die. I was scared to death."

Mia was startled by his candidness. *I was scared to death.* Another surprise. She never would have expected him to admit that. Ever. But then again, this man had been surprising her right from the start.

"I don't know how parents handle it," he said, pushing down on top of the kettle as if that would make the water heat faster. "I mean, here's this kid that you love more than life itself, right? And suddenly she's so sick she can't even stand up." His voice tightened.

"The thing that kills me is that if I had been the only

one left in the world, if it had been up to me and me alone, we wouldn't've made it to that hospital. I'd still be here, trying to figure out a way to get her down those stairs." He turned suddenly, slamming his hand down on top of the counter in frustration and anger. "I *hate* feeling so damned helpless!"

His shoulders looked so tight, his face so grim. Mia wrapped her arms around herself to keep from reaching for him. "But you're not the only one left in the world. You're *not* alone."

"But I *am* helpless."

"No, you're not," she told him. "Not anymore. You're only helpless if you refuse to ask for help."

He laughed, an exhale of bitter air. "Yeah, right—"

"Yeah," she said earnestly. "*Right.* Think about it, Alan. There are things that we all don't do, things that we probably couldn't do—look at your shirt," she commanded him, stepping closer. She reached out and touched the soft cotton of his T-shirt. She lifted it, turning it over and bringing the factory-machine-sewn hem into the light from the kitchen window. "You didn't sew this shirt, did you? Or weave the cotton to make the fabric? Cotton grows in fields—you knew that, right? Somehow a whole bunch of people did something to that little fluffy plant to make it turn into this T-shirt. Does it mean that you're helpless just because you didn't do it yourself?"

Mia was standing too close to him. She could smell his musky, masculine scent along with some kind of decadently delicious aftershave or deodorant. He was watching her, the light from the window casting shadows across his face, making his features craggy and harsh. His eyes gleamed colorlessly, but the heat within them didn't need a color to be seen. She released her hold on his T-shirt but she didn't back away. She didn't want to back away, even if it meant spontaneous combustion from the heat in his eyes.

"So what if you can't make your own clothes?" she continued. "The good people at Fruit of the Loom and Levi's will make them for you. So what if you can't carry Tasha down the stairs. *I'll* carry her for you."

Frisco shook his head. "It's not the same."

"It's *exactly* the same."

"What if you're not home? What then?"

"Then you call Thomas. Or your friend, what's-his-name...Lucky. And if they're not home, you call someone else. Instead of this," she said, gesturing toward the list on his refrigerator, "you should have a two-page list of friends you can call for help. Because you're only helpless if you have no one to call."

"Will they run on the beach for me?" Frisco asked, his voice tight. He stepped closer to her, dangerously closer. His body was a whisper away from hers, and she could feel his breath, hot and sweet, moving her hair. "Will they get back in shape for me, get reinstated as an active-duty SEAL for me? And then will they come along on my missions with me, and run when I need to run, and swim against a two-knot current when I need to swim? Will they make a high-altitude, low-opening jump out of an airplane for me? Will they fight when I need to fight, and move without making a noise when I need to be silent? Will they do all those things that I'd need to do to keep myself and the men in my unit alive?"

Mia was silent.

"I know you don't understand," he said. The teakettle started to hiss and whistle, a lonely, high-pitched keening sound. He turned away from her, moving toward the stove. He hadn't touched her, but his presence and nearness had been nearly palpable. She sagged slightly as if he had been holding her up, and backing away, she lowered herself into one of his kitchen chairs. As she watched, he removed the kettle from the heat and took two mugs down from the cabinet. "I wish I could make you understand."

"Try."

He was silent as he opened the cabinet again and removed two tea bags. He put one into each mug, then poured in the steaming water from the kettle. He set the kettle back onto the stove and was seemingly intent on steeping the tea bags as he began, haltingly, to speak.

"You know that I grew up here in San Felipe," he said. "I also told you that my childhood wasn't a barrel of laughs. That was sort of an understatement. Truth was, it sucked. My old man worked on a fishing boat—when he wasn't too hungover to get out of bed. It wasn't exactly like living an episode of *Leave it to Beaver,* or *Father Knows Best.*" He looked at her, the muscle in his jaw tight. "I'm going to have to ask you to carry the mugs of tea into the living room for me."

"Of course." Mia glanced at him from the corner of her eyes. "That wasn't really so hard, was it?"

"Yes, it was." With both crutches securely under his arms, Frisco led the way into the living room. He switched on only one lamp and it gave the room a soft, almost golden glow. "Excuse me for a minute," he said, then vanished down the hallway to his bedroom.

Mia put both mugs down on the coffee table in front of the plaid couch and sat down.

"I wanted to check on Tash," he said, coming back into the living room, "and I wanted to get *this.*" He was holding a paper bag—the bag the doctor had given him at the hospital. He winced as he sat down on the other side of the long couch and lifted his injured leg onto the coffee table. As Mia watched, he opened the bag and took out a syringe and a small vial. "I need to have my leg up. I hope you don't mind if I do this out here."

"What exactly is it that you're doing?"

"This is a local painkiller, kind of like novocaine," he explained, filling the syringe with the clear liquid. "I'm going to inject it into my knee."

"*You're* going to *inject* it into… You're kidding."

"As a SEAL, I've had training as a medic," he said. "Steve gave me a shot of cortisone in the hospital, but that won't kick in for a while yet. This works almost right away, but the down side is that it wears off after a few hours, and I have to remedicate. Still, it takes the edge off the pain without affecting my central nervous system."

Mia turned away, unable to watch as he stuck the needle into his leg.

"I'm sorry," he murmured. "But it was crossing the border into hellishly painful again."

"I don't think I could ever give myself a shot," Mia admitted.

He glanced over at her, his mouth twisted up into a near smile. "Well, it's not my favorite thing in the world to do, either, but can you imagine what would have happened tonight if I'd taken the painkiller Steve wanted to prescribe for me? I would never have heard Tasha fall out of bed. She'd still be in there, on the floor, and I'd be stupid, drooling and unconscious in my bed. This way, my knee gets numb, not my brain."

"Interesting philosophy from a man who drank himself to sleep two nights in a row."

Frisco could feel the blessed numbing start in his knee. He rolled his head to make his shoulders and neck relax. "Jeez, you don't pull your punches, do you?"

"Four-thirty in the morning is hardly the time for polite conversation," she countered, tucking her legs up underneath her on the couch and taking a sip of her tea. "If you can't be baldly honest at four-thirty in the morning, when can you be?"

Frisco reached up with one hand to rub his neck. "Here's a baldly honest truth for you, then—and it's true whether it's 0430 or high noon. Like I said before, I'm not drinking anymore."

She was watching him, her hazel eyes studying him, looking for what, he didn't know. He had the urge to turn away or to cover his face, afraid that somehow she'd be able to see the telltale signs of his recent tears. But instead, he forced himself to hold her gaze.

"I can't believe you can just quit," she finally said. "Just like that. I mean, I look at you, and I can tell that you're sober, but…"

"The night we met, you didn't exactly catch me at my best. I was…celebrating my discharge from the Navy— toasting their lack of faith in me." He reached forward, picked up his mug of tea and took a sip. It was too hot and it burned all the way down. "I told you—I don't make a habit out of drinking too much. I'm not like Sharon. Or my father. Man, he was a bastard. He had two moods— drunk and angry, and hung over and angry. Either way, my brothers and Sharon and I learned to stay out of his way. Sometimes one of us would end up in the wrong place at the wrong time, and then we'd get hit. We used to sit around for hours thinking up excuses to tell our friends about where we got all our black eyes and bruises." He snorted. "As if any of our friends didn't know exactly what was going on. Most of them were living the same bad dream.

"You know, I used to pretend he wasn't really my father. I came up with this story about how I was some kind of mercreature that had gotten tangled in his nets one day when he was out in the fishing boat."

Mia smiled. "Like Tasha pretending she's a Russian princess."

Her smile was hypnotizing. Frisco could think of little but the way her lips had felt against his, and how much he wanted to feel that sweet sensation again. He resisted the urge to reach out and touch the side of her beautiful face. She looked away from him, her smile fading, suddenly shy, as if she knew what he was thinking.

"So there I was," Frisco continued with his story, "ten years old and living with this nightmare of a home life. It was that year—the year I was in fourth grade—that I started riding my bike for hours on end just to get out of the house."

She was listening to him, staring intently into her mug as if it held the answers to all of her questions. She'd kicked off her sneakers and they lay on their side on the floor in front of her. Her slender legs were tucked up beneath her on the couch, tantalizingly smooth and golden tan. She was wearing a gray hooded sweatshirt over her cutoffs. She'd had it zipped up at the hospital, but at some point since they'd returned home, she'd unzipped it. The shirt she wore underneath was white and loose, with a small ruffle at the top.

It was her nightgown, Frisco realized. She'd simply thrown her clothes on over her nightgown, tucking it into her shorts and covering it with her sweatshirt.

She glanced up at him, waiting for him to continue.

Frisco cleared the sudden lump of desire from his throat and went on. "One day I rode my bike a few miles down the coast, to one of the beaches where the SEALs do a lot of their training exercises. It was just amazing to watch these guys." He smiled, remembering how he'd thought the SEALs were crazy that first time he'd seen them on the beach. "They were always wet. Whatever they were doing, whatever the weather, the instructors always ran 'em into the surf first and got 'em soaked. Then they'd crawl across the beach on their bellies and get coated with sand—it'd get all over their faces, in their hair, everywhere. And *then* they'd run ten miles up and down the beach. They looked amazing—to a ten-year-old it was pretty funny. But even though I was just a kid, I could see past the slapstick. I knew that whatever they were going to get by doing all these endless, excruciating endurance tests, it had to be pretty damn good."

Mia had turned slightly to face him on the couch. Maybe it was because he knew she was wearing her night-gown under her clothes, or maybe it was the dark, dangerous hour of the night, but she looked like some kind of incredible fantasy sitting there like that. Taking her into his arms and making love to her would be a blissful, temporary escape from all of his pain and frustration.

He knew without a shadow of a doubt that one kiss would melt away all of her caution and reserve. Yes, she was a nice girl. Yes, she wanted more than sex. She wanted love. But even nice girls felt the pull of hot, sweet desire. He could show her—and convince her with one single kiss—that sometimes pure sex for the sake of pleasure and passion was enough.

But oddly enough, he wanted more from this woman than the hot satisfaction of a sexual release. Oddly enough, he wanted her to understand how he felt—his frustration, his anger, his darkest fear.

Try, she'd said. Try to make her understand.

He was trying.

"I started riding to the naval base all the time," he continued, forcing himself to focus on her wide green eyes rather than the soft smoothness of her thighs. "I started hanging out down there. I snuck into this local dive where a lot of the off-duty sailors went, just so I could listen to their stories. The SEALs didn't come in too often, but when they did, man, they got a hell of a lot of respect. A *hell* of a lot of respect—from both the enlisted men *and* the officers. They had this aura of greatness about them, and I was convinced, along with the rest of the Navy, that these guys were gods.

"I watched 'em every chance I could get, and I noticed that even though most of the SEALs didn't dress in uniform, they all had this pin they wore. They called it a Budweiser—it was an eagle with a submachine gun in one claw and a trident in the other. I found out they got that pin after they went through a grueling basic training session called BUD/S. Most guys didn't make it through BUD/S, and some classes even had a ninety-percent dropout rate. The program was weeks and weeks of organized torture, and only the men who stayed in to the end got that pin and became SEALs."

Mia was still watching him as if he were telling her the most fascinating story in all of the world, so he continued.

"So one day," Frisco told her, "a few days before my twelfth birthday, I saw these SEALs-in-training bring their IBSs—their little inflatable boats—in for a landing on the rocks over by the Coronado Hotel. It was toward the end of the first phase of BUD/S. That week's called Hell Week, because it *is* truly hell. They were exhausted, I could see it in their faces and in the way they were sitting in those boats. I was sure they were all going to die. Have you seen the rocks over there?"

She shook her head, no.

"They're deadly. Jagged. And the surf is always

rough—not a good combination. But I saw these guys put their heads down and do it. They could've died—men *have* died doing that training exercise.

"All around me, I could hear the tourists and the civilian onlookers making all this noise, wondering aloud why these men were risking their lives like that when they could be regular sailors, in the regular Navy, and not have to put themselves in that kind of danger."

Frisco leaned closer to Mia, willing her to understand. "And I stood there—I was just a kid—but I *knew.* I knew why. If these guys made it through, they were going to be SEALs. They were going to get that pin, and they were going to be able to walk into any military base in the world and get automatic respect. And even better than that, they would have self-respect. You know that old saying, 'Wherever you go, there you are'? Well, I knew that wherever they went, at least one man would respect them, and that man's respect was the most important of all."

Mia gazed back at Frisco, unable to look away. She could picture him as that little boy, cheeks smooth, slight of frame and wire thin, but with these same intense blue eyes, impossibly wise beyond his tender years. She could picture him escaping from an awful childhood and an abusive father, searching for a place to belong, a place to feel safe, a place where he could learn to like himself, a place where he'd be respected—by others and himself.

He'd found his place with the SEALs.

"That was when I knew I was going to be a SEAL," he told her quietly but no less intensely. "And from that day on, I respected myself even though no one else did. I stuck it out at home another six years. I made it all the way through high school because I knew I needed that diploma. But the day I graduated, I enlisted in the Navy.

And I made it. I did it. I got through BUD/S, and I landed my IBS on those rocks in Coronado.

"And I got that pin."

He looked away from her, staring sightlessly down at his injured knee, at the bruises and the swelling and the countless crisscrossing of scars. Mia's heart was in her throat as she watched him. He'd told her all this to make her understand, and she *did* understand. She knew what he was going to say next, and even as yet unspoken, his words made her ache.

"I always thought that by becoming a SEAL, I escaped from my life—you know, the way my life *should* have turned out. I should've been killed in a car accident like my brother Rob was. He was DUI, and he hit a pole. Or else I should've got my high school girlfriend pregnant like Danny did. I should have been married with a wife and child to support at age seventeen, working for the same fishing fleet that my father worked for, following in the old bastard's footsteps. I always sort of thought by joining the Navy and becoming a SEAL, I cheated destiny.

"But now look at me. I'm back in San Felipe. And for a couple nights there, I was doing a damned good imitation of my old man. Drink 'til you drop, 'til you feel no pain."

Mia had tears in her eyes, and when Frisco glanced at her, she saw that his jaw was tight, and his eyes were damp, too. He turned his head away. It was a few moments before he spoke again, and when he finally did, his voice was steady but impossibly sad.

"Ever since I was injured," he said softly, "I feel like I've slipped back into that nightmare that used to be my life. I'm not a SEAL anymore. I lost that, it's gone. I don't know who I am, Mia—I'm some guy who's less than whole, who's just kind of floating around." He shook his head. "All I know for sure is that my self-respect is gone, too."

He turned to her, no longer caring if she saw that his eyes were filled with tears. "That's why I've got to get it all back. That's why I've got to be able to run and jump and dive and do all those things on that list." He wiped roughly at his eyes with the back of one hand, refusing to give in to the emotion that threatened to overpower him. "I want it back. I want to be whole again."

CHAPTER ELEVEN

MIA COULDN'T HELP herself. She reached for Frisco.

How could she keep her distance while her heart was aching for this man?

But he caught her hand before she could touch the side of his face. "You don't want this," he said quietly, his eyes searching as he gazed at her. "Remember?"

"Maybe we both need each other a little bit more than I thought," she whispered.

He forced his mouth up into one of his heartbreakingly poignant half smiles. "Mia, you don't need me."

"Yes, I do," Mia said, and almost to her surprise, her words were true. She did need him. Desperately. She had tried. She had honestly tried not to care for this man, this *soldier.* She'd tried to remain distant, aloof, unfeeling, but somehow over the past few days, he had penetrated all of her defenses and gained possession of her heart.

His eyes looked so sad, so soft and gentle. All of his anger was gone, and Mia knew that once again she was seeing the man that he had been—the man all of his pain and bitterness had made him forget how to be.

He could be that man again. He was *still* that man. He simply needed to stop basing his entire future happiness on attaining the unattainable. She couldn't do that for him. He'd have to do it for himself. But she *could* be with him now, tonight, and help him remember that he *wasn't* alone.

"I can't give you what you want," he said huskily. "I know it matters to you."

Love. He was talking about love.

"That makes us even." Mia gently freed her hand from his, and touched the side of his face. He hadn't shaved in at least a day, and his cheeks and chin were rough, but she didn't care. She didn't care if he loved her, either. "Because I can't give you what *you* want."

She couldn't give him the power to become a SEAL again. But if she could have, she would.

She leaned forward and kissed him. It was a light kiss, just a gentle brushing of her lips against his.

Frisco didn't move. He didn't respond. She leaned forward to kiss him again, and he stopped her with one hand against her shoulder.

She was kneeling next to him on the couch, and he looked down at her legs, at the soft cotton of her nightgown revealed by her unzipped sweatshirt and finally into her eyes. "You're playing with fire," he said quietly. "There may be an awful lot of things that I can't do anymore, but making love to a beautiful woman isn't one of them."

"Maybe we should start a new list. Things you *can* still do. You could put 'making love' right on the top."

"Mia, you better go—"

She kissed him again, and again he pulled back.

"Dammit, you *told* me—"

She kissed him harder this time, slipping her arms up around his neck and parting his lips with her tongue. He froze, and she knew that he hadn't expected her to be so bold—not in a million years.

His hesitation lasted only the briefest of moments before he pulled her close, before he wrapped her in his arms and nearly crushed her against the hard muscles of his chest.

And then he was kissing her, too.

Wildly, fiercely, he was kissing her, his hot mouth gaining possession of hers, his tongue claiming hers with a breathtaking urgency.

It didn't seem possible. She had only kissed him once before, on the beach, yet his mouth tasted sweetly familiar and kissing him was like coming home.

Mia felt his hands on her back, sweeping up underneath her sweatshirt and down to the curve of her bottom, pulling her closer, seeking the smooth bareness of her legs. He shifted her weight toward him, pulling her over and on top of him, so that she was straddling his lap as still they kissed.

Her fingers were deep in his hair. It was incredibly, decadently soft. She would have liked to spend the entire rest of her life right there, kissing Alan Francisco and running her hands through his beautiful golden hair. It was all she needed, all she would ever need.

And then he shifted his hips and she felt the hardness of his arousal pressing up against her and she knew she was wrong. She both needed and wanted more.

He pulled at her sweatshirt, pushing it off her shoulders and down her arms. He tugged her nightgown free from the top of her shorts, and she heard herself moan as his work-roughened hands glided up and across the bare skin of her back. And then he pulled away from her, breathing hard.

"Mia." His lean, handsome face was taut with frustration. "I want to pick you up and take you to my bed." But he couldn't. He couldn't carry her. Not on crutches, not even with a cane.

This was not the time for him to be thinking about

things he couldn't do. Mia climbed off of him, slipping out of his grasp. "Why don't we synchronize watches and plan to rendezvous there in, say…" She pretended to look at an imaginary watch on her wrist. "Oh two minutes?"

His face relaxed into a smile, but the tension didn't leave his eyes. "You don't need to say 'oh.' You could say 0430, but two minutes is just two minutes."

"I know that," Mia said. "I just wanted to make you smile. If that hadn't worked, I would have tried this…." She slowly pulled her nightgown up and over her head, dropping it down into his lap.

But Frisco's smile disappeared. He looked up at her, his gaze devouring her bare breasts, heat and hunger in his eyes.

Mia was amazed. She was standing half-naked in front of this man that she had only known for a handful of days. He was a soldier, a fighter who had been trained to make war in more ways than she could probably imagine. He was the toughest, hardest man she'd ever met, yet in many ways he was also the most vulnerable. He'd trusted her enough to share some of his secrets with her, to let her see into his soul. In comparison, revealing her body to him seemed almost insignificant.

And she could stand here like this, she realized, without a blush and with such certainty, because she was absolutely convinced that loving this man was the right thing to do. She'd never made love to a man before without a sense of unease, without being troubled by doubts. But she'd never met a man like Alan Francisco—a man who seemed so different from her, yet who could look into her eyes, and with just a word or a touch, make her feel so totally connected to him, so instantly in tune.

Mia had never considered herself an exhibitionist before, but then again, no one had ever looked at her the way Frisco did. She felt her body tighten with anticipation under the scalding heat of his gaze. It was seductive, the way he looked at her—and nearly as pleasurable as a caress.

She reached up, slowly and deliberately, taking her time as she unfastened her ponytail, letting him watch her as she loosened her long hair around her shoulders, enjoying the sensation of his eyes on her body.

"You're not smiling," she whispered.

"Believe me, I'm smiling inside."

And then he did smile. It was half crooked and half sad. It was filled with doubt and disbelief, laced with wonder and anticipation. As she gazed into his eyes, Mia could see the first glimmer of hope. And she felt herself falling. She knew in that single instant that she was falling hopelessly and totally in love with this man.

Afraid he'd see her feelings in her eyes, she picked up her sweatshirt from the floor and turned, moving quickly down the hall to his bedroom. To his bed.

Frisco wasn't far behind, but she heard him stop at Natasha's room and go inside to check on the little girl.

"Is she all right?" she asked as he came in a few moments later. He closed the door behind him. And locked it.

He stood there, a dark shape at the far end of the room. "She's much cooler now," he said.

Mia crossed to the window and adjusted the blinds slightly, allowing them both privacy and some light. The dim light from the landing streamed up in a striped pattern across the ceiling, giving the ordinary room an exotic glow. She turned back to find Frisco watching her.

"Do you have protection?" she asked.

"Yes. It's been a while," he admitted, "but...yes."

"It's been a while for me, too," she said softly.

"It's not too late to change your mind." He moved away from the door, allowing her clear access to make an escape. He looked away, as if he knew that his gaze had the power to imprison her.

"Why would I want to do that?"

He gave her another of his sad smiles. "A sudden burst of sanity?" he suggested.

"I want to make love to you," she said. "Is that really so insane?"

He looked up at her. "You could have your choice of anyone. Anyone you want." There was no self-pity in his voice or on his face. He was merely stating a fact that he believed was true.

"Good," she said. "Then I'll choose you."

Frisco heard her soft words, but it wasn't until she smiled and moved toward him that they fully sank in.

Mia wanted him. She wanted *him*.

The light from the outside walkway gleamed on her bare skin. Her body was even more beautiful than he'd imagined. Her breasts were full and round—not too big, but not too small, either. He ached to touch her with his hands, with his mouth, and he smiled, knowing he was going to do just that, and soon.

But she stopped just out of his reach.

Holding his gaze, she unfastened her shorts and let them glide down her legs.

He'd seen her in her bathing suit just that afternoon— he was well aware that her trim, athletic body was the closest thing to his idea of perfection he'd ever seen. She wasn't voluptuous by any definition of the word—in fact, some men might've found her too skinny. Her hips were slender, curving in to the softness of her waist. She was willowy and gracefully shaped, a wonderful combination of smooth muscles and soft, flowing lines.

Frisco sat down on the edge of the bed and she turned toward him. He reached for her and she went willingly into his arms, once again straddling his lap.

"I think this is where we were," she murmured and kissed him.

Frisco spun, caught in a vortex of pleasure so intense, he couldn't keep from groaning aloud. Her skin was so smooth, so soft beneath his hands, and her kisses were near spiritual experiences, each one deeper and longer than the last, infusing him with her joyful vitality and sweet, limitless passion.

She tugged at his T-shirt, and he broke free from their embrace to yank it up and over his head. And then she was kissing him again, and the sensation of her bare skin against his took his breath away.

He tumbled her back with him onto the bed, pulling her down on top of him, slipping his hand between them to touch the sweet fullness of her breasts. Her nipples were taut and erect with desire and he pulled her to his mouth, laving her with his tongue, suckling first gently then harder as she gasped her pleasure, as she arched her back.

"I like that," she breathed. "That feels so good...."

Her whispered words sent a searing flame of need through him and he pulled her even closer.

His movement pressed her intimately, perfectly against his arousal and she held him there tightly for a moment. He could feel her heat, even through her panties and his shorts. He wanted to touch her, to taste her, to fill her completely. He wanted her all. He wanted her now. He wanted her forever, for all time.

Her hair surrounded them like a sensuous, sheer, black curtain as he kissed her again, as she began to move on top of him, slowly sliding against the hard length of him.

Oh, man, if she kept this up, he was going to lose it before he even got inside of her.

"Mia—" he groaned, his hands on her hips, stilling her movement.

She pulled back to look down at him, her eyes heavy-lidded with pleasure and desire, a heart-stoppingly sexy smile curving her lips. Flipping her long hair back over one shoulder, she reached for the button at the waistband of his shorts. She undid it quickly, deftly, then slid back, kneeling over his thighs to unfasten the zipper.

His arousal pressed up, released from his shorts, and she covered him with her delicate hands, gazing down into his eyes, touching him through his briefs.

She looked like some kind of extremely erotic fantasy kneeling above him, wearing those barely-there panties, the white silk contrasting perfectly with the gleaming golden color of her smooth skin. Her long, thick hair fell around her shoulders, several strands curving around her beautiful breasts.

Frisco reached for her, wanting to touch all of her, running his hands down her arms, caressing her breasts.

She pulled his shorts and his briefs down, watching his eyes and smiling at the pleasure on his face as her hands finally closed around him, closing her eyes in her own ecstasy as his hand tightened on her breast.

She leaned forward and met his lips in a hard, wild kiss, then pulled away, leaving a trail of kisses from his mouth, down his neck, to his chest, as with one hand she still held him possessively.

Her hair swept across him in the lightest of caresses and Frisco bit back a cry as her mouth moved even lower, as he nearly suffocated in a wave of exquisite, mind-numbing pleasure.

This was incredible. This was beyond incredible, but

it wasn't what he wanted. He reached for her, roughly pulling her up and into his arms.

"Didn't you like that?" She was laughing—she knew damn well that he'd liked it. She knew damn well that she'd come much too close to pushing him over the edge.

He tried to speak, but his voice came out as only a growl. She laughed again, her voice musical, her amusement contagious. He covered her mouth in the fiercest of kisses, and he could feel laughter and sheer joy bubbling up from inside of her and seeping into him, flowing through his veins, filling him with happiness.

Happiness. Dear God, when was the last time he'd felt happy? It was odd, it was weird, it was *beyond* weird, because even remembering back to when he had been happy, before his injury, he had never associated that particular emotion with making love. He'd felt desire, he'd felt sexual satisfaction, he'd felt interested, amused, in control or even out of control. He'd felt confident, self-assured and powerful.

But he'd never felt so unconditionally, so inarguably *happy.* He had never felt anything remotely like this.

He'd also never made love to a woman who was, without a doubt, his perfect sexual match.

Mia was openly, unabashedly sexy and unembarrassed by her powerful sensuality. She was unafraid to take the lead in their lovemaking. She was confident and daringly fearless and bold.

If it hadn't been for that glimpse she'd given him in the hospital lobby of her sensual side, he never would have expected it. She was so sweet natured, so gentle and kind. She was *nice.* She was the kind of woman a man would marry, content to spend the rest of his life surrounded by her quiet warmth.

But Mia didn't carry her quietness with her into the bedroom. And she wasn't warm—she was incredibly, scaldingly, moltenly hot.

His hands swept down the smooth expanse of her stomach, down underneath the slip of silk that covered her. She was hot and sleek and ready for him, just as he'd known she would be. She arched up against his fingers, pushing him deeply inside of her, pulling his head toward her and guiding his mouth to her breast.

"I want to get on top of you," she gasped. "Please—"

It was an incredible turn-on—knowing this fiercely passionate woman wanted him so completely.

He released her, rolling onto his side to reach into the top drawer of his bedside table. He rifled through the clutter, and miraculously his hand closed on a small foil packet. He tore it open and covered himself as Mia pushed down her panties and kicked her legs free. And then she *was* on top of him.

She came down, and he thrust up, and in one smooth, perfect, white-hot movement, he was inside of her.

The look on her face was one he knew he'd remember and carry with him to his grave. Her eyes were closed, her lips slightly parted, her head thrown back in sheer, beautiful rapture.

He was making her feel this way.

She opened her eyes and gazed down at him, searching his face for God knew what. Whatever she was looking for, she seemed to have found it, because she smiled at him so sweetly. Frisco felt as if his heart were suddenly too large to fit inside of his chest.

She began to move on top of him, slowly at first. Her smile faded, but still she looked into his eyes, holding his gaze.

"Alan…?"

He wasn't sure he could speak, but he moistened his lips and gave it a try. "Yeah…?"

"This is really good."

"Oh, yeah." He had to laugh. It came bubbling up from somewhere inside of him, and he recognized his laughter as belonging to her.

She was moving faster now and he tried to slow her down. He wanted this to last forever, but at the rate they were going… But she didn't want to slow down, and he could refuse her nothing.

He pulled her down on top of him and kissed her frantically, fighting for his tenuous control. But he was clinging to the side of a cliff, and his fingerhold was slipping fast.

"Alan…" She gasped his name as she clutched him tightly, and he felt the first waves of her tumultuous release.

Frisco went over the edge. But instead of falling, he sailed upward, soaring impossibly high, higher than he'd ever gone before. Pleasure rocketed through him, burning him, scorching him, leaving him weak and stunned, shattered and depleted—yet still filled, completely and thoroughly, with happiness.

Mia's long, soft hair was in his face and he closed his eyes, just breathing in the sweet scent of her shampoo as he slowly floated back to earth.

After a moment, she sighed and smiled—he could feel her lips move against his neck. He wondered if she could feel his own smile.

Mia lifted her head, pulling her hair from his face. "Are you still alive?"

He felt his smile get broader as he met her eyes. Hazel was his new favorite color. "Definitely."

"I think we can safely add 'making love' to the list of things that you can still do," she said with a smile.

His knee. Man, he hadn't thought about his knee since he'd locked his door behind them. He *still* didn't want to think about it, and he fought to hold on to the peacefulness of this moment.

"I don't know," he said. "Maybe we should make sure that it wasn't some kind of fluke. Maybe we better try it again."

Mia's smile turned dangerous. "I'm ready when you are."

Frisco felt a surge of desire course through him, hot and sweet. "Give me a few minutes…."

He kissed her, a slow, deep kiss that promised her unlimited pleasure.

Mia sighed, pulling back to look at him again. "I'd love to stay, but…"

"But…?"

She smiled, running her fingers through his hair. "It's after six in the morning, Alan. I don't think it's smart for me to be here when Natasha wakes up. She's had enough turbulence recently in her life, without her having to worry about whether she's got to compete with me for your time and affection."

Frisco nodded. Mia was probably right. He was disappointed to see her leave so soon, but he had to consider the kid.

Mia slipped out of his arms and out of his bed. He turned onto his side to watch her gather her clothes from his floor.

"You called me Alan again," he said.

She looked up at him in surprise as she slipped on her shorts. "Did I? I'm sorry."

"You think of me as Alan, don't you?" he asked. "Not Frisco."

She zipped up her sweatshirt and then came and sat down next to him on the bed. "I like your name," she admitted. "I'm sorry if it keeps slipping out."

He propped himself up on one elbow. "It slipped out a lot while we were making love."

"God, I hope that didn't ruin it for you." She was half-serious.

Frisco laughed. "If you had called me Bob, that might've ruined it, but..." He touched the side of her face. "That was the first time in a long time that I've actually enjoyed being called Alan. And I *did* enjoy it."

She closed her eyes briefly, pressing her cheek against the palm of his hand. "Well, I certainly enjoyed calling you Alan, that's for sure."

"Who knows," he murmured, tracing her lips with his thumb. "If we keep this up, I might even get used to it."

Mia opened her eyes and gazed at him. "Do you...want to keep this up?" she asked. All teasing was gone from her voice, and for the first time all night, she sounded less than certain.

Frisco couldn't respond. It wasn't her question that shocked him—it was his own immediate and very certain answer. Yes. God, yes.

This was dangerous. This was extremely dangerous. He didn't want to feel anything but pleasure and satisfaction when he thought about this woman. He didn't want anything more than neighborly, casual, no-strings sex.

Yet there was no way he could let her walk out of here thinking that one night had been enough. Because it hadn't. Because the thought of her leaving simply to go home was hard enough to tolerate. He didn't want to think about how he would feel if she ever left for good. He *couldn't* think about that.

"Yes," he finally answered, "but I have to be honest, I'm not in any kind of place right now where I can—"

She silenced him with a kiss. "I want to, too," she told him. "That's all we both need to know right now. It doesn't have to be any more complicated than that."

But it *was* more complicated than that. Frisco knew just from looking at her. She cared for him. He could see it in her eyes. He felt a hot flash of elation that instantly turned to cold despair. He didn't want her to care for him. He didn't want her to be hurt, and if she cared too much, she would be.

"I just want to make sure you don't go turning this into some kind of fairy tale," he said quietly, unable to resist touching the soft silk of her hair, praying that his words weren't going to sting too badly. Still, a small sting now was better than a mortal wound in the long run. "I know what we've got going here looks an awful lot like *Beauty and the Beast,* but I need more than a pretty girl to turn me back into a prince—to make me whole again. I need a whole hell of a lot more to do that. And I've got to be honest with you, I…"

He couldn't say it. His throat closed on the words, but he had to make sure she understood.

"I'm scared that the doctors are right," he admitted. "I'm scared that my knee is as good as it's going to get."

Mia's beautiful eyes were filled with compassion and brimming with emotion. "Maybe it would be a good thing if you could admit that—if you could accept your limitations."

"A *good* thing…?" He shook his head, exhaling his disbelief. "If I give up trying, I'm condemning myself to a lifetime of this limbo. I'm not dead, but I'm not really alive, either."

Mia looked away from him, and he knew what she was thinking. He'd certainly seemed full of life when they'd made love, just a short time ago. But this wasn't about sex. This wasn't about her. "I need to know who I am again," he tried to explain.

Her head came up and she nearly burned him with the intensity of her gaze. "You're Lieutenant Francisco, from San Felipe, California. You're a man who walks with a cane and a hell of a lot of pain because of that. You're a Navy SEAL—you'll always be a SEAL. You were when you were eleven years old. You will be when you die."

She cupped his face with her hands and kissed him—a sweet, hot kiss that made him almost believe her.

"I haven't really known you that long," she continued, "but I think I know you well enough to be certain that you're going to win. You're not going to settle for any kind of limbo. I know you're going to do whatever it takes to feel whole again. I know you'll make the right choices. You *are* going to live happily ever after. Just don't give up." She kissed him again and stood up. "I'll see you later, okay?"

"Mia—"

But she was already closing his door quietly behind her.

Frisco lay back in his bed and gazed up at the ceiling. She had such faith in him. *Just don't give up.* She seemed convinced he would do whatever it took to get back into active duty.

He used to have that kind of faith, but it was worn mighty thin from time and countless failure, and now all of his doubts were showing through. And over the past several days, those doubts had grown pretty damn strong. It was becoming as clear as the daylight that was streaming in through his blinds that his recovery was not something that was in his control. He could bully himself, push himself to the edge, work himself until he dropped, but if his knee couldn't support his weight, if the joint was unable to move in certain ways, he would be doing little more than slamming his head against a stone wall.

But now he had Mia believing in him, believing he had what it would take to overcome his injury, to win, to be an active-duty SEAL again.

She cared more about him than she was letting on. Frisco knew without a doubt that she wouldn't have made love to him without feeling *some*thing for him. Was she falling in love with him? It was entirely likely—she was softhearted and kind. He wouldn't be the first down-on-his-luck stray she took into her heart.

Somehow he'd fooled her into thinking he was worth her time and emotion. Somehow he'd tricked her into believing his pipe dream. Somehow she'd bought into his talk of happily ever after.

He closed his eyes. He wanted that happily ever after. He wanted to stand up from this bed and walk into the bathroom without having to use his cane. He wanted to lace up his running shoes and clock himself five miles before breakfast. He wanted to head over to the naval base and join the team for some of their endless training. He wanted to be back in the game, to be ready for anything and everything, ready to be sent out at a moment's notice should the Alpha Squad be needed.

And he wanted to come home after a tough assignment to the sweetness of Mia's arms, the heaven of her kisses and the warm light of love in her eyes.

God, he wanted that.

But would Mia want him if he failed? Would she want

to spend her time always waiting for him to catch up? Would she want to be around a man trapped forever in the limbo between what he once was and what he hoped never again to be?

You're not going to settle for any kind of limbo, she'd told him. *I know you're going to do whatever it takes to feel whole again.*

You're going to win.

But what if he didn't win? What if his knee didn't allow him to rejoin the SEALs? And in his mind, rejoining the SEALs was the only way to win. Anything short of that, and he'd be a loser.

But Mia had faith in him.

He, however, no longer had her confidence. He knew how easy it was to lose when things were out of his control. And as much as he wanted it to be, his recovery was *not* in his control.

Frisco's knee began to throb, and he reached for his painkiller.

He wished he had something that would work as quickly and effectively to ease the ache in his heart.

CHAPTER TWELVE

THE MAN CALLED Dwayne was walking across the condo parking lot.

Mia was in her kitchen, standing at the sink, and she just happened to look up and see him.

Not that he was easy to miss. His size called immediate attention to himself. He was wearing another well-tailored suit and a pair of dark sunglasses that didn't succeed in hiding the bandage across the bridge of his nose or the bruises on his face.

Mia went into her living room, where Natasha was sitting on the floor, working with painstaking care on a drawing. Crayons and paper were spread out in front of her on the wicker coffee table.

Trying to look casual, Mia locked and bolted her door, and then closed the living room curtains.

Dwayne's presence here was no coincidence. He was looking for Frisco. Or Natasha. But he wasn't going to find either of them.

Tasha didn't do more than glance up at Mia as she turned on the lamp to replace the sunlight that was now blocked by the curtains.

"Need more juice?" Mia asked the little girl. "You know, you'll get better faster if you have more juice."

Tasha obediently picked up her juice box and took a sip.

Frisco had knocked on Mia's door at a little after eleven. She almost hadn't recognized him at first.

He was wearing his dress uniform. It fit him like a glove—white and starched and gleaming in the midmorning sun. The rows and rows and rows of colored bars on his chest also reflected the light. The effect was blinding. Even his shoes seemed to glow.

His hair was damp from a shower and neatly combed. His face was smooth shaven. He looked stern and unforgiving and dangerously professional. He looked like some kind of incredibly, breathtakingly handsome stranger.

And then he smiled. "You should see the look on your face."

"Oh, really? Am I drooling?"

Heat flared in his eyes, but then he turned and looked down, and Mia saw that Tasha was standing next to him.

"May we come in?" he asked.

Mia pushed open the screen. Tasha was already feeling much better. The little girl was quick to show Mia the second medal she'd had pinned to her T-shirt, awarded for following Frisco's rules all morning long. Of course, she'd been asleep nearly all morning long, but no one mentioned that.

She'd recovered from her high fever with the remarkable resilience of a small child. The antibiotic was working, and Tasha was back in action, alert and energetic.

Frisco touched Mia gently and lightly as he came inside—just a quick sweep of his fingers down her bare arm. It was enough to take her breath away, enough to remind her of the love they'd made just a few short hours ago. Enough to let her know he remembered, too.

He was wondering if she would mind watching Tasha for a few hours, while he went to the detox hospital and tried to see his sister. That was why he was all dressed up. He figured he had a better shot at getting past the "no visitors" rule if he looked like some kind of hero. One way or another, he was hell-bent on finding out exactly why Dwayne was after Sharon.

Mia volunteered to watch Natasha in Frisco's condo, but he'd told her he'd rather Tasha stay here at her place—he'd feel less as if he were bothering her. And despite Mia's reassurances otherwise, her condo was where they'd ended up.

Now she had to wonder—had Frisco expected Dwayne to come looking for him again? Was that why he'd insisted she and Tash stay at her place instead of his?

Resisting the urge to peer out from behind her closed curtains to see if Dwayne was climbing up the stairs, Mia sat down next to Tasha. "What are you drawing?" she asked.

Her heart was drumming in her chest. Dwayne was going to ring Frisco's doorbell, and realize that no one was home. What then? Would he try the neighbors' doors in an attempt to find out where the man had gone? What if he rang her bell? What was she going to tell Tasha? How was she going to explain why she wasn't going to answer her door?

And, dear God—what if Frisco came home while Dwayne was still there?

Natasha carefully selected a red crayon from the brand-new box Frisco had bought her. "I'm making a medal," she told Mia, carefully staying within the lines she had drawn. "For Frisco. He needs a medal today, too. We were in the kitchen, and he dropped the milk and it spilled on the floor. He didn't say any bad words." She put the crayon back and took another. "He wanted to—I could tell—but he didn't."

"He's going to like that medal a lot," Mia said.

"And then," Natasha continued, "even though he was mad, he started to laugh." She chose another crayon. "I asked him if milk felt all funny and squishy between his toes, but he said he was laughing because there was something funny on the refrigerator. I looked, but I didn't see anything funny. Just a piece of paper with some writing on it. But I can't read, you know."

"I know." Mia had to smile, despite her racing heart. "He laughed, huh?" Before she'd left Frisco's condo early this morning, she'd started a new list and stuck it onto his refrigerator, next to his other list. Her new list included some of the things he *could* still do, even with his injured leg. She'd listed things like sing, hug Tasha, laugh, read, watch old movies, lie on the beach, do crossword puzzles, breathe and eat pizza. She'd begun and ended the list, of course, with "make love." And she'd peppered it thoroughly with spicy and sometimes extremely explicit suggestions—all of which she was quite sure he was capable of doing.

She was glad he'd laughed. She liked it when he laughed.

She liked it when he talked to her, too. He'd revealed quite a bit of himself last night. He had admitted he was afraid his knee wasn't going to get any better. Mia was almost certain he had been voicing his fears aloud for the very first time.

Frisco's friend Lucky had told her there was an instructor position waiting for Frisco at the base. Sure, it wasn't the future he'd expected or intended, but it *was* a future. It would take him out of this limbo that he feared. It would keep him close to the men he admired and respected. It would make him a SEAL again.

Mia went to the window. She moved the curtain a

fraction of an inch then quickly dropped it back into place as she saw Dwayne pulling his large girth up the stairs.

She stood by her front door, listening intently, heart hammering. She could hear the faint sound of Frisco's doorbell through the thin wall that separated their two condos. It rang once, twice, three times, four.

Then there was silence.

Mia waited, wondering if the man had gone away, or if he was out in the courtyard—or standing in front of her own door.

And then she heard the sound of breaking glass. There was another sound, a crash, and then several more thumps—all coming from inside Frisco's condominium.

Dwayne had gone inside. He'd broken in, and from the sound of things, the son of a bitch was destroying Frisco's home.

Mia leaped for her telephone and dialed 911.

POLICE CARS—THREE of them—were parked haphazardly in the condominium lot.

Frisco threw a ten-dollar bill at the taxi driver and pulled himself and his crutches as quickly as he could out of the cab.

His heart was in his throat as he raced into the courtyard. People were outside of their units, standing around, watching the police officers, several of whom were outside of both his and Mia's condos.

Both doors were open wide and one of the uniformed officers went into Mia's place.

Still on his crutches, Frisco took the stairs dangerously fast. If he lost his balance, he'd seriously hurt himself, but he wasn't going to lose his balance, dammit. He needed to get up those stairs.

"Mia," he called. "Tash?"

Thomas King stepped out of Mia's condo. "It's okay, Navy," he said. "No one was hurt."

But Frisco didn't slow down. "Where are they?"

"Inside."

He went in, squinting to adjust his eyes to the sudden dimness. Despite Thomas's reassurance, he had to see with his own eyes that they were okay. Mia was standing near the kitchen, talking to one of the policewomen. She looked all right. She was still wearing the shorts and sleeveless top she'd had on earlier. Her hair was still back in a single braid. She looked calm and composed.

"Where's Tasha?"

She looked up at him and a flurry of emotions crossed her face and he knew she wasn't quite as composed as she looked. "Alan. Thank God. Tasha's in my office, playing computer games. She's fine." She took a step toward him as if she wanted to reach for him, but stopped, glancing back at the police officer, as if she were embarrassed or uncertain as to his reception.

Frisco didn't give a damn who was watching. He wanted her in his arms, and he wanted her *now*. He dropped his crutches and pulled her close, closing his eyes and breathing in her sweet perfume. "When I saw those police cars…" He couldn't continue. He just held her.

"Excuse me," the policewoman murmured, slipping past them and disappearing out of the open condo door.

"Dwayne came looking for you," Mia told him, tightening her arms around his waist.

Dwayne. He held her tighter, too. "Dammit, I shouldn't have left you alone. Are you sure he didn't hurt you?"

"I saw him coming and we stayed inside," she said, pulling back to look up at him. "Alan, he totally trashed your living room and kitchen. The rest of the apartment's okay—I called the police and they came before he went into the bedrooms, but—"

"He didn't talk to you, didn't threaten you or Tash in any way?"

She shook her head. "He ran away when he heard the police sirens. He never even knew we were next door."

Frisco felt a rush of relief. "Good."

Her eyes were wide. "Good? But your living room is wrecked."

"To hell with my living room. I don't care about my living room."

He gazed down into her eyes, and at her beautiful lips parted softly in surprise, and he kissed her.

It was a strange kiss, having nothing to do with attraction and desire. He wasn't kissing her because he wanted her. He kissed her because he wanted to vanquish the last of his fears. He wanted to convince himself without a doubt that she truly was all right. It had nothing to do with sex and everything to do with the flood of emotions he'd felt while running up those stairs.

Her lips were warm and sweet and pliant under his own. She kissed him eagerly, both giving and taking comfort in return.

When they finally pulled apart, Mia had tears in her eyes. She wiped at them, forcing an apologetic smile. "I was scared out of my mind that Dwayne was going to somehow find you before you got home—"

"I can handle Dwayne."

She looked away, but not before he caught a glimpse of the skepticism in her eyes. He felt himself tense with frustration, but stopped himself from reacting. Why shouldn't she doubt his ability to protect himself? Just yesterday, she'd watched Dwayne beat the crap out of him.

He pulled her hand up, positioning it on the outside of his jacket, just underneath his left arm. There was surprise on her face as she felt the unmistakable bulge of his shoulder holster and sidearm.

"I can handle Dwayne," he said again.

"Excuse me, Lieutenant Francisco…?"

Frisco released Mia and turned to see one of the cops standing just inside the door. He was an older man, balding and gray with a leathery face and a permanent squint to his eyes from the bright California sun. He was obviously the officer in charge of the investigation.

"I'm wondering if we might be able to ask you some questions, sir?"

Mia bent down and picked up Frisco's crutches, her head spinning.

A gun. Her lover was carrying a *gun*. Of course, it made sense that he would have one. He was a professional soldier, for crying out loud. He probably had an entire collection of firearms. She simply hadn't thought about it before this. Or maybe she hadn't *wanted* to think about it. It was ludicrous, actually. She, who was so opposed to violence and weapons of any kind, had fallen in love with a man who not only wore a gun, but obviously knew how to use it.

"Thanks," he murmured to her, positioning his crutches under his arms. He started toward the policeman. "I'm not sure I can give you any answers," he said to the man. "I haven't even seen the damage yet."

Mia followed him out the door. Thomas was still standing outside. "Will you stay with Tasha for a minute?" she asked him.

He nodded and went inside.

She caught up with Frisco as he was stepping into his

condo. His face was expressionless as he gazed at what used to be his living room.

The glass-topped coffee table was shattered. The entertainment center that had held his TV and a cheap stereo system had been toppled forward, away from the wall. The heavy wood of the shelves was intact, but the television was smashed. All of his lamps were broken, and the ugly plaid couch had been slashed and shredded, and wads of white stuffing and springs were exposed.

His dining area and kitchen contained more of the same. His table and chairs had been knocked over and the kitchen floor was littered with broken glasses and plates swept down from the cabinets. The refrigerator was open and tipped forward, its contents smashed and broken on the floor, oozing together in an awful mess.

Frisco looked, but didn't say a word. The muscle in his jaw moved, though, as he clenched his teeth.

"Your…friend ID'd the man who broke in as someone named Dwayne…?" the policeman said.

His *friend*. As Mia watched, Frisco's eyes flickered in her direction at the officer's tactful hesitation. The man could have called her his neighbor, but it was obvious to everyone that she was more than that. Mia tried not to blush, remembering the bright-colored condom wrapper that surely still lay on Frisco's bedroom floor. These police officers had been crawling all over this place for the past twenty-five minutes. They surely hadn't missed seeing that wrapper—or the way Frisco had pulled her possessively into his arms when he'd arrived. These were seasoned cops. They were especially good at deductive reasoning.

"I don't know anyone named Dwayne," Frisco told the policeman. He unbuttoned his jacket, and carefully began maneuvering his way through the mess toward his bedroom. "Mia must've been mistaken."

"Alan, I saw—"

He glanced at her, shaking his head, just once, in warning. "Trust me," he murmured. Mia closed her mouth. What was he doing? He knew damn well who Dwayne was, and she *wasn't* mistaken.

"I appreciate your coming all the way down here, Officer," he said, "but I won't be pressing charges."

The policeman was respectful of Frisco's uniform and his rows of medals. Mia could hear it in the man's voice. But he was also obviously not happy with Frisco's decision. "Lieutenant, we have four different witnesses who saw this man either entering or leaving your home." He spread his hands, gesturing to the destruction around them. "This is no small amount of damage that was done here this afternoon."

"No one was hurt," Frisco said quietly.

Mia couldn't keep quiet. "No one was hurt?" she said in disbelief. "Yesterday someone was hurt…." She bit her lip to keep from saying more. Yesterday that man had sent Frisco to the hospital. His name had been Dwayne then, and it was still Dwayne today. And if Frisco had been home this afternoon…

But *trust me,* he'd whispered. And she did. She trusted him. So she had swallowed her words.

But her outburst had been enough, and for the first time since he'd stepped inside his condo, Frisco's face flashed with emotion. "This is not something that's going to go away by arresting this bastard on charges of breaking and entering and vandalism," he told her. "In fact, it'll only make things worse." He looked from Mia to the cop, as if aware he'd nearly said too much. With effort, he erased all signs of his anger from his face and when he spoke again, his voice was matter of fact. "Like I said, I don't want to press charges."

He started to turn away, but the policeman wouldn't let him go. "Lieutenant Francisco, it sounds like you have some kind of problem here. Maybe if you talked to one of the detectives in the squad...?"

Frisco remained expressionless. "Thank you, but no. Now, if you don't mind, I want to change my clothes and start cleaning up this mess."

"I don't know what's going on here," the cop warned him, "but if you end up taking the law into your own hands, my friend, you're only going to have a bigger problem."

"Excuse me." Frisco disappeared into his bedroom, and after a moment, the policeman went out the door, shaking his head in exasperation.

Mia followed Frisco. "Alan, it *was* Dwayne."

He was waiting for her at his bedroom door. "I know it was. Hey, don't look at me that way." He pulled her inside and closed the door behind her, drawing her into his arms and kissing her hard on the mouth, as if trying to wipe the expression of confusion and apprehension off her face. "I'm sorry if I made you feel foolish in front of the police—claiming you were mistaken that way. But I didn't know what else to say."

"I don't understand why you won't press charges."

She looked searchingly up at him and he met her gaze steadily. "I know. Thanks for trusting me despite that." His face softened into his familiar half smile and he kissed her again, more gently this time.

Mia felt herself melt. His clean-shaven cheeks felt sensuously smooth against her face as she deepened their kiss, and she felt a hot surge of desire. His arms tightened around her, and she knew he felt it, too.

But he gently pushed her away, laughing softly. "Damn, you're dangerous. I've got a serious jones for you."

"A…jones?"

"Addiction," he explained. "Some guys get a traveling jones—they can't stay in one place for very long. I've had friends with a skydiving jones, can't go for more than a few days without making a jump." He crossed to his closet and leaned his crutches against the wall, turning back to smile at her again. "Looks like I've got myself a pretty severe Mia Summerton jones." His voice turned even softer and velvet smooth. "I can't go for more than an hour or two without wanting to make love to you."

The heat coursing through her got thicker, hotter. *I've got a serious jones for you*—the words weren't very romantic. Yet, when Frisco said it, with his husky voice and his liquid-fire eyes, and that incredibly sexy half smile… it was. It was pure romance.

He turned away from her, somehow knowing that if he looked at her that way another moment longer, she'd end up in his arms, and they'd wind up in his bed again.

And there was no time for that now, as nice as it would have been. Thomas was back at her condo, watching Natasha. And Mia was still waiting for Frisco's explanation.

"Why won't you press charges?" she asked again.

She sat down on his bed, watching as he took off his jacket and hung it carefully in the closet.

"I saw Sharon," he told her, glancing back at her, his eyes grim and his smile gone. He was wearing a white shirt, and the dark nylon straps of his shoulder holster stood out conspicuously. He unfastened the holster and tossed it, gun included, next to her onto his bed.

Mia couldn't help but stare at that gun lying there like that, several feet away from her. He'd treated it so casually, as if it weren't a deadly weapon, capable of enabling him to take a human life with the slightest effort.

"It turns out that she *does* owe Dwayne some money. She says she 'borrowed' about five grand when she moved out of his place a few months ago." He hopped on one leg over to the bed and sat down next to her. Bending down, he pulled off his shoes and socks. His shirt was unbuttoned, revealing tantalizing glimpses of his tanned, muscular chest. But even that wasn't enough to pull Mia's attention away from the gun he'd thrown onto the bed.

"Please—I'd like it if you would move this," she interrupted him.

He glanced at her, and then down at his holstered gun. "Sorry." He picked it up and set it down, away from her, on the floor. "I should've known you wouldn't like firearms."

"I don't dislike them. I *hate* them."

"I'm a sharpshooter—*was* a sharpshooter, I'm a little rusty these days—and I know firearms so well, I'd be lying if I told you I hated them. I'd also be lying if I told you I didn't feel more secure when I'm carrying. What I do hate is when weapons get into the wrong hands."

"In my opinion, *any* hands are the wrong hands. Guns should be banned from the surface of the earth."

"But they exist," Frisco pointed out. "It's too late to simply wish them away."

"It's not too late to set restrictions about who can have them," she said hotly.

"Legally," he added, heat slipping into his voice, too. "Who can have them *legally*. The people who shouldn't have them—the bad guys, the criminals and the terrorists—they're going to figure out some way to get their hands on them no matter *what* laws are made. And as long as *they* can get their hands on firearms, I'm going to make damn sure that I have one, too."

His jaw was set, his eyes hard, glittering with an intense blue fire. They were on opposite sides of the fence here, and Mia knew with certainty that he was no more likely to be swayed to her opinion than she was to his.

She shook her head in sudden disbelief. "I can't believe I'm…" She looked away from him, shocked at the words she almost said aloud. *I can't believe I'm in love with a man who carries a gun.*

He touched her, gently lifting her hand and intertwining their fingers, correctly guessing at half of what she nearly said. "We're pretty different from each other, huh?"

She nodded, afraid to look into his eyes, afraid he'd guess the other half of her thoughts, too.

He smiled wryly. "Where do you stand on abortion? Or the death penalty?"

Mia smiled despite herself. "Don't ask." No doubt their points of view were one hundred and eighty degrees apart on those issues, too.

"I like it this way," he said quietly. "I like it that you don't agree with everything that I think."

She *did* look up at him then. "We probably belong to opposite political parties."

"Is that so bad?"

"Our votes will cancel each other out."

"Democracy in action."

His eyes were softer now, liquid instead of steel. Mia felt herself start to drown in their blueness. Frisco wasn't the only one who had a jones, an addiction. She leaned forward and he met her in a kiss. Her hands went up underneath his open shirt, skimming against his bare skin, and the sensation made them both groan.

But when Mia would've given in, when she would have fallen back with him onto his bed, Frisco made himself pull away. He was breathing hard and the fire in his eyes was unmistakable. He wanted her as much as she wanted him. He may have been addicted, but he had a hell of a lot of willpower.

"We have to get out of here," he explained. "Dwayne's going to come back, and I don't want you and Tasha to be here when he does."

"I still don't understand why you won't press charges," Mia said. "Just because your sister owes this guy some money, that doesn't give him the right to destroy your condo."

Frisco stood up, shrugging out of his shirt. He wadded it into a ball and tossed it into the corner of his room, on top of his mountain of dirty laundry. "His name is Dwayne Bell," he told her. "And he's a professional scumbag—drugs, stolen goods, black-market weapons— you name it, he's involved. And he doesn't earn six figures a year by being nice about unpaid loans."

He glanced at her as he unfastened and stepped out of his pants. Mia knew she shouldn't be staring. It was hardly polite to stare at a man dressed only in utilitarian white briefs, but she couldn't look away.

"Sharon lived with him for about four months," he told her, hopping toward his duffel bags and searching through them. "During that time, she worked for him, too. According to Sharon, Dwayne has enough on her to cause real trouble. If he was arrested for something as petty as breaking and entering, he'd plea-bargain and give her up for dealing drugs, and *she'd* be the one who'd end up in jail."

Mia briefly closed her eyes. "Oh, no."

"Yeah."

"So what are we going to do?"

He found a pair of relatively clean shorts and came back to the bed. He sat down and pulled them on. "*We're* going to get you and Tasha out of here. Then *I'm* going to come back and deal with Dwayne."

Deal with Dwayne? "Alan—"

He was up again, slipping his shoulder holster over his arm and fastening it against his bare skin. "Do me a favor. Go into Tash's room and grab her bathing suit and a couple of changes of clothes." He bent down and picked up one of his empty duffel bags and tossed it to her.

Mia caught it, but she didn't move. "Alan…"

His back was to her as he searched his closet, pulling out a worn olive-drab army fatigue shirt, its sleeves cut short, the ends fraying. He pulled it on. It was loose and he kept it mostly unbuttoned. It concealed his gun, but still allowed him access to it. He could get to it if he needed it when he "dealt with Dwayne." Unless, of course, Dwayne got to his own gun first. Fear tightened Mia's throat.

He turned to face her. "Come on, Mia. Please. And then go pack some of your own things."

She felt a flash of annoyance, hotter and sharper than the fear. "It's funny, I don't recall your *asking* me to come along with you. You haven't even told me where you're going."

"Lucky has a cabin in the hills about forty miles east of San Felipe. I'm going to call him, see if we can use his place for a few days."

Lucky. From Frisco's former SEAL unit. He was Frisco's friend—no, they were more than just friends, they were…what did they call it? Swim buddies.

"I'm asking for your help here," he continued quietly. "I need you to come along to take care of Tash while I—"

"Deal with Dwayne," she finished for him with exasperation. "You know I'll help you, Alan. But I'm not sure I'm willing to go hide at some cabin." She shook her head. "Why don't we find someplace safe for Tasha to go? We could…I don't know, maybe drive her down to my mother's. Then I could come with you when you go to see Dwayne."

"No. No way. Absolutely not."

Her temper flared. "I don't want you to do this alone."

He laughed, but there was no humor in it. "What, do you really think *you're* gonna keep Dwayne from trying to kick my butt again? Are you going to lecture him on nonviolence? Or maybe you'll try to use positive reinforcement to teach him manners, huh?"

Mia felt her face flush. "No, I—"

"Dwayne Bell is one mean son of a bitch," Frisco told her. "He doesn't belong in your world—and you don't belong in his. And I intend to keep it that way."

She folded her arms across her chest, holding her elbows tightly so he wouldn't see that her hands were shaking with anger. "And which of those worlds do *you* belong in?"

He was quiet for a moment. "Neither," he finally said, unable to look her in the eye. "I'm stuck here in limbo, remember?"

Positive reinforcement. To use positive reinforcement to award positive behavior meant being as consistently blasé as possible when negative behavior occurred. Mia closed her eyes for a moment, willing herself not to fall prey to her anger and lash out at him. She wanted to shake some sense into him. She wanted to shout that this limbo he found himself in was only imagined. She wanted to hold him close until he healed, until he realized that he

didn't need a miracle to be whole again—that he could
be whole even if his knee gave out and he never walked
another step again.

Wallowing in despair wouldn't do him a damn bit of
good. And neither would her yelling at or shaking or
even comforting him. Instead, she kept her voice carefully
emotionless. "Well," she said, starting for the door with
the duffel bag he'd tossed her, "I'll get Tasha's stuff." She
turned back to him almost as an afterthought, as if what
she was about to say to him didn't matter so much that
she was almost shaking. "Oh, and when you call Lucky
to ask about the cabin, it would be smart to tell him about
all this, don't you think? *He* could go with you when you
find Dwayne. He could watch your back, and *he* probably
wouldn't resort to lectures on nonviolence as means of
defense." She forced herself to smile, and was surprised
to find she actually could. His insult had been right on
target—and it wasn't entirely unamusing.

"Mia, I'm sorry I said that."

"Apology accepted—or at least it will be if you call
Lucky."

"Yeah," Frisco said. "I'll do that. And I'll…" It took
him a great deal of effort to say it, but he did. "I'll ask
him for help."

He was going to ask for help. Thank God. Mia wanted
to take one of the colorful medals from his dress uniform
and pin it on to his T-shirt. Instead, she simply nodded.

"Then I'll stay with Tasha at Lucky's cabin," she said,
and left the room.

CHAPTER THIRTEEN

NATASHA PUSHED OPEN the cabin's screen door, but then stopped, looking back at Frisco, who was elbow deep in dinner's soapy dishes. "Can I go outside?"

He nodded. "Yeah, but stay on the porch. It's getting dark." She was out the door in a flash, and he shouted after her, "Hey, Tash?"

She pressed her nose against the screen, peering in at him.

"Good job remembering to ask," he said.

She beamed at him and vanished.

He looked up to find Mia watching him. She was sitting on the couch, a book in her lap, a small smile playing about the corners of her mouth.

"Good job remembering to praise her," she told him.

"She's starting to catch on."

"Sure you don't want me to help over there?" she asked.

Frisco shook his head. "You cooked, I clean. It's only fair."

They'd arrived at Lucky's cabin just before dinnertime. It had been close to six years since Frisco had been up here, but the place looked almost exactly the same.

The cabin wasn't very big by any standards—just a living room with a fireplace and a separate kitchen area, two small bedrooms—one in the back, the other off the living room, and an extremely functional bathroom with only cold running water.

Lucky kept the place stocked with canned and dried goods—and enough beer and whiskey to sink a ship. Mia hadn't said a word about it, but Frisco knew she wondered about the temptation. She still didn't quite believe that alcohol wasn't a problem for him. But he'd been up here dozens of times with Lucky and some of the other guys from Alpha Squad, and he'd had cola while they made short work of a bottle of whiskey and a six pack of beer.

Still, he knew that she trusted him.

This afternoon, she'd followed his directions without so much as a questioning look as he'd asked her to leave the narrow back road and pull her car onto what was little more than a dirt path. They'd already been off the highway for what seemed like forever, and the dirt road wound another five miles without a sign of civilization before they reached an even smaller road that led to Lucky's cabin.

It was, definitely, in the middle of nowhere.

That made it perfect for SEAL training exercises. There was a lake not five hundred yards from the front porch, and countless acres of brush and wilderness surrounding the place.

It was a perfect hideout, too. There was no way on earth Dwayne Bell would find them here.

"How's your knee?"

Frisco glanced up to find that Mia had come to lean against the icebox, watching as he finished scouring the bottom of the pasta pot. He rinsed the suds from the pot by dunking it in a basin of clear, hot water, nodding his reply. "It's…improved," he told her. "It's been about eight hours since I've had to use the painkiller, and…"

He glanced at her again. "I'm not about to start running laps, but I'm not in agony, either."

Mia nodded. "Good." She hesitated slightly, and he knew what was coming.

"When you spoke to Lucky..."

He carefully balanced the pot in the dish drain, on top of all the others. He knew what she wanted to know. "I'm meeting him tomorrow night," he said quietly. "Along with a couple other guys from Alpha Squad. The plan is for Thomas to come up in the afternoon and give me a lift back into San Felipe. You and Tash will hang out here."

"And what happens when you actually find Dwayne?"

He released the water from the sink and dried his hands and arms on a dish towel, turning to look down into her eyes. "I'm going to give him a thousand bucks and inform him that the other four thousand Sharon owes him covers the damages he caused by breaking into my condo. I intend to tell him that there's no amount of money in the world that would make retribution for the way he hit Natasha before she and Sharon moved out, and he's damned lucky that I'm not going to break him in half for doing that. I'm also going to convince him that if he so much as comes near Tash or Sharon or anyone else I care about, I will hunt him down and make him wish that he was dead."

Mia's eyes were wide. "And you really think that will work?"

Frisco couldn't resist reaching out and touching the side of her face. Her skin was so deliciously soft beneath his fingers. "Yeah," he said. "I think it'll work. By giving Dwayne some money—a substantial amount of money, despite the fact that it's only a fifth of what Sharon took— he doesn't walk away with nothing. He saves face." He paused. Unless this situation was more complicated than that. Unless there was something that Sharon hadn't told him, something she hadn't been quite honest about. But Mia probably didn't need to know that he was having doubts.

Unfortunately, she read his hesitation accurately. "What?" she asked, her gaze searching his face. "You were going to say more, weren't you?"

He wanted to pull her close, to breathe in the sweet scent of her clean hair and luxuriate in the softness of her body pressed against his. He wanted that, but he couldn't risk touching her again. Even the sensation of her smooth cheek beneath his fingers had been enough to ignite the desire he felt whenever she was near—hell, whenever he so much as *thought* about her. If he pulled her into his arms, he would kiss her. And if he kissed her, he wouldn't want to stop.

"I got the sense Sharon wasn't one-hundred-percent honest with me," he finally admitted. Mia had been straightforward with him up to this point, sometimes painfully so. He respected her enough to return the favor. "I don't know—maybe I'm just being paranoid, but when I find Dwayne, I'm going to be ready for anything."

Mia's gaze dropped to his chest, to that hidden place near his left arm where his sidearm was snugly ensconced in his shoulder holster. Frisco knew exactly what she was thinking. He was going to go meet Dwayne with that weapon Mia disliked so intensely tucked under his arm. And it was that weapon that would help make him ready for anything.

She looked up at him. "Are you going to take that thing off when we make love tonight?"

When we make love tonight. Not if. When. Frisco felt the hot spiral of anticipation. Man, he'd hoped, but he hadn't wanted to assume. It was fine with him, though, if *she* wanted to assume that they were going to share a bed again tonight. It was more than fine.

"Yeah," he said, his voice husky. "I'll take it off."

"Good." She held his gaze and the air seemed to crackle around them.

He wanted to reach for her, to hold her, kiss her. He could feel his body's reaction to her nearness, to the soft curve of her lips, to the awareness in her eyes.

He wanted Mia now, but that wasn't an option—not with Tasha out sitting on the porch swing, rocking and singing a little song to herself. He tried to calculate the earliest he could get away with putting Tash to bed, tried to figure how long it would take her to fall asleep. Twilight was falling, and the cabin was already shadowy and dark. Even with no electricity, no bright lights and TV to distract the little girl, he had to guess it would be another hour at least before she'd agree to go to bed, another half hour after that before she was asleep.

He tried to glance surreptitiously at his watch, but Mia noticed and smiled. She didn't say a word, but he knew she was aware of everything he'd been thinking.

"Do you know where Lucky keeps the candles?" she asked, stepping away from him. "It's starting to get pretty dark."

He gestured with his head as he positioned his crutches under his arms. "In the cabinet next to the fireplace. And there's a kerosene lantern around here somewhere."

"Candles will be fine," Mia said, crossing to the cabinet. She threw him a very sexy smile over her shoulder. "I like candlelight, don't you?"

"Yeah," Frisco agreed, trying not to let his thoughts drift in the direction of candlelight and that big double bed in the other room. This next hour and a half was going to be the longest hour and a half of his entire life if he started thinking about Mia, with her long dark hair and her gorgeous, luminous eyes, tumbled onto that bed, candlelight gleaming on her satin smooth skin.

Mia found a box of matches on the fireplace mantel, well out of Tasha's reach, and lit one candle after another, placing them around the room. She looked otherworldly with the flickering candles sending shadows and light dancing across her high cheekbones, her full, graceful lips and her exotically tilted eyes. Her cutoff shorts were threadbare denim, and they hugged her backside sinfully snugly. Her hair was up in a braid. Frisco moved toward her, itching to unfasten it, to run his fingers through her silken hair, longing to see her smile, to hear her laughter, to bury himself in her sweetness and then hold her in his arms all night long. He hadn't had a chance to do that after they'd made love in the early hours of the morning, and now he found he wanted that more than he could believe.

She glanced at him again, but then couldn't look away, trapped for a moment by the need he knew was in his eyes.

"Maybe candlelight isn't such a good idea," she whispered. "Because if you keep looking at me like that I'm going to…"

"Oh, I hope so." Frisco moved closer, enough to take the candle from her hand and set it down on the fireplace mantel. "Whatever you're thinking about doing—I hope so."

Mia's heart was hammering. Lord, when he looked at her with such desire in his eyes, every nerve ending in her body went on red alert. He touched her lightly, brushing his thumb across her lips and she felt herself sway toward him, but he dropped his hand. She knew she shouldn't kiss him—not here, not now. Natasha was outside and she could come in at any moment.

She could read the same thoughts in Frisco's dark blue eyes. But instead of backing away as she'd expected, he lowered his head and kissed her anyway.

He tasted seductively sweet, like the fresh peaches they'd picked up at a local farm stand and sampled after dinner. It was a hard kiss, a passionate kiss, despite the fact that he kept both hands securely on the grips of his crutches, despite that the only place he touched her was her lips.

It was more than enough.

For now, anyway.

He pulled back and she found herself gazing into eyes the color of blue fire. And then she found herself reaching up, pulling his incredible lips down to hers again. She was wrong. Once was *not* enough.

"Are you gonna kiss again?"

Mia sprang away from Frisco as if she'd been burned.

She turned to see Natasha standing in the doorway, watching them. How long the child had been there, she couldn't begin to guess. She felt her cheeks flush.

Frisco smiled at Tasha. If he were the least bit perturbed, he was hiding it well. "Not right now."

"Later?"

His gaze flickered to Mia, and she could see genuine amusement lurking there. "I hope so."

Natasha considered this, head tilted to one side. "Thomas said if you broke Mia's heart, he was gonna kick you in the bottom." She sat down haughtily on the couch—the perfect Russian princess. "He really said something else, but I don't say bad words."

The muscles in the side of Frisco's face twitched, but

somehow he managed to hide his smile. "Well, Thomas and you don't have to worry. I have no intention of—"

"I made you a medal," Tash told him. "For not saying bad words, too. And for not drinking that smelly stuff," she added, almost as an afterthought, wrinkling her nose. She looked up at Mia. "Can I give it to him now?"

"Oh, Tasha, I'm afraid we left it back in my living room. I'm sorry…"

"It's beautiful," Tasha told Frisco, completely seriously. "You can have it when we go back. I'll give you the salute now, though, okay?"

"Sure…"

The little girl stood up and snapped off a military salute that would have impressed the meanest, toughest drill sergeant.

"Thanks, Tash." Frisco's voice was husky.

"Dwayne kissed Mommy and gave her a broke heart instead of getting married," she told them. "Are you going to get married?"

Frisco was no longer unperturbed. "Whoa, Tash, didn't we have this conversation already? And didn't we—"

"I would rather have a broke heart than Dwayne for a daddy," Tasha announced. "Why is it dark in here? Why don't we turn the lights on?"

"Remember that I told you there wasn't any electricity up here?"

"Does that mean that the lights are broke?"

Frisco hesitated. "It's kind of like that—"

"Is the TV broke, too?"

The little girl was looking up at Frisco, her eyes wide with horror. Frisco looked back at her, his mouth slightly open. "Oh, damn," he said, breaking her rule.

"Sweetie, there *is* no television up here," Mia said.

Natasha looked as if the end of the world were near, and Frisco's expression was nearly identical.

"I can't fall asleep without the TV on," Tasha whispered.

FRISCO FORCED HIMSELF not to overreact as he went into Tash's bedroom for the third time in less than a half an hour. Yes, he'd seen Tasha in action on the night he'd accidentally turned off the TV set. She clearly depended on the damned thing to provide soothing background noise and light. She found it comforting, dependable and consistent. Wherever she'd been before this in her short life, there'd always been a television.

But she was a five-year-old. Sooner or later, exhaustion would win and she'd fall asleep. True, he'd hoped it would be sooner, but that was life. He'd have to wait a few more hours before Mia was in his arms. It wasn't *that* big a deal.

At least that's what he tried to convince himself.

As he sat on the edge of one of the narrow beds in the tiny back bedroom, Tasha looked up at him with wide, unhappy eyes. He kissed the top of her head. "Just *try* to sleep, okay?"

She didn't say a word. She just watched him as he propelled himself out of the room on his crutches.

Mia was sitting on one end of the couch that was positioned in front of the fireplace, legs curled up underneath her. Candlelight flickered, and she looked deliciously sexy. Carefully supporting his injured knee, he sat down, way at the other end of the couch.

"You're being very patient with her," she said softly.

He smiled ruefully. "You're being very patient with us both."

"I didn't come up here only for the great sex," she

told him, trying to hide a smile. She failed and it slipped free.

"I had about two hours of sleep this morning, total," he said, his voice low. "I should be exhausted, but I'm not. I'm wide-awake because I know the kid's going to fall asleep, and I know that when she does, I'm going to take you into the other room, take off your clothes and make love to you, the way I've been dying to do again since you walked out of my bedroom this morning."

He held her gaze. His own was steady and hot, and her smile quickly faded.

"Maybe we should talk about something else," she suggested breathlessly, and he forced himself to look away.

She was quiet for several long moments. Frisco could hear the second hand of her watch ticking its way around the dial. He could hear the cool night breeze as it swept through the trees. He heard the soft, almost inaudible creaking of the cabin as it lost the heat it had taken from the hot summer sun.

"I'm sorry I left the medal Tasha made for you at home," Mia finally said, obviously changing the subject. "We were in such a hurry, and I just didn't even think. She spent a long time on it. She told me all about what happened when you dropped the milk."

Frisco couldn't help but think about that new list that Mia had attached to his refrigerator—the list of things he could still do, even with his injured knee. He'd seen it for the first time as he'd been mopping up the spilled milk. It had taken the edge off his anger, turning his frustration into laughter and hot, sweet anticipation. Some of the things she'd written down were mind-blowingly suggestive. And she was dead right. He *could* do all of those things. And he intended to, as soon as he got the chance....

He forced himself to focus on their conversation. Tasha. The medal she had made for him. But the little girl had said it was for more than his recently cleaned-up language. "I didn't think she'd notice that I haven't been drinking," he confessed. "I mean, I haven't been making that big a deal about it. I guess it's kind of…sobering, if you'll pardon the pun, that she *did* notice."

Mia nodded, her eyes gentle. "She hasn't said anything to me about it."

He lowered his voice even further, so that if Tasha were still awake, she wouldn't hear. "I ordered that couch."

Mia looked confused, but then recognition flashed in her eyes, and she clamped a hand over her mouth to keep from laughing out loud. "You mean the…?"

"Pink one," Frisco finished for her. He felt a smile spreading across his own face. "Yep. The other one was destroyed, and I figured what the hell? The kid wants it so badly. I'll just make sure she takes it with her when she goes."

When she goes. The thought was not a pleasant one. In fact, it was downright depressing. And that was strange. When Tash first arrived, he could think of nothing but surviving, about making the best of a bad situation until the time that she would go. It hadn't taken long for that to change. It was true that having the kid around made life more complicated—like right now for instance, when he desperately wanted her to fall asleep—but for the first time in years he was forced to think about something other than his injury. He was forced to stop waiting for a chance to live again, and instead actually do some living.

The truth was, he'd adored Tasha from the moment she'd been born.

"I helped deliver her. Did you know that?" he asked Mia.

"Natasha?" she said. "I didn't know."

"Lucky and I were on leave and he drove out to Arizona with me to see Sharon. She was about to have the baby, and we were about to be shipped out to the Middle East for God knows how long. She was living in this trailer park about forty miles east of Tucson. Twenty minutes after we arrived, she went into hard labor. The nearest hospital was back in Tucson, so we got her into my truck and drove like hell."

He smiled. "But Sharon never does anything the easy way. She must've had the shortest labor in history. We had to pull off the road because Tasha wasn't going to wait."

As Mia watched, Frisco was silent for a moment. She knew he was reliving that event, remembering.

"It was incredible," he said quietly. "When that baby came out, it was... It was one of the high points of my life."

He shook his head, the expression on his face one of wonder and awe, even after all this time. "I'd never seen a miracle before, but I saw one that day. And when Lucky put that tiny baby in my hands... She was all red and wrinkly, and so *alive*—this little new life, only a few seconds old."

He glanced up at her, his smile tinged with embarrassment. "Sounds pretty corny, huh?"

Mia shook her head, unable to answer him, unable to speak. It wasn't corny. It was incredibly, heart-wrenchingly sweet.

"I held Tasha all the way to the hospital," he continued. "Sharon was out of it—which is pretty much her standard condition. So I wrapped that baby in my T-shirt and held

her for what seemed like forever because she was crying,
and Sharon was crying and the really stupid thing was
that it was all I could do not to cry, too." He was quiet for
a moment. "But I finally got Tasha quieted down. I sang
to her and talked to her, promised her that the hardest part
of her life was over. She'd been born, and that's always
rough, but if I had anything to say about it, it was going
to be a breeze for her from here on in. I told her I'd take
care of her, and I'd take care of her mom, too.

"And then we got to the hospital, and the nurses came
out to take her away, and I didn't want to let her go." He
forced a smile, and it made him look impossibly sad. "But
I did."

He looked down at his injured knee. "And three hours
later, the CO called in all of SEAL Team Ten, and Alpha
Squad shipped out on an emergency rescue mission."

"That's when you were wounded," Mia said.

It wasn't a question, but he glanced at her and nodded.
"Yeah. That's when I was wounded." He was clenching
his teeth and the muscle in the side of his jaw worked.
"I didn't keep any of those promises I made to that little
baby. I mean, I sent Sharon money, but…" He shook his
head and forced another smile. "So I'm buying the kid a
pink couch, hoping that'll make up for all those years I
wasn't around." His smile became more genuine. "Lucky
was going to go over with some of the guys and finish
getting the place cleaned up. He'll be there to take delivery. I told him about the couch, but I'm not sure he
believed me." He laughed. "He'll believe me when he
sees it, huh?"

Mia didn't know whether to laugh or cry. Every flicker
of emotion on Frisco's face, every glint of pain or sorrow
or joy in his eyes, every word that he spoke, every word

that he shared with her filled her heart with a feeling of longing so deep, she could barely breathe.

She loved him.

He was everything she didn't need. His wounds were so deep and so catastrophic. She could handle his physical limitations. For her own self, she didn't give a damn whether or not he needed a cane or crutches or even a wheelchair to get around. In her mind, his emotional limitations were far more crippling. It was his emotional baggage—the bitterness and anger he carried with him— that had the bulk and the weight to engulf her and drag her down, too.

Still, despite that, she loved him.

Mia felt her eyes flood with tears, and she turned away, not wanting him to see. But he did, and he leaned forward, his eyes filled with concern.

"Mia…?"

She silently cursed her volatile emotions as she wiped her eyes. "I'm sorry. I'm…being silly."

He tried to make light of it. "It *is* pretty silly to cry over a pink couch."

"I'm not crying about the couch. I'm crying…" Mia made the mistake of glancing up into his eyes, and now she was trapped, unable to look away, held as much by the gentleness of his concern as by the fire and the intensity that was also in his gaze. "Because you've complicated my life beyond belief," she whispered.

He knew what she meant. He understood her unspoken message. Mia could see comprehension in his eyes, so she said the words aloud. "I'm falling in love with you, Alan."

Frisco's heart was in his throat. He'd suspected that Mia cared, but there was a big difference between a vague suspicion and hearing the words directly from her mouth. Falling. In love. With *him*.

Dear God, was she blind? How could she possibly be falling in love with this dried husk of a man he'd become? How could beautiful, lighthearted, joyful Mia possibly love someone who wasn't whole?

Her words should have elated him. Instead, he felt only despair. How could she *love* him?

He could hear Mia's watch ticking, its second hand traveling full circle again and again.

Finally she stood and crossed to the screen door, gazing out into the night as if she knew how much her softly spoken honesty had thrown him.

He had to say something. He knew from the tight set of her back that she wanted him to say something, *any*thing, but he couldn't think of a single response. "You're crazy" seemed inappropriate, as did "You're wrong."

"Frisco?"

He turned to see Natasha standing in the hallway. Her nightgown was several sizes too large, and it hung almost all the way down to the ground. She was holding her stuffed bear by one of its raggedy arms. Her hair was tangled around her face, and her eyes were filled with tears.

"I can't sleep," she told him. "It's too quiet. Too *nothing*. I don't like it. I can't hear *any*thing at all."

Frisco glanced at Mia, who had turned back, but wouldn't meet his eyes. Man, she'd just spilled her guts to him, and he hadn't responded. He'd said nothing, done nothing. At least he had to tell her that her declaration had totally blown him away.

"Tash, go on back into bed," he said. "I'll be there in a sec, but I need to talk to Mia first—"

Mia interrupted him. "No, it's okay. Alan, we can talk

later." She forced a smile, but her eyes looked so sad. "It was…bad timing on my part."

She looked away, and there was silence in the room. Frisco could hear his own heart beating, and Tasha's slight snuffle and that damned ticking watch….

The idea came to him in a flash.

Frisco pulled himself to his feet. "Come on." He led the way back into Tasha's bedroom. The little girl followed, but Mia didn't move. He stuck his head back out the door. "You, too," he told her.

He could see uncertainty in her eyes. "Maybe I should just wait out here…."

"Nope, we need you. Come on." He went back into the bedroom. "Back in bed, Tash."

Mia stood in the doorway, letting her eyes get used to the dark. She'd been in this bedroom, helping Tasha put on her nightgown. Even though it was dark, she could identify the different shapes that were the furniture. The bed Tasha had climbed into was against one wall. Another bed was directly opposite it. There was a small table and a chest of drawers, and several long windows that were open to the soft breezes of the summer night.

Frisco was sitting on the other bed, his back against the wall. "Come here," he said to Mia quietly.

She stepped hesitantly into the room, and he gently took her arm and pulled her down in front of him on the bed so that she was sitting between his legs, her back leaning against his chest. He looped his arms around her waist, holding her firmly in place.

She fought him for all of a half a second before giving in to the decadently glorious feeling of his arms around her. She let her head fall back against his shoulder and allowed herself the luxury of enjoying the sensation of his rough chin against her temple.

She knew she'd surprised him with her statement of love. Shoot, she'd surprised herself. But when he'd failed to react in any way at all, she'd assumed that unless she could somehow explain her feelings, he was intending to push her away.

But right now, he was doing anything but pushing her away. He was holding her close.

His lips brushed her cheek and she fought the sudden urge to cry again. Maybe the fact that she was falling in love with him didn't frighten him quite so much as she'd imagined. Maybe now that he'd had several minutes to get used to the idea, he actually *liked* it. Maybe...

"Tasha thinks it's absolutely silent in here," he said, his voice raspy and warm in the cool darkness.

"It *is*." The little girl sat up in the other bed.

"Gotta lie down," Frisco told her. "This will only work if you lie down."

She obeyed, but then popped right up again. "What are we doing?"

"*You* are lying down in your bed," he told her, waiting as she did so, amusement in his voice. "*We* are here to check on this odd silence you claim is in this room. And it's odd because it's far from silent out in the living room. And it's sure as he—*heck* not silent outside the cabin."

"It's *not?*" Tasha sat up again. This time she caught herself, and lay back down before Frisco could scold her.

"No way. Shh. Lie *very* still and listen."

Mia found herself holding her breath as Frisco and Tasha fell silent.

"Man," Frisco said after a moment. "You're wrong, Tash. This is one of the noisiest rooms I've ever been in."

The little girl sat up. "Noisy...?"

"Lie down," he commanded. "And listen again."

Again the silence.

"Listen to the wind in the trees," Frisco said quietly. Mia closed her eyes, relaxing even farther into his embrace, loving the sensation of his arms around her and his breath against her ear as his voice floated out across the darkness. "Listen to the way the leaves whisper together when a breeze comes through. And there's a branch—it's probably dead. It keeps bumping against the other branches, trying to shake itself free and drop to the ground. Do you hear it?"

"Yeah," breathed Tasha.

Mia did, too. But just a moment ago, she hadn't even been aware of the noise at all. Another gust swept by, and she heard the sound of the leaves in the wind. Whispering, Frisco had said. His descriptions were poetic in their accuracy.

"And the crickets," Frisco said. "Hear them? And there must be some kind of locust out there, too, making their music, putting on a show. But they'll hush right up if a stranger comes around. The story the insects tell is the loudest when their music stops."

He was quiet again.

"Someone must be camping around the other side of the lake," he said quietly. "I can hear a dog barking—whining, probably tied up somewhere. And—shhh! Listen to that rumble. Must be train tracks not too far from here. Freight's coming through."

Sure enough, in the distance, Mia could hear the faint, lonely sound of a train whistle.

It was amazing. Although she made her living teaching U.S. history, she considered herself an artist, raised around artists, brought up surrounded by artists' sensitivities and delicate senses of detail. She'd never be able to paint like her mother, but she wasn't a half-bad photographer, able to catch people's quirks and personalities on film. On top of being an artist, she considered herself a liberal feminist, in tune with her world, always willing to volunteer at the local church homeless shelter, sensitive to the needs of others. She was a modern, sensitive, artistic, creative woman—who had never taken the time to truly stop and *listen* to the sounds of the night.

Unlike this big, stern-faced, gun-carrying, flesh-and-blood version of G.I. Joe, who ignored physical pain as if his heart and soul were made of stone—who had the patience to listen, and the sensitivity to hear music in the sound of the wind in the trees.

Mia had been amazed at herself for falling for a rough, tough professional soldier. But there was so much more to this man besides the roughness and toughness. So much more.

"The night is *never* silent," Frisco said. "It's alive, always moving, always telling a story. You just have to learn to hear its voice. You've got to learn how to listen. And once you learn how to listen, it's always familiar, always like being home. At the same time, it's never boring. The voice might always be the same, but the story it tells is always changing."

Another breeze shook the leaves, carrying with it the sound of that distant dog barking. It was remarkable.

"And that's only *outside* the cabin," he told them. "Inside, there's a whole pile of noises, too. Inside the cabin, *you* become part of the night's story."

"I can hear you breathe," Tasha said. Her voice sounded sleepy and thick.

"That's right. And I can hear *you* breathing. And Mia, too. She keeps holding her breath, thinking that'll help her be more quiet, but she's wrong. Every time she exhales and then sucks in another big breath, it's ten times as loud. If you don't want to be heard, you need to breathe slowly and shallowly. You need to become part of the night, breathing along with its rhythms."

Mia could hear the distinct sound of his lips curving up into a smile. She didn't need to see his face to know it was one of his funny half smiles.

"Every now and then I can hear Mia's stomach rumble. I don't know, Tash—maybe we didn't feed her enough at dinner," Frisco continued. "And I can also hear the second hand on her watch. It's making a hell—heck—of a racket."

"Maybe it's *your* watch that you hear," Mia countered softly, feeling much too noisy. Her breathing, her stomach, her watch…next he was going to tell her that he could hear her heart beating. Of course, due to her present position, pressed firmly against him, her heart was pounding loudly enough to be heard across the entire state.

"My watch has LED's," he breathed into her ear. "It's silent."

She had to ask. "Where did you learn to listen like this?"

He was quiet for a moment. "I don't know. I did a lot of night details, I guess. When it's just you and the night, you get to know the night pretty well."

Mia lowered her voice. "I've never known anyone like you."

His arms tightened around her. "The feeling is…very mutual."

"Are you gonna kiss?" Tasha's voice was *very* drowsy sounding.

Frisco laughed. "Not in front of you, kid."

"Thomas told me if you and Mia had a baby, it would be my cousin."

"Thomas is certainly full of all kinds of information, isn't he?" Frisco released his hold on Mia, giving her a gentle push up and off the bed. "Go to sleep now, Tash. Remember, you've got the night keeping you company, all right?" He picked his crutches up off the floor.

"All right. I love you, Frisco."

"Love you, too, Tash."

Mia turned away as Frisco bent over the little girl's bed and gave her a quick kiss.

"Sit with me for a minute?" the little girl asked.

Mia heard Frisco sigh. "All right. Just for a minute."

Mia went into the living room, listening to wind in the trees, listening to the sound of her own breathing, the ticking of her watch. She stood at the screen door, looking out into the night, aware of the flames from the candles leaping and flickering behind her.

It may have been one minute or ten, but when she finally heard Frisco follow her out into the living room, she didn't turn around. She was aware of him watching her, aware that he didn't move any closer, but instead stopped, not even crossing to sit down on the couch.

She felt nervous at his silence, and she kicked herself for letting her feelings slip out the way they had. She hadn't been thinking. If she *had* been, she would've remembered that love wasn't on his agenda.

Still, the way he'd held her as they'd sat together in Tasha's room...

She took a deep breath and turned to face him. "I didn't mean to scare you. You know... Before."

"You didn't." He shook his head, as if he were aware he wasn't telling her the truth. "You *did*. I just... I don't..." It was his turn to take a deep breath. "Mia, I don't understand."

"What part are you having problems with?" she asked,

taking refuge in her usual cheekiness. "The part where I said I love you, or… Well, no, that was the only part, wasn't it?"

He didn't laugh. He didn't even crack a smile. "A few days ago, you didn't even like me."

"No. A few days ago, I didn't like the person I thought you were," she told him. "I was wrong, though—you're incredible. I meant it when I said I've never met anyone like you. You're funny and smart and—"

"Dammit, stop," he said, pushing himself forward on his crutches, but then stopping in the middle of the room as if he were unsure of where to go, what to do. He ran one hand through his hair, leaving it messy—a visual testament to his frustration.

"Why? It's true. You're wonderful with Tasha. You're gentle and patient and kind, yet at the same time I don't doubt your ability to be anything *but* gentle in more aggressive situations. You're a soldier with an absolute code of honor. You're sensitive and sweet, yet you've got a willpower that's made of stone. You're—"

"Physically challenged," Frisco ground out through clenched teeth. "Don't leave *that* out."

CHAPTER FOURTEEN

"YES, YOU'RE PHYSICALLY challenged, but you're also strong enough to deal with it." Mia took a step toward Frisco, and then another and another until she was close enough to touch him, until she *was* touching him.

When Mia touched him, it was so easy to forget about everything. When she touched him, the entire world went away. He pulled her toward him, needing the sanctuary of her kiss, but afraid she might take his silence for agreement. He stopped himself and forced himself to pull back.

"Mia, you don't understand. I—"

She kissed him. She kissed him, and he was lost. He was lost, but he was also suddenly, miraculously found.

She was fire in his arms, fire beneath his lips. She was an explosion of all that he wanted—only she wasn't out of reach. She was right here, well within his grasp.

Frisco heard himself groan, heard his crutches clatter to the floor, heard her answering sound of satisfaction as he kissed her harder now—deeper, longer, hotter kisses filled with all of his need and desire.

And then she pulled back. "Make love to me."

It wasn't an entreaty he needed to hear twice. "I'll check on Tash," he said hoarsely.

She slipped out of his arms. "I'll take some candles into our bedroom."

Candles. Candlelight. Yes. Frisco picked up his crutches

and moved as silently as he could toward the room where Tasha was sleeping. He could hear the child's slow and steady breathing before he even reached the doorway.

She was asleep.

For how long, he couldn't say. She might wake up in an hour or two. In fact, she'd *probably* wake up in an hour or two and be scared and confused. But for right now, she was asleep. For right now, he had the freedom to lock himself in that other bedroom with Mia and indulge in physical pleasures the likes of which he'd gotten a taste of early this morning.

For Mia, their joining would be more than mere physical satisfaction. Mia loved him. She actually believed that she loved him.

But sooner or later, just like Tasha, Mia would wake up, too. And then she'd see him without those rose-colored glasses that she always wore. She'd realize that he had been lying—lying both to her and even to himself.

His knee wasn't going to get any better. Steve Horowitz was right. Frisco had come as far as he could. He'd fought hard and long, but to keep fighting would only damage his joint further. It would be counterproductive. It would put him back into a wheelchair—maybe even for the rest of his life.

It was time to accept that which he'd denied for so many years.

He was permanently disabled. He wasn't going to be a SEAL ever again.

The truth crashed down around him, crushing him, squeezing him, and he nearly cried out.

He had to tell Mia. She said she loved him, but would she love him if she knew the truth?

He wasn't Lt. "Frisco" Francisco of SEAL Team Ten. He was Alan Francisco, disabled civilian. He didn't even

know who Alan Francisco was. How could she possibly
love him if he no longer knew who he was?

He had to tell her. Yet at the same time, he didn't want
her to know. He couldn't bear the thought of her looking at
him with pity in her beautiful hazel eyes. He couldn't bear
to say the words aloud. It was hard enough to admit he
was temporarily disabled. But *permanently* disabled…

Mia's hair was down loose around her shoulders and
she was smiling as she came toward him. He closed his
eyes as she began unbuttoning his shirt, tugging him
toward the bed at the same time.

She took his crutches and laid them on the floor. Then
she gently pushed him down so that he sat on the bed,
and swept his shirt off his shoulders.

"Mia…" he rasped.

"Get rid of the gun, will you?" she murmured, pressing
feathery light kisses against his neck.

He unbuckled his shoulder holster and slipped it and
his sidearm into the top drawer of a rickety old bedside
table. He tried again, and again his voice sounded hoarse
and strained. "Mia. About my knee…"

She lifted her head, gazing directly into his eyes. "Does
it hurt?"

"No, it's all right. It's not—"

"Shh," she whispered, covering his mouth with hers.
"We've already talked enough tonight."

She kissed him again and he let himself drown in her
sweetness. He'd tried to tell her, but she didn't want to
talk. And he really didn't want to say any of those awful
truths aloud.

She was offering him a temporary escape, and he
reached for it eagerly. He grabbed it with both hands
and held on tight to the magic of right here and right

now. In Mia's arms, reality vanished, leaving only sheer perfection, only pure pleasure.

The outside world, with all of its problems and harsh truths disappeared.

But only for an hour or two.

He rolled back with her onto the bed, covering her with his body, kissing her, determined to take that hour or two and use it to its fullest.

He pulled her shirt up and she helped get it over her head. She was wearing a bra, and the black satin and lace against her skin was enticingly sexy, but not nearly as sexy as the candlelight would be, flickering across her bare breasts. He unfastened the front clasp, freeing her from its restraints.

He made a sound, deep in his throat as he touched her, and she pushed herself up onto her elbows. "Is your knee all right? Maybe I should be on top."

Her eyes were a swirl of yellow and brown, flecked with bits of green and concern.

"No," he murmured, lowering his mouth to where his hands had been just moments before, lightly encircling one hard bud of a nipple with the tip of his tongue.

He heard her sudden inhale of pleasure, felt her legs tighten around him and her hips rise to meet him. But just as quickly as she'd reacted, she released the pressure of her legs. "Alan, please, I don't want to accidentally hurt you…."

He was balancing on his left leg. It was awkward, but with practice, he knew he would become more graceful. "You're not going to hurt me," he told her.

"But what if—"

"Mia, you're going to have to trust me on this, okay? Trust me enough to know that I'll tell you if I'm in pain. Right now, I'm not in pain." He pressed himself against her, fitting his arousal to her most intimately, to prove his point.

She moaned, arching up against him. "I *do* trust you."

Her words broke through the many layers of his desire—a pinprick of reality breaking through to this dreamworld. She trusted him. She *loved* him. His stomach tightened with remorse and despair, into a solid, cold block of deceit.

But her fingers were unfastening his shorts and her mouth covered his in a breathtaking kiss, warming him, melting him—at least a little bit, at least for a little while.

He awkwardly moved back, pulling her shorts and panties down her smooth, silky legs. She lay back against the pillows, her long dark hair fanning out across the white sheets, her eyes on fire as she gazed unsmilingly up at him. She was naked and so vulnerable in that position, yet she didn't try to cover herself. She didn't even move. She just waited. And watched as he pushed down his own shorts, as he released himself from his briefs.

She smiled then, gazing first at his arousal and then up into his eyes.

She watched, unmoving, as he covered himself, the heat in her eyes growing stronger, even more molten. She shifted her hips, opening herself even further to him, her invitation obvious.

Frisco inched himself forward, brushing the inside of her ankle with his mouth, trailing kisses up the smoothness of one calf while he caressed the soft inside of her other leg with his hand. He lifted his head when he reached her knees. She was up on her elbows again, her breasts rising and falling with each rapid breath. Her lips were parted and her hair tumbled down around her shoulders. As he met her eyes, she smiled a hot, sweet smile.

"Don't stop there," she told him.

Her smile was contagious and Frisco found himself grinning back at her before he lowered his head and continued his journey.

He heard her gasp, heard her soft cry of pleasure as he reached his destination. Her hands were in his hair, the softness of her thighs against his face as he tasted her sweet pleasure.

Maybe this would be enough.

The thought flashed through his mind as he took her higher, as he brought her closer to the brink of release.

Maybe he could find contentment or even happiness spending the rest of his life as Mia's lover. He could live forever in her bedroom, waiting for her to return from work, ready and willing to give her pleasure whenever she so desired.

It was, of course, a ridiculous idea.

How could she love a man who did nothing but hide?

Yet, hide was exactly what he'd been doing for the past few years. The truth had been there to see if he hadn't been so damn busy hiding from it.

Yeah, he was a real expert at evading the truth.

"Alan, please…" Mia tugged at his shoulders, pulling him up.

He knew what she wanted, and he gave it to her, filling her completely with one smooth thrust.

She bit down on her lip to keep from crying out, rising up to meet him.

His own pleasure was so intense, he had to stop, resting his forehead against hers while he struggled to maintain control.

"We fit together so well," she whispered into his ear, and when he lifted his head, he could see all of her love for him shining in her eyes.

And he knew at the moment that there was no way he could continue to deceive her. He had to tell her the truth. Not now. He couldn't tell her now. But soon. Very soon.

She began to move slowly underneath him and he matched her pace, watching her eyes, memorizing the pleasure on her face. He knew that once she knew the truth, she was as good as gone. How could he expect her to stay? He'd walk away from himself, if only he could.

"You're so serious tonight," she murmured, reaching up to touch the side of his face.

He tried to smile, but he couldn't, so he kissed her instead.

Her kiss was like magic, carrying him away to a place where there was only pleasure and light, where darkness and despair were set aside, if only temporarily.

They moved together faster now and even faster, bodies slick with heat and desire. There was no room between them for anything but the giving and taking of pleasure. Or love.

Frisco felt Mia's body tighten around him, felt her muffle her cries of passion with a deep, searing kiss. His body responded instantly to the sounds and sensations of her release, and he exploded with a fireball of pleasure that flared with a white-hot light behind his closed eyes.

The brilliant light brought clarity, and clarity brought another unwanted truth. He loved her.

He loved her.

Oh, Lord, he didn't love her. He *couldn't* love her.

His emotions were confused, and that, combined with the chemicals his body released at his climax, had given him this odd sensation that he had mistaken for love. It was nothing, and it would no doubt fade the same way his intense feelings of satisfaction and pleasure would eventually diminish.

Frisco slowly became aware of the soft hissing sounds of the candles' flames, of the ticking of Mia's watch from where it lay across the room on the dresser, of Mia's slow and steady breathing.

Damn, he was twice as big as she—he was crushing her. He rolled off of her, gathering her into his arms and cradling her close.

She sighed, opening drowsy eyes to smile up at him before she snuggled against his shoulder.

"Mia," he said, wondering how to tell her, how to begin. But she was already asleep.

It was not a big surprise that she was asleep—she'd been up all of the previous night, helping him take Tasha to the hospital. Like him, she'd probably only had around a two-hour nap in the morning. And then she'd had to endure the upset of Dwayne Bell's destructive visit to his apartment....

He gazed down at her, curled up against him, her hand pressed against his chest, covering his heart.

And that odd feeling that was surely just a strange chemical reaction made his heart feel tight and sore.

But that didn't mean that he loved her.

It didn't mean anything at all.

"WHERE'S TASH?"

Frisco came out of the bathroom with his hair still wet from his shower, dressed only in a pair of shorts slung low on his lean hips, a towel around his neck. His question was phrased casually, but Mia couldn't miss the undercurrent of tension that seemed to flow from the man.

He looked tired, as if he hadn't slept well last night. He hadn't been in bed with her when she'd awoken this morning. She had no idea how early he'd gotten up. Or why he'd gotten up at all.

She'd fallen asleep in his arms last night. She would have loved to have awakened that same way.

Mia set her book down on the end table, first marking her page with a leaf Natasha had brought inside to show her.

"Tasha's outside," she told him. "She asked, and I told her she could play right out front. I hope that's all right."

He nodded, sitting down across from her on the couch. He looked more than tired, Mia realized. He looked worn-out. Or burned-out and beaten down. He looked more like the grim angry man she'd first met. The glimpses of laughter and good humor and joy he'd let her see over the past several days were once again carefully hidden.

"I wanted a chance to talk to you while Tash was outside," he said, his voice uncommonly raspy. But then he didn't say anything else. He just cleared his throat and gazed silently into the cold fireplace.

"Well, Tasha's outside," Mia finally murmured. "And I'm listening."

He glanced up at her, briefly meeting her eyes and flashing one of his crooked smiles. "Yeah," he said. "I know. I'm just…you know, trying to find the right words." He shook his head and the flash of pain in his eyes nearly took her breath away. "Except there are no right words."

Mia couldn't believe what she was hearing. What had happened between last night and this morning? Last night they'd made love so perfectly, hadn't they? Or maybe it had only been perfect for her. He'd been quiet, almost subdued—she'd even commented on it. She leaned forward, wanting to reach for him, but suddenly, horribly afraid of his rejection.

He'd been honest with her, and told her he didn't love her. She in turn had told herself she didn't care, but that had been a lie. She *did* care. She wanted him to love her, and she'd foolishly hoped that the sex they shared would at least hold his attention until she could somehow, some way, make him love her, too.

She couldn't bear to know the answer, but still, she had to ask. "Are you trying to dump me?"

His blue eyes flashed as he looked up at her. "Hell, no! I'm... I'm trying to figure out how to tell you the truth." He held her gaze this time, and Mia was nearly overpowered by the sadness she saw there, mixed in among his quietly burning anger.

She wanted to reach for him, but his anger held her back. "Whatever it is, it can't be *that* bad, can it?"

"My knee's not going to improve," he said quietly, and she realized there were tears in his eyes. He gestured to his crutches. "This is as good as it's going to get. Hobbling around on crutches or with a cane."

Alan was finally facing the truth. Mia felt her own eyes flood with tears. Her heart was in her throat, filling her with relief. This wasn't about her, wasn't about *them*. It was about him.

She was so glad. He was facing the truth, and once he looked it in the eye, he could finally move forward.

At the same time, she grieved for him, knowing how hard it must've been for him to reach his conclusion.

He looked away from her, and his voice dropped even lower. "I'm not going to be a SEAL again. That's over. I have to accept the fact that I'm...permanently disabled."

Mia wasn't sure what to say. She could see the anger
and bitterness beneath the pain in his eyes, and she realized that by telling her this, he was probably uttering
these words aloud for the very first time. She decided to
keep her mouth shut and simply let him talk.

"I know I told you that I was going to work past this,"
he said. "I know I made that list that's on my refrigerator,
and if wanting something badly enough was all I needed
to make it happen, damn, I'd be doing wind sprints right
now. But my knee was destroyed and all the wishing and
wanting in the world isn't going to make it better. This is
it for me."

He looked up at her as if he wanted her to comment. Mia said the only thing she possibly could in the
circumstances.

"I'm sorry."

But he shook his head. "No," he said tightly. "*I'm* sorry.
I made you think that there would be something more. I
let you believe that I had some kind of future—"

She couldn't let that one pass. "You *do* have a future.
It's just not the one you thought you'd have back when
you were eleven years old. You're strong, you're tough,
you're creative—you can adapt. Lucky told me there's an
instructor job waiting for you. If you wanted, you could
choose to teach."

Frisco felt a burning wave of anger and frustration
surge through him, devouring him. Teach. Man, how
many times had he heard *that?* He could teach, and then
watch his students graduate out of his classroom and do
the things he would never do again. "Yeah, I'll pass on
that barrel of laughs, thanks."

But Mia didn't let up. "Why? You'd be a *great* teacher.
I've seen how patient you are with Natasha. And Thomas.
You have an incredible rapport with him. And—"

His temper flared hotter, but the anger didn't succeed in covering up his hurt. There was nothing about this that didn't hurt. He felt as if he were dying. Whatever part of him that hadn't died back when his leg was nearly blown off, was dying now.

"Why the hell do *you* care what I do?" It wasn't exactly the question he was burning to ask her, but it would do for now.

She was shocked into silence, and gazed at him with her luminous eyes. "Because I love you—"

He swore, just one word, sharp and loud. "You don't even know me. How could you *love* me?"

"Alan, I *do* know—"

"*I* don't even know who I am anymore. How the hell could you?"

She nervously moistened her lips with the tip of her tongue, and Frisco felt his rage expanding. Dear God, he wanted her. He wanted her to stay. He wanted her to love him, because, dear Lord, he was in love with her, too.

The tight, uncomfortable feeling in his chest had never faded. He'd awakened repeatedly throughout the night to find it burning steadily, consuming him. It wasn't going to go away.

But she was. She was going to go away. Because, really, how could she love him? She was in love with a phantom, a shadow, an echo of the man he used to be. And sooner or later, even if he didn't tell her, she'd figure it out. Sooner or later she'd realize he was scamming her—that he'd been scamming her all along. And sooner or later, she would realize that she'd made a mistake, that he wasn't worth her time and laughter, and she would leave.

And then he'd be more alone than ever.

"Why should I bother to teach when I can sit home

and watch TV and collect disability pay?" he asked roughly.

"Because I know that would *never* be enough for you." Her eyes were hot, her voice impassioned. How could she possibly have such faith in him?

Frisco wanted to cry. Instead he laughed, his voice harsh. "Yeah, and teaching's right up my alley, right? I certainly fit the old adage—'Those who can, do. Those who can't, teach.'"

She flinched as if he had struck her. "Is that *really* what you think about teachers? About *me?*"

"It wouldn't be an adage if there weren't some truth to it."

"Here's another adage for you—'Those who are taught, do. Those who teach, shape the future.'" Her eyes blazed. "I teach because I care about the future. And children *are* the future of this world."

"Well, maybe I *don't* care about the future," he shot back. "Maybe I don't give a damn about *any*thing anymore."

She raised her chin. "I know that's not true. You care about Tasha. And I know, even though you won't admit it, that you care about me."

"You're as hopeless as I was when it comes to wishful thinking," he lied, wanting to push her over the edge, needing her to get mad enough to walk away, wanting her to stay forever, and knowing that she never would. How could she? He was nothing now, nobody, no one. "It's typical. You only see what you want to see. You moved to San Felipe from Malibu, thinking you're going to save the world by teaching underprivileged kids all about American history, when what those kids *really* need to learn is how to get through another day without some kid from the rival gang gunning them down when they walk to the store.

"You took one look at me and figured maybe I was worth saving, too. But just like the kids in your school, I don't need what you're teaching."

Her voice shook. "You're so wrong. You need it more than anyone I've ever met."

He shrugged. "So stick around, then. I guess the great sex is worth putting up with your preaching."

Mia looked dazed, and he knew he'd dealt their relationship the death blow. When she stood up, blinking back a fresh flood of tears, her face was a stony mask.

"You're right," she said, her voice trembling only slightly. "I don't know who you are. I thought I did, but..." She shook her head. "I thought you were a SEAL. I thought you didn't quit. But you have, haven't you? Life isn't working out exactly the way you planned it, so you're ready to give up and be bitter and angry and collect disability pay while you drink away the rest of your life, sitting on your couch in your lousy condominium, feeling sorry for yourself."

Frisco nodded, twisting his lips into a sad imitation of a smile. "That's right. That just about sums up my big plans for my exciting future."

She didn't even say goodbye. She just walked out the door.

CHAPTER FIFTEEN

"Yo, Navy, was that Mia I saw heading west, driving like she was behind the wheel of the Batmobile?"

Frisco looked up grimly from the peanut butter and jelly sandwich he was making for Natasha as Thomas King pushed open the screen door.

"Hey, Martian girl," the lanky teenager greeted Tash with one of his rare smiles.

"Thomas!" Tasha launched herself at the kid and immediately burst into tears. "Frisco yelled and yelled at Mia, and she went away!"

Thomas staggered back under the sudden unexpected weight of the little girl, but he managed to shift her into a position easier to hold on to. His dark eyes sought confirmation from Frisco over the top of Tasha's head. "Is that right?"

Frisco had to look away. "In a nutshell."

"I didn't want Mia to go," Tasha wailed. "And now she'll never come back!"

Thomas shook his head in disgust. "Oh, perfect. I come up here thinking *I'm* the one bearing bad news, and it turns out you guys have already done yourselves in without any outside help." He turned to the little girl still wailing in his arms. "You. Martian. Turn off the siren. Stop thinking only about yourself, and start thinking about Uncle Navy over here. If Ms. S. doesn't come back, *he'll* be the big loser, not you."

To Frisco's surprise, Tasha actually stopped crying.

"And you, Navy. Check yourself into a hospital, man. It's time to get your head examined." Thomas lowered Tasha to the floor and picked up the plate that held her lunch. "This yours?" he asked her.

She nodded.

"Good," Thomas said, handing it to her. "Go sit on that funny-looking swing on the porch while you eat this. I need to talk to Uncle Crazy here, all right?"

Tasha's lips were set at heavy pout, but she followed the teenager's order. As the screen door closed behind her, Thomas turned back to Frisco.

But instead of berating him about Mia's AWOL status, Thomas said, "Your friend Lucky gave me a call. Apparently something came up. Said to tell you he's out of the picture until 2200 hours tomorrow night—whenever the hell *that* is. I mean, ten o'clock is ten o'clock—there's no need to get cute."

Frisco nodded. "It's just as well—I'm going to need to find someone to take care of Tash, now that…" Mia's gone. He didn't finish the sentence. He didn't need to.

"I don't know what went down between you two," Thomas said, reaching into the bag of bread and pulling out two slices and laying them directly onto the counter. He pulled the peanut butter jar closer and began spreading the chunky spread onto the bread, "But you oughta know that Ms. S. doesn't hang out with just anyone. I've known her for four years, and as far as I know, there's only been one other guy besides you that she's said good-night to after breakfast, if you know what I mean. She's been selective, Uncle Fool, and she's selected *you*."

Frisco closed his eyes. "I don't want to hear this."

"Plugging your fingers in your ears so that you can't hear it doesn't change the truth, my man," Thomas told him, adding a thick layer of sweet, sticky strawberry jam to his sandwich. "I don't know what she told you, but she wouldn't've let you get so close if she didn't love you, with a capital *L*. I don't know what the hell you did to make her fall for you, but you'll be the biggest ass in the world if you don't take advantage of—"

Frisco's temper frayed. "I'm not going to stand here and be lectured by some kid!"

Thomas took a bite of his sandwich and chewed it thoughtfully as he gazed at Frisco. "Why are you always so angry, Navy?" he finally asked. "You know, I used to be just like you. I used to live and breathe anger. I thought it was the only way to stay alive. I was the meanest son of a bitch on the block. I didn't join a gang because I didn't *need* a gang—everyone was scared of me. I was tough enough to go solo. And I was on an express bus straight to hell. But you know what? I got lucky. I got the new teacher for history the year I was fifteen. I was six months away from dropping out, and Ms. S. did something no one ever did before. She looked me in the eye and somehow saw through all that anger, down to who I was underneath."

Thomas gestured at Frisco with his sandwich. "I remember, it was the day I pulled a knife on her. She told me to put the blade away and never bring it back to school again. She said I hid behind anger because *I* was the one who was scared—scared that everyone was right, that I was worthless and good for nothing.

"I mocked her, but she just smiled. She told me that she'd seen some of my test scores, and from what she saw, not only was I going to graduate from high school, but I was going to be valedictorian." He shook his head. "She didn't give up on me, and when I turned sixteen, I kind of just kept putting off dropping out. I kept telling myself that I'd stay for another week, 'cause of the free lunches." He looked at Frisco. "If I hadn't lucked out and had Ms. Summerton for a teacher, I would've ended up in jail. Or dead."

"Why are you telling me this?"

"Because you don't seem to realize what was directly under your nose, Uncle Blindman."

Frisco used his crutches to propel himself away from the kitchen counter, his movements jerky. "I *do* know. You're wrong."

"Maybe. But one thing I'm right about is whatever it is you're scared of, whatever you're hiding under your anger, it's nothing compared to the fear you *should* be feeling about losing Ms. Mia Summerton. Be afraid of that, Navy, be *very* afraid."

FRISCO SAT ON the couch, with his back to the cabinet that held enough whiskey to sink a ship.

It wouldn't take much. All he had to do was pull himself to his feet, set his crutches in place and then he'd be standing in front of that very same cabinet. The door would pop open with a pull of one hand...

Thomas and Natasha were down at the lake, not due to return until late afternoon, when they were all scheduled to leave for San Felipe. But right now there was no one around to protest. And by the time they returned, it would be too late. By then, Frisco wouldn't give a damn what anyone thought, what anyone said.

Not even little Tasha with her accusing blue eyes.

He closed his eyes. He would welcome the oblivion that a bottle of whiskey would bring. It would erase the picture he had in his mind of Mia's face right before she walked out the door.

He'd needed to tell her the truth. Instead he'd insulted

her avocation and made it seem as if their relationship had been based purely on sex.

Why? Because he was so damned afraid that she would leave.

In fact, he *knew* Mia would leave. So he'd pushed her away before she could leave on her own initiative.

Very clever. He prophesied his own doom, and then went and made damn sure it happened. Self-sabotage, it was called in all the psychology textbooks.

Savagely Frisco pulled himself to his feet and set his crutches underneath his arms.

MIA PULLED HER CAR OVER the side of the road, swearing like a sailor.

She couldn't believe that she'd allowed herself to fall into such a classic trap. It had been *years* since she'd made this kind of mistake.

For the past few years, she'd been successful—she'd been able to work with and get through to the toughest, hardest cases in the high school. And she'd been able to do that by being thick-skinned.

She'd looked countless angry, hurt, and painfully frightened young men and women in the eyes. She'd let all of their harsh, insulting, sometimes shockingly rude words bounce off of her. She'd met their outbursts with calm and their verbal assaults with an untouchable neutrality. They couldn't hurt her if she didn't let them.

But somehow she'd let Alan Francisco hurt her.

Somehow she'd forgotten how to remain neutral in the face of this man's anger and pain.

And, God, he was in so much pain.

Mia closed her eyes against the sudden vision of him on the night they'd taken Tasha to the hospital. She'd seen him sitting on his bed, bent over from pain and grief, hands covering his face as he wept.

This morning Alan's darkest fears had been realized. He'd admitted—both to himself and to her—that he wasn't ever going to get his old life back. He wasn't going to be a SEAL again. At least not a SEAL on active duty. He'd come face-to-face with a harsh reality that had to have shattered the last of his dreams, crushed out the final flicker of his hope.

Mia knew Alan didn't love her. But if ever there was a time that he needed her, it was now.

And she'd let his angry words hurt her.

She'd run away.

She'd left him alone and on the edge—with only a five-year-old child and several dozen bottles of whiskey for comfort.

Mia turned her car around.

FRISCO STARED AT the bottle and the glass he'd set out on the kitchen counter.

It was a rich, inviting amber color, with an instantly familiar aroma.

All he had to do was pick up the glass and he'd crawl into that bottle for the rest of the afternoon—maybe even for the rest of his life. He'd forget everything that he wasn't, everything that he couldn't be. And when he woke up, dizzy and sick, when he came eye to eye with what he'd become, well, he'd just have another drink. And another and another until once again he reached oblivion.

All he had to do was pick up that glass and he'd fulfill his family legacy. He'd be one of those good-for-nothing Francisco boys again. Not that they'd know any better, people had said, the way the father sits around drinking himself into an early grave....

That was his future now, too. Angry. Alcoholic. Alone.

Mia's face flashed in his mind. He could see her beautiful hazel eyes, her funny smile. The hurt on her face as she walked out the door.

He gripped the edge of the counter, trying to push the image away, trying not to want what he knew he couldn't have.

And when he looked up, there was that glass and that bottle, still sitting on the counter in front of him.

Hey, why fight destiny? He was pegged to follow this path right from the start. Yeah, he'd temporarily escaped by joining the Navy, but now he was back where he'd started. Back where he belonged.

At least he'd had the integrity to know that Mia didn't deserve to spend her life in his personal hell. At least he had *that* much up on his old man.

Man, he loved her. Pain burned his stomach, his chest—rising up into his throat like bile.

He reached for the glass, wanting to wash away the taste, wanting not to care, not to need, not to feel.

I thought you were a SEAL. I thought you didn't quit.

Mia might as well have been standing in the room with him, her words echoed so loudly in his head.

"I'm not a SEAL anymore," he answered her ghostly presence.

You'll always be a SEAL. You were when you were eleven years old. You will be when you die.

The problem was, he'd already died. He'd died five years ago—he was just too stubborn and stupid to know it at the time. He'd lost his life when he'd lost his future. And now he'd lost Mia.

By choice, he reminded himself. He'd had a choice about that.

You do have a future. It's just not the one you thought you'd have back when you were a boy.

Some future. Broken. Angry. Less than whole.

I know you're going to do whatever it takes to feel whole again. I know you'll make the right choices.

Choices. What choices did he have now?

Drink the whiskey in this glass. Polish off the rest of the bottle. Kill himself slowly with alcohol the way his old man had. Spend the rest of his miserable life in limbo, drunk in his living room, with only the television for company.

He didn't want that.

You're strong, you're tough, you're creative—you can adapt.

Adapt. That's what being a SEAL had been all about. Sea, air or land, he'd learned to adapt to the environment, adapt to the country and the culture. Make changes to his method of operation. Break rules and conventions. Learn to make do.

But adapt to *this?* Adapt to forever walking with a cane? Adapt to knowing he would remain forever in the rear, away from the front lines and the action?

It would be so hard. It would be the hardest thing he'd ever done in his entire life. Whereas it would be so damn easy just to give up.

It would've been easy to give up during Hell Week, too, when he'd done the grueling training to become a SEAL. He'd had the strength to keep going when all around him strong men were walking away. He'd endured the physical and psychological hardships.

Could he endure this, too?

I know you'll make the right choice.

And he *did* have a choice, didn't he? Despite what he'd thought, it came down to the very basic of choices.

To die.

Or to live.

Not just to be or not to be, but rather to do or not to do. To take charge or to lie back and quit.

But dammit, Mia was right. He *was* a SEAL, and SEALs *didn't* quit.

Alan Francisco looked down at the whiskey in his hand. He turned and threw it into the sink where the glass shattered and the whiskey trickled down the drain.

He chose life.

MIA'S CAR BOUNCED as she took the potholed dirt road much too fast.

She wasn't far now. Just another few miles until the turnoff that would lead directly to the cabin.

Determinedly, she wiped the last traces of her tears from her face. When she walked back in there, when she looked Alan in the eye, he was going to see only her calm offer of comfort and understanding. His angry words couldn't hurt her because she wouldn't let them. It would take more than that to drive her away.

She slowed as she rounded a curve, seeing a flash of sunlight on metal up ahead of her.

It was another car, heading directly toward her, going much too fast.

Mia hit the brakes and pulled as far to the right as she could, scraping the side of a tree as the other car went into a skid.

She watched it plunge down a sloping embankment, plowing through the underbrush and coming to a sudden jarring stop as it hit a tree.

Mia scrambled to unfasten her seat belt, fumbling in her haste to get out of her car and down to the wreck.

It was almost entirely hidden in the thick growth, but

she could hear someone crying. She pushed away branches to get to the driver's side door, yanking it open.

Blood. There was blood on the man's forehead and face, but he was moving and…

Dwayne Bell. The man in the driver's seat was Dwayne Bell. He recognized her at the exact moment she recognized him.

"Well, now, it's the girlfriend. Isn't *this* convenient," he said in his thick Louisiana drawl. He reached up to wipe the blood from his eyes and face.

Natasha. The crying sound came from *Natasha*. What was *she* doing here…?

"Dammit, I think I must've hit my head on the windshield," Dwayne said.

Mia wanted to back away, to run, but Natasha was belted into the front seat. Mia couldn't simply just leave her there. But maybe Dwayne had hit his head hard enough to make him groggy…. Maybe he wouldn't notice if…

Mia quickly went around to the other side of the car. Tasha already had her seat belt unfastened and was up and in Mia's arms as soon as the door was opened.

"Are you okay?" she asked, smoothing back Tasha's hair from her face.

The little girl nodded, eyes wide. "Dwayne hit Thomas," she told Mia, tears still streaming down her face. "He fell down and was all bloody. Dwayne made him dead."

Thomas…? Dead? No…

"I screamed and screamed for Thomas to help me—" Tasha hiccuped "—but he wouldn't get up and Frisco couldn't hear me and Dwayne took me in his car."

Thomas was unconscious maybe, but not dead. Please God, not dead. Not Thomas King….

Moving quickly, Mia carried Natasha around the car and up the embankment, praying Dwayne was too dizzy to notice, hoping that if she didn't turn around to check, he wouldn't—

"Where you going in such a hurry, darlin'?" Dwayne drawled.

Mia froze. And turned around. And found herself staring down the muzzle of a very big, very deadly-looking gun.

Dwayne held a handkerchief to his forehead, but his gun hand was decidedly steady as he hefted his bulk out of the car.

"I think we'll take your car," he told her with a gap-toothed smile. "In fact, you can drive."

FRISCO KNEW SOMETHING was wrong. The woods were too quiet. There was no echo of laughter or voices from the lake. And he'd never known Tasha to be silent for long.

The footpath down to the water wasn't easy to navigate on crutches, but he moved as quickly as he could. And as he neared the clearing—out of force of habit—he drew his sidearm from his shoulder holster. He moved as silently as he could, ready to drop his right crutch should the need arise to use it.

He saw Thomas, crumpled on the beach, blood on his face.

There was no sign of Tasha—or anyone else. But there were fresh tire tracks at the boat drop. Whoever had been here had gone.

And taken Tasha with them.

Frisco holstered his weapon as he moved quickly toward Thomas.

The kid stirred as Frisco touched him, searching for

a pulse. He was alive, thank God. His nose was bleeding and he had a nasty-looking gash on the back of his head. "Tasha," he gasped. "The fat man took Tash."

The fat man.

Dwayne Bell.

Took Tasha.

Frisco had been at the cabin, wrestling with his demons while Dwayne had been down here kicking the living daylights out of Thomas and kidnapping Tash. Guilt flooded him, but he instantly pushed it aside. He'd have time to feel guilty later. Right now he had to move fast, to get Tasha back.

"How long ago?" Frisco tore a piece of fabric from his shirttail and used it to apply pressure to the back of Thomas's head as he helped the kid sit up.

"I don't know. He hit me hard and I went down." Thomas let out a stream of foul language that would've made a SEAL take notice. "I tried to fight it—I heard Tasha screaming for me, but I blacked out. Dammit. Dammit!" There were tears in his eyes. "Lieutenant, she's scared to death of this guy. We gotta find her and get her back."

Frisco nodded, watching as Thomas forced away his dizziness and crawled to the lake to splash water onto his face, washing away the blood. The kid probably had a broken nose, but he didn't so much as say ouch. "Can you walk, or should I get your car and bring it around?"

Thomas straightened up, wobbling only slightly. "I can walk." He felt his pockets and swore again. "The fat man took my car keys."

Frisco started up the path that led back to the cabin. "So we'll hot-wire it." He looked back. "Tell me if I'm going too fast for you." Now *that* was a switch, wasn't it?

"*You* know how to hot-wire a car?"

"It's something we're taught in the SEAL teams."

"Shoot," Thomas said. "I could be a SEAL."

Frisco looked back at him and nodded. "Yeah, you could."

CHAPTER SIXTEEN

"I NEED YOUR HELP."

Frisco looked out the open car window, up at Lt. Joe Catalanotto, the Commanding Officer of SEAL Team Ten's Alpha Squad. Cat looked like he was ready to ship out on some high-level security training mission. He was dressed in fatigues and a black combat vest and wore his long dark hair back in a ponytail.

"Right now?" Cat asked, bending slightly to look inside the car, his sharp gaze taking in Thomas's battered appearance and bloody T-shirt.

"Yeah," Frisco said. "My sister's kid's been snatched. Sharon got herself in too deep with a drug dealer. He's the one that took the kid. I need help finding him and getting her back."

Joe Cat nodded. "How many guys you need?"

"How many you got?"

Frisco's former CO smiled. "How's all seven of Alpha Squad?"

Seven. Those seven were the six guys Frisco had served with—along with his own replacement. That was one man he *wasn't* looking forward to working with. But he nodded anyway. Right now he needed all the help he could get to find Natasha. "Good."

As Frisco watched, Cat slipped a microthin cellular phone from the pocket of his vest and dialed a coded number.

"Yeah, Catalanotto," he said. "Cancel Alpha Squad's flight out. Our training mission has been delayed—" he glanced up at the cloudless blue sky "—due to severe weather conditions. Unless otherwise directed, we'll be off base as of 1600 hours, executing local reconnaissance and surveillance training." He snapped the phone shut and turned back to Frisco. "Let's pay a visit to the equipment room, get the gear we need to find this guy."

"WHOA, FRISCO, NICE couch!"

With the exception of the glaringly pink couch, Frisco's apartment was starting to look like command central.

Lucky had finished cleaning the place up and had moved the sofa in yesterday. Now, under Joe Cat's command, Bobby and Wes—Bob, tall and built like a truck; Wes, short and razor thin, but inseparable since BUD/S training had made them swim buddies—had moved aside all unessential furniture and set the small dining room table in the center of the living room.

"You've gotta do the rest of the room in pink, too—it suits you, baby!" Six and a half feet tall, black and built like a linebacker, Chief Daryl Becker—nicknamed Harvard—possessed an ivy league education and a wicked sense of humor. He carried a heavy armload of surveillance gear, which he began to set up on the table.

Blue McCoy was the next to arrive. The blond-haired SEAL brought several large cases that made the muscles in his arms stand out in high relief. Assault weapons—God forbid they'd need to use them. Even the normally taciturn executive officer and second in command of Alpha Squad couldn't resist commenting on the pink couch.

"I'm dying to meet this new girlfriend of yours," Blue

said in his soft Southern drawl. "Please tell me that sofa there belongs to her."

Mia.

Where the hell was she? She should have been back long before him.

But her apartment was still locked up tight. Frisco had gone out to check at least five times since he'd arrived. He'd even left a message on her answering machine, thinking she might phone in. He hadn't apologized—he'd need to do that in person. He'd simply told her that he was looking for Tash. Please call him.

"Okay," Harvard said, finishing hooking the computers and other equipment to Frisco's phone line. "We're all set. When this Dwayne calls, you keep him talking and we'll pinpoint his location in about forty seconds."

"*When* Dwayne calls. *If* Dwayne calls." Frisco couldn't keep his frustration from buzzing in his voice. "Dammit, I *hate* waiting."

"Gee, I forgot how much fun it was to work with the King of Impatience," Lucky said, coming in the door. Another man followed him. It was Ensign Harlan Jones, aka Cowboy—the hotheaded young SEAL who'd replaced Frisco in the Alpha Squad. He nodded a silent greeting to Frisco, no doubt subdued both by the seriousness of a kidnapped child and the strangeness of being in the home of the man whose place he'd taken for his own.

"Thanks for coming," Frisco said to him.

"Glad to be able to help," Cowboy replied.

Frisco's condo had never seemed so small. With eight large men and Thomas there, there was barely room to move. But it was good. It was like old times. Frisco had missed these guys, he realized. He just wished Natasha hadn't had to be kidnapped to bring them all together again.

And that had entirely been up to him. *He'd* been the one keeping his distance, pushing the squad away. Yeah, the fact that he wasn't one of them anymore stuck in his throat. Yeah, it made him jealous as hell. But this was better than nothing. It was better than quitting....

"You got anything to eat?" Wes asked, heading for the kitchen.

"Hey, Frisco, mind if I crash on your bed?" Bobby asked, also not waiting for an answer before he headed down the hall.

"Who hit *you* in the face with a baseball bat?" Lucky asked Thomas, who'd remained silent and off to one side until now.

The kid was leaning back against the wall and he looked as if he should be sitting if not lying down. "Dwayne," he answered. "And it was the barrel of his gun, not a baseball bat."

"Maybe you should go home," Lucky suggested. "Take care of that—"

Thomas turned to give the other man a cool, appraising look. "Nope. I'm here until we get the little girl back."

"I think Alpha Squad…"

"I'm *not* leaving."

"…can probably handle—"

Frisco cut in. "The kid stays," he said quietly.

Blue stepped forward. "Your name's Thomas, right?" he said to the boy.

"Thomas King."

Blue held out his hand. "Pleased to meet you," he drawled. The two shook. "If you're going to be helping us, why don't I show you how some of this equipment works?"

Frisco sat down on the pink sofa next to Joe Cat as Blue and Harvard began giving Thomas a crash course in tracing phone calls. "I can't just sit here waiting," he said. "I've got to do something."

Wes came back out of the kitchen, having overheard Frisco's remark. "Why don't you make yourself a nice cup of hot tea," he teased in a lispingly sweet voice, "and curl up on your nice pink couch with your favorite copy of *Sense and Sensibility* to distract you?"

"Hey," Harvard boomed in his deep, subbass voice. "I heard that. I *like* Jane Austen."

"I do, too," Cowboy interjected.

"Whoa," Lucky said. "Who taught *you* to read?"

The room erupted in laughter, and Frisco restlessly stood up, pushing his way out the door and onto the landing. He knew that humor was the way the men of Alpha Squad dealt with stress and a tense situation, but he didn't feel much like laughing.

He just wanted Natasha back.

Where was she right now? Was she scared? Had Dwayne hit her again? Dammit, if that bastard as much as *touched* that little girl...

Frisco heard the screen door open behind him and turned to see that Joe Cat had followed him.

"I want to go talk to my sister again," Frisco told the CO. "I think there's more to this than she's told me."

Cat didn't hesitate. "I'll drive you over. Just let me tell the guys where we're going." He stepped back into Frisco's condo, then came back out, nodding to Frisco. "Let's go."

As they headed down to the parking lot, Frisco glanced back one last time at Mia's lifeless condo. Where *was* she?

MIA CARRIED TASHA across the well-manicured lawn to the front door of the big Spanish-style house.

This was ludicrous. It was broad daylight, they were
in the middle of a seemingly affluent, upper-middle-class
suburb. Down the street, several landscapers cleaned up
a neighbor's yard. Should she scream for help, or try to
run?

She did neither, well aware of that very large gun
Dwayne Bell carried concealed in his pocket. If she had
been alone, she might have risked it. But not with Natasha
in her arms. Still, it gave her a chill to know that she could
clearly identify the address where they'd been brought,
and the man who'd brought them here.

"Shouldn't you have blindfolded us?" she asked as
Dwayne opened the door.

"Can't drive if you're blindfolded. Besides, you're here
as my guests. There's no need to make this more unpleasant than it has to be."

"You have a curious definition of the word *guest,* Mr.
Bell," Mia said as Dwayne shut the door behind her. The
inside of the house was dark with all the shades pulled
down, and cool from an air conditioner set well below
seventy degrees. She could hear canned laughter from
a television somewhere in the big house. Tasha's arms
tightened around her neck. "I've never held someone at
gunpoint simply to invite them into my home. I think
hostage is a more appropriate term."

"Actually, I prefer the word *collateral,*" the overweight
man told her.

A man appeared, walking toward them down the hall
from a room that might've been a kitchen. His jacket was
off and he wore a gun in a shoulder holster very similar
to Frisco's. He spoke to Dwayne in a low voice, glancing
curiously at Mia and Natasha.

"Have Ramon take care of it," Dwayne said loudly

enough for Mia to overhear. "And then I want to talk to you both."

There were at least two other men in the house—at least two of them carrying weapons. Mia looked around as Dwayne led them up the thickly carpeted stairs, trying to memorize the layout of the house, determined to gather any information that would be valuable for Frisco when he came.

Frisco would find them. Mia knew that as surely as she knew that the late-afternoon sun would soon slip beneath the horizon.

And then he would come.

"THE STAKES ARE higher than I thought," Frisco said tightly, coming out into the drug-and-alcohol rehab center's waiting room. Joe Catalanotto rose to his feet. "Sharon didn't steal five thousand from Bell—she stole *fifty* thousand. She fudged his bookkeeping—didn't think he'd notice."

He headed for the door, toward the parking lot and Joe Cat's jeep.

"Can she pay it back?" Cat asked.

Frisco snorted. "Are you kidding? It's long gone. She used most of it to pay off some gambling debts and blew the rest on drugs and booze." He stopped, turning to Cat. "Let me borrow your phone. Sharon gave me the address where she used to live with Bell," he told Cat as he dialed the number of the cellular phone link they'd set up back at his apartment.

The line was picked up on the first ring.

"Becker here." It was Harvard.

"It's just me, Chief," Frisco said. "Any calls?"

"Nothing yet. You know we would have relayed it directly to you if there were."

"I've got an address I want to check out. It's just outside of San Felipe, in Harper, the next town over to the east. Have Lucky and Blue meet me and Cat over there, all right?" He gave Harvard the street address.

"I've got that location on my computer," Harvard told him. "They're on their way, soon as I print them out a map. You need directions?"

Cat was listening in. "Tell H. to send a copy of that map to the fax in my jeep."

Frisco stared at Joe Cat. "You have a *fax* machine in your *jeep*?"

Cat smiled. "CO privileges."

Frisco ended the call and handed the phone back to Cat. But Cat shook his head. "You better hold on to it. If that ransom call comes in…"

Frisco met his friend's eyes. "If that ransom call comes in, we better be able to trace it," he said grimly.

"And pray that we're not already too late. Sharon told me Dwayne Bell has killed in revenge for far less than fifty thousand dollars."

"No one's home," Lucky reported as he and Blue McCoy silently materialized alongside Cat's jeep, down the street from the house Sharon had lived in with Dwayne Bell.

"I went through a basement window," Blue told Frisco and Joe Cat. "From what I could see from just a quick look around, Dwayne Bell doesn't live there anymore. There were kids' toys all over the place, and there was mail on the kitchen counter addressed to Fred and Charlene Ford. Looks like Bell moved out and these other folks moved in."

Frisco nodded, trying not to clench his teeth. It would've been too easy if Bell had been there. He'd known that coming out here was a long shot to start with.

Cat was looking at him. "What do you want to do?"

Frisco shook his head. Nothing. There was nothing they *could* do now but wait. "I want the phone to ring."

"He'll call and we *will* get Natasha back," Lucky said with far more confidence than Frisco felt.

MIA TRIED THE window of the tiny bedroom where she and Tasha were being held. It was sealed shut. They wouldn't get out that way, short of breaking the glass. And even if they *could* break it without Dwayne and his goons hearing them, there was a *long* drop down to the ground.

Tasha sat on the bed, knees hugged tightly to her chest, her blue eyes wide as Mia made her way around the room.

The closet was minuscule—there was no way out there.

There were no secret doors, no hidden passages, no air ducts in the walls or crawl spaces underneath the throw rug. There was no hidden telephone with which she could make a furtive call for help, no gun in the dresser drawer that she could use to defend them.

The door was locked with a bolt on the outside.

They weren't going anywhere until Dwayne or his goons unlocked it.

There was nothing to do now but wait.

THE PHONE RANG.

They were halfway back to the condo, when the cell phone in Frisco's pocket chirped and vibrated against his leg. Joe Cat quickly pulled the jeep over to the side of the road as Frisco flipped the phone open.

"Frisco."

It was Harvard. "Call's coming in," he reported tersely.

"I'm linking it directly to you. Remember, if it's Bell, keep him talking."

"I remember."

There were several clicks, and then the soft hiss of an open line.

"Yeah," Frisco said.

"Mr. Francisco." It was Dwayne Bell's lugubrious voice. "You know who I am and why I'm calling, I assume."

"Let me talk to Tasha."

"Business before pleasure, sir," Bell said. "You have twenty-four hours to return to me the money that your charming sister stole. Fifty thousand, plus another ten in interest."

"It's going to take me longer than twenty-four hours to get together that kind of—"

"I'm already being very generous out of sentimentality for what Sharon and I once shared. It's nearly six. If I don't have cash in hand by 6:00 p.m. tomorrow, I'll kill the girl. And if I don't have it by midnight, then I'll kill the child. And if you go to the police, I'll kill them both, and take your sister to prison with me."

"Whoa," Frisco said. "Wait a minute. What did you say? Both? The girl, *then* the child...?"

Bell laughed. "Oh, you don't know? Your girlfriend is a guest in my house as well as the brat."

Mia. Hell, Bell had Mia, too.

"Let me talk to her," Frisco rasped. "I want proof they're both still all right."

"I anticipated that." He must have turned away from the phone because his voice was suddenly distant. "Bring them in."

There was a pause and a click, and then Mia's voice came on the line. "Alan?"

The sound was boomy and Frisco knew Bell had

switched to a speaker phone. "I'm here," he said. "Are you all right? Is Tash with you?"

Lucky appeared silently outside Joe Cat's car window. As Frisco glanced at him, he pointed to his own cellular phone and signaled a thumbs-up.

Harvard had gotten the trace. They had a location.

"Yes," Mia was saying. "Listen, Alan. My parents have money. Go to them. Remember I told you they live near the country club in Harper?"

No, she'd told him her parents lived in Malibu.

"Just be careful of my dad—he's a little nuts, with all those guns he has in his collection, and his two bodyguards."

Harper. Guns. Two bodyguards. Damn, she had the presence of mind to tell him where they were and how many men there were guarding them.

"That's enough," Bell cut in.

"My parents have the money you want," Frisco heard Mia say sharply. "How is Alan going to get it if I don't tell him where to go?"

"I have the address," Frisco told her. "I'll take care of the money, you take care of Tasha. Tash—are you okay?"

"I wanna go home." Natasha's voice was wobbly.

"She doesn't have her medicine, so if her temperature goes up again, put her in the bathtub and cool her down. Do you understand?" Frisco said to Mia as quickly as he could. "Stay with her in the bathroom. And talk to her so she's not scared. You know how she gets when it's too quiet. I know she's too little to listen to the sounds of the night the way I can."

Man, he hoped she understood. If Mia and Tasha kept talking, the SEALs would be able to use high-tech, high-powered microphones to help pinpoint their location

inside of the house. Frisco would need that information
before he could figure out the best way to launch their
attack against Bell and his men.

"Mia, I'll get that money soon. Right now, in fact, all
right?"

"All right. Alan, be careful." Her voice shook slightly.
"I love you."

"Mia, I—"

The line went dead. Frisco clicked off the telephone,
cursing Dwayne Bell, cursing himself. But what, exactly,
had he intended to say?

I love you, too.

God, the words had been right on the tip of his tongue.
Forget about the fact that Cat and Lucky and Blue were
listening in. Forget about the fact that a relationship with
him was the last thing Mia needed.

But if after all he'd said and done she could still love
him... No, she didn't *need* a relationship with him, but
maybe, just maybe she wanted it.

God knows he did, despite the fact that he may well
have burned his bridges with the awful things he'd said to
her. Burned? Damn, he'd bombed the hell out of them.

Still, she'd told him that she *loved* him.

"We got it—273 Barker Street in Harper," Lucky
leaned in the window to say. "Harvard's faxing a map and
leaving Thomas at headquarters to relay any other calls.
He and the rest of the squad will meet us over there."

Frisco nodded, hope flooding through him as he turned
to Joe Cat. "Let's move."

Mia's stomach hurt as one of Dwayne Bell's cohorts
followed her and Natasha back up the stairs.

Take care of Tasha, Frisco had told her. He'd given her
as much carefully disguised information in his message

as she'd tried to give him. *Stay with her in the bathroom. Put her in the bathtub.* If bullets started to fly, bullets like the ones that could be fired from Dwayne's enormous gun, bullets that could pass through walls and still have enough force to kill, then the bathtub, with its hard enamel, would be the safest place.

He'd told her to talk to Tasha. Why? *Talk to her so she's not scared.* Why would he want them to talk? It didn't make sense. But it didn't have to make sense. He'd asked—she'd do it.

Right now, Frisco had said. *I have the address.* Mia knew without a doubt that he was on his way. Somehow he'd found them. He'd be here soon.

She stopped in front of the open bathroom door, turning to look back at the man with the gun. "We need to use the bathroom."

He nodded. "Go ahead. Don't lock the door."

Mia drew Tasha inside the tiny room, closing the door behind her, taking a quick inventory.

Pedestal sink, grimy tub with a mildewed shower curtain, a less-than-pristine-looking toilet.

The window was tiny and sealed shut, the same as the window in the bedroom.

There was a narrow linen closet that held a few paper-wrapped rolls of toilet paper and several tired-looking washcloths and towels.

Mia took one of the washcloths from the closet and turned on the warm water in the sink, holding the small square of terry cloth underneath. "Okay, Tash," she said. "We're going to try to fool Dwayne and his friends into thinking that you're really sick, and that you might throw up, okay?"

The little girl nodded, her eyes wide.

"I need you to take a deep breath and hold it in for

as long as you can—until your face turns *really* red, all right?"

Tasha nodded again, drawing in a big breath as Mia wrung out the washcloth.

"Now, this is going to be warm against your face, but we want you to feel kind of warm and sweaty so Dwayne will believe you've got a fever, okay?"

The little girl stood staunchly as Mia pressed the warm cloth against her forehead and cheeks. By the time Tasha exhaled, she was flushed and quite believably clammy.

"Can I get a drink?" she asked, turning on the cold water.

"Sure," Mia said. "But remember to look sick, okay?" She waited until Tash was done at the sink before she opened the bathroom door. "Excuse me. I think we better stay in here. Tasha's got a fever and—"

Behind her came the awful sound of retching, and Mia turned to see Tasha leaning over the toilet, liquid gushing from her mouth.

"Oh, hell!" the man with the gun said in disgust, backing away and closing the bathroom door.

"Natasha," Mia started to say, alarmed.

But Tasha turned to look at Mia with a wicked light in her eyes. "I put lots of water in my mouth and spit it out," she whispered. "Do you think we fooled him?"

There was a sound from outside the door, and Mia opened it a crack. It was the man with the gun.

"I'm putting a bolt on the outside of this door," he said gruffly. "You're gonna have to stay in here. Dwayne don't want no mess. Can I get the kid some blankets or something?"

Mia nodded. "Blankets would be great."

She closed the door and turned back to Natasha, giving the little girl a big thumbs-up.

Now she had to keep talking. For some reason, Frisco wanted her to keep talking.

And she prayed that after this was all over, he'd still be alive to explain exactly why.

CHAPTER SEVENTEEN

"I'VE GOT SOMETHING," Harvard said, fine-tuning the dials of the ultrasensitive microphone that was aimed at the Barker Street house. "Sounds like a woman and a kid singing—I think it's 'The Alphabet Song.'"

He held out his padded earphones and Frisco slipped them on, staring out the darkened glass window in the side of Harvard's van at the house they were watching.

It was them. It had to be them. And then the song ended, and he heard Tash speak.

"Mia, why are we sitting in the bathtub?"

"Because your uncle thought we'd be safest here."

"'Cause Dwayne wants to make us dead, like he did to Thomas?"

"Honey, Frisco's not going to let that happen."

"Because he loves us?" the child asked.

Mia hesitated. "Yes," she finally said. "Because he loves…us."

Frisco knew she didn't believe what she was telling Tash. And why should Mia think he loved her after the terrible things he'd said? The thought of it made his chest ache. He handed the headphones back to Harvard. "It's them, Chief," he said. "Can you pinpoint their location?"

"Back of the house," Harvard told him, turning his dials. "I've got a TV up much too loud in the front of the house, along with sounds of someone eating."

Frisco nodded. That was a start. He'd have a better idea of Mia and Tash's exact location after Blue, Cowboy and Lucky checked in from their sneak and peek. In the early hours of the dusk, the three SEALs were checking over the yard and exterior of the house, looking for alarms or booby traps—anything that would tip Bell off as to their presence.

And Wes and Bobby were scanning with an infrared device that would help place the locations of Mia and Tash and their kidnappers. Bell and two others—that's what Mia had managed to tell him. All armed.

Three lowlifes against eight SEALs. There was no way the SEALs could lose.

Except for the fact that Frisco was determined that the SEALs would not open fire. Not with Mia and Tasha in the house, even despite the fact that they were protected by the bathtub. Because God help him if something went wrong and one of the two people he loved most in all of the world wound up in the cross fire.

No, they were going to have to do this by stealth—which currently was not one of his strengths. There was no way in hell he could climb up the side of the house silently.

"Hey! I found an extra headset and vest in the back of my jeep." Joe Catalanotto climbed into the van, tossing both in Frisco's direction.

"Man, do you know how long it's been since I've worn one of these?" Frisco asked, holding up the vest and lightweight headphones.

Cat nodded. "Yeah," he said. "I *do* know. Put 'em on. Blue and Lucky are starting to report in. You're gonna want to hear what they're saying."

Frisco slipped on the black combat vest. It was a newer version of the heavy-duty vest he'd damn near worn out during his five years as a SEAL. It was made from lighter fabric than his old vest and was more comfortable.

It felt good. He slipped on the headset and adjusted the lip microphone, plugging the wire into the radio unit in the vest. He adjusted the frequency and—

"...ly nothing in the yard." It was Blue McCoy, speaking in a low voice. "No extra alarms or movement sensors—nothing. The alarm on the house is Mickey Mouse—Lucky already overrode it. There's also a trellis in the back—it's perfectly placed. Like an engraved invitation to the second floor.

"I'm already up there." This was Cowboy's voice. "Windows seem tight. But there's a third floor—probably an attic. Windows there look good and loose. Easy access."

"I got movement on the infrared," Bobby's deep voice reported. "Two are still stationary on the second floor, and three are downstairs, in the front of the structure, although one is moving now toward the back."

"That's Cliff," Harvard reported. "He just told his homeboy Ramon that he's going into the kitchen to get more salsa for his corn chips. They're watching something on an adults-only channel. Not much dialogue but lots of cheesy music."

Blue's voice again. "The house has seven rooms downstairs. A living room in the southeast corner. A dining room to the immediate west, and a kitchen and some kind of rec room stretches along the entire back of the house."

Frisco grabbed paper and pen and sketched a rough floor plan as Blue continued to describe the layout, and the location of all doors and windows.

"Cat, you want me to insert through the attic?" Cowboy asked.

"It's Frisco's show," Cat replied, turning to look at him.

Frisco looked up from his drawing and shook his head. "Not yet. Report back to the van," he said, speaking into his mike for the first time in five years. "Everyone but Bobby. I want you to stay on the infrared, Bob. I need to be dead sure that Mia and Tash aren't moved from that upstairs room."

"You got it," Bobby replied.

It only took a few minutes for the rest of Alpha Squad to appear from the shadows and gloom of the early evening.

Frisco's plan was simple.

"I want Cat and Lucky to go in through the attic windows and work their way down to the second floor where Mia and Tash are held. The rest of us will make a silent entry through this back door." He pointed down to his drawing. "Except for Bobby, who's going to stay glued to the infrared and Harvard who's gonna keep listening in."

"Bor-ring," Bob's voice sounded over their headsets from somewhere out in the yard.

"Someone's got to do it," Joe Cat told him.

"Yeah, but why me? I mean, come on, a damn paraplegic in a wheelchair could handle *this* job…."

There was a sudden silence in the van. Nobody looked at Frisco or his crutches. Nobody so much as moved.

Bobby realized what he'd said and he swore softly. "Frisco, man—I didn't mean that the way it sounded…. I wasn't thinking."

"As usual," Wes added.

Frisco sat down, looking up at the uncomfortable expression on the faces of his friends.

"It makes sense for me to switch places with Bob," he said quietly. "Doesn't it?"

Joe Catalanotto was the first to look up and into his eyes. "This isn't going to be a difficult operation," he said. He glanced over at Blue. "We figured—"

And suddenly it was all clear to Frisco. "You figured you could let me play soldier one last time, huh?" he said, knowing that he spoke the truth. "You figured you could babysit me, and the fact that I can't run and can barely walk without crutches wouldn't put the squad in that much danger."

Cat respected him enough not to try to lie. But he couldn't bring himself to agree, either. So instead, he said nothing. But the answer was written plainly on his face.

"But still, my being there is going to put the squad in some danger," Frisco said.

"It's nothing we can't handle—"

"But if I'm not part of the team that goes in the back door, the chances of a snafu happening decreases."

"It's not that big a deal—"

Frisco pulled himself to his feet. "Bob, when we get ready to go, I'll switch with you."

Bob sounded as if he were in agony. "Frisco, I didn't mean to—"

"You'll have to wait until I get out there, because I want eyes on that infrared scanner at all times."

Lucky stepped forward. "Hey, buddy, we know how important it is for you to go in there and—"

"Working in a team means recognizing individual team members' strengths and weaknesses," Frisco told him evenly. "As much as I want to be the one to protect Mia and Natasha, I know I can't climb in the attic window. And the fact is, I have no business trying to sneak in that back door, either. I'll man the infrared." He took a deep breath. "Blue, you've got the point. You're in command once you're inside the house." He knew he could trust Blue McCoy to make the right decisions to apprehend Dwayne and his two men with the least amount of gunplay. "Okay, let's get into position."

One by one, the SEALs slipped out of the van, fading into the darkness of the night.

Frisco turned to Joe Cat. "Don't move Mia and Tash downstairs until you receive an all clear."

Cat nodded. "We'll wait for your signal."

Frisco clumsily swung himself out of the van and started toward the shrubs at the edge of the yard where Bobby and the infrared scanner were hidden. But Joe Cat stopped him.

"You know, it takes a real man to put others' welfare and safety before his own pride," Cat said.

"Yeah, right. I'm one hell of a hero," Frisco said. "Excuse me while I go hide in the bushes while the rest of you guys risk death to rescue my niece and my girlfriend."

"We both know that what you just did was impossibly hard and incredibly heroic," Cat countered. "If that were Ronnie in that house, I'm not sure I would've been able to assign myself out of the action."

"Yes, you would've," Frisco said quietly. "If you knew that putting yourself in the assault force would not only risk the lives of your men, but risk Ronnie's life..." He shook his head. "I had no choice. You would've had no choice, too."

Joe Cat nodded. "Maybe." He paused. "I'd like to think so."

"I'm counting on you to take care of Mia and Tash," Frisco said.

"These guys aren't going to hear us coming. If we do this right, the risk is minimal."

And doing it right meant that he wasn't in the way. Damn, as much as Frisco hated that, he knew it was true.

"Hey, you said it yourself. Working as a team means recognizing team members' strengths and weaknesses," Joe said as if he could read Frisco's mind. When Frisco would have nodded and turned away, Joe Cat stopped him again. "You can still be part of SEAL Team Ten, Lieutenant. God knows we need your strengths. I've got one hell of a shortage of dependable instructors and way too many raw recruits coming into the SEAL Teams to be able to teach 'em properly. You have a wealth of information to pass on to these kids. You could virtually have your pick of subjects to teach."

Frisco was silent. Teach. *Those who can, do. Those who can't, teach.* Except, what was it that Mia had said? *Those who are taught, do. Those who teach, shape the future.*

"And as for your weaknesses…" Joe Cat continued. "Do you remember the very end of Hell Week? You weren't in my boat team, but I know you probably heard the story. I was a half a day away from the end of the ordeal, and I got a stress fracture in my leg. Talk about pain. It was hell, but I wouldn't quit. I wasn't gonna quit after I'd come that far. But I was *damn* close to being taken out. One of the instructors—a real bastard nicknamed Captain Blood—was about to call for the medics and have me removed."

Frisco nodded. "I remember hearing that."

"But then Blue and the other guys who were left in my boat team told Captain Blood that I was okay, that I could make it. In fact, they said I'd run a mile down the beach to prove it. And the captain looked at me and told me if I could run that mile, he'd let me stay in 'til the end.

"There was no way in hell I could *walk,* let alone run, but Blue and the other guys picked me up, and they ran that mile carrying me."

Frisco *had* heard that story. With their incredible show of unity and loyalty, Cat and Blue and the rest of their boat team were rewarded by having the hard-nosed instructor announce them secure nearly six hours before the official end of Hell Week. It was unprecedented.

Joe Cat reached out and squeezed Frisco's shoulder. "Right now you're letting us carry *you.* But don't think there's no way you can carry us in return, my friend. Because you can. By teaching those recruits who are going to back us up someday, you'd be shouldering more than your share."

Frisco was silent. What could he say?

"Think about it," Cat said quietly. "At least think about it."

Frisco nodded. "I will—after you get Mia and Natasha safely out of that house."

"I know you meant after *we* get them out of there. All of us—working as a team."

Frisco smiled. "Right. Slip of the tongue."

FROM WHERE HE sat, Frisco could see the light coming from an upstairs window. This window was smaller than the others—it had to be the bathroom.

Mia and Natasha were on the other side of those panes of glass. So close, yet so damn far.

As he watched the infrared scanner, the reddish-orange spots that were the Alpha Squad moved closer to the house. Two who had to be Lucky and Cat moved up onto the house.

The other four—Blue, Bobby, Wes and Cowboy—were motionless now, waiting for Frisco's command.

Inside the house, according to his scanner, nothing had changed. Dwayne and his men were still in the living room. Mia and Tash were still upstairs.

Mia and Tash.

Both of them had given him unconditional love. Funny, he had no problem accepting it from the kid, but from Mia...

Frisco hadn't believed it was possible. It still seemed much too good to be true. She was filled with such joy and life while he was the poster model for despair. She had such strength of purpose while he was floundering and uncertain.

He hadn't told her he loved her. He could have. But instead he'd attacked her, attacked her avocation. He'd pushed her away. Yet still she loved him.

Was it possible that she'd somehow seen the desperate, frightened man that hid beneath the anger and pain of his verbal attack? Thomas had told him she'd done the same with him, making a critical difference in his life, altering his destiny, shaping his future.

Those who are taught, do. Those who teach, shape the future.

Frisco could picture Mia telling him that, her eyes blazing with passion and fire. She believed it so absolutely.

And right then, as Alpha Squad waited for his signal to move into Dwayne Bell's house, Frisco knew just as absolutely that he wanted a second chance.

His entire life was full of second chances, he realized. Another man might have died from the wounds he'd received. Another man would never have made it out of that wheelchair.

Another man would let Mia Summerton get away.

He thought of that list that she'd posted on his refrigerator—all the things he could still do. There *was* so much he could still do, although some of it was going to be extremely hard.

Like not being an active-duty SEAL. That was going to be damned hard. But it was going to be damned hard whether he spent the rest of his life drinking in his living room, or if he signed on as an instructor. His disappointment and crushed hopes would be a tough weight to carry, a rough road to walk.

But he was a SEAL. Tough and rough were standard operating procedure. He'd come this far. He could—and he would—make it the rest of the way.

"Okay," Frisco said into his lip microphone. "The three targets haven't moved. Let's get this done. Quietly and quickly, Alpha Squad. Go."

There was no response over his headset, but he saw the shapes on the infrared scanner begin to move.

Blue clicked once into his lip mike when the downstairs team were all inside.

"Moving slow in the attic," he heard Joe Cat breathe. "Beams are old—don't want 'em to creak."

"Take as long as you need," Frisco told him.

It seemed to take an eternity, but Frisco finally heard Cat report, "In place."

He and Lucky were outside the upstairs bathroom door. That was Blue's signal to move.

Frisco heard the flurry of movement and the sound of four automatic weapons being locked and loaded. That was when the noise started.

"Hands up," Blue shouted, his normally smooth voice hard and clipped. "Come on—let me see 'em. Hands on your heads!"

"Come on, get 'em up!" It was Cowboy. "Come on—*move!*"

"What the…" Frisco could faintly hear Dwayne's voice as he was picked up over all four microphones.

"Move it! Down on the floor, faces against the rug. Let's *go.*" That was Bobby, along with an accompanying crash as he helped someone down there.

"Who the hell are you?" Dwayne kept asking. "Who the hell are you guys?"

"We're your worst nightmare," Cowboy told him, and then laughed. "Hell, you don't know *how* many years I've been waiting to say that line!"

"We're Alan Francisco's friends," Frisco heard Blue tell Dwayne. "Okay, Frisco, Mr. Bell and his associates have all been relieved of their weapons."

"Take 'em out into the front yard and tie 'em up, Blue," Frisco ordered. He had already moved across the yard and was nearly inside the house. "H., use that fancy equipment of yours to dial 911. Let's get the police garbage removal squad to take away the trash. Cat, this is my official all clear. Let's get Mia and Tasha out of there."

THE BATHROOM DOOR swung open, and Mia stared up into the face of an enormous dark-haired stranger carrying an equally enormous gun.

He must've seen the surge of panic in her eyes because he quickly aimed the gun down toward the floor. "Lt. Commander Joe Catalanotto of the Alpha Squad." He identified himself in a rather unmistakable New York accent. "It's all right now, ma'am, you're safe."

"Dwayne's been detained—permanently." Another man poked his head in the door. It was Lucky O'Donlon. Both men were wearing army fatigues and some kind of black vest.

"Are you okay?" the dark-haired man—Joe—asked.

Mia nodded, still holding Tasha close. In the distance, she could hear the sound of sirens. "Where's Alan? Is he all right?"

Lucky smiled, coming forward to give them both a hand out of the bathtub. "He's downstairs, waiting for the police to arrive. They're not going to be real happy to see us here, doing their job for them, so to speak."

"I pretended to throw up so the bad man would lock us in the bathroom," Natasha told Lucky proudly.

"That's very cool," he told her, perfectly straight-faced. But when he looked up at Mia, there was a glint of amusement in his eyes. "Barfing kid as weapon," he said to her under his breath. "The thought makes the strongest man tremble with fear. Good thinking."

"I want to see Alan," she said.

The man named Joe nodded. "I know he wants to see you, too. Come on, let's go downstairs."

"How many SEALs are here?" she asked Joe as Lucky, Tasha in his arms, led the way down the stairs.

"All of Alpha Squad," he told her.

"How did you ever get him to agree to let you help?"

"He asked us."

Mia stared at Joe. Alan asked *them* for help? They didn't volunteer and he grudgingly accept? God, she'd been so afraid he'd come here on his own and get himself killed….

"It's hard for him, but he's learning," Joe said quietly. "Give him time. He's gonna be okay."

"Frisco!" Tasha shouted.

Mia stopped halfway down the stairs, watching as the little girl wriggled free from Lucky's arms and launched herself at Alan Francisco.

He was dressed similarly to the other SEALs, complete

with black vest and some kind of headphone thing. His
crutches clattered to the living room floor as he caught
Tasha in his arms.

From across the room, over the top of Tasha's head,
Alan looked up at Mia. Their eyes met and he smiled one
of his sad, crooked, perfect smiles.

Then, God help her, she was rushing toward him,
too—as shamelessly as Natasha had.

And then she was in his arms. He held her as tightly
as he could with Tasha still clinging to him, too.

"I'm sorry," he whispered into her ear. "Mia, I'm so
sorry."

Mia wasn't sure if he was apologizing for his angry
words or Dwayne's abducting them. It didn't matter. What
mattered was they were safe and he was safe and he had
actually *asked* for help....

Flashing lights marked the arrival of police squad cars,
and Frisco loosened his hold on Mia and let Tasha slide
down to the floor.

"Can we talk later?" Frisco asked.

Mia nodded. "I was coming back, you know," she told
him. "To the cabin. To talk to you—talk, not fight. That
was when Dwayne nearly ran me off the road."

Her beautiful hazel eyes were shining with unshed
tears. She had been coming back to the cabin. She loved
him enough to swallow her pride.

And suddenly later wasn't good enough. Suddenly
there were things he had to tell her, things that couldn't
wait.

Frisco knew in that moment that even if right then and
there, in a miraculous act of God, he suddenly regained
full use of his injured leg, he would still be less than
whole.

He knew with a certainty that took his breath away that

it was only when he was with this incredible woman that he was truly complete.

Oh, he knew he could live without her—the same way he knew he could live without ever running again. It would be hard, but he could do it. It wasn't as if she'd saved him. She hadn't—he'd done that himself. With a little help. It had taken Natasha to nudge him back to the world of the living. And once there, Mia's warmth and joy had lit his path, helping him out of his darkness.

Frisco knew he'd probably never run again. But he also knew that he didn't have to live without Mia.

That was something he had at least a small amount of control over.

And he could start by telling her how he felt.

But there wasn't any time. The police had arrived, and the uniformed officers were less than pleased that the SEALs had taken matters into their own hands. Joe Cat had intercepted the officer in charge and was trying to calm him down, but back-up had to be called along with the police captain.

And instead of telling Mia that he loved her, Frisco turned to Lucky. "Do me a favor, man, and walk Mia and Tash out to Harvard's van. I want to get them out of here, but I've got to set one thing straight with the police before we leave."

"Absolutely."

Frisco picked up his crutches, positioning them under his arms as he looked back at Mia. "I'll try not to take too long."

She gave him a tremulous smile that added so much weight and meaning to her words. "That's okay. We'll wait."

Frisco smiled back at her, suddenly almost ridiculously happy. "Yeah," he said. "I know. But I don't want to keep you waiting any longer."

"I TOLD THE police captain that Sharon was willing to testify against Bell," Frisco told Harvard and Mia as they climbed out of the van and started toward the condo courtyard. "With her help, they can ID Bell as the perpetrator in a number of unsolved robberies and possibly even a murder."

"Sharon saw Dwayne *kill* someone?" Mia asked Frisco in a low voice.

He nodded, glancing at Harvard who was carrying a drowsy Tasha. But her five-year-old ears were as sharp as ever and she lifted her head. "I saw Dwayne kill someone, too," Tasha told them, her eyes filling with tears. "I saw him kill Thomas."

"Thomas isn't dead," Frisco said.

"Yes, he is," Tasha insisted. "Dwayne hit him and made him bloody, and he didn't get back up."

"Thomas is waiting for you, princess, up in the condo."

"Oh, thank God," Mia said. "Is he really all right?"

"A little shaky, maybe," Frisco said, "but, yeah. He's okay."

All signs of her drowsiness gone, Tasha squirmed free from Harvard's arms. Like a flash, she ran up the stairs. But the condo door was locked, and she pounded on it.

As Mia watched, it swung open, and sure enough, there was Thomas King, looking a little worse for wear. Tasha launched herself at him, and nearly knocked the teenager over.

"Hey, Martian girl," Thomas said casually and matter-of-factly, as if they'd run into each other on the street. But he held the child tightly. That and the sudden sheen of tears in his eyes gave him away.

"I thought you were dead," she told him, giving him a resounding kiss on the cheek. "And if you were dead, then you couldn't marry me."

"*Marry* you?" Thomas's voice slipped up an octave. "Whoa, wait a minute, I—"

"A Russian princess has to marry a king," Tasha told him seriously.

"You're kind of short," Thomas told her. "I'm not so sure I want a wife who's that *short*."

Tasha giggled. "I'll be taller, silly," she told him. "I'll be sixteen."

"Sixteen…" Thomas looked as if he were choking. "Look, Martian, if you're still interested when you're *twenty*-six, give me a call, but until then, we're friends, all right?"

Natasha just smiled.

"All right," Thomas said. "Now, come on inside and see what Navy bought for you."

They disappeared inside the house, and Mia could hear Tasha's excited squealing. She turned to Frisco, who was painstakingly pulling himself up the stairs. "Is it the couch?"

Frisco just shook his head. "Man, I forgot all about it."

"I didn't," Harvard said, laughter in his voice.

Curiosity overcame Mia, and she hurried to Frisco's door. And laughed out loud. "You got it," she said. "The couch. Dear Lord, it's so…"

"Pink?" Frisco volunteered, amusement and chagrin glinting in his eyes as he followed her inside.

Tasha was sitting in the middle of the couch, her ankles delicately crossed—the perfect Russian princess, despite the fact that her hair was tangled and her face dirty and tear streaked.

Harvard started packing up the array of equipment, and Thomas moved to help him.

"This stuff is so cool," Mia heard Thomas tell Harvard. "What do I have to do to become one of you guys?"

"Well, you start by joining the Navy," Harvard said. "And you work your butt off for about three years, and maybe, just maybe, then you'll be accepted into the BUD/S training."

"Hey," Frisco said to Natasha. "Don't I get a hug? Or any thanks?"

Tasha looked at him haughtily. "Russian princesses *don't* say thank you or give hugs."

"Wanna bet?" He sat down on the couch next to the little girl and pulled her into his arms.

She giggled and threw her arms around his neck. "Thank you, thank you, thank you, thank you, thank you—"

Frisco laughed. Mia loved the sound of his laughter. "Enough already," he said. "Go wash your face and get ready for bed."

Tash stood up, casting a look of longing back at the sofa.

"Don't worry," Frisco told her. "It'll be here in the morning."

"You bet it will," Harvard interjected. "And the morning after that, and the morning after *that...*"

"I don't know," Mia said. "It's starting to grow on me." She held out her hand to Tasha. "Come on. I'll help you."

Frisco watched them disappear into the bathroom. Tasha was dragging, clearly exhausted. It wouldn't be long before she was sound asleep. He turned back to Harvard. "Need help getting that stuff together?"

Harvard grinned, reading his mind. "All done. We're out of here. Gee, sorry we can't stay."

Frisco held out his hand, and Harvard clasped it. "Thanks, man."

"It was good seeing you again, Francisco. Don't be a stranger."

"I won't be," Frisco told his friend. "In fact, I'll probably be coming over to the base in a few days to talk to Cat."

Harvard smiled, his powerful biceps flexing as he easily lifted pounds and pounds of heavy equipment. "Good. See you then."

He followed Thomas outside and closed the door behind them.

The sudden silence and stillness was deafening. Frisco started toward Tasha's room, but stopped short at the sight of Mia quietly closing the little girl's door.

"She's already asleep," she told him. "She was exhausted."

Mia looked exhausted, too. Maybe this wasn't a good time to talk. Maybe she just wanted to go home.

"Do you want a cup of tea?" Frisco asked, suddenly horribly uncertain.

She took a step toward him. "All I want right now is for you to hold me," she said quietly.

Frisco carefully leaned his crutches against the wall and slowly drew her into his arms. She was trembling as she slipped her arms around his waist. He pulled her closer, held her tighter and she rested her head against his chest and sighed.

"Did you really ask the Alpha Squad for help?" she asked.

"Is that so hard to believe?"

Mia lifted her head. "Yes."

He laughed. And kissed her. She tasted so sweet, her lips were so soft. He'd been crazy to think he could ever give her up.

"Were you really coming back to the cabin?" he asked her.

She nodded.

"Why? You said damn near all that there was to say pretty concisely. Your vision of the way my future might've been was pretty accurate—although I'm willing to bet you didn't picture me drinking myself to death on a pink couch."

"The way your future might've been…?"

There was such hope in her eyes, Frisco had to smile. "That's not my future, Mia," he told her. "That was my past. It was my father who drank himself into oblivion every night in front of the TV set. But I'm not my old man. I'm a SEAL. You were right. I'm still a SEAL. And it's only my knee that got busted, not my spirit."

"Oh, Alan…."

"Yeah, it hurts to know I'm not going to go on the active-duty list, but that's the hand fate dealt me. I'm done wallowing," he told her. "Now I'm going to get on with my *true* future. I'm going to talk to Joe Cat about that instructor position. And I've got Tash to think about, because Sharon's gonna have to do time on those DUI charges even if the man she hit lives…."

Mia was crying. She was crying *and* she was laughing.

"Hey," Frisco said. "Are you all right?"

"I'm great," she told him. "And so are you. You made it, Alan. You're whole again." Her eyes filled with a fresh flood of tears. "I'm so happy for you."

He was whole? Frisco wasn't quite so sure. "I'm going to look for another place to live," he told her, searching her eyes. "I figure if I sell this place, I can maybe get something a little closer to the base, maybe something on the water—something on the ground floor. Something big enough for me and Tash and maybe...you, too...?"

"Me?" she whispered.

He nodded. "Yeah, I mean, if you want to...."

"You want me to live with you...?"

"Hell, no. I want you to *marry* me."

Mia was silent. Her eyes were wide and her lips slightly parted. She didn't say a word, she just stared at him.

Frisco shifted his weight nervously. "I know you're probably speechless with joy at the thought of spending the rest of your life with a man who owns a pink couch and—"

"Do you love me?"

Frisco could see from her eyes that she honestly didn't know. How could she not know? Well, he realized, because for starters, he'd never actually said the words....

"You know, up at the cabin, when I said all those horrible things...?"

Mia nodded.

"What I *really* meant to say was that I'd fallen absolutely in love with you, and that I was terrified—both of what I was feeling, and of the thought of you ruining the rest of your life by spending it with me."

She was indignant. "How could you have thought that?"

He smiled. "I still think it—I just figure I'll work really hard to keep you happy and smiling, and you won't even notice. You also won't notice that when we vote, we cancel each other out."

"Democracy in action," Mia said.

"And maybe, someday—if you want—we could add 'making babies' to that list you started on my refrigerator," he told her. "What do you say?"

"Yes," Mia told him, emotion making her voice tremble. "I say oh, yes."

Frisco kissed her.

And he was whole.

* * * * *

EVERYDAY,
AVERAGE JONES

* * *

For my big sister,
Carolee Brockmann.
And for my mom,
Lee Brockmann,
who likes even the ones
that never sell.

ACKNOWLEDGMENTS

Thanks to Candace Irvin, who helped clear up
a great deal of confusion about rank and pay grade
and U.S. Navy life in general.

My eternal thanks to my tall, dark and dangerously
funny friend Eric Ruben, who called me up one day
and said, "Hey, Suz, I just read a great article about
Navy SEALs. You should check it out."
(I did, and the rest, as they say, is history.)

Thanks also to the EAJ Project volunteers from the Team
Ten list (http://groups.yahoo.com/group/teamten/)
for their proofreading skills: Group Captain
Rebecca Chappell, Jolene Birum, Joan Detzner,
Nancy Fecca, Ginny Ann Jakob, Annie Lewis,
Leah Long, Gail Reddin, Vivian L. Weaver and
Deborah Wooley.

Special thanks to the Frisco's Kid Project volunteers,
who got left out of the acknowledgments for that book:
cocaptains Rebecca Chappell and Agnes Brach,
Miriam Caraway, Maureen Cleator,
Nicole Ione Cottles, Anne Dierkes, Melody Jacobson,
Leah Long, Kelly Ludwig, Nadine Mayhew
and Lauri Uzee. Hooyah, gang! Thanks so much
to all of you for helping out.

Thanks to the real teams of SEALs, and to all the
courageous men and women in the U.S. military who
sacrifice so much to keep America the land of the free
and the home of the brave. And last but not least,
a heartfelt thank-you to the wives, husbands,
children and families of these real-life military heroes
and heroines. Your sacrifice is deeply appreciated!

Any mistakes I've made or liberties I've taken
in writing this book are completely my own.

CHAPTER ONE

IT WAS EXTREMELY likely that she was going to die.

And with every hour that passed, her chance of making it out of this godforsaken country any way other than inside a body bag was slipping from slim to none.

Melody Evans sat quietly in the corner of the little windowless office that had become her prison, writing what she hoped would not be her final words in a letter to her sister.

Dear Brittany, I'm scared to death of dying....

She was terrified of the finality of a single bullet to the head. But she was even more afraid of the other sort of death that possibly awaited her. She'd heard of the kinds of torture that were far too prevalent in this part of the world. Torture, and other archaic, monstrous practices. God help her if they found out she was a woman....

Melody felt her pulse kick into overdrive, and she took slow, deep breaths, trying to calm herself.

Remember the time you took me sledding up at the apple orchards? Remember how you got on the sled behind me, and told me in that supertheatrical voice you sometimes used that we were either going to steer a straight course down the hill through the rows of trees— or die trying?

Her older sister had always been the adventurous one. Yet it was Brittany who was still at home in Appleton, living in the same four-story Godzilla of a Victorian house that they'd grown up in. And it was Melody who, in a moment of sheer insanity, had accepted the job of administrative assistant to the American ambassador and had moved overseas to a country she hadn't even known existed until six months ago.

I remember thinking as we plunged down the hill—God, I couldn't have been more than six years old, but I remember thinking—at least we'll die together.

I wish to God I didn't feel so alone....

"You don't really think they're going to let you *send* that, do you?" Kurt Matthews's acerbic voice dripped scorn.

"No, I don't." Melody answered him without even looking up. She knew she was writing this letter not for Brittany, but for herself. Memories. She was writing down some childhood memories, trying to give herself a sense of that peace and happiness she'd known once upon a time. She was writing about the way she'd always tried so desperately to keep up with a sister nearly nine years older than she was. She skipped over the sibling infighting and petty arguments, choosing to remember only Britt's patience and kindness.

Britt always used to make such a big deal over Melody's birthday. This year, even though Mel was thousands of miles from the New England charm of their hometown in Massachusetts, Britt had sent a huge box of birthday surprises. She'd taken care to send it far enough in advance, and Melody had received it four days ago—more than a week before her twenty-fifth birthday.

She was glad now that she hadn't followed Britt's written orders and instead had opened the pile of presents in advance of the so-called special day. Britt had sent five new pairs of warm socks, a thick woolen sweater and some new athletic shoes. Those were the practical gifts.

The fun gifts included the newest Garth Brooks CD, Tami Hoag's latest romantic thriller, a jar of real peanut butter and two videotapes on which Brittany had recorded the past three months' episodes of *ER*. It was America-in-a-box, and Melody had both laughed and cried at her older sister's thoughtfulness. It was the best birthday present she'd ever received.

Except now it looked as if she wouldn't live to see those episodes of *ER*. Or her twenty-fifth birthday.

Kurt Matthews was ignoring her again. He'd gone back to his asinine discussion with Chris Sterling. They were trying to figure out just how much CNN would pay them for the exclusive rights to their story after the deal between the terrorists and the U.S. government was made and they were released.

Matthews, the fool, actually had the gall to say that he hoped the talks weren't going too smoothly. He seemed to think that the monetary value of their story would increase with the length of their ordeal. And so far, they'd only been held for two days.

He—or Sterling, either, for that matter—didn't have a clue as to the seriousness of this situation.

Melody, on the other hand, had done research on this particular terrorist group who had overthrown the entire government in an unexpected coup early Wednesday morning. They'd taken the American embassy by storm shortly after that. They were terrorists, and the U.S. didn't negotiate with terrorists. Right now, they were only talking. But if the talking didn't end, and end soon, this group of zealots was not likely to continue to show their three civilian hostages the same amount of respect and creature comfort they had to date. Provided, of course, that one could call being locked in a tiny, nearly airless office with two idiots, irregular deliveries of food and water and a washroom facility that no longer worked "comfortable."

Matthews and Sterling both seemed to think they were being held under rather dire conditions.

But Melody knew better.

She closed her eyes, trying to force away the image of the cold dankness of an underground cell. When she'd left Appleton to take this job at the embassy, she'd had no idea that the desert could be so cold during the winter months. It was March now—early spring—and it could still be chilly at night.

She focused instead on her feet. They were warm, clad in a pair of the socks and the cross trainers Brittany had sent. They'd be taken from her—both shoes and socks— before she was thrown into that dark cell.

Lord, she had to stop thinking like that. It wasn't going to do her a bit of good.

Still, the image of the prison cell was better than the other picture her overactive imagination cooked up: three American infidels, dead at the hands of their captors.

COWBOY WATCHED THE back of the American embassy through high-powered binoculars. The place was jumping with tangos, arriving and leaving at apparently unscheduled times.

"Cat," he said almost silently into his lip microphone.

Capt. Joe Catalanotto, commander of SEAL Team Ten's Alpha Squad, was positioned on the other side of the building. He was cooling his heels with the five other members of the team, having set up temporary camp in an abandoned apartment. The owner of the unit was no doubt some smart son of a bitch who had grabbed his TV and run, realizing the obvious negatives in owning real estate so close to a building that could go up in flames at any moment.

For Alpha Squad's purposes, the apartment was perfect. The master-bedroom window had a nifty view of the front of the embassy. With one of the other SEALs seated in an easy chair in front of that window, and with Cowboy positioned somewhat less comfortably on a rooftop overlooking the back, they could track the tangos'—SEAL slang for terrorists—every move.

"Yeah, Jones." Cat's flat New York accent came in loud and clear over the headphones Ensign Harlan Jones, otherwise known as Cowboy, was wearing.

Cowboy said only one word. "Chaos." He had made himself invisible on the roof, but he was well aware that the windows were opened on the floor directly below him, so when he spoke, he was as concise and as quiet as possible. He kept his binoculars trained on the building, moving from one broken window to the next. He could see movement inside, shadowy figures. The place was huge—one of those old mothers of a building, built during the middle of the previous century. He didn't doubt for a moment that the hostages were secured in one of the inner chambers.

"Copy that," Catalanotto said, a trace of amusement in his voice. "We see it from this side, too. Whoever these clowns are, they're amateurs. We'll go in tonight. At oh-dark-hundred."

Cowboy had to risk a full sentence. "I recommend we move now." He could hear Cat's surprise in the silence that grew longer and longer.

"Jones, the sun'll be going down in less than three hours," the captain finally said. The SEALs worked best at night. They could move almost invisibly under the cover of darkness.

Cowboy switched the powerful lenses to the infrared setting and took another quick scan of the building. "We should go now."

"What do you see that I don't see, kid?" Joe Cat's question was made without even a trace of sarcasm. Yeah, Cat had a wagonload of experience that Cowboy couldn't begin to compete with. And yeah, Cat had recently gotten a pay raise to O-6—captain—while Cowboy was a measly O-1, an ensign. But Captain Joe Catalanotto was the kind of leader who took note of his team's individual strengths and used each man to his full ability. And sometimes even beyond.

Every man on the team could see through walls, provided they had the right equipment. But no one could take the information that equipment provided and interpret it the way Cowboy could. And Cat knew that.

"At least fifty T's inside."

"Yeah, that's what Bobby tells me, too." Cat paused. "What's the big deal?"

"The pattern of movement."

Cowboy heard Cat take over Bobby's place at the bedroom window. There was silence, and then Cat swore. "They're making room for something." He swore again. "Or some*one*."

Cowboy clicked once into his lip mike—an affirmative. That's what he thought, too.

"They're clearing out the entire east side of the building," Joe Cat continued, now able to see what Cowboy saw. "How many more tangos are they expecting?"

It was a rhetorical question, but Cowboy answered it anyway. "Two hundred?"

Cat swore again and Cowboy knew what he was thinking. Fifty T's were manageable—particularly when they were of the Three Stooges variety, like the ones he'd been watching going in and out of the embassy all day long. But two hundred and fifty against seven SEALs... Those odds were a little skewed. Not to mention the fact that the SEALs didn't know if any of the soon-to-be-arriving tangos were real soldiers, able to tell the difference between their AK-47s and their elbows.

"Get ready to move," he heard Cat tell the rest of Alpha Squad.

"Cat."

"Yeah, Jones?"

"Three heat spots haven't moved much all day."

Catalanotto laughed. "Are you telling me you think you've located our hostages?"

Cowboy clicked once into his lip mike.

Christopher Sterling, Kurt Matthews and Melody Evans. Cowboy had been carrying those names inside his head ever since Alpha Squad was first briefed on this mission in the plane that took them to their insertion point—a high-altitude, low-opening parachute jump from high above the desert just outside the terrorist-controlled city.

He'd seen the hostages' pictures, too.

All of the men in Alpha Squad had held on to the picture of Melody Evans for a little bit longer than necessary. She couldn't have been more than twenty-two, twenty-three at most—hardly more than a kid. In the photo, she was dressed in blue jeans and a plain T-shirt that didn't show off her female figure but didn't quite manage to hide it, either. She was blue-eyed with wavy blond hair that tumbled down her back and a country-fresh, slightly shy smile and sweet face that reminded each and every one of them of their little sisters—even those of 'em like Cowboy who didn't *have* a little sister.

And Cowboy knew they were all thinking the same

thing. As they were sitting there on that plane, waiting to reach their destination, that girl was at the mercy of a group of terrorists who weren't known for their humanitarian treatment of hostages. In fact, the opposite was true. This group's record of torture and abuse was well documented, as was their intense hatred of all things American.

He hated to think what they might do—had already done—to this young woman who could've been the poster model for the All-American Girl. But all day long, he'd kept a careful eye on the three heat sources he suspected were the hostages. And all day long, none of them had been moved.

"Fourth floor, interior room," he said quietly into his mike. "Northwest corner."

"I don't suppose in your free time you found us a way into the embassy?" Cat asked.

"Minimal movement on the top floor," Cowboy reported. Those windows were broken, too. "Roof to windows—piece a cake."

"And gettin' to the roof?" The south-of-the-Mason-Dixon-line voice that spoke over his headphones was that of Lt. Blue McCoy, Alpha Squad's point man and Joe Cat's second in command.

"Just a stroll from where I'm at. Connecting roofs. Route's clear—I've already checked."

"Why the hell did I bother bringing along the rest of you guys?" Cat asked. Cowboy could hear the older man's smile in his voice. "Good job, kid."

"Only kind I do," Cowboy drawled.

"That's what I really love about you, Junior." Senior Chief Daryl Becker, also known as Harvard, spoke up, his deep voice dry with humor. "Your humility. It's rare to find such a trait in one so young."

"Permission to move?" Cowboy asked.

"Negative, Jones," Cat replied. "Wait for Harvard. Go in as a team."

Cowboy clicked an affirmative, keeping his infrared glasses glued to the embassy.

It wouldn't be long now until they went inside and got Melody Evans and the others out.

IT HAPPENED SO quickly, Melody wasn't sure where they came from or who they were.

One moment she was sitting in the corner, writing in her notebook, and the next she was lying on her stomach on the linoleum, having been thrown there none too gently by one of the robed men who'd appeared out of thin air.

She felt the barrel of a gun jammed into her throat, just under her jaw, as she tried to make sense of the voices.

"Silence!" she was ordered in more languages than she could keep track of. "Keep your mouths shut or we'll shut 'em for you!"

"Dammit," she heard someone say in very plain English, "the girl's not here. Cat, we've got three pieces of luggage, but none of them's female."

"If none of them's female, one of 'em's a tango. Search 'em and do it right."

English. Yes. They were definitely speaking American English. Still, with that gun in her neck, she didn't dare lift her head to look up at them.

"Lucky, Bobby and Wes," another voice commanded, "search the rest of this floor. Find that girl."

Melody felt rough hands on her body, moving across her shoulders and down her back, sweeping down her legs. She was being searched for a weapon, she realized. One of the hands reached up expertly to feel between her legs as another pushed its way up underneath her arm and around to her chest. She knew the exact instant that each hand encountered either more or less than their owner expected, because whomever those hands belonged to, he froze.

Then he flipped her onto her back, and Melody found herself staring up into the greenest eyes she'd ever seen in her life.

He pulled off her hat and touched her hair, then looked at the black shoe polish that had come off on his fingers. He looked down at the mustache she had made from some of her own cut hair darkened with mascara and glued underneath her nose. He smiled as he looked back into her eyes. It was a smile that lit his entire face and made his eyes sparkle.

"Melody." It was more of a statement than a question.

But she nodded anyway.

"Ma'am, I'm Ensign Harlan Jones of the U.S. Navy SEALs," he said in a soft Western drawl. "We've come to take you home." He looked up then, speaking to one of the other hooded men. "Cat, belay that last order. We've found our female hostage, safe and sound."

"ABSOLUTELY NOT." Kurt Matthews folded his arms across his narrow chest. "They said if any of us attempted an escape, they'd kill us all. They said if we did what we were told, and if the government complied with their modest list of demands, we'd be set free. I say we stay right here."

"There's no way we can get out of here undetected," the other man—Sterling—pointed out. "There's too many of them. They'll stop us and then they'll kill us. I think it's safer to do what they said."

Cowboy shifted impatiently in his seat. Negotiating with damn fools was not one of his strengths, yet Cat had left him here to try to talk some sense into these boneheads as the rest of the squad went to carry out the rest of their mission—the destruction of several extremely confidential files in the ambassador's personal office.

He knew that if worse came to worst, they'd knock 'em over the head if they had to and carry 'em out. But it would be a lot easier to move through the city, working their way toward the extraction point, *without* having to carry three unconscious bodies over their shoulders.

Not for the first time in the past twenty minutes, he found himself staring at Melody Evans.

He had to smile. And admire the hell out of her. There was no doubt in his mind that her quick thinking had saved her own life. She'd disguised herself as a man. She'd cut her long hair short, blackened it with shoe polish to hide its golden color and glued some kind of stragglylooking mustache thing onto her face.

Even with her hair shorn so close to her head and that ridiculous piece of hair stuck underneath her nose, she was pretty. He couldn't imagine that he'd looked at her when they'd first come in and not seen right away that she was a woman. But he hadn't. He'd thrown her onto the floor, for God's sake. And then he'd groped her, searching for hidden weapons.

She glanced at him as if feeling his eyes on her, and he felt it again—that flash of sexual awareness that jolted to life between them. He held her gaze, boldly letting his smile grow wider, letting her take a good long look at this mutual attraction that hovered in the very air around them.

That photo he'd seen had made her look like someone's little sister. But meeting Melody Evans face-to-face made him well aware—and grateful—of the fact that while she may indeed have been someone's little sister, she sure as hell wasn't *his*.

With the exception of the silly mustache, she possessed damn near everything he liked most in a woman. She was tall and slender with a body that he knew firsthand was trim in some places, soft in others. Her face was pretty despite her lack of makeup and the smudges of shoe polish that decorated her forehead and cheeks and hid the shining gold of her hair. She had a small nose, a mouth that looked incredibly soft and crystal blue eyes surrounded by thick, dark lashes. Clear intelligence shone in those eyes. Tears had shown there, too, moments after he'd introduced himself to her. But despite that, she hadn't let herself cry, much to Cowboy's relief.

As he watched, she rubbed her left shoulder, and he knew whatever pain she was experiencing was his fault. That shoulder was where she'd landed when he'd first come in and thrown her onto the floor.

"I'm sorry we had to treat you so roughly, ma'am," he said. "But in our line of work, it doesn't pay to be polite and ask questions first."

"Of course," she murmured, glancing almost shyly at him. "I understand—"

Matthews drowned her out. "Well, *I* don't understand, and you can be damned sure your superiors are going to hear about this little incident. Holding the ambassador's staff at gunpoint and subjecting us to a body search!"

Cowboy didn't get a chance to defend Alpha Squad's actions because Melody Evans stood up and defended them for him. "These men came into this embassy look-ing for *us*," she said hotly. "They're risking their lives to be here right now—the same way they risked their lives when they opened that locked door and came into this room. They had no idea who or what was on the other side of that door!"

"Surely they could've seen just from looking that we were Americans," Matthews countered.

"Surely there's never been a terrorist who dresses up as a hostage and hides with his captives, waiting to blow away any rescuers," she lit into him. "And of course there's *never* been an American who's been brainwashed or coerced or bribed into defecting to the other side!"

For the first time since they'd let the hostages up off the floor, Kurt Matthews was silent.

Cowboy had to smile. He liked smart women—women who didn't suffer fools. And this one was more than smart. She was strong and clearly courageous, too—able to stand up and defend that which she believed in. He admired the swift action she took to disguise herself in the face of sheer disaster. Surely a woman with that much fight in her could be made to see how important it was that she leave here—and leave soon.

"Melody," he said, then corrected himself. "Miss Evans, it's now or never, ma'am. These tangos aren't gonna let you go, and you know that as well as I do. If you let these gee—*gentlemen,* talk you into staying here, you're all as good as dead. Forgive me for being so blunt, ma'am, but that's the God's truth. It would make *our* job a whole hell of a lot easier if you would simply trust us to get you safely home."

"But Chris is right. There's only a few of you and so many of them."

Count on a woman to play devil's advocate and switch sides just when he was convinced he had a solid ally. Still, when she fixed those baby blues on him, his exasperation dissolved into sheer admiration. It was true, the odds didn't appear to be in their favor. She had every right to be concerned, and it was up to him to convince her otherwise.

"We're Navy SEALs, ma'am," he said quietly, hoping she'd heard of the special forces teams, hoping word of SEAL Team Ten's counterterrorist training had somehow made its way to whatever small town she'd grown up in.

But his words didn't spark any recognition in her eyes.

The taller man, Chris Sterling, shook his head. "You say that as if it's some kind of answer, but I don't know what that means."

"It means they think they're supermen," Matthews said scornfully.

"Will you *please* let Ensign Jones talk?" Melody said sharply, and Matthews fell silent.

"It means that even with only seven of us and fifty of them, the odds are still on *our* side," Cowboy told them, once again capturing Melody's gaze and holding it tightly. *She* was the one who was going to talk these other idiots into seeing reason. "It also means that the U.S. government has totally given up all hope of getting you out through negotiation or settlement. They don't send us in, Melody," he said, talking directly to her, "unless they're desperate."

She was scared. He could see that in her eyes. He didn't blame her. There was a part of him that was scared, too. Over the past few years, he'd learned to use that fear to hone his senses, to keep him alert and giving a full hundred and fifty percent or more. He'd also learned to hide his fear. Confidence bred confidence, and he tried to give her a solid dose of that feeling as he smiled reassuringly into Melody's ocean blue eyes.

"Trust us," he said again. "Trust *me*."

She turned back to the other hostages. "I believe him," she said bluntly. "I'm going."

Matthews stood up, indignant, menacing. "You stupid bitch. Don't you get it? If you try to escape, they'll kill *us!*"

"Then you better come, too," Melody said coolly.

"No!" His voice got louder. "No, we're staying here, right, Sterling? *All* of us. These steroid-pumped sea lions or whatever they call themselves can go ahead and get themselves killed, but we're staying right here." His voice got even louder. "In fact, since Mr. Jones seems to want so badly to die, I can give him a hand and shout for the guards to come and turn him into hamburger meat with their machine guns *right now!*"

MELODY DIDN'T SEE the broad-shouldered SEAL move, let alone raise his hand, but before she could blink, he was rather gently lowering Kurt Matthews onto the floor.

"By the way, it's *Ensign* Jones," he said to the now unconscious man. He flexed the fingers of the hand he'd used to put Matthews into that state and flashed an apologetic smile in Melody's direction before he looked up at Chris Sterling. "How about you?" he asked the other man as he straightened up to his full height. "You want to walk out of this embassy, or do you want to get carried out like your buddy here?"

"Walk," Sterling managed to say, staring down at Matthews. "I'll walk, thanks."

The door swung silently open, and a big black man—taller even than Ensign Harlan Jones—stepped into the room. Harvard. He was the one Ensign Jones had called Harvard. "You ready, Junior?"

"Zeppo, Harpo and Groucho here need robes," Jones

told the other man, sending a quick wink in her direction. "And sandals."

Groucho. She fingered her false mustache. He'd gestured toward Matthews when he'd said Harpo. Harpo. The silent Marx brother. Melody laughed aloud. Chris Sterling looked at her as if she was crazy to laugh when at any moment they could be killed, but Jones gave her another wink and a smile.

Kevin Costner. *That's* who Jones looked like. He looked like a bigger, beefier, much younger version of the Hollywood heartthrob. And she had no doubt he knew it, too. That smile could melt hearts as well as bolster failing courage.

"Melody, I'm afraid I'm going to have to ask you to take off those kicks, hon."

Hon. Honey. Well, she'd certainly gone from being called Miss Evans and ma'am to hon awfully fast. And as far as taking off her shoes... "These are new," she told him. "And warm. I'd rather wear them, if you don't mind."

"I *do* mind," Jones told her apologetically. "Check out the bottoms of my sandals, then look at the bottoms of those things you're wearing."

She did. The brand name of the athletic shoes was emblazoned across the bottoms, worked into the grooved and patterned-to-grip soles of the sneakers.

"Everyone else in this city—and maybe even in this entire country—has sandals like mine," he continued, lifting his foot to show her the smooth leather sole. "If you go out wearing *those,* every time you take a step you'll leave a unique footprint. It will be the equivalent of signing your name in the dirt. And *that* will be like leaving a sign pointing in our direction that says Escaped American Hostages, Thisaway."

Melody took off the sneakers.

"That's my girl," he said, approval and something else warming his voice. He squeezed her shoulder briefly as he turned his attention to several more men who were coming silently into the room.

That's my girl.

His soft words should have made her object and object strenuously. Melody *wasn't* a girl. Jones couldn't have been more than a few years older than she was at most, and he would never have let anyone call him a *boy.*

And yet there was something oddly comforting about his words. She *was* his girl. Her life was totally in his hands. With his help, she could get out of here and return to the safety of Appleton. Without his help, she was as good as dead.

Still, she couldn't help but notice that little bit of something else that she'd heard in his voice. That subtle tone that told her he was a man and she was a woman and he wasn't ever going to forget that.

She watched Ensign Jones as he spoke quietly to the other SEALs. He certainly was a piece of work. She couldn't believe those smiles he kept giving her. Here they were, deep inside an embassy overrun with terrorists, and Jones had been firing off his very best bedroom smile in her direction. He was as relaxed as a man leaning against a bar, offering to buy her a drink, asking for her sign. But this wasn't a bar, this was a war zone. Still, Jones looked and acted as if he were having fun.

Who *was* this guy? He was either very stupid, very brave or totally insane.

Totally insane, she decided, watching him as he took a bundle of robes from another of the SEALs. Underneath his own robe, he wore some kind of dark-colored vest that appeared to be loaded with all kinds of gear and weaponry. He had what looked to be a lightweight, nearly invisible set of headphones on his head, as well as an attached microphone similar to, but smaller than, something a telephone operator would wear. It stretched out on a hinged piece of wire or plastic and could be maneuvered directly in front of his mouth when he needed to talk.

What kind of man did this kind of thing for a living?

Jones tossed one of the robes to Chris Sterling and the other to her, along with another of those smiles.

It was hard to keep from smiling back.

As Melody watched, Jones spoke to someone outside the room through his little mike and headphones as he efficiently and quickly dressed the still-unconscious Kurt Matthews in the third robe.

He was talking about sandals. Sandals, apparently, were a bit harder to procure than the robes had been. At least it was difficult to find something in her size.

"She's going to have to go in her socks," one of the other SEALs finally concluded.

"It's cold out there," Jones protested.

"I don't care," Melody said. "I just want to *go*."

"Let's do it," the black man said. "Let's move, Cowboy. Cat controls the back door. Now's the time."

Jones turned to Melody. "Put the kicks back on. Quickly."

"But you said—"

He pushed her down into a chair and began putting the sneakers on her feet himself. "Lucky, got your duct tape?"

"You know I do."

"Tape the bottom of her foot," Jones ordered, thrusting the tied shoe on Melody's right foot toward the other SEAL.

The SEAL called Lucky got to work, and Jones himself began taping the bottom of her left sneaker, using a roll of silvery gray duct tape he, too, had been carrying in his vest.

They were covering the tread, making sure that when she walked, she wouldn't leave an unusual footprint behind.

"It might be slippery." Jones was kneeling in front of her, her foot on his thigh, as if he were some kind of fantasy shoe salesman. "And we're going to have to make sure that if you wear it through, we tape 'em up again, okay?"

Melody nodded.

He smiled. "Good girl." He moved his mike so that it was in front of his mouth. "Okay, Cat, we're all set. We're coming out." He turned to Melody. "You're with me, okay? Whatever happens, stick close to me. Do exactly what I say, no questions. Just do it, understand?"

Melody nodded again. She was his girl. She couldn't think of anything else she wanted to be right at that particular moment in time.

"If shots are fired," he continued, and for once his face was serious, his eyes lit with intensity rather than amusement or attraction, "get behind me. I will protect you. In return, I need two hundred percent of your trust."

Melody couldn't tear her gaze away from those neon green eyes. She nodded.

Maybe this man was insane, but he was also incredibly brave. He'd come into this terrorist stronghold to help rescue her. He'd been safe and sound, but he chose to give that up and risk his life for hers. *I will protect you.*

As bold and as confident as his words were, the truth was that the next few minutes could see them both killed.

"In case something goes wrong," she began, intending to thank him. God knows if something went wrong, she wouldn't have the chance to thank him. She knew without a doubt that he would die first—taking bullets meant for her.

But he didn't let her finish. "Nothing's gonna go wrong. Joe Cat's got the door. Getting out of this latrine's gonna be a piece of cake. Trust me, Mel."

He took her hand, pulling her with him out into the hall.

Piece of cake.

She almost believed him.

CHAPTER TWO

SOMETHING WAS WRONG.

Melody could tell from the seriousness with which
the man Ensign Jones called Joe Cat was talking to the
shorter, blond-haired man named Blue.

They'd made it safely out of the embassy just as Jones
had promised. They'd come farther than she'd ever
thought possible. They'd traveled across and outside the
limits of the city, up into the hills, moving quietly through
the darkness.

The danger had not ended when they left the embassy.
The city was under military rule, and there was a predusk
curfew that was strictly enforced. If they were spotted
by one of the squads patrolling the streets, they would
be shot without any questions.

More than once, they'd had to hide as a patrol came
within inches of them.

"Close your eyes," Jones had murmured into her ear
as the soldiers had approached. "Don't look at them. And
don't hold your breath. Breathe shallowly, softly. They
won't see us, I promise."

Melody's shoulder had been pressed against him, and
she leaned even closer, taking strength from his solid
warmth. And from the thought that if she died, at least
she wouldn't die alone.

After that, each time they had to hide, he'd slipped
one arm around her, keeping his other arm free for his

deadly-looking assault weapon. Melody had given up her pretense of being strong and independent. She'd let him hold her—let him be big and strong, let herself take comfort from his strength. She'd tucked her head underneath his chin, closing her eyes and listening to the steady beating of his heart kick into overdrive, breathing softly and shallowly as he'd told her.

So far they hadn't been caught.

Jones came and sat next to her now.

"We've got a problem," he said bluntly, not trying to hide the truth from her.

Her trust in him went up to just over a thousand percent. He wasn't trying to pretend everything was hunky-dory when it so obviously was not.

"The chopper's a no-show," he told her. In the moonlight, his expression was serious, his mouth grim instead of curling up into his usual smile. "They're ten minutes late. We're getting ready to split up. We can't keep moving together. Come daybreak, a group this size is going to get noticed. And it won't be long before the tangos realize you and Pete and Linc got away."

Pete and Linc. The men who made up two-thirds of the Mod Squad. Even at his most serious, this man couldn't resist making a joke of sorts. "Ten minutes isn't that long," Melody countered. "Shouldn't we just wait?"

Jones shook his head. "*One* minute isn't that long. Ten is too long. The chopper's not coming, Mel. Something went wrong, and our waiting here is putting us in danger." He lifted one of her feet, looking at the bottom of her sneaker. "How's that duct tape holding up?"

"It's starting to wear through," Melody admitted.

He handed her his roll of tape. "Can you put on another layer yourself? We need to be ready to leave here in about three minutes, but right now I want to put in my two cents about our next move."

Melody took the tape from him as he stood up.

Split up. He'd said they were going to split up. Melody felt a sudden rush of panic. "Jones," she called softly, and he paused, looking back at her. "Please. I want to stay with you."

She couldn't see his eyes in the shadows, but she saw him nod.

DAWN WAS BEGINNING to light the eastern sky before they stopped moving.

Harvard had the point and he'd traveled twice as far as Cowboy and Melody had during the night. He'd continuously moved ahead, silently scouting out the best route to take, then doubling back to report what he'd seen.

Cowboy was glad to have H. on his team. Moving through hostile territory would've been tricky enough for two SEALs on their own. Add a female civilian into the equation, and that mission got significantly harder. Getting across the border was going to be a real pain in the butt.

He glanced at Melody. The small smile she gave him both worried and elated him.

It was obvious she trusted him. He hadn't been the only one in Alpha Squad to hear her say that she wanted to stay with him. Under normal circumstances, such an overheard remark would've been subject to merciless teasing. Cowboy Jones, notorious lady-killer, strikes again.

But every one of those other men knew that the lady's words only verified that Cowboy had done his job and done it well. It wasn't easy to gain the complete confidence and trust of a former hostage. Kurt Matthews, for instance, hadn't bonded to Cowboy in quite the same way.

Still, the girl trusted him. He saw it in her eyes every time he looked at her. He knew without a doubt that in the course of a few short hours, he had become the most important person in her world.

He'd spent quite a bit of time studying the psychology of hostages and the emotions and fears involved in a rescue mission such as this one. He'd spent twice as much time learning what to expect from himself—his own behavior and psychological reactions when faced with life-and-death situations.

And what worried him most about Melody Evans's smile was not the fact that he'd become the center of her universe. No, what worried him most was that she had somehow managed to become the center of *his.*

He knew it could happen. The danger added to the tremendous responsibility of preserving another's life and multiplied by a very natural and honest sexual attraction sometimes resulted in an emotional response above and beyond the norm.

He'd first been aware of his inappropriate response to this girl when they'd hidden from the city's patrols. She'd huddled close and he'd put his arm around her—nothing wrong with that. She'd rested her head against his chest—and there was nothing wrong with her drawing strength and support from him that way, either.

But then, beneath the pungent odor of the shoe polish she wore on her hair, beneath the more subtle yet no less sharp odor of fear that surrounded all of the former hostages, he'd smelled something sweet, something distinctly female.

And then, right then, when the curfew patrol was inches away from them, when they were nanoseconds away from being discovered and killed, he'd felt Melody relax. The tension among the other hostages and the SEALs could've been cut with a knife, but Melody had damn near fallen asleep in his arms.

He knew in that instant that she trusted him more completely than anyone had ever trusted him before. Her faith in him was strong enough to conquer her fear. Her life was in his hands, and she'd placed it there willingly, trusting that if she died it would be because there was no other way out.

And just like that, as they hid behind trash in one of the city's back alleys, Cowboy's entire life changed. He felt his pulse rate accelerate out of control, felt his body respond to her nearness.

He might've been able to dismiss it as mere sexual desire except that it happened over and over again—even when she wasn't touching him. All this girl had to do was smile at him, and he got that same hot, possessive rush.

Cowboy knew he should have mentioned the way he was feeling to Joe Cat before they split into three smaller groups. But he didn't. He didn't want to risk Cat's pulling him away from Melody. He wanted to make damn sure she got out of this armpit of a country alive. As much as he trusted his teammates, he knew the only way he'd be certain of that was to stay close, to take care of her himself.

With Harvard's help.

As the sun climbed above the horizon, they sat for a moment in the growing warmth outside a shallow cave Harvard had found cut into a desolate outcropping of rocks.

Once they warmed up, they'd spend the daylight hours here, out of the sun and out of sight of anyone wandering the foothills. Come nightfall, they would set out again, heading steadily north.

"I'll take the first watch," Cowboy told Harvard.

Melody was sitting next to him, near the entrance to the cave, her head back, eyes closed, face lifted toward the warmth of the sun. He touched her arm lightly, ready to pass her his canteen, but she didn't move. She was exhausted, but she hadn't complained once, all night long.

"Maybe you should get her settled first," Harvard said in a low voice.

"Am I suddenly not here?" Melody asked, opening her eyes and surprising them both.

Harvard laughed, a low, rich chuckle. "Sorry," he said. "I thought you were asleep."

"Where are we heading?" she asked. Her eyes were nearly the same shade of blue as the cloudless sky. "Up to the coast?" They flashed in Cowboy's direction as he handed her the canteen.

As their fingers touched, he felt an instant connection, a flood of electricity. And he knew damn well she felt it, too.

She was covered with dust from the road, smeared with shoe polish and utterly bone weary. Yet at the same time, she managed to be the most beautiful woman Cowboy could ever remember seeing. Damn, he shouldn't be feeling this way. After this was over, he would have to go in for a psychological review, work with the unit shrink and try to pinpoint what it was, exactly, that he'd done wrong. Find out when it was that he'd let her get under his skin...

Harvard nodded. "We're going for the ocean." He glanced at Cowboy. They hadn't had much time to discuss their route. "I thought it would be easier to leave the country by boat."

"Or plane, Senior Chief," Cowboy interjected. "Get us home a whole hell of a lot faster."

Harvard caught and held his gaze, and Cowboy knew the older man was thinking the same thing he was. They'd both studied a map of this country during the briefing. There was a major city directly between their current position and the ocean. According to the map, that city had an airfield. Maybe instead of skirting the city, they should get close enough to check out that airfield.

"With any luck, it'll be a military base," Cowboy said aloud. "We're the last people they'll be expecting to show up there."

Harvard nodded. "The best defense is a strong offense."

"Do you two always communicate through non sequiturs?" Melody asked.

Harvard stood up. "Junior thinks we should steal a plane tonight, and crazy as it sounds, I agree. But right now I've got a combat nap scheduled." He paused before going into the cave, turning back to Melody. "You've got dibs on whatever soft ground is in there, milady," he said.

But she shook her head. "Thanks, but...I want to get warm first," she told him. She glanced at Cowboy and a faint blush spread along her cheeks as if she realized how transparent she was. No one was fooled. It was clear she wanted to be out here with her own personal hero.

Cowboy felt it again. That hot rush of emotion.

Harvard paused just inside the cave. "Don't let her fall asleep out here," he instructed Cowboy. "And make sure you get your Texan butt in the shade before too long, too.

I don't want you two pigment-challenged types unable to move come dusk because of a sunburn."

"Yes, Mother," Cowboy droned.

"And wake me in four." Harvard headed toward the back of the cave. "No more, no less."

Cowboy looked at Melody and smiled. "Hell, I thought he'd *never* leave."

She blushed again.

"You okay?" he asked, both wishing she wasn't sitting quite so far away and glad as hell for the distance between them. God help him if he actually got her into his arms when it *wasn't* a life-and-death situation.

"I wish I could wash my face," she told him.

Cowboy shook his head in apology. "We've got to save the water I've got for drinking," he told her.

"I know," she said. "I just wish it, that's all."

The sun was warming the air considerably, and Cowboy loosened his robe and even unfastened the black combat vest he wore underneath.

Her next words surprised him. "I thought we'd be dead by now."

"Tomorrow at this time, we'll be on America-friendly soil."

She shifted her legs and winced slightly, then pulled her feet closer to untie her sneakers. "You say that with such conviction."

"Have I been wrong yet?" he countered.

She looked up at him, and her eyes were so wide, Cowboy felt as if he might fall into them and drown. "No," she said.

She turned away from him then, looking down as she started to slip off her sneakers.

That was when Cowboy saw the blood on her socks. The entire backs of her socks were stained. She saw it, too, and stopped trying to take off her sneakers. She pulled her feet underneath her as if she intended to hide the blood from him.

"Are you really from Texas?" she asked.

Cowboy was shocked. She was. She was planning to not tell him that her new sneakers had rubbed her heels raw. She wasn't going to mention that her feet were *bleeding,* for God's sake. Every step she'd taken last night had to have been sheer agony, but she hadn't said a word.

"Yeah," he managed to say. "Fort Worth."

She smiled. "You're kidding. How did someone from Fort Worth end up in the navy?"

Cowboy looked her squarely in the eye. "I know that your feet are bleeding," he said bluntly. "Why the hell didn't you tell me about that, like twelve *hours* ago?" His voice came out sounding harsher, sharper than he'd intended.

And although her smile faded and her face went a shade paler, she lifted her chin and met his gaze just as steadily. "Because it wasn't important."

"I have a medical kit. I could have wrapped 'em. All you had to do was say something!"

"I didn't want to slow us down," she said quietly.

Cowboy took his medikit from his combat vest as he stood up. "Are you going to take those sneakers off, or do you want me to do it for you?"

As he knelt in front of Melody, he could see her pain reflected in her face as she silently slid her feet out of her sneakers. Her eyes welled with tears, but she fought them, blinking them back, once again refusing to cry.

Her knuckles were white, hands clasped tightly in her lap, as he pulled off one sock and then the other as gently as he could.

"Actually," he said quietly, hoping to distract her with

his words, "I didn't move to Fort Worth until I was about twelve. Before that, I lived damn near everywhere in the world. My old man's career Navy, and wherever he was stationed, that's where we lived."

She had extremely nice feet—long and slender, with straight toes. She had remnants of green polish on her toenails, as if she'd tried hastily to remove it but hadn't gotten it all off. He liked the idea of green nail polish. It was different. Intriguing.

Sexy.

Cowboy pulled his attention back to the task at hand. He rested her feet on his thigh as he opened his canteen and used some of their precious water to clean off the blood. He felt her stiffen as he touched her, and his stomach twisted as he tried his best to be gentle.

"He just made full admiral," he continued, telling her about his father. "He's stationed up in D.C. these days. But Mom still lives in Fort Worth, which just about says it all, considering that Fort Worth is about as landlocked a city as you can get."

He gave her a quick smile to offset the depressing undertones of his story. Yeah, his home life had sucked. His father had been by-the-book Navy. The old man was a perfectionist—harsh and demanding and cold. He'd run his family the same way he'd commanded his ships, which, to both his young son and his wife, left much to be desired.

"So what made *you* join the Navy?" she asked, bracing herself for the antibiotic ointment he was about to spread on her raw and broken skin.

"Actually, the old guy manipulated me into it," Cowboy told her with a grin, applying the ointment as quickly as he could. "You don't make admiral without having *some* kind of smarts, and old Harlan the first is nobody's fool."

He wiped the ointment off his hands on the bottom edge of his robe, then dug in his kit for bandages. "After I graduated from high school, my old man wanted me to go to college and then into the U.S. Navy's officer's program. I flipped him the bird and set off for my own glowing future—which I was sure I'd find on the rodeo circuit. I spent about a year doing that—during which time the old man squirmed with embarrassment. Even in retrospect, that makes it damn well worth it."

He smiled up into Melody's eyes. "He started sending me letters, telling me about the problems he was having with 'those blasted Navy SEALs.' I knew when he was much younger, before I was born, he'd gotten into the BUD/S program and went through the training to become a SEAL. But he was one of the eighty-five percent who couldn't cut it. He was flushed out of the program— he wasn't tough enough. So every time he wrote to me, I could see that he was carrying around this great big grudge against the SEAL units."

"So you joined the SEALs to tick him off," Melody guessed.

Cowboy nodded, his grin widening. "And to show him that I could do something better than him—to succeed where he'd failed." He chuckled. "The crafty old son of a bitch broke down and cried tears of joy and pride the day I got my budweiser—my SEAL pin. I was floored— I'd rarely seen the old guy smile, let alone weep. Turns out that by joining the SEALs, I'd put myself exactly where he wanted me to be. He didn't hate the SEAL units the way he'd let me believe. He admired and respected them—and he wanted me to know what it felt like to achieve my potential, to be one of 'em. Turns out dear old Dad loved me after all."

She was looking at him as if he was some kind of hero. "You're amazing," she said softly. "For you to realize all that and come to terms with him that way..."

"One of my specialties is psychology," he told her with a shrug. "It's really not that big a deal."

All he had to do was to lean forward and he could kiss those soft, sweet lips. She wouldn't object. In fact, he could tell from the sudden spark of heat in her eyes that she would welcome the sensation of his mouth on hers.

Instead, he looked away, bandaging her feet in silence. Yes, one of his specialties was psychology, and he knew exactly the kind of problems even just one kiss could cause. But maybe, just maybe, after he'd brought her to safety...

"You should get some sleep," he told her quietly.

Melody glanced toward the cave. "Can I stay here, up near the entrance?"

Near him.

Cowboy nodded. "Sure," he said quietly, moving out of the sun and back into the shade himself. He found a fairly flat, fairly comfortable rock to lean against as he stretched his legs out in front of him, his HK MP5-K held loosely in his arms.

He kept his eyes on the distant horizon as she wrapped herself in her robe and settled down, right on the ground, not far from him. He wished he had a bedroll or a blanket to give her. Hell, he wished he had dinner reservations at some fancy restaurant and the room key to some four-star hotel to give her. He wished he could fall with her back onto some soft hotel bed and...

He pushed that thought far, far away. This wasn't the time or place for such distractions.

It wasn't long before the sound of her breathing turned slow and steady. He glanced at her and his heart clenched.

In sleep, she looked barely more than seventeen, her lashes long and dark against the smoothness of her cheeks. It didn't take much to imagine what she'd look like with that black shoe polish washed out of her hair. The boyishly short cut she'd given herself to hide her femaleness only served to emphasize her slender neck and pretty face.

Cowboy knew with a grim certainty that seemed to flow through him and out into the timeless antiquity of the moonlike landscape that he was going to bring this girl back home where she belonged. Or he was going to die trying.

Melody was sleeping on her side, curled into a ball with the exception of one arm that was stretched out and reaching toward him. And as he looked closer, he saw that in her tightly clasped fist she was holding on to the very edge of his robe.

"SHOULDN'T HE BE back by now?"

Melody heard the anxiety in her voice, saw a reflection of it in the darkly patient eyes of the man Jones called Harvard.

"I'm sorry," she murmured.

"Junior's doing his job, Melody," Harvard told her calmly. "This is something he does well—you're going to have to trust him to do it and return in his own good time."

The *this* that Ensign Jones was doing was to creep undetected into a terrorist-held air base. It was only a small air base, he'd told her as if that would reassure her, with only a dozen aircraft of any type out on the field. He was going over the barbed-wire fence to make sure that the dilapidated hangars didn't hold some fancy high-tech machine that could come roaring up into the sky and shoot them down as they made their getaway.

After Jones had checked out the hangar, he was going to sneak out into the airfield and select the biggest, fastest, most powerful plane of all to use for their escape. And after he did that, he was going to meet them here.

Then all three of them would go back over the fence and roar off in a stolen plane into the coming sunrise.

After he came back. *If* he came back.

"You call him Junior," she said, desperate for *some*-thing to talk about besides Jones's whereabouts. "But that other man, Joe Cat, he called Ensign Jones *kid*. And everyone else called him Cowboy. Doesn't *any*one call him Harlan?"

Harvard smiled. His straight white teeth flashed, re-flecting a beam of moonlight that streamed in through one of the cracks in the boarded-up windows. "His mom does. But that's about it. He *hates* being called Harlan. I only call him that when I want to make him *really* mad. It's his father's name, too. His father is Admiral Harlan Jones."

"I know. He told me."

Harvard lifted his eyebrows. "No kidding. Told you about his old man. I'm surprised, but…I guess I shouldn't be—Junior's always been full of surprises." He paused. "I worked closely with the senior Jones quite a few years ago. I know the admiral quite well. I guess that's why I call his son Junior *Junior*."

"And the other men call him Cowboy because he's from Texas?"

"Legend has it he came to BUD/S wearing an enormous rodeo ring and a cowboy hat." Harvard laughed softly.

"BUD/S," Melody repeated. "That's where SEALs go for training?"

"Not necessarily where, but what," he corrected her. "It's the training program for SEAL wanna-be's. Junior walked into this particular session out in California wearing everything but a pair of spurs, and the instructors took one look at him and named him Cowboy. The nickname stuck."

Melody wished he would come back.

She closed her eyes, remembering the way Jones had gently awakened her as the sun was starting to set. He'd given her a sip of water from his canteen and some kind of high-protein energy bar from a pocket of his vest.

He'd also given her his sandals.

He must've spent most of the time he'd been on watch cutting down the soles and reworking the leather straps to fit her much smaller feet. At first she refused them, but he'd pointed out that they wouldn't fit him now anyway.

Jones was barefoot at this very moment. Barefoot and somewhere on that air base with God only knows how many terrorists—

"Where are you from, Miss Melody Evans?" Harvard's rich voice interrupted her grim thoughts.

"Massachusetts," she told him.

"Oh yeah? Me, too. Where exactly?"

"Appleton. It's west of Boston. West and a little north."

"I grew up in Hingham," Harvard told her. "South shore. My family's still there." He smiled. "Actually, there's not much of my family left. Everyone's gone off to college, with the exception of my littlest sister. And even she heads out this September."

"I don't even know your real name," Melody admitted.

"Becker," he told her. "Senior Chief Daryl Becker."

"Did you really go to Harvard?"

He nodded. "Yes, I did. How about you? Where'd you go to school?"

Melody shook her head. "This isn't working. I know you're trying to distract me, but I'm sorry, it's just not working."

Harvard's brown eyes were sympathetic. "You want me to be quiet?"

"I want Jones to come back."

Silence. It surrounded her, suffocated her, made her want to jump out of her skin.

"Please don't stop talking," she finally blurted.

"First time I worked with the junior Harlan Jones was during a hostage rescue," Harvard told her, "back, oh, I don't know, about six years ago."

Melody nearly choked. "You've been doing this sort of thing for six *years?*"

"More than that."

She gazed into his eyes searchingly, looking for an explanation. *Why?* "Risking your life for a living this way is *not* normal."

Harvard laughed. "Well, none of us ever claimed to be that."

"Are you married?" she asked. "How does your wife stand it?"

"I'm not," he told her. "But some of the guys are. Joe Cat is. And Blue McCoy."

"They're somewhere out in the countryside tonight,

hiding from the terrorists, the way we are," she realized. "Their wives must *love* that."

"Their wives don't know where they are."

Melody snorted. "Even better."

"It takes a strong man to become a SEAL," Harvard told her quietly. "And it takes an even stronger woman to love that man."

Love. Who said anything about *love?*

"Does SEAL stand for something, or is it just supposed to be cute?" she asked, trying to get the subject back to safer ground.

"It stands for Sea, Air and Land. We learn to operate effectively in all of those environments." He laughed. "Cute's not a word that comes to mind when *I* think about the SEAL units."

"Sea, air and land," she repeated. "It sounds kind of like the military equivalent of a triathlon."

Harvard's head went up and he held out a hand, motioning for her to be silent.

In a matter of an instant, he had changed from a man casually sitting in the basement entrance of a burned-out building to a warrior, every cell in his body on alert, every muscle tensed to fight. He held his gun aimed at the door, raising it slightly as the door was pushed open and...

It was Jones.

Melody forced herself not to move toward him. She forced herself to sit precisely where she was, forced herself not to say a word. But she couldn't keep her relief from showing in her eyes.

"Let's move," he said to Harvard.

There was blood on his robe—even Harvard noticed it. "Are you all right?" he asked.

Jones nodded dismissively. "I'm fine. Let's do it. Let's get the hell out of here."

Melody didn't want to think about whose blood that was on his robe. She didn't want to think about what he'd been through, what he'd had to do tonight to guarantee her safety.

There was blood on his bare feet, too.

"Are we going to do this by stealth or by force?" Harvard asked.

"By stealth," Jones answered. His smile was long gone. "Unless they see us. Then we'll use force. And we'll send 'em straight to hell."

He looked directly at her, and in the moonlight his eyes looked tired and old. "Come on, Melody. I want to take you home."

THEY WERE HALFWAY to the plane before they were spotted.

Cowboy knew it was really only a question of when—not if—they were seen. It had to happen sooner or later. There was no way they could take a plane from an airfield without *some*one noticing.

He'd just hoped they wouldn't be noticed until they were taxiing down the runway.

But nothing else had gone right tonight, starting with his surprising four terrorists in the hangar. He'd had *some* luck, though—only one of them had had an automatic weapon, and it had jammed. If it hadn't, he wouldn't be running toward the plane now. He wouldn't be doing much of anything. Instead, he was racing across the sun-cracked concrete. He was both pulling Melody Evans along and trying to shield her with his body from the bullets he knew were sure to accompany the distant cries to halt.

He'd dispatched the four men in the hangar efficiently and silently. As a SEAL, he was good at many things, and taking out the enemy was something he never shied from. But he didn't like it. He'd never liked it.

"You want to clue me in as to where we're going?" Harvard shouted.

"Twelve o'clock," Cowboy responded. And then there it was—a tiny Cessna, a mere mosquito compared to the bigger planes on the field.

Harvard's voice went up an octave. "Junior, what the *hell...?* I thought you were going to swipe us the biggest, meanest, fastest—"

"Did you want to take the 727?" Cowboy asked as he grabbed for the handle of the door, swung it open and gave Melody a boost inside. "It was this or the 727, and *I* sure as hell didn't want to be a sitting duck out on the runway, waiting for those jet engines to warm up."

He'd run the checklist when he'd been out here earlier, so he merely pulled the blocks and started the engine. "This way, I figured we'd be a smaller target in the air, too, in case the tangos want to give their antiaircraft toys a test run."

But Harvard wasn't listening. He was standing, legs spread, feet braced against the ground, firing his AK-47 in a sweeping pattern, keeping the wolves at bay.

"Do you know how to fly a plane?" Melody shouted over the din.

"Between me and H., there's nothing we can't pilot." Cowboy reached back behind him, pushing her head down as a bullet broke the back window. "Stay down!"

He gunned the engine, using the flaps to swing the plane in a tight, quick circle so that the passenger door was within Harvard's grasp.

He took off before H. even had the door fully open,

let alone had climbed in. They headed down toward the edge of the field at a speed much too fast to make the necessary U-turn to get onto the main runway.

"I assume you've got another plan in mind," Harvard said, fastening his seat belt. He was a stickler for things like personal safety. It seemed almost absurd. Forty men were shooting at them, and H. was making sure his seat belt was on correctly.

"We're not using the runway," Cowboy shouted, pushing the engine harder, faster. "We're going to take off... right...*now!*"

He pulled back the stick and the engine screamed as they climbed at an impossibly steep angle to avoid hitting the rooftops of nearby buildings.

Cowboy heard Harvard shout, and then, by God, they were up. They were in the air.

He couldn't contain his own whoops of excitement and success. "Melody, honey, I *told* you we were going to get you home!"

Melody cautiously raised her head. "Can I sit up now?"

"No, it's not over yet." Harvard was much too grim as he looked over his shoulder, back at the rapidly disappearing airfield. "They're going to send someone after us—try to force us down."

"No, they're not," Cowboy said, turning to grin at him. God, for the first time in hours, he could smile again.

They were flying without lights, heading due east. This godforsaken country was so tiny that at this rate of speed, with the wind behind them, they'd be in friendly airspace in a matter of minutes. It was true they'd covered a great deal of the distance last night. But this was by far the easiest way of crossing the border.

"Aren't we flying awfully low?" Melody asked.

"We're underneath their radar," Cowboy told her. "As soon as we're across the border, I'll bring 'er up to a higher altitude."

Harvard was still watching their six, waiting for another plane to appear behind them. "I don't know how you can be so convinced they're not going to follow, Jones."

"I *am* convinced," Cowboy told him. "What do you think took me so long earlier tonight? I didn't stop for a sandwich in the food commissary, that's for damn sure."

Harvard's eyes narrowed. "Did you...?"

"I did."

Harvard started to laugh.

"What?" Melody asked. "What did you do?"

"How many were there?" Harvard asked.

Cowboy grinned. "About a dozen. Including the 727."

Melody turned to Harvard. "What did he do?"

He swung around in his seat to face her. "Junior here disabled every other plane on that field. Including the 727. There are a whole bunch of grounded tangos down there right now, hopping mad."

Cowboy glanced back into the shadows, hoping to see her smile. But as far as he could tell, her expression was serious, her eyes subdued.

"We are crossing the border," Harvard announced. "Boys and girls, it looks as if we are nearly home!"

ENSIGN HARLAN COWBOY Junior Kid Jones landed the little airplane much more smoothly and easily than he'd taken off.

Melody could see the array of ambulances and Red Cross trucks zooming out across the runways to meet them in the early dawn light. Within moments, they would taxi to a stop and climb out of the plane.

She wanted four tall glasses of water, no ice, lined up in front of her so that she could drink her fill without stopping. She wanted a shower in a hotel with room service. She wanted the fresh linens and soft pillows of a king-size bed. She wanted clean clothes and a hairdresser to make some sense out of the ragged near scalping she'd given herself.

But before she had any of that, she wanted to hold Harlan Jones in her arms. She wanted to hold him tightly, to thank him with the silence of her embrace for all that he had done for her.

He'd done so much for her. He'd given her so much. His kindness. His comforting arms. His morale-bolstering smiles. His encouraging words. His sandals.

And, oh yeah. He'd killed for her, to keep her safe, to deliver her to freedom.

She'd seen the blood on his robe, seen the look in his eyes, on his face. He'd run into trouble out alone on the air base and he'd been forced to take enemy lives. And the key word there was not *enemy*. It was *lives*.

Melody was long familiar with the expression "All's fair in love and war." And this *was* a war. The legal government had been overthrown and the country had been invaded by terrorist forces. They'd threatened American lives. She knew full well that it was a clear-cut case of "them" or "us."

What shook her up the most was that this was what Cowboy Jones did. This was what he *did,* day in, day out. He'd done it for the past six years and he'd continue to do it until he retired. Or was killed.

Melody thought about that blood on Jones's robe,

thought about the fact that it just as easily could have been his own blood.

All was fair in love and war.

But what were the rules if you were unlucky enough to fall in love with a warrior?

Jones cut the engine, then pushed the door open with his bare feet. But instead of climbing out, he turned around to face Melody, giving her his hand for support as she moved up through the cramped cabin and toward the door.

He slid down out of the plane, then looked up at her.

He'd taken off his blood-streaked robe, but he still wore that black vest with its array of velcroed pockets. It hung open over a black T-shirt that only barely disguised his sweat and grime. His face was streaked with dirt and dust, his hair matted against his head. There was shoe polish underneath his chin and on his neck—from where she'd burrowed against him, stealing strength and comfort from his arms.

But despite his fatigue, his eyes were as green as ever. He smiled at her. "Do I look as…ready for a bath as you do?"

She had to smile. "Tactfully put. Yes, you certainly do. And as for me—I think I'm more than ready to be a blonde again and wash this stuff out of my hair."

"But before you do, maybe I could send my shoes over to your hotel room for a touch-up…?"

Melody laughed. Until she looked down at his feet. They were still bare. They looked red and sore.

"You and Harvard saved my life," she whispered, her smile fading.

"I don't know about H.," Jones told her, gazing up into her eyes, "but as far as I'm concerned, Miss Evans, it was purely my pleasure."

Melody had to look away. His eyes were hypnotizing. If she didn't look away, she'd do something stupid like leap into his arms and kiss him. She glanced out at the line of cars approaching them. Was it possible that Jones had cut the engine and stopped the plane so far away from the terminal in order to let them have these few moments of privacy?

He reached for her, taking her hands to help her down from the plane.

"What's going to happen next?" she asked.

He pulled just a little too hard, and she fell forward, directly into his arms. He held her close, pressing her against his wide chest, and she held him just as tightly, encircling his waist with her arms and holding on as if she weren't ever going to let go. His arms engulfed her, and she could feel him rest his cheek against the top of her head.

"Jones, will I see you again?" she asked. She needed to know. "Or will they take you away to be debriefed and then send you back to wherever it was you came from?"

She lifted her head to look up at him. The trucks were skidding to a stop. She was going to have to get into one of those trucks, and they would take her someplace, away from Harlan Jones, maybe forever....

Her heart was pounding so hard she could barely hear herself think. She could feel his heart, too, beating at an accelerated rate.

"I'll tell you what's going to happen," he said, gazing into her eyes unsmilingly. "Second thing that's going to happen is that they're going to put you in one ambulance and me and H. in another. They'll take us to the hospital, make sure we're all right. Then we'll go into a short debriefing—probably separately. After that's done, you'll be taken to whatever hotel they're keeping the top brass in these days, and I'll go into a more detailed debriefing. After we both get cleaned up, I'll meet you back at the hotel for dinner—how's that sound?"

Melody nodded. That sounded very good.

"But the first thing that's going to happen," he told her, his mouth curving up into that now familiar smile, "is this."

He lowered his head and kissed her.

It was an amazing kiss, a powerful kiss, a no-holds-barred kind of kiss. It amplified all of the heat she'd seen in Harlan Jones's bedroom eyes over the past forty-eight hours. God, had it only been forty-eight hours? She felt as if she'd known this man for at least a lifetime. She felt, too, as if she'd wanted him for every single second of that time.

He kissed her even harder, deeper, sweeping his tongue into her mouth. It was a kiss that was filled with a promise of ecstasy, of lovemaking the likes of which she'd never known. The entire earth dropped out from under her feet, and she clung to him, giddy and dizzy and happier than she'd ever been in her entire life, returning his kisses with equal abandon. He wanted her. This incredible man honestly, truly *wanted* her.

His lips were warm, his mouth almost hot. He tasted sweet, like one of those energy bars he'd shared with her. Melody realized that she was laughing, and when she pulled back to look at him, he was smiling, too.

And then, just as he'd said, she was tugged gently away from him toward one of the ambulances as he was led toward another.

He kept watching her, though, and she held his gaze right up until the moment that she was helped into the back of the emergency vehicle. But before she went in, she glanced at him one last time. He was still watching her, still smiling. And he mouthed a single word. "Tonight."

Melody couldn't wait.

CHAPTER THREE

Seven months later

MELODY COULDN'T WAIT.

She had to get home, and she had to get home *now*.

She looked both ways, then ran the red light at the intersection of Route 119 and Hollow Road. But even then, she knew she wasn't going to make that last mile and a half up Potter's Field Road.

Melody pulled over to the side and lost her lunch on the shoulder of the road, about half a mile south of the Webers' mailbox.

This wasn't supposed to be happening anymore. She was supposed to be done with this part of it. The next few months were supposed to be filled with glowing skin and a renewed sense of peace, and yeah, okay, maybe an occasional backache or twinge of a sciatic nerve.

The morning sickness was supposed to have stopped four months ago. Morning sickness. Hah! She didn't have morning sickness—she had every-single-moment-of-the-day sickness.

She pulled herself back into her car and, after only stalling twice, slowly drove the rest of the way home. When she got there, she almost didn't pull into the driveway. She almost turned around and headed back toward town.

There was a Glenzen Bros. truck parked out in front

of the house. And Harry Glenzen—one of the original Glenzen brothers' great-great-grandsons—was there with Barney Kingman. Together the two men were affixing a large piece of plywood to the dining-room window. Or rather to the frame of what *used* to be the dining-room window.

Melody had to push her seat all the way back to maneuver her girth out from behind the steering wheel.

From inside the house, she could hear the unmistakable roar of the vacuum cleaner. Andy Marshall, she thought. Had to be. Brittany was going to be mad as a hornet.

"Hiya, Mel," Harry called cheerfully. "How about this heat wave we're having, huh? We've got a real Indian summer this year. If it keeps up, the kids'll be able to go trick-or-treating without their jackets on."

"Hey, Harry." Melody tried not to sound unenthusiastic, but this heat was killing her. She'd suffered all the way through July and August and the first part of September. But it was October now, and October in New England was supposed to be filled with crisp autumn days. There was nothing about today that could be called even remotely crisp.

She dragged herself up the front steps of the enormous Victorian house both she and her sister had grown up in. Melody had moved back in after college, intending to live rent free for a year until she decided what she wanted to do with her life, where she wanted to go. But then her mom had met a man. A very nice man. A very nice, *wealthy* man. Before Melody could even blink, her mother had remarried, packed up her things and moved to Florida, leaving Mel to take care of the sale of the house.

It wasn't long after that that Brittany filed for divorce.

After nearly ten years of marriage, she and her husband, Quentin, had called it quits and Britt moved in with Melody.

Melody never did get around to putting the house on the market. And Mom didn't mind. She was happier than Melody had ever seen her, returning to the Northeast for a month each summer and inviting her two daughters down to Sarasota each winter.

They were just two sisters, living together. Melody could imagine them in their nineties, still living in the same house, the old Evans girls, still unmarried, eccentric as hell, the stuff of which town legends were made.

But soon there would be three of them living together in this big old house, breaking with that particular tradition. The baby was due just in time for Christmas. Maybe by then the temperature would have finally dropped below eighty degrees.

Melody opened the front door. As she lugged her briefcase into the house, she heard the vacuum cleaner shut off.

"Mel, is that you?"

"It's me." Melody looked longingly toward the stairs that led to her bedroom. All she wanted to do was lie down. Instead, she took a deep breath and headed for the kitchen. "What happened?"

"Andy Marshall happened, *that's* what happened," Britt fumed, coming into the cheery yellow room through the door that connected to the dining room. "The little juvenile delinquent threw a baseball through the dining-room window. We have to special order the replacement glass because the damn thing's not standard-sized. The little creep claimed the ball slipped out of his hand. He says it was an accident."

Mel set her briefcase on the kitchen table and sank into one of the chairs. "Maybe it was."

Britt gave her such a dark look, Melody had to laugh. "It's not funny," Brittany said. "Ever since the Romanellas took that kid in, it's been chaos. Andy Marshall has a great big Behavior Problem, capital *B*, capital *P*."

"Even kids with behavior problems have accidents," Melody pointed out mildly, resting her forehead in the palm of her hand. God, she was tired.

Her sister's eyes softened. "Oh, hell. Another bad day?"

Melody nodded. "The entire town is getting used to seeing my car pulled over to the side of the road. Nobody stops to see if I'm okay anymore. It's just, 'Oh, there's Melody Evans hurling again.' Honk, honk, 'Hey, Mel!' and then they're gone. I feel like a victim of the boy-who-cried-wolf syndrome. One of these days, I'm going to be pulled to the side of the road in hard labor, giving birth to this baby, and no one's going to stop to help me."

Brittany took a glass down from the cabinet, filling it with a mixture of soda water and ginger ale. "Push those fluids. Replace what you've lost," she said, Andy Marshall finally forgotten. "In this weather, your number-one goal should be to keep yourself from becoming dehydrated."

Melody took the glass her sister was pressing on her. Her stomach was still rolling and queasy, so she only took a small sip before she set it down on the table. "Why don't you go upstairs and change out of your nurse's uniform before you forget you're not at work any longer and try to give me a sponge bath or something?" she suggested.

Britt didn't smile at her pitiful attempt at a joke. "Only if *you* promise to lie down and let me take care of dinner." Melody's sister had to be the only person in the world who could make an offer to cook dinner sound like a dire threat.

"I will," Melody promised, pushing herself out of the chair. "And thank you. I just want to check the answering machine. I ordered the latest Robert Parker book from the library and Mrs. B. thought it might be back in today. I want to see if she called." She started toward the den.

"My, my, you *do* have quite a wild and crazy lifestyle. Spending Friday night at home with a book again. Honestly, Mel, it's something of a miracle that you managed to get pregnant in the first place."

Mel pretended not to have heard that comment as she approached the answering machine. There were only two messages, but one of them was a long one. She sat down as the tape took forever to rewind.

…it's something of a miracle that you managed to get pregnant in the first place…something of a miracle…

She leaned her head back and closed her eyes, remembering the look in Harlan Jones's eyes as she'd met him at the door to her hotel room.

Cleaned up and wearing a naval dress uniform, he'd looked like a stranger. His shoulders were broader than she remembered. He seemed taller and harder and thoroughly, impossibly, devastatingly handsome.

She'd felt geeky and plain, dressed in too conservative clothes from the American shop in the hotel. And at the same time, she felt underdressed. The store had had nothing in her bra size except for something in that old-fashioned, cross-your-heart, body-armor style her grandmother used to wear, so she'd opted to go without. Suddenly, the silky fabric of the dress felt much too thin.

At least her hair was blond again, but she'd cut it much too short in her attempt to disguise herself. It would take weeks before she looked like anything other than a punk-rock time traveler from the early 1980s.

"I ordered room service," she'd told him shyly. "I hope you don't mind if we stay in…."

It was the boldest thing she'd ever done. But Jones's smile and the rush of heat in his eyes left no room for doubt. She'd done the right thing.

He'd locked the door behind him and pulled her into his arms and kissed her and kissed her and *kissed* her….

"Hi, Melody, this is Mrs. Beatrice from the Appleton Public Library," said the cheery voice on the tape, interrupting Melody's thoughts. "The book you requested is here. We've got quite a waiting list for this one, so if you aren't interested any longer, please give me a call! Hope you're feeling better, dear. I heard the heat's due to break in a day or two. I know when I was carrying Tommy, my eldest boy, I simply could not handle any temperature higher than seventy-two. Tom Senior actually went out and bought an air conditioner for me! You might want to think about something like that. If you want, I could send both Toms over to help you girls install it. Call me! Bye now!"

Girls. Sheesh.

That's my girl.

With determination, Melody pushed that thought out of her head.

The machine beeped, and a different voice, a male voice with the slightest of drawls, began to talk.

"Yeah, hi, I hope this is the right number. I'm looking for Melody Evans…?"

Melody sat forward. Dear God, it couldn't be, could it? But she knew exactly who it was. This was one voice she was never going to forget. Ever. Not until the day she died.

"This is Lt. Harlan Jones, and Mel, if you're listening, I, uh, I've been thinking about you. I'm going to be stationed here on the East Coast, in Virginia, for a couple of months, and um…well, it's not that far from Boston. I mean, it's closer than California and it's a *whole* hell of a lot closer than the Middle East and…"

On the tape, he cleared his throat. Melody realized she was sitting on the edge of her seat, eager for his every word.

"I know you said what you said before you got on the plane for Boston back in March, but…" He laughed, then swore softly, and she could almost see him rolling his eyes. "Hell, as long as I'm groveling, I might as well be honest about it. Bottom line, honey—I think about you all the time, *all* the time, and I want to see you again. Please call me back." He left a number, repeating it twice, and then hung up.

The answering machine beeped and then was silent.

"Oh. My. God."

Melody looked up to see Brittany standing in the doorway.

"Is this guy trying to win some kind of title as Mr. Romantic, or what?" her sister continued. "He is totally to die for, Mel. That cute little cowboy accent—where's he from anyway?"

"Texas," Melody said faintly. Lieutenant. He'd called himself Lt. Harlan Jones. He'd gotten a promotion, been awarded a higher rank.

"That's right. Texas. You told me that." Britt sat down across from her. "Mel, he wants to see you again. This is *so* great!"

"This is *not* so great!" Melody countered. "I can't see

him—are you kidding? God, Britt, he'll take one look at me and…"

Brittany was looking at her as if she'd just confessed to murdering the neighbors and burying them in their basement. "Oh, Melody, you didn't—"

"He'll know," Melody finished more softly.

"You didn't tell him you're pregnant?"

Mel shook her head. "No."

"You didn't tell him you're having his baby—that he's fathered your child?"

"What was I supposed to do? Write him a postcard? And where was I supposed to send it? Until he called, I didn't even know where he was!" Until he called, she didn't even know if he was still alive. But he was. He was still alive….

"Melody, that was a very, very, *very* bad thing to do," Brittany said as if she were five years old again and had broken their mother's favorite lamp by playing ball in the house. "A man has a right to know he's *knocked up* his girlfriend!"

"I'm not his girlfriend. I never was his girlfriend."

"Sweetie, you're having this man's baby. You may not have been his girlfriend, but you weren't exactly strangers!"

Melody closed her eyes. No, they were anything but strangers. They'd spent three days in that hotel room in that Middle Eastern city whose name she couldn't pronounce, and another three days in Paris. In the course of those six amazing days, they'd made love more times than she could count—including once in the miniature bathroom on board the commercial flight that had taken them north to France.

That was her doing. She'd wanted him so badly, she couldn't bear to wait until they touched down and took a taxi to their hotel. The plane was nearly empty—she'd thought no one would notice if they weren't in their seats for just a little while.

So she'd lured Jones to the back of the plane and pulled him into the tiny bathroom with her.

After three days, she had learned enough of his secrets to drive him wild with just a touch. And Jones—he could light her on fire with no more than a single look. It wasn't long before the temperature in that little room skyrocketed out of control.

But Jones didn't have a condom. He'd packed his supply in his luggage. And she didn't have one, either….

Making love that way was not the smartest thing either of them had ever done.

Brittany went to the answering machine and rewound the message, playing it again and writing down the phone number he left. "What does he mean by 'I know you said what you said before you got on the plane for Boston…'? What's he talking about?"

Melody stood up. "He's talking about a *private* conversation we had before I came home."

Brittany followed her out of the room. "He's implying that *you* were the one who broke off whatever it was you had going."

Melody started up the stairs. "Britt, what I said to him is not your business."

"I always just assumed that he dumped you, you know. 'So long, babe, it's been fun. Time for me to go rescue some other chick who's being held hostage.'"

Melody turned and faced her sister, looking down at her from her elevated position on the stairs. "He's not that type of man," she said fiercely.

She could practically see the wheels turning in Brittany's head. "Now you're defending him. Very interesting.

Fess up, Sis. Were you the one who dumped him? Jeez, I never thought you'd turn out to be the love-'em-and-leave-'em type."

"I'm not!" Melody started up the stairs again, exhaling noisily in frustration. "Look, nobody dumped *any*one, all right? It was just a…fling! God, Britt, it wasn't real—we hardly even knew each other. It was just…sex, and lust, and *relief*. A whole *lot* of very passionate relief. The man saved my life."

"So naturally you decide to bear his child."

Melody went into her bedroom and turned to shut the door, but Brittany blocked her.

"That's what you told him before you got on the plane home, isn't it? That crap about sex and lust and passionate relief? You told him you didn't want to see him again, didn't you?"

Mel gave up and sat down wearily on her bed. "It's not crap. It's true."

"What if you're wrong? What if this man is your missing half, your one true love?"

She shook her head vehemently. "He's *not*." God, over the past seven months, she'd asked herself the same question. What if…?

It was true that she missed her Navy SEAL. She missed him more than she was willing to admit. There were nights that she ached for his touch, that she would have died for a glimpse of his smile. And those amazing green eyes of his haunted her dreams.

But what she felt wasn't love. It *wasn't*.

Brittany sat next to her on the bed. "As much as you talk about passionate relief, sweetie, I just don't see you as the type to lock yourself in a hotel room with any man for six solid days unless he means something special to you."

Melody sank back against her pillows. "Yeah, well, you haven't met Harlan Jones."

"I'd *like* to meet Harlan Jones. Everything you've told me about him makes him sound like some kind of superman."

"There you go," Melody said triumphantly, sitting back up again. "That's my point exactly. He's some kind of superhero. And I'm just a mere mortal. What I felt for him wasn't love. It was hero worship. Jones saved my life. I've never met anyone like him before—I probably never will again. He was amazing. He could do *any*thing. Pilot a plane. Bandage my feet. Cut his sandals down to fit me yet make them look like new. He spoke four different languages, *four!* He knew how to scuba dive and skydive and move through the center of an enemy compound without being seen. He was smarter and braver and— God!—*sexier* than any man I've ever known, Britt. You're right, he *is* a superman, and I couldn't resist him—not for one day, not for six days. If he hadn't been called back to the States, I would've stayed with him for *sixteen* days. But that has nothing to do with real love. That was hero worship. I couldn't resist Harlan Jones any more than Lois Lane could resist Superman—and *that's* one relationship that could never be called healthy, or normal, either."

Brittany was silent.

"I still think it's wrong not to tell him about the baby," she finally said, setting the paper with Jones's phone number on Melody's bedside table. She stood up and crossed the room, pausing with her hand on the doorknob. "Call him and tell him the truth. He deserves to know."

Brittany left the room, closing the door behind her.

Melody closed her eyes. Call Jones.

The sound of his voice on her answering machine had sparked all sorts of memories.

Like finding the bandage he wore under his shirt on the back of his arm. They had been in her hotel room and she had been in the process of ridding him of that crisp white dress uniform, trailing her lips across every piece of skin she exposed. She'd pushed his jacket and then his shirt over his shoulders and down his arms, and there it was—big and white and gauze and covering a "little" gash he'd had stitched up at the hospital that morning.

When she pressed, he told her he'd been slashed with a knife, fighting off the men he'd surprised in the hangar at the air base.

He'd been *stabbed,* and he hadn't bothered to mention it to either Harvard or Melody. He'd simply bandaged the wound himself, right then and there, and forgotten about it.

When she asked to see it, he'd lifted the gauze and shown her the stitches with a shrug and a smile. It was no big deal.

Except the "little" gash was four *inches* long. It was angry and inflamed—which also was no big deal to Jones, since the doctor had given him antibiotics. He'd be fine in a matter of days. Hours.

He'd pulled her back on top of him, claiming her mouth with a gentleness astonishing for a man so strong, intertwining their legs as he took a turn ridding her of more of *her* clothes.

And it was then Melody knew for dead certain their love affair was not going to be long-term.

Because there was no way this incredible man—for whom rescuing strangers deep inside a terrorist strong-hold and getting sliced open in a knife fight was all in a casual day's work—would ever remain interested in someone like drab little Melody Evans for long.

He would be far better off with a woman reminiscent of

Mata Hari. Someone who would scuba dive and parasail with him. Someone strong and mysterious and daring.

And Melody would be better off with an everyday, average guy. Someone who would never *forget* to mention it when he was slashed by a knife. Someone whose idea of excitement was mowing the lawn and watching the Sunday afternoon football game on TV.

She curled up on her side on her bed, staring at the piece of paper that Brittany had left on her bedside table.

Still, she had to call him back.

If she didn't call him, he'd call here again, she was sure of it. And God help her if he spoke to Brittany and she let slip Melody's secret.

Taking a deep breath, Melody reached for the paper and the phone.

COWBOY WAS IN Alpha Squad's makeshift office, trying to get some work done.

Seven desks—one for each member of the squad—had been set up haphazardly down at one end of an echoy metal Quonset hut. This hut was a temporary home base to work out the details of a training mission. Except this time, the members of Alpha Squad were the trainers, not the trainees. Within a few months, a group of elite FinCOM agents were being sent down from D.C. to learn as much as they could of SEAL Team Ten's successful counterterrorist operations.

They needed the desks, and the computers and equipment set up on top of them, to plan out their own little version of BUD/S training for these Finks.

Joe Catalanotto had pulled strings with his admiral pal, Mac Forrest, to make arrangements for Lt. Alan Francisco, one of the top BUD/S training instructors, to meet them out here in Virginia. Joe Cat was hoping Frisco would be able to organize the jumble of notes and training ideas the squad had come up with to date.

Frisco was a former member of Alpha Squad who had been pulled off the active-duty list with a knee injury more than five years ago. Cowboy had been filling in for a missing member of the squad when Frisco had been injured. That had been Cowboy's first time in the field, his first time in a real war zone—and he'd been sure that it was going to be his last. Cowboy was certain that Joe Cat, the squad's commander, had seen his hands shaking as they set a bomb to blow a hole in the side of an embassy.

It had been another embassy rescue....

Melody Evans's wide blue eyes flashed into his head, but Cowboy gently pushed the image away. He'd been thinking about Mel too much lately, and right now he was writing up a summary of the information he was intending to share with the FinCOM agents. At Cat's request, he was in charge of presenting the psychological profile of a terrorist to the Finks. The key to success when dealing with terrorists lay in understanding their reasoning and motivation—how their minds worked. And with all of the cultural, environmental and religious differences, their minds worked very differently from the average white-bread American FinCOM agent.

Frisco was going to arrive Monday morning, and although it was only Friday, Cowboy was pushing to get his report finished today. After working nearly nonstop over the past seven months, he was hoping to take a few days of leave this weekend.

Mel's face popped into his thoughts again. He'd left a message on an answering machine he'd hoped was hers. Please, dear Lord, let her call him back.

Again he took a deep breath and focused his thoughts on his report. It was important to him that this summary be as complete as possible. Alan "Frisco" Francisco was going to be the man to read it, and Cowboy wanted to make the best impression he could.

Because when it was determined that Frisco's injury was permanent, Cowboy had been assigned to Alpha Squad at Joe Cat's request, as the man's replacement.

Cowboy still felt a little uncomfortable when Frisco was around. He knew the man missed being in the action, and here he was, his official replacement. And if Frisco hadn't been hurt, Cowboy probably wouldn't be working with the elite seven-member Alpha Squad. Cowboy had benefited from Frisco's tragedy, and both men damn well knew it. As a result, when they were together, they tippy-toed around each other, acting especially polite. Cowboy was hoping that would change as the two men worked closely together over the next few months.

Right now, he appeared to be the only man in the room who was actually working. Blue McCoy and Harvard were checking out the Web site for Heckler & Koch, the German weapon manufacturer. Even Joe Catalanotto had his feet up on his desk as he talked on the phone with his wife, Veronica. Their son's first birthday was quickly approaching, but from what Cowboy couldn't help but overhear, it sounded as if Joe was more interested in planning a separate, very different, very *private* party for the parents of the birthday boy, to be held after all the guests had gone home and little Frankie Catalanotto was tucked into his crib.

The rest of the guys were sitting around the "office," trying to come up with ways to truly torment the poor Finks.

"We start the whole thing off with a twenty-five-mile run," Wesley was suggesting.

One desk over, Lucky O'Donlon was playing some kind of computer game complete with aliens and exploding starships and roaring sound effects.

"No, I read the rule book," Bobby countered loudly to be heard over the sound of the alien horde. "These guys—and gals—are going to be put up at the Marriott while they're here. I don't think they're going to let us run 'em for five miles, let alone twenty-five."

That got Lucky's attention. "FinCOM's sending *women* out here?"

"That's what I heard," Bobby said. "Just one or two out of the bunch of them."

Lucky smiled. "One or two is all we need. One for me and one for Cowboy. Oh, but wait. I almost forgot. Cowboy's sworn off women. He's decided to become a priest—or at least live like one. But then again, maybe a little one-on-one with a pretty young FinCOM agent is all he needs to get him back in the game."

Cowboy couldn't let that go. Lucky had been teasing him mercilessly about his current celibacy for months. "I don't criticize the way you live, O'Donlon," he said tightly. "I'd appreciate it if you'd show me the same courtesy."

"I'm just curious, Cowboy, that's all. What's going on? Did you honestly find God or something?" Lucky's eyes were dancing with mischief. He didn't realize that he'd pushed Cowboy to his limit. "I seem to remember a certain Middle Eastern country and a certain pretty little former hostage you seemed intent upon setting some kind of world record with. I mean, come on. It was kind of obvious what you were up to when you went to meet her for dinner and then didn't come back for six days." Lucky laughed. "She sure must've been one hell of a good—"

Cowboy stood up, his chair screeching across the concrete floor. "That's enough," he said hotly. "You say one more word about that girl and you're going to find the very next word you say is going to be said without any teeth."

Lucky stared at him. "God, Jones, you're serious! What the hell did this girl do to you?" But then he grinned, quick to turn anything and everything into a joke. "Do you think if I asked real nice, I could get her to do it to me, too?"

Cowboy was moments from launching himself at the blond-haired SEAL when Harvard stepped between them, holding up one hand, silently telling Cowboy to freeze.

The big man fixed Lucky with a steady, dangerous gaze. "You're nicknamed Lucky because with all the truly asinine things that come out of your mouth, you're lucky to still be alive, is that right, O'Donlon?"

Lucky wisely returned his attention to his computer game, glancing up at Cowboy with disbelief still glimmering in his eyes. "Sorry, Jones. Jeez."

Cowboy slowly sat back down, and as Joe Cat hung up the phone, a complete silence fell, broken only by the sounds of Lucky's computer game.

What the hell did this girl do to you?

Cowboy honestly didn't know.

Surely it was some kind of witchcraft. Some kind of enchantment or spell. It had been seven months, seven *months,* and he couldn't so much as glance at another woman without comparing her, unfavorably, to Melody Evans.

Melody. Shoot, she'd had his head spinning from the moment she'd opened her hotel-room door for him.

Her hair was so light, he'd nearly laughed aloud. He knew she was a blonde from her picture, but until he saw her, he really hadn't been able to imagine it. Cut short the way it was, it accentuated the delicate shape of her face and drew attention to her long, graceful neck.

She was gorgeous. She'd gotten hold of some makeup and wore just a trace of it on her eyes and a touch of lipstick on her sweet lips. It highlighted her natural beauty. And it told him without a doubt that she had anticipated and prepared for this dinner as much as he had.

She was wearing some kind of boxy, shapeless, too large dress that she must've had sent up from one of the hotel shops. On any other woman, it would've looked as if she was playing dress-up in her mother's clothes. But on Mel, it looked sexy. The neckline revealed her delicate collarbone, and the silky material managed to cling to her slender body, revealing every soft curve, every heart-stopping detail. Her legs were bare, and she wore the sandals he'd made for her on her feet.

Nail polish. She had pink nail polish on her toes. Probably hadn't been able to get any green.

He'd stood there in the doorway, just looking at her, knowing that despite all he'd silently told himself about the basis for the emotion behind hostage-and-rescuer relationships, he was lost. He was truly and desperately lost.

He'd wanted this woman more than he'd ever wanted anyone….

Wes's voice broke the silence. "You think they're gonna put *us* up in the Marriott, too?" the shortest member of Alpha Squad wondered aloud.

Bobby, Wes's swim buddy, built like a restaurant refrigerator, shook his head. "I didn't see anything about that in the FinCOM rule book."

"What FinCOM rule book?" Joe Cat's husky New York accent cut through the noise of exploding spacecraft. "Blue, you know anything about a *rule* book?"

"No, sir."

"This morning, FinCOM sent over something they're calling a rule book," Bobby told their commanding officer.

"Let me see it," Cat ordered. "O'Donlon, kill the volume on that damn thing."

The computer sounds disappeared as Bobby sifted through the piles of paper on his desk. He uncovered the carefully stapled booklet FinCOM had sent via courier and tossed the entire express envelope across the room to Cat. Cat caught it with one hand.

The phone rang and Wesley picked it up. "Alpha Squad Pizza. We deliver."

Catalanotto pulled out the booklet and the cover letter. He quickly skimmed the letter, then opened the booklet to the first page and did the same. Then he laughed—a snort of derision—and ripped both the book and the letter in half. He stuffed it back into the envelope and tossed it back to Bob.

"Send this back to Maryland with a letter that tells the good people of FinCOM no rule books. No rules. Sign my name and send it express."

"Yes, sir."

"Hey, Cowboy."

Cowboy looked up to see Wes holding up the telephone receiver, hand securely over the mouthpiece. "For you," Wesley said. "A lady. Someone named Melody Evans."

Suddenly, the room was so quiet, Cowboy could have heard a pin drop.

But then Harvard clapped his hands together. "Okay,

coffee break," he announced loudly. "Everyone but Junior outside. Let's go. On the double."

Cowboy held the phone that Wes had handed him until the echo from the slamming door had faded away. Taking a deep breath, he put the receiver to his ear.

"Melody?"

He heard her laugh. It was a thin, shaky laugh, but he didn't care. Laughter was good, wasn't it? "Yeah, it's me," she said. "Congratulations on making lieutenant, Jones."

"Thanks," he said. "And thanks for calling me back. You sound…great. How are you?" He closed his eyes tightly. Damn, he sounded like some kind of fool.

"Busy," she said without hesitation, as if it was something she'd planned to say if he asked. "I've been incredibly busy. I'm working full-time as an AA for the town attorney, Ted Shepherd. He's running for state representative, so it's been crazy lately."

"Look, Mel, I don't want to play games with you," he told her. "I mean, we've never been anything but honest with each other, and I know you said you didn't want to see me again, but I can't get you out of my head. I want to get together."

There. He'd said it.

He waited for her to say something, but there was only silence.

"I can get a weekend pass and be up in Massachusetts in five hours."

More silence. Then, "Jones, this weekend is really bad for me. The election's only a few weeks away and… It's not a good time."

Now the silence belonged to him.

He had two options here. He could either accept her excuses and hang up the phone, or he could beg.

He hadn't begged back in March. He hadn't dropped to his knees and pleaded with her to reconsider. He hadn't tried to convince her that everything she'd told him about their passion being false, about their relationship being based on the adrenaline rush of her rescue, was wrong.

He was a psych specialist. Everything she said made sense—everything but the incredible intensity of his feelings for her. If those feelings weren't real, he didn't know what real was.

But his pride had kept him from saying everything he should have said. Maybe if he'd said it then, she wouldn't have walked away.

So maybe he should beg. It wouldn't kill him to beg, would it? But if he was going to beg, it would have to be face-to-face. No way was he going to do it over the phone.

"Nothing's changed," Melody said softly. "Ours wasn't a relationship that could ever go anywhere."

I miss you, Mel. Cowboy closed his eyes, unable to say the words aloud.

"It was nice hearing your voice, though," Melody said.

She said she was busy this weekend. Maybe it wasn't just a transparent excuse. Maybe she *was* busy. But even busy people had to grab a sandwich for lunch. He'd take that weekend pass, head up to Boston, rent a car and drive out to Appleton.

And then, face-to-face, he'd get down on the ground and beg.

"Yeah," Cowboy said, "yeah—it was nice talking to you."

"I'm sorry, Jones," she said quietly, and the line was disconnected.

Cowboy slowly hung up the phone.

For all these months, he'd sat around, waiting to get over this girl. It was definitely time to stop waiting and take some action.

He saved his file on the computer, then set it up to print. As the laser printer started spewing out his psych summary, Cowboy pushed his chair back from his desk.

He left the Quonset hut and headed toward the barracks where the unmarried members of Alpha Squad were being housed. He would pack a quick bag, do the necessary paperwork for a weekend pass, then bum a ride to the air base.

As Cowboy pulled open the screen door, the inner door opened, too, and he nearly walked into Harvard. The older man took one look at the grim set to Cowboy's mouth, then sighed.

"No good, huh?" Harvard stepped back to let Cowboy into the Spartanly decorated bunk room.

Cowboy shook his head. "Senior Chief, I need a weekend pass and information on flights heading north to Boston."

Harvard smiled. "Way to go, Junior. You pack your things, I'll handle the paperwork. Meet you by the gate in fifteen."

Cowboy forced a smile of his own. "Thanks, H."

First thing tomorrow, he'd be face-to-face with Melody Evans.

She didn't want to see him because she knew damn well that if she saw him, she wouldn't be able to resist the pull of the attraction that lingered between them. Face-to-face, she wouldn't be able to resist him any more than he could resist her.

And by this time tomorrow, he'd have her back in his arms. And maybe, if he played his cards right, if he got humble and got down on his knees and begged, maybe then he'd have her back in his life for as long as it took for him to be satisfied—to get over her once and for all.

For the first time in a long time, Cowboy's smile actually felt real.

CHAPTER FOUR

MELODY SPOTTED HIM from across the town common
and her heart nearly stopped.

The Romanellas' new foster kid, Andy Marshall, was
fighting with two boys who had to be at least three years
older and a foot and a half taller than he was.

The three kids were in the shadows of the trees at the
edge of the town playground. As Melody watched, Andy
was knocked almost playfully to the ground as the two
older boys laughed. But the kid rolled into the fall like
an accomplished stunt fighter and came up swinging.
His fist connected with the nose of one of the other boys,
sending the taller one staggering back.

Melody could hear the bellow of pain from inside her
car. She heard the shouts change from taunting laughter
to genuine anger, and she knew that Andy was on the
verge of getting the spit kicked out of him.

She took a quick left onto Huntington Street and another left the wrong way into the Exit Only marked drive
of the playground parking lot, leaning on her horn as she
went.

"Hey!" she shouted out the car window. "You boys!
Stop that! Stop fighting *right now!*"

One of the older boys—Alex Parks—savagely back-
handed Andy with enough force to make Melody's own
teeth rattle before he and his friend turned and ran.

As Melody scrambled to pull her girth from the front

seat of her car, Andy tried to run, too, but he couldn't. He couldn't do better than to push himself up onto his hands and knees on the grass.

"Oh, Andy!" Melody crouched down next to him. "Oh, God! Are you all right?"

She reached for him, but he jerked away and she backed off.

His knees and elbows were raw, and his nose was bleeding pretty steadily. He had a scrape on his cheek underneath his left eye, and his lip was already swollen and split. His brown hair was messy and clotted with dirt and bits of grass, and his T-shirt was bloody and torn.

He'd had the wind knocked out of him and he struggled to regain his breath as tears of pain and humiliation filled his eyes.

"Go away," he growled. "Just leave me alone!"

"I can't do that," Melody told him evenly. "Because we're neighbors. And here in Appleton, neighbors look out for each other."

She sat down in the grass, crossing her legs tailor-style, fighting a familiar wave of nausea, thankful they were sitting in the shade.

He was checking the watch he wore on his skinny left wrist, examining the protective surface over the clock face and holding it to his ear to be sure it was still ticking.

"Did they break it?" Melody asked.

"What's it to you?" he sneered.

"Well, you seem more concerned with your watch than with the fact that you're bleeding, so I thought—"

"You're the unwed mother, right?"

Melody refused to acknowledge the tone of his voice. He was being purposely rude so that she wouldn't know he was on the verge of dissolving into tears. She ignored both the rudeness and the threatening tears. "In a nutshell, yeah, I guess I am. My name's Melody Evans. I live next door to the Romanellas. We met last week, when Vince and Kirsty brought you home with them."

He sat down, still catching his breath. "You know, they talk about you. They wonder exactly who knocked you up. Everyone in town talks about you all the time."

"Except when they're talking about you," Melody pointed out. "Between the two of us, we've got the gossips working full-time, haven't we? A foster child from the big, bad city who blows up lawn mowers. There's probably a betting pool guessing how long it'll be before the police become involved in your discipline."

Her bluntly honest words surprised him, and he actually looked at her. For a brief moment, he actually met her eyes. His own were brown and angry—far too angry and bitter for a twelve-year-old. But then he looked away.

"The hell with them," he said harshly. "I won't be here long anyway."

Melody feigned surprise. "Really? Vince told me you were going to be staying with him and Kirsty at least until next September—that's almost a year." She fished in her handbag for some tissues. She wished she had a can of ginger ale in her bag, too. She was trying to make friends with this kid, and God knows throwing up on him wouldn't win her big points.

"A year." Andy snorted. "Yeah, right. I'll be gone in a month. Less. A week. That's all most people can take of me."

She handed him a wad of tissues for his nose. "Gee, maybe you should try a different brand of mouthwash."

There was another flash of surprise in his eyes. "You're a laugh riot," he said scornfully, expertly stemming the flow of blood. He seemed to be a pro at repairing the damage done him in fistfights.

"You're a sweet little bundle of charm and good cheer yourself, munchkin."

He held her gaze insolently. He was James Dean and Marlon Brando rolled into one with his heavily lidded eyes and curled lip. He'd successfully concealed all of his pain and angry tears behind a "who cares?" facade. "I broke your window yesterday."

"I know." Melody could play the "who cares?" game, too. "Accidents happen."

"Your sister didn't think it was an accident."

"Brittany wasn't born with a lot of patience."

"She's a witch."

Melody had to laugh. "No, she's not. She's got something of a volatile temper, though."

He looked away. "Whatever."

"Volatile means hot. Quick to go off."

"Duh. I know *that*," he lied.

She handed him more tissues, wishing she could pull him into her arms and give him a hug. He was skinny for a twelve-year-old, just a narrow slip of a little boy. His injuries from the fight—and probably from the battles he'd been fighting all of his life—went far deeper than a split lip, a bloody nose and a few scrapes and scratches. Still, although he may have looked like a child, his attitude was pure jaded adolescent, and she gave him a smile instead.

"You're prettier than what's-her-name, the witch," he said, then snorted again. "But look what being prettier got you. Preggo."

"Actually, being careless got me...preggo. And to tell you the truth," Melody said seriously, "not using a condom could've gotten me far more than just pregnant.

These days, you have to use a condom to protect yourself against AIDS. But I'm sure you already know that. Smart men never forget—not even for a minute."

Andy nodded, acting ultracool, as if sitting around and talking about condoms was something he did every day. It was clear he liked being spoken to as if he were an adult.

"What was the fight about?"

"They insulted me." He shrugged. "I jumped them."

"You jumped *them?* Andy, together those boys weigh four times more than you."

He bristled. "They insulted me. They were making up stories about my mother, saying how she was a whore, turning tricks for a living, and she didn't even know who my father was—like I was some kind of lousy bastard." He glanced down at her belly. "Sorry."

"I know who the father of my baby is."

"Some soldier who saved your life."

Melody laughed. "Gee, you're up to speed on the town gossip after only a few days, aren't you?"

Another shrug. "I pay attention. My father's a soldier, too. He doesn't give a damn about me, either."

Doesn't give a damn. Melody closed her eyes, fighting another wave of nausea. She hadn't exactly given Harlan Jones a chance to give a damn, had she?

"So you gonna keep it or give it away?"

The baby. Andy was talking about the baby. "I'm going to keep it. Him." Melody forced a smile. "I think he's a boy. But I don't know for sure. I had an ultrasound, but I didn't want to know. Still, it just...*he* feels like a boy to me."

As if on cue, the baby began his familiar acrobatic routine, stretching and turning and kicking hard.

Melody laughed, pressing her hand against her taut

belly and feeling the ripple of movement from both inside and out. It was an amazing miracle—she'd never get used to the joy of the sensation. It made her sour stomach and her dizziness fade far away.

"He's kicking," she told Andy. "Give me your hand— you've got to feel this."

Andy gave her a skeptical look.

"Come on," she urged him. "It feels *so* cool."

He wiped the palm of his hand on his grubby shorts before holding it out to her. She held it down on the bulge close to her belly button just as the baby did what felt like a complete somersault.

Andy pulled back his hand in alarm. "Whoa!" But then he hesitantly reached for her again, his eyes wide.

Melody covered his hand with hers, pressing it down once again on the playground-ball tightness of her protruding stomach.

Andy laughed, revealing crooked front teeth, one of which was endearingly chipped. "It feels like there's some kind of alien inside of you!"

"Well, there sort of is," Melody said. "I mean, think about it. There's a person inside of me. A human being." She smiled. "A little, wonderful, *lovely* human being." And if she was lucky, that little human being would take after his mother. Her smile faded. If she was really lucky, she wouldn't have to spend the rest of her life gazing into emerald green eyes and remembering….

"Are you okay?" Andy asked.

It was ironic, really. *He* was the one who looked as if he'd been hit by a train. Yet he was asking if *she* was all right. Underneath the tough-guy exterior, Andy Marshall was an okay kid.

"Yeah, I'm fine." Melody forced another smile. "I just get dizzy and…kind of queasy sometimes."

"You gonna barf?"

"No." Melody took a deep breath. "Why don't we go get you cleaned up?" she suggested. "Maybe I should take you over to the hospital…?"

He pulled away, slipping instantly back into surly James Dean mode. "No way."

"You've got dirt ground into your knee." Melody tried to sound reasonable. "It's got to be washed. All of your scrapes have to be washed. My sister's a nurse. She could—"

"Yeah, like I'd ever let the Wicked Witch of the West touch *me*."

"Then let me take you home to Kirsty—"

"No!" Beneath his suntan and the dirt, Andy's face had gone pale. "I can't go there looking like this. Vince said…." He turned abruptly away from her.

"He told you no more fighting," Melody guessed. Violence wasn't in her next-door neighbor's vocabulary.

"He said I got into another fight, I'd get it." Andy's chin went out as he pushed himself to his feet. "No way am I gonna let him take his belt to me! Hell, I just won't go back!"

Melody laughed aloud. "Vince? Take his belt to you?"

"I'm outta here," Andy said. "It's not like anyone's gonna miss me, right?"

"Andy, Vince doesn't even *wear* a belt." Vince Romanella might've looked like the kind of guy who would react with one of his big, beefy fists rather than think things through, but in the three years he and his wife had been foster parents, he'd never raised a hand to a child. What Andy was going to "get" was a trip to his bedroom tonight, where he would sit alone, writing a five-page essay on nonviolent alternatives to fighting.

But before she could tell Andy that, he was gone, walking quickly across the field, trying his best to hide a limp.

"Andy, wait!"

She started after him. He glanced back at her and began to run.

"Shoot, Andy, wait for me!"

Melody broke into a waddling trot, supporting her stomach with her arms.

He had to stop at Main Street and wait for a break in the traffic before he could cross.

"Andy, Vince isn't going to *hit* you!"

But he didn't hear her. He darted across the road and started running down the street.

Melody picked up her own pace, feeling like one of the running dinosaurs in *Jurassic Park*. With each step she took, the sky should have rumbled and the earth should have shook.

"Andy! Wait! Somebody stop Andy Marshall—please!"

She was light-headed and dizzy and within nanoseconds of losing what little breakfast she'd forced down earlier this morning. But no one seemed to notice her calls of help. No one seemed to be paying one bit of attention to the gigantically pregnant woman chasing the twelve-year-old boy.

No one except the exceptionally tall, exceptionally broad-shouldered man on the corner. Sunlight gleamed off sun-streaked brown hair that was pulled back into a ponytail at the nape of his neck. He was dressed similarly to just about all the other Saturday-morning antique shoppers who crowded the quaint little stores that surrounded the common. He wore a muted green polo shirt and a pair of khaki Dockers that fit sinfully well.

Seemingly effortlessly, he reached out and grabbed

Andy around the waist. He moved with the fluid grace of a trained warrior, and as he moved, Melody recognized him instantly. He didn't have to come any closer for Melody to know that his shirt accentuated the brilliant green of his eyes.

Lt. Harlan "Cowboy" Jones had come to Appleton to find her. Blackness pressed around Melody, taking out her peripheral vision and giving her the illusion of looking at Jones through a long, dark tunnel.

"Is this the kid you wanted, ma'am?" he called across the street to her, his voice carrying faintly over the roaring in her ears. He didn't realize he'd found her. He didn't recognize her new, extralarge, two-for-the-price-of-one size.

Melody felt nausea churning inside of her, felt dizziness swirling around her, and she did the only thing she could possibly do, given the circumstances.

She carefully lowered herself down onto the grass of the Appleton Common and fainted.

"WHAT'S WRONG WITH you?" Cowboy scolded the squirming kid as he carried him across the street. "Making your mama chase after you like that."

"She's not my mother," the kid spit. "And you're not my father, so let go of me!"

Cowboy looked up and blinked. That was odd. The woman had been standing right behind the blue Honda sedan. She was blond and hugely, heavily pregnant, but somehow she had managed to vanish.

He took a few more steps and then he saw her. She was on the ground, on the grass behind the parked cars, lying on her side as if she'd stopped to take a nap, her long hair hanging like a curtain over her face.

The kid saw her, too, and stopped struggling. "God, is she dead?" His face twisted. "Oh, God, did I kill her?"

Cowboy let go of the kid and moved fast, kneeling next to the woman. He slid his hand underneath her hair and up to the softness of her neck, searching for a pulse. He found one, but it was going much too fast. "She's not dead."

The kid was no longer trying to run away. "Should I find a phone and call 911?"

Cowboy put his hand on the woman's abdomen, wondering if she was in labor, wondering if he'd even be able to feel her contractions if she was. He knew quite a bit about first aid—enough to qualify as a medic in most units. He knew the drill when it came to knife wounds, gunshot wounds and third-degree burns. But unconscious pregnant women were way out of his league. Still, he knew enough to recognize shock when he saw it. He brushed her hair out of her face to check her eyes, glancing up at the kid. "Is the hospital far away?"

"No, it's right here in town—just a few blocks north."

Cowboy looked back to check the woman's eyes, and for several long, timeless seconds, he couldn't move.

Dear, dear God, it was Melody. It was *Melody*. This immensely pregnant woman was *Melody. His* Melody. *His...*

He couldn't breathe, couldn't speak, could hardly even think. Melody. *Pregnant?*

The implication nearly knocked him over, but then his training kicked in. Keep going, keep moving. Don't analyze more than you have to. Don't think if it's gonna slow you down. Act. Act and react.

His rental car was on the corner of Main Street. "We can probably get her to the hospital faster ourselves." His voice sounded hoarse. It was a wonder he could speak at all. He handed his car keys to the kid with the split lip. "I'll carry Mel, you unlock the car door."

The kid stared at him as he lifted Melody up and into his arms. "You know her?"

A hell of a question, considering he'd gone and gotten her pregnant. "Yeah. I know her."

She roused slightly as he carried her down the street toward his car. "Jones…?"

"Yeah, honey, I'm here."

The kid dropped the keys twice but finally managed to get the passenger door open.

"Oh, God, you are, aren't you?" Melody closed her eyes as he affixed the seat belt around her girth.

Cowboy felt light-headed himself. She looked as if she were hiding a watermelon underneath her dress. And he'd done that to her. He'd sent his seed deep inside of her and now she was going to have his baby. And if he didn't hurry, she was going to have his baby in the front seat of this car.

"Hang on, Mel. I'm taking you to the hospital."

Cowboy turned around to order the kid into the back seat, but the kid was gone. He did a quick sweep of the area and spotted the boy at ten o'clock, running full speed across the common. Melody had no doubt been chasing him for a reason, but no matter what that reason was, getting her to the hospital had to take priority.

The kid had left Cowboy's car keys on the front seat, thank God. Cowboy scooped them up as he slid behind the wheel, then started the engine with a roar.

Melody was *pregnant* and the baby had to be his. Didn't it? Had it truly been nine months since the hostage rescue at the embassy? He did a quick count but came up with only seven months. He must have counted wrong.

He pushed all thoughts away as he searched the street for a familiar blue hospital sign. Don't think. Act. He'd have plenty of time to think after he was certain Mel was going to be okay.

The kid had been right—the hospital was nearby. Within moments, Cowboy pulled up to the emergency room entrance.

He took the shortest route to the automatic E.R. doors—over the hood of the car—and helped the sliding doors open faster with his hands. "I need some help," he shouted into the empty corridor. "A wheelchair, a stretcher, *some*thing! I've got a lady about to have a baby here!"

The startled face of a nurse appeared, and Cowboy moved quickly back to the car, opening the door and lifting Melody into his arms. Even with the added weight of her pregnancy, she still felt impossibly light, improbably slender. She still felt so familiar. She still fit perfectly in his arms. God, how he'd missed her.

He was met at the door by a gray-haired nurse with a wheelchair who took one look at Mel and called out, "It's Melody Evans. Someone call Brittany down here, stat!"

"She's unconscious," Cowboy reported. "She's come out of it once but slipped back."

The nurse pushed the chair away. "She'd only fall out of this. Can you carry her?"

"Absolutely." He tossed his car keys to a security guard. "Move my car for me, will you, please?"

He followed the woman through a set of doors and into the emergency room where they were joined by another woman—this one a doctor.

"She's preregistered, but we will need your signature on a form before you go," the nurse told him as they moved briskly toward a hospital bed separated from a row of other beds by only a thin, sliding curtain.

"I'm not going anywhere," Cowboy said.

"Can you tell me when the contractions started?" the doctor asked. "How far apart they are?"

"I don't know," he admitted as he set Melody on the bed. "She was out cold when I found her. She must have just keeled over, right by the side of the road."

"Did she hit her head when she fell?" The doctor examined Melody quickly, lifting her eyelids, checking her eyes and feeling the back of her head for possible injury.

"I don't know," Cowboy said again, feeling a surge of frustration. "I didn't see her fall."

The nurse had already slipped a blood-pressure cuff on Mel's arm. She pumped it up and took a reading. "Blood pressure's fine. Pulse seems steady."

Melody looked so helpless lying there on that narrow bed. Her face was so pale. Her hair was so much longer than it had been in Paris. Of course, his hair was a lot longer, too.

It had been a long time since he'd seen her.

But it had only been seven months. Not nine.

Was it possible that she'd already been two months pregnant in Paris? He couldn't believe that. He *wouldn't* believe that. Of course the baby was his. She'd told him it had been close to a year since she'd broken up with her last serious boyfriend and…

Melody's eyelashes flickered.

"Well, hello," the doctor said to her. "Welcome back."

As Cowboy watched, Melody gazed up at the doctor, her brow wrinkled slightly with confusion. "Where am I?" she breathed.

"At County Hospital. Do you remember blacking out?"

Melody closed her eyes briefly. "I remember…" She opened them, sitting up suddenly, turning to look around the room until her gaze fell directly on Cowboy. "Oh, God. You're real."

"I'd say hi, how are you, but that's kind of obvious." Cowboy did his best to keep his voice low and even. She was in no condition to be yelled at—even if she damn well deserved it. "It looks as if you have some news you forgot to tell me yesterday when we spoke on the phone."

Her cheeks flushed, but she lifted her chin. "I'm pregnant."

He moved closer. "I noticed. When were you planning to tell me?"

She lowered her voice. "I thought you told me SEALs were trained never to assume anything. Yet here you are, assuming my condition has something to do with you."

"Are you telling me it doesn't?" He knew without a doubt that that baby was his. He couldn't imagine her with somebody else. The idea was ludicrous—and unbearable.

"How far apart are the contractions?" the doctor asked as the nurse gently pushed Melody back down on the hospital bed.

"Are you telling me it doesn't?" Cowboy said again, knowing he should just step back and give the doctor space but needing to know if Melody was actually going to look him in the eye and lie to him.

She looked from the doctor to Cowboy and back. "The…what?"

"Contractions." The doctor spoke slowly and clearly. "How far apart are they?"

"Sir, I'm going to have to ask you to wait outside," the nurse murmured to him.

"And, ma'am, I'm going to have to decline that request. I'm staying right here until I know for sure Melody's all right."

Melody was shaking her head. "But I'm not—"

"Mel, what happened?" Another nurse came bursting through the door. She didn't wait for an answer before turning to the doctor. "It's nearly two months too soon. Have you given her something to stop the contractions? How far is she dilated?"

"I'm not having—"

"I've given her nothing," the doctor reported calmly. "If she's having contractions, they're *very* far apart. I haven't even done a pelvic exam."

"Sir, her sister's here now. Please wait outside," the older nurse murmured, trying to push him gently toward the door.

Cowboy didn't budge. So this was Mel's sister. Of course. Mel had told him she was a nurse.

"I don't *need* a pelvic exam," Melody protested loudly. "I'm not having contractions at all. I was running after Andy Marshall and I got a little dizzy, that's all."

Her sister nearly jumped down her throat. "You were *running!*"

Melody sat up again, turning toward Cowboy. "You caught Andy for me. I saw you. Is he here?"

"No. I'm sorry. He ran away while I was getting you into my car."

"Shoot! *Shoot!*" Melody turned toward her sister. "Brittany, you've got to call the Romanellas for me. Andy's going to run away because he thinks Vince is going to take his belt to him for getting into another fight!"

But Brittany was looking at Cowboy, noticing him for the first time. Her eyes were a different shade of blue than Mel's. Her face was sharper, more angular, too, but it was clear the two women were closely related. "Who the hell are you?"

"That depends on the baby's due date," he answered.

"What?"

"He brought Melody in," the other nurse told her. "I've been trying to tell him—"

"Can we focus on *Melody* for a minute?" the doctor asked, gently trying to push Melody back down onto the bed. "I'd like to do that pelvic anyway—make sure that fall didn't do anything it shouldn't have."

The gray-haired nurse was persistent. "Sir, now you *really* must wait outside."

Brittany was still looking at him, her eyes narrowed in speculation. "Her due date, huh?"

Melody sat up again. "If we don't hurry, Andy Marshall will be gone!"

"December first," Brittany told Cowboy. She looked him over more carefully, from the tips of his boots to the end of his ponytail. "My God, you're what's-his-name, the SEAL, aren't you?"

December first. That made more sense. Melody *wasn't* due now—she *wasn't* about to have the baby. With her slender frame and petite build she only *looked* as if she were going to pop any minute.

December... Cowboy quickly counted back nine months to... March. He'd been in the Middle East in March performing that hostage rescue. And after that, he'd spent six solid days in heaven.

He met Melody's eyes. She knew without a doubt that he'd done the easy math and put two and two together—

or, more accurately, one and one. And in this case, one and one had very definitely made three.

"I'm Lieutenant Harlan Jones," he said, holding Melody's gaze, daring her to deny what he was about to say. "I'm the baby's father."

JONES WAS WAITING for her in the hospital lounge.

Melody took a deep breath when she saw him, afraid that she might pass out again. She'd more than half expected him to be long gone.

Brittany tightened her grip on her arm. "Are you okay?" her sister whispered.

"I'm scared," Melody whispered back.

Britt nodded. "This isn't going to be easy for either of you. Are you sure you don't want me to stick around?"

Jones was standing by the windows, leaning against the frame, looking out over the new housing development going up on Sycamore Street. He looked so tall, so imposing, so stern.

So impossibly handsome.

Melody could see the muscles in the side of his jaw jumping as he clenched his teeth. She saw the muscles in his forearms tighten and flex as he slipped his hands into the back pockets of his pants. She knew firsthand the strength and power of those arms. She knew how incredibly gentle he could be, as well.

Jones looked so odd in civilian clothes—particularly these pants and this shirt that had such a blandly yuppie style. But she realized that she'd never seen him out of uniform. He'd worn black BDUs under his robe during the rescue. And after that, she'd only seen him in—or out of—his dress uniform.

These oddly conservative clothes might be the way he dressed all the time when he was off duty. Or they might have been something he'd specially chosen to wear for this surprise visit.

Talking about surprises…

As she watched, he closed his eyes and rubbed his forehead with one hand, as if he had a headache and a half. And why shouldn't he? He'd come here obviously hoping to sweet-talk his way back into her bed. He'd gotten far more than he'd bargained for—that was for sure.

She could see the lines of stress clearly etched on his face.

He'd smiled and laughed his way through the six days they'd spent together. But then his pager had gone off, and he'd told her he needed to return to California. He'd smiled as he kissed her in the airport, making promises she knew he wouldn't keep. He'd smiled—right up until the point where she told him she didn't want to see him again. And as he struggled to understand her many reasons for making a clean break, he looked so grim and imposing—rather like the way he looked right now.

It was as if no time had passed at all. It was as if they were right back where they'd left off.

Except for the obvious differences. His hair was longer. Hers was, too. And instead of being three days pregnant and ignorant of the fact, she was now seven months along.

Melody rubbed her extended belly nervously, afraid of what he was going to say, afraid of the tension she could see in his face and in the tightness of his shoulders.

The early-afternoon sunshine lit his face, giving his hair an even more sun-streaked look.

She remembered how soft his hair had felt beneath her fingers. It had grown down past his shoulders now—rich and gleamingly golden brown. Freed from its restraint, it would hang wavy and thick around his face, making him look like one of those exotic men who graced the covers of the historical romances she liked to read so much.

He straightened up as he saw her coming. A flick of his green eyes took in Brittany, too, and Melody knew he was wondering if they were going to have this conversation with an audience. She saw him straighten his shoulders and clench his teeth a little more tightly, and she knew he intended to say what he had to say whether or not her sister was listening.

But, "I've got to get back to work," Britt announced. She narrowed her eyes at Jones. "Will you see that she gets home safely?"

Jones nodded, managing only a ghost of his usual five-thousand-watt smile. "That's my specialty."

"Okay," Brittany said, backing away. "Then I'm out of here. It was nice finally meeting you, Lieutenant Jones."

"Likewise, ma'am."

Melody had forgotten how polite Cowboy Jones could be. She'd forgotten how green his eyes were, how good he smelled, how sweet his lips had tasted... No, she hadn't forgotten that. She had simply tried to forget.

"Are you really all right?" Jones asked. His smile was gone again, and he gazed searchingly into her eyes, looking for what, she didn't know. "They don't want to keep you here overnight or anything? Do more tests...?"

She shook her head, suddenly shy, suddenly wishing that Brittany hadn't walked away. "I didn't have much breakfast, and being hungry combined with chasing Andy across the common made me light-headed. It hasn't been an easy pregnancy—I've had trouble keeping food down almost right from the start."

"I'm sorry."

Melody glanced up at him. *I'll bet you are.* She forced a smile. "Brittany wouldn't let me leave until I had lunch. Did you have something to eat?"

"Yeah. I grabbed a sandwich from the cafeteria." He was uncomfortable, too. "Do you want to sit down?"

"No, I want to… I want to go home. If you don't mind."

He shook his head. "I don't mind. It might be easier to talk someplace less public." He led the way toward the double doors. "My car's out this way."

"Are you still with SEAL Team Ten?" she asked, realizing as they stepped out into the warm afternoon sunshine that she had about a million questions to ask him.

"Yes, ma'am."

God, they'd regressed all the way back to "ma'am." "How's Harvard?"

"He's fine. He's good. The entire squad's in Virginia— for the next few months, at least."

"Say hello for me next time you see him."

"I will." He gestured with his head. "Car's over here."

"Have you heard from Crash?" Melody waited as he unlocked and opened her door for her.

Cowboy's swim buddy, Crash, was as dark and mysterious as his odd nickname implied. They'd met him by chance at the hotel in Paris. Crash wasn't a member of Alpha Squad, or even SEAL Team Ten. In fact, Cowboy hadn't been absolutely certain *where* the SEAL he'd called his best friend back in BUD/S training was assigned. Except for the accidental meeting, it had been years since they'd even seen each other, but the ongoing mutual trust and respect between the two men had been obvious.

"I got some email from him just last week. Nothing much—just a hi, how are ya, I'm still alive. But when I wrote to him, the mail all bounced back, undeliverable. Need help getting in?" He watched her maneuver her unwieldy body into the bucket seat.

She shook her head. "It looks more awkward than it really is. Although ask me again when we get to my house—I won't refuse a hand getting out."

Jones leaned over so that he was at her eye level. "I can't believe you still have two more months to go." He quickly backpedaled. "Not to imply that you're not telling the truth or..." He closed his eyes, swearing softly. When he opened them again, his eyes were a startling shade of green against the tan of his face. "What I was *trying* to say was that if that baby gets much bigger, it's going to be a real struggle for you to give birth." He paused. "I want you to know that from the moment I saw you, Mel, I didn't doubt for a minute that the baby was mine."

"Jones, you don't have to—"

"You haven't denied that I'm right."

"I haven't said anything either way!"

"You don't have to." Jones straightened up and closed the car door. As Melody watched, he crossed around the front and unlocked the driver's-side door. "I called your neighbor—Vince Romanella—about that kid. He said to relax—that he'd find him. Andy. That's the kid's name."

The subject of whose baby she was carrying seemed to have been temporarily and quite intentionally dropped. "I know," Melody said as he climbed in and started the car. "Brittany told me you called Information to get Vince's number. Thank you for doing that."

"It was no problem." He took a left as he pulled out of the driveway.

"Don't you want me to give you directions?"

Jones glanced at her. "I know where you live. I checked a map and went out there this morning, but you weren't home." He smiled slightly, politely, as if they were strangers. "Obviously."

Melody couldn't stand it anymore. "Look, I think you should just drop me off and drive away." He was silent, so she took a deep breath and went on. "You can pretend you don't know. Pretend you never came to Appleton. Just… drive into Boston and catch the next flight to Virginia and don't look back. *Don't* say hi to Harvard for me. Don't say anything. You can tell the guys I wouldn't see you and…"

She had to stop and clear her throat. He was holding on to the steering wheel so tightly, his knuckles were white, but he still didn't speak.

"I know you didn't ask for this, Jones. I know this was not what you were thinking when we spent that time together. It wasn't what I was thinking, either, but I've had a chance to deal with it. I've had time to fall in love with this little baby, and I'm okay about it now. I'm *excited* about it. It may not have been what I wanted seven months ago, but I do want it now. But your being here messes things up."

He pulled into her driveway and, leaving the engine running, turned toward her. "It was on the flight to Paris, wasn't it? That's when it happened."

The look in his eyes was so intense, Melody felt as if he had X-ray vision and could see deep inside of her. She prayed that he couldn't. She prayed that he wouldn't know how close she was to throwing up even as she desperately tried to send him away forever.

"Drive away," she said again, steeling herself, purposely making her words as harsh as she possibly could.

"And don't look back. I don't need you, Jones. And I don't want you."

He looked away, but not before she saw a flare of hurt in his eyes. Her heart nearly broke, but she forced herself to go on. It was better this way. It had to be better this way.

"I know for a fact that the last thing *you* need is this baby and me, tying you down in any way at all. All you can possibly do by sticking around is to complicate things. I have money. I have enough saved so that I can spend the next four years at home with the baby. My mother's already started a trust fund for him, for college. There's nothing you can give him that I haven't already thought of and provided."

He tried to cover his hurt with a cynical smile. "Well, hell, honey. Don't hold back. Tell me how you *really* feel."

She felt like a total bitch. But she had to do this. She had to make him leave before he got some crazy idea of "doing right" by her. "I'm sorry. I just didn't think now was the time to play games."

He exhaled in what might've been a laugh, but there wasn't much humor in it. "I'd say we pretty much covered the game-playing seven months ago."

Melody flushed, knowing precisely to what he was referring. They'd left their hotel room only once each night—for dinner. They'd gone out onto the winding, romantic streets of both those foreign cities and had let their insatiable desire for one another drive them half-mad. They'd kissed and touched and gazed into each other's eyes in a silent contest of wills. Who would be the first to give in and beg the other to return to their room to make giddy, passionate love?

Jones had had no shame, sliding his hand up her skirt,

along the inside of her thigh to touch her intimately beneath the curtained privacy of a thick restaurant tablecloth. She had lost the battle that night but won the next when he did the same, only to discover she'd gone out without her panties on—without even the smallest scrap of lace to cover her. And when she smiled into his eyes right there in the restaurant and opened herself to his exploring fingers…

They'd taken a taxi back to the hotel that night, even though the restaurant had only been a short three-block walk away.

It had happened similarly on that flight to France. What began as an innocent conversation about favorite books and movies with a four-star general also heading to Paris took on more meaningful undercurrents. Jones had thought it best to hide the nature of their relationship, and sitting side by side without touching soon had them both totally on edge.

Jones had had to reach past her to shake the general's hand, and his arm brushed her breast. The sensation nearly sent her through the roof—a fact she knew that he had not missed.

She'd countered by leaning across him to get a look out the window at the countryside below and letting her fingers brush his thigh.

He'd stretched his legs and accidentally bumped into her.

She'd excused herself and went into one of the tiny bathrooms. When she returned and sat back down, she looked through her handbag in the pretense of searching for some chewing gum. She opened her bag carefully, revealing its contents—including a white bit of satin and lace—only to Jones and not the general. While she'd been gone, she'd once again removed her panties, knowing full

well Jones would recognize the same article of clothing
he'd taken such pains to remove earlier that morning,
causing them to have to rush to get to the airport on
time.

Melody felt her blush deepen. Who would've thought
she'd have done such things, such daring, provocative,
sexually aggressive things like that?

She'd liked it, though. She'd loved the way Jones had
made her feel as if she was the sexiest woman in the
world. She loved the way he'd needed her so desperately,
the way he couldn't seem to get enough of her.

On that flight to Paris, she'd lured him into the tiny
bathroom. She hadn't realized he wasn't carrying any
condoms. And he had thought she had some in her purse.
But once they were together in that hot little closet of
a room, the need to sate their searing desire had taken
priority over the fact they had no protection.

Jones had roughly pushed her skirt up her thighs and
she had wrapped her legs around him as he thrust deeply
inside her and took her to heaven. He'd pulled out in an
attempt to keep her from getting pregnant, but Melody
was well aware that as a form of birth control, the with-
drawal method was far less than foolproof.

Still, she'd convinced herself that one time wouldn't
matter. Surely they could cheat just once. Surely the odds
were in their favor. And heck, luck had been on their side
so far. Besides, she'd told herself, she wanted Jones badly
enough to be willing to face the consequences.

As she glanced at him now, she knew he was remembering that little airplane bathroom, too. He was remembering the taste of her, the scent of her, the slick heat that
surrounded him, carrying them both to ecstasy.

God knows *she'd* never forget the incredible waves of
pleasure that engulfed her as he gritted his teeth, fighting

to keep himself from releasing all of his seed deep inside her.

He cleared his throat not once but twice before he could speak. "At least the sex was the greatest I've ever had in my life. I mean, it would've been real anticlimactic—no pun intended—to find out that I got you pregnant after having only mediocre sex."

Melody laughed. She couldn't stop herself. It was so like Jones to search for the positives in a no-win situation. But then her eyes filled up and she opened the car door, afraid she was going to burst into tears.

Somehow she managed to scramble up and out of the bucket seat. She closed the door, then he climbed out, too. But he stood with his door open, engine still running, as he looked at her over the top of the car.

"Jones, we had fun together. I can't deny that. But I told you back in March and I'm telling you again—what we shared is not enough to base any kind of real relationship on." Her voice shook slightly, and she fought to steady it. "So good luck. God bless. Don't think I won't remember you. I will." She forced a smile. "I brought home a souvenir."

Jones shook his head. "Melody, I can't—"

"Please. Do me a favor and don't say anything," she begged him. "Just…leave and think about it for a week or two. Don't say anything until you've given yourself time to really think it through. This whole concept— my pregnancy—is still so new to you. I'm giving you a chance to walk away. No strings attached. Give yourself time to think about what that means before you say or do anything rash." She turned and headed toward the house.

He didn't follow, thank God.

She nearly dropped her keys as she unlocked the door.

As she went inside, he was still standing there, half in and half out of his car.

As she shut the door behind her, she heard the car door slam. And then, through the window, she saw him drive away.

With any luck at all, he'd do as she asked and think about his options. And if her luck held, he would realize that she was dead serious about this easy way out she was giving him. And that would be that. He wouldn't call, he wouldn't write.

She would never see Lt. Harlan Jones of the U.S. Navy SEALs again.

The baby kicked her, hard.

CHAPTER FIVE

COWBOY THOUGHT MEL was going to faint again, merely at the sight of him.

He opened the screen door, ready to catch her, but Melody stepped out on the porch rather than let him into the house.

"What are you doing here?" She sounded breathless, shocked, as if she'd actually expected him to take her advice and leave town.

He met her eyes squarely, forcing himself to keep breathing as the enormity of what he was about to do seemed to set itself down directly on his chest. "I think you can probably figure it out."

Melody sat on the edge of one of the plastic lounge chairs that hadn't yet been moved inside for the coming winter. "Oh, God."

He'd put on his white dress uniform, hat and all. He'd even shined his shoes for the occasion. This was not your everyday, average social call.

"Sweetie, who's…?" Brittany's voice trailed off as she came to look out the screen.

"Good evening, ma'am." Cowboy was uncertain if the covered porch was considered indoors or out. He took off his hat, deciding that the ceiling above his head had to count for something. And he didn't want to risk being rude. God knows he was going into this with enough points against him already.

Brittany did a double take. "Are those all *medals?*" she asked.

"Yes, ma'am."

Melody wasn't looking at him. She was staring off into space, across the front yard and down the road that led into town. She looked worn-out and about as unhappy as he'd ever seen her. Even in the Middle East, in the midst of all the danger and death, she hadn't looked this defeated.

Her sister pushed open the screen door. "God, you've got—there must be...*how* many?"

"Lucky thirteen, ma'am."

"*Thirteen* medals. My God."

She leaned even closer to look and Cowboy cleared his throat. "If you'll excuse us, Brittany...? You see, I came over here tonight to ask Melody to marry me."

He managed to get the words out without choking. Dear God, what was he doing here? The answer came swiftly: he was doing the only thing he could do now. He was doing the right thing.

Melody looked up at him, clearly surprised he'd be so forthcoming.

He smiled at her, praying he didn't look as terrified as he felt. She'd told him back in Paris that she couldn't resist his smile. He held out his hand, too. "What do you say we go for a walk?"

But she didn't reach for him. In fact, she all but slapped at his hand. "Didn't you hear *any*thing I said this afternoon?"

It seemed as if over the past seven months, she'd somehow learned to resist him.

"I'll just go and, um, go." Brittany faded back into the house.

"'You don't need me.'" Cowboy repeated Melody's

words. "'You don't want me. You've got it all figured out. You and you alone can give this baby everything he or she needs.' Except you're wrong. Without me, you can't give this child legitimacy. And you can't be his father."

His words came out sounding a whole lot more bitter than he'd intended, and as he watched, her eyes filled with tears.

"I didn't say those things purposely to hurt you, Jones," she told him quietly. "I just thought... I wanted to give you a chance to escape. To get away from here free and clear. I wanted to keep you from doing exactly what you're doing right now. I thought if I could make you see that I truly, honestly don't need you to support me or the baby—"

"You actually thought I'd just walk away?" Cowboy felt sick to his stomach.

Her tears almost overflowed, but she fiercely blinked them back. "I thought if I could convince you that I'm absolutely not your responsibility—"

"You truly believed I'd just turn around and go back to the Alpha Squad and never even *think* of you again?" Cowboy sat down heavily in the chair directly across from hers. "Honey, you don't know me very well."

Melody leaned forward. "That's the point. We don't know each other at all. We were together for...what? Eight days? During which time we actually *talked* for all of eight hours? That's not enough to build a relationship on, let alone a *marriage!*"

Even tired, even with the seriousness of this argument keeping her from smiling, she was lovely.

There was a trail of freckles across her nose and cheeks, making her look as if she had slowly ripened in the summer sun. Her pregnancy had added a lushness to her body, a womanly fullness to her breasts and hips that had been almost boyishly slender before. Even her face was fuller, less little-girl cute and more grown-woman beautiful.

Cowboy wanted to touch her. He was dying to press his hand against the tautness of her stomach, to feel the reality of her baby—*his* baby—beneath his fingers.

They'd done this together. They'd created this baby in the cramped bathroom of that 747 to Paris. It had to have happened then. It was the only time they hadn't used protection. Hell, it was the only time in thirteen years he'd had sex without a condom.

He could still remember the dizzying swiftness with which he had thrown aside a lifetime of precaution and control. And he could also remember the heart-stoppingly exquisite sensation when he'd driven himself deep inside her.

Damn, but he wanted to do that again. And over and over again...

Cowboy cleared his throat, unable to hide the heat he knew was in his eyes as he looked at her. "It's just that, well, let me put it this way. I could think of far worse ways to spend the rest of my life than being married to you."

Married. Damn, the word still made him feel faint.

She held his gaze with eyes the color of a perfect summer sky. They were so familiar, those eyes. He'd dreamed about her eyes more times than he could count. He'd dreamed about sitting right here, across from her on the front porch of her house and gazing at her.

He'd dreamed that he'd touch her. He'd trail one finger down the silky smoothness of her cheek and she would smile and open her arms to him. And then, finally, after all these months of starving for the taste of her lips, he would kiss her and...

But here in real life, he didn't dare reach for her. And she didn't smile. She simply looked away.

But not before he saw it—the undeniable answering heat of attraction that flashed across her face. There was still a spark between them. Despite everything she'd said, she was not unaffected by his presence. But it just wasn't enough.

"I can't think of anything worse," she said softly, "than to get married for the wrong reason."

"And you don't think that little baby you're carrying is a right enough reason?"

Melody lifted her chin in the air in that gesture of defiance that was so familiar. "No, I don't. Love is the only reason two people should get married."

He was about to speak, but she stopped him. "And I *know* you don't love me, so don't insult my intelligence by even trying to pretend that you do. People don't really fall in love at first sight—or even after eight days. Lust, yes, but not love. Love takes time. The kind of love you base a long-term relationship on—a relationship like marriage—needs to grow over a course of weeks and months and even *years*. What we experienced during my rescue and those days following it had nothing to do with love. Love is about normal things—about sharing breakfast and then going off to work. It's about working in the yard together on the weekend. It's about sitting on the back porch and watching the sunset."

"When I go off to work, I don't come back for four weeks," Cowboy said quietly.

"I know." She gave him a very sad smile. "That's not what I want from a husband. If I'm going to get married, it's going to be to a man whose idea of risking his life is to mow the lawn near the hornet's nest."

Cowboy was silent. He'd never been one for long

speeches. He'd never been the type for philosophizing or debating some minute detail of an issue the way Harvard could do for hours at a time.

But at this crucial moment, Cowboy wished he had Harvard's talent for waxing eloquent. Because he knew how he felt—he just wasn't certain he'd be able to find the right words to explain.

"Sometimes, Mel," he started slowly, hesitantly, "you've got to take what life dishes out. And sometimes that's real different from what you hoped for or what you expected. I mean, I didn't exactly picture myself getting married and starting a family for a whole hell of a lot of years, but here I am, sitting here with a diamond ring in a box in my pocket."

"I'm not going to marry you," she interrupted. "I don't want to marry you!"

His voice rose despite his intentions to stay calm. "Yeah, well, honey, I'm not that excited about it myself." He took a deep breath and when he spoke again his voice was softer. "But it's the right thing to do."

She pressed the palm of her hand against her forehead. "I knew it. I knew you were going to start with 'the right thing.'"

"You bet I'm starting with it. Because *I* believe that baby—*my* baby as well as yours, Mel—deserves a name."

"He'll have a name. He'll have *my* name!"

"And he'll grow up in this little town with everyone knowing he's a bastard. Yeah, you're really looking out for him, aren't you?"

Anger flashed in her eyes. "Stop with the Middle Ages mentality. Women are single mothers all the time these days. I can take care of this baby by my—"

"I know. I heard you. You've got it all figured out.

You've got his college education handled. But you know, there *is* one thing you can't provide for this kid, and that's a chance for him to know his father. *I'm* the only one who can make sure this kid grows up knowing that he's got a father who cares."

Cowboy couldn't believe the words that had come out of his mouth. He was glad he was sitting down. A father who cared. Hell, he actually sounded as if he knew what he was talking about—as if he knew anything at all about how to make sure this unborn child would grow up believing that he was loved.

In truth, he was clueless. His own father had been a dismal failure in that regard. By-the-book U.S. Navy, Admiral Jones was a perfectionist. He was harsh and demanding and cold and—with the exception of Cowboy's joining the SEALs—was never happy with anything he ever did. With the old man as his only real role model, Cowboy wasn't sure he was ready to get within a hundred feet of an impressionable child.

Still, he didn't have any choice, did he? He drew the ring box from his pocket and snapped the lid open. He held it out to her. "Mel, you gotta marry me. This isn't just about you and me anymore."

Melody couldn't bring herself even to look at the ring.

She clumsily pushed herself to her feet, fighting to keep from crying. She'd made a mistake—assuming Jones wouldn't care. She'd misjudged him—thinking his good-time, pleasure-seeking, no-strings disposition would win out over his sense of responsibility.

But a sense of responsibility didn't make for a happy home.

"The worst thing we can do for this baby is enter into a marriage neither one of us wants," she said. "What kind of home life could we possibly give him when we don't even know if we like each other?"

That seemed to floor Jones. He swore softly, shaking his head. "I like you. I sort of thought you liked me, too." He laughed in disbelief. "I mean, come on…"

She stopped, her hand on the screen door. "I did like you," she told him. "I liked you a whole lot when you were the only thing standing between me and death when we were inside that embassy. And I liked you even more when you made love to me, after we were back and safe. But there's a whole lot more to you besides your abilities as a Navy SEAL and your considerable talent in bed. And I don't know *that* part of you at all. And you don't know me, either. Let's be honest—you don't."

Let's be honest. Except she wasn't—not really. She *did* like Cowboy Jones. She admired and respected him, and every time he opened his mouth, every minute longer he hung around, she liked him more and more.

It wouldn't take much for her feelings to grow into something stronger.

And that would be trouble, because adventure and excitement were this man's middle names. There was no way he would be satisfied with a marriage to someone as unadventurous and unexciting as Melody Evans. And after the novelty of doing the right thing wore off, they'd both be miserable.

By then, he'd be bored with her, and she—fool that she was—would be hopelessly in love with him.

Melody looked up at him as she opened the door and stepped inside. "So, no, Lieutenant Jones, I'm not going to marry you."

"I NEED A ROOM."

The elderly woman behind the counter at the local inn

could have been a SEAL team's point man. Cowboy could
tell that she missed nothing with her shrewd, sweeping
gaze. She quickly took in his naval uniform, his perfectly
shined shoes, the pile of medals that decorated his chest.
No doubt she was memorizing the color of his eyes and
hair and taking a mental picture of his face—probably for
reference later when she watched *Top Cops* or another of
those reality-based TV shows just to make sure the uniform wasn't an elaborate disguise when, in fact, he was
wanted for heinous crimes in seven different states.

He gave her his hundred-dollar smile.

She didn't blink. "How many nights?"

"Just one, ma'am."

She pursed her lips, making her face look even longer
and narrower, and slid a standard hotel-room registration
form across the counter to him. "You're from Texas?"

Cowboy paused before picking up the pen. His accent
wasn't that obvious. "You have a good ear, ma'am."

"That was a question, young man," she told him
sternly. "I was asking. But you are, aren't you? You're
that sailor from Texas."

Another elderly woman, this one as round and short
as the other was tall and narrow, came out of the back
room.

"Oh, my," she said, stopping short at the sight of him.
"It's him, isn't it? Melody's Navy fellow."

"He wants to stay the night, Peggy," the stern-faced
woman intoned, disapproval thickening her voice. "I'm
not sure I want his type in our establishment. Having
all kinds of rowdy parties. Getting all of the local girls
pregnant."

All of the…?

"Hannah Shelton called to say he just bought a

diamond ring at Front Street Jeweler's," the round lady—Peggy—said. "On credit."

Both women turned to look at him.

"About time," the tall one sniffed.

"Did he give it to her?" Peggy wondered.

It was odd—the way they talked about him as if he weren't there, even as they stood staring directly at him.

He decided the best course would simply be to ignore their comments. "I'd like a room with a telephone, if possible," he said as he filled out the registration form. "I need to make some out-of-state calls. I have a calling card, of course."

"None of our rooms have private phones," the tall lady informed him.

"Our guests are welcome to use the lobby phone." Peggy gestured across the room toward an antique sideboard upon which sat an equally antique-looking rotary phone.

The lobby phone. Of course. God forbid a conversation go on in this building that Peggy and the bird lady not know about.

"You *did* buy it as an engagement ring, didn't you?" the tall woman asked, narrowing her eyes, finally confronting him directly. "With the intention of giving it to Melody Evans?"

Cowboy tried his best to be pleasant. "That's private business between Ms. Evans and me."

"Thank God, Lieutenant! You're still here!" Brittany came bursting through the inn's lobby door. "I have to talk to you."

"It's Brittany Evans." Peggy stated the obvious to her dour-faced companion.

"I can see that. She wants to talk to the sailor."

"Do you have a few minutes?" Mel's sister asked Cowboy.

He shrugged. "Yeah, sure. Although I'm not sure if the Spanish Inquisition has finished with me."

She laughed, and he could see traces of Melody in her face. The wave of longing that hit him was overpowering. Why couldn't this have been easy? Why couldn't he have arrived in Appleton to find Melody happy to see him—and not seven months pregnant?

But "why couldn't" scenarios were of no help to him now. He couldn't change the past—that wasn't in his control. And difficult as it seemed, he somehow had to change Mel's mind. He had to make her see that they really only had one choice here.

As he'd walked away with that diamond ring still in his pocket, it occurred to him that he'd been taking the wrong tack. He shouldn't have tried to argue with Melody. He should've spent all of his energy sweet-talking her instead. He should've tried to seduce his way back into her life.

Yeah, sure, great sex probably *wasn't* enough to base a long-term relationship on. But great sex combined with a soon-to-be-born baby were grounds for a definite start.

Brittany turned to the two old ladies, fixing them with a pointed finger and a glare. "Peggy. Estelle. If either one of you breathes so much as a word about the fact that I came here to talk to Lieutenant Jones, and my sister hears about it, I swear I will take my chain saw to your rosebushes. Is that understood?"

Estelle didn't seem convinced, lifting her hawklike nose in the air. "She'd never do it."

Peggy wasn't quite so certain. "She might."

Brittany grabbed Cowboy's arm. "Come on, Lieutenant. Let's take a walk."

He scooped his duffel bag off the floor and followed her out into the early-evening dusk.

There was a chill in the air as the sun dipped below the horizon. After weeks of unseasonably warm weather, autumn was definitely on its way.

Melody's sister marched in silence until they were a good fifty feet away from the front porch of the inn. At that point, Cowboy ventured to speak. "I doubt they can hear us from this distance. Although I suppose they could be tracking us via some KH-12 SATCOM." At her frown of confusion, he explained, "Spy satellite. It'd be right up their alley."

Brittany laughed, rolling her eyes and crossing the street, taking them onto the town common. "God, I can just picture Peggy and Estelle down in some high-tech studio in their basement, with little headsets on over their purple hair, gleefully monitoring the private conversations going on all over town."

"Seems they do pretty well all by themselves. In fact, they could probably teach the staff at NAVINTEL a thing or two about information gathering."

Appleton was a perfect little New England town, complete with eighteenth-century clapboard houses that surrounded a picture-perfect, rectangular-shaped common. The common was covered with thick green grass and crisscrossed with sidewalks. Benches and stately trees were scattered here and there. Brittany led the way toward one of the benches.

"This town has a gossip network like you wouldn't believe. We've got the highest busybody per capita ratio in the entire state."

Cowboy swore softly. "That must've been really tough on Melody—I mean, when her pregnancy started to show. There was probably a lot of talk."

"Actually, she didn't give anyone a chance to talk. Come on, let's sit. I've been on my feet, running all day." Brittany sank onto the white-painted bench, and Cowboy sat beside her.

From a playground, way down at the other end of the green, he could hear the sounds of children laughing. Someday his kid would play there. His *kid*. He felt a cold streak of fear run down his spine. How could he have a kid? He wasn't ready to stop being a kid himself.

"Melody went all the way into the city to buy a home pregnancy test," Brittany continued. "She knew if she bought it here in town, word would've been out within two minutes of leaving the store. When the test turned up positive, she didn't have to think for very long before deciding that an abortion wasn't the right choice for her. And giving the child up for adoption was also out of the question. So there she was, pregnant, about to be a single mother. She realized that sooner or later her condition was going to be obvious to the entire town, so she…"

She broke off, chuckling and shaking her head. "I'm sorry—I still can't quite believe she did this. But my little sister crashed one of Estelle Warner's Ladies' Club meetings. The Ladies' Club is really just a cover name for Gossipers Anonymous. I usually don't go—Estelle and I aren't exactly friends—but I was there that day, drumming up support for the hospital's AIDS awareness program.

"At first I thought Melody was there to give me support, but when Hazel Parks opened the floor for new topics of discussion, Mel stood up. She cleared her throat and said, 'I would like you all to know that I have no intention of getting married, but I am, however, two months pregnant.' She didn't even give anyone time to gasp in shock. She just kept going. She gave 'em the facts—that you were the father and that she intended to keep the baby."

"She stood there," Brittany went on, "looking all those gossipmongers in the eye, and offered to answer any questions they might have about her condition and her plans. She even passed around a picture of you."

Cowboy shook his head in admiration. "She told them the truth. And once the truth was out, no one could speculate." He paused. "God, I wish she'd told me, too. I wish..."

He should've called her at the beginning of the summer. He should have swallowed his pride a whole hell of a lot sooner and picked up the phone. He should have been there. He should have known right from the start.

"Although Estelle and Peggy pretend to disapprove, I've got to admit even *they've* been pretty supportive. They even threw Mel a baby shower that the entire Ladies' Club turned out for." Brittany gazed at him. "There's been some talk, but not a lot. And most of it's concerned you."

Cowboy sighed. "And here I am, showing up in town, throwing the gossip squad into an uproar. No wonder Melody wanted me to leave as quickly as possible. I'm just making things worse for her, aren't I?"

"I heard what you said to my sister this evening out on the porch," Brittany said baldly. "And I heard what she said to you, about not needing you. Don't you believe her for a second, Lieutenant. She pretends to be so tough and resilient. But I know better.

"She's been depressed and unhappy ever since she came back from Paris," Brittany told him. "And she may believe with all of her heart that marrying you won't make her any happier, but I've got to tell you, today in the hospital, I watched her when she looked at you. And for the first time in more than half a year, she actually seemed alive again. Don't let her chase you away, Lieutenant."

Cowboy looked at the woman sitting next to him and smiled. "I wasn't about to go anywhere. In fact, I was planning to knock on your door again first thing in the morning."

Brittany took a deep breath. "Good. Okay. I'll plan not to be home."

"And, by the way, since I'm getting a strong hint here that we're allies, you should know that my friends call me Cowboy."

She lifted one eyebrow. "Cowboy. Is that because you're from Texas or because you're some kind of hotshot?"

"A little of each."

Brittany laughed. "Doesn't it figure? Somehow I always imagined Melody spending the rest of her life with an accountant—not one of the X-Men."

Cowboy smiled ruefully. He wished he could feel as certain that Melody was going to see things his way. And despite his belief that getting married was the only solution, he wished that the thought of vowing to remain faithful and true to one woman for the rest of his life didn't scare him half to death.

He'd been so enchanted by Melody that he hadn't been able to stop thinking about her those months they'd been apart. He'd loved making love to her. But she was right. He hadn't come all the way to Appleton to pledge his undying love. He'd come to renew their affair. He'd come to have sex, not to get married.

But now he had to convince Mel to marry him.

That would be hard enough to do even if he didn't

have his own doubts and fears. And he was running out of time. His leave was up at 0900 Monday morning.

Cowboy closed his eyes at the sheer impossibility of this situation. Compared to this mess, a hostage rescue was a piece of cake.

CHAPTER SIX

MELODY WAS A hostage in her own home.

Of course, she was a hostage to her own stupidity and foolishness, but knowing that didn't make it any better. In fact, it made it worse.

Cowboy Jones had been sitting out on her front porch for more than two hours now. He'd rung her doorbell while she was getting dressed to go to the late service at the Congregational Church. She'd wrapped her robe around herself and rushed into Brittany's room, intending to beg her sister to tell him she wasn't home.

But Brittany's bed was neatly made. She was long gone. There was a note on the kitchen table saying that she'd forgotten to tell Melody, but she'd promised to work a friend's shift at the hospital. She wouldn't be home until late.

So Melody had hidden from Jones. She'd taken the chicken's way out and she hadn't answered the door at all. And Jones had made himself comfortable out on the porch, apparently determined to wait all day for her to come back home.

So if she went out now, she'd be forced to admit that she truly had been home all this time. Assuming, of course, that he didn't already know that.

She tried to catch up on her reading, tried not to let herself be unnerved by the fact that this man she had shared such intimacies with was sitting within shouting distance. She tried to convince herself that those twinges of frustration and longing she felt were the result of her being unable to work in her garden. She'd planned to spend the afternoon out in the sunshine and fresh air.

Instead, she was here. Locked inside her house.

Melody slowly opened the window in the room she was making into a nursery, careful not to make any noise. It *was* a glorious day—cool and crisp. She pressed her nose to the screen and took a deep breath.

There was no way she could possibly have caught a whiff of Harlan Jones's hauntingly familiar and utterly masculine scent, was there? Of course not. Not all the way up here on the third floor. She was imagining things. She was remembering—

"Hey."

The sound of a voice in the yard made her jump back, away from the window. But it was only Andy Marshall, crossing over from the Romanellas' yard.

"That's not an Army uniform, is it?" He wasn't talking to her. He hadn't even seen her, and she moved closer to the window to peer down at the boy. "My old man's in the Army."

"I'm Navy," Jones replied from beneath the roof of the porch.

"Oh." There was disappointment in Andy's voice. "Then I guess you don't know my father."

"I guess not." Jones sounded sleepy, his Western drawl more pronounced. Melody could picture him sitting back in one of her lounge chairs, feet up and eyes half-closed, like a lion sunning himself. Relaxed, but dangerously aware of everything going on around him.

"Looks pretty damn uncomfortable, buttoned all the way up like that," Andy commented.

"It's not that bad."

"Yeah, well, you look like a monkey. You'd never get me into one of those things, not in a million years."

"Probably not. Only the smartest, toughest and strongest men get into the SEAL teams. You probably wouldn't come close."

Out on the lawn, Andy took a step back. "The hell with you."

Jones yawned. "The hell with you, too. If you don't want to be insulted, don't insult *me*. But the fact is, SEAL training is tough. Most guys don't have what it takes and they end up dropping out of the program. They run away—the way you did yesterday."

Melody winced. Ouch. Jones wasn't pulling his punches.

"And you're like some kind of god, right?" Andy bristled with outrage. "Because you made it through?"

Jones laughed. "That's right. My pay grade is O-3, but my rank is God. Anytime you feel like it, just go right ahead and grovel and bow down to my magnificence. And if you don't believe me, go to the library and read anything you can get your hands on about BUD/S—the SEAL training program. Of course, in your case, you're probably going to have to learn to read first."

Melody watched Andy, certain that he was going to turn and run away. But to her surprise, the boy laughed and sat down on the steps leading up to the porch.

"You think you're pretty funny, don't you?" he retorted.

"Hey, I'm a god—I don't need to be funny. The mortals laugh even when I make a bad joke."

"Is it really that tough—you know, the training?"

"It's insane," Jones said. "But you know what I learned from doing it?"

"What?"

"I can do anything." Jones paused and Melody could picture his smile. "There's no job that's too tough. There's no task that's impossible. If I can't climb over it, I'll swim around it. If I can't swim around it, I'll blow the damn thing up and wade through the rubble."

Melody closed her eyes. Jones had already done the very same thing to her life. He'd blown it up and now was wading through the rubble.

"So you're the guy who knocked up Melody Evans, huh?" Andy asked.

Jones was silent for several long seconds. And when he spoke, there wasn't even the slightest trace of amusement or laughter in his voice. "You want to rephrase that question so that I'm certain you meant absolutely no disrespect to the woman I intend to marry? You can dis me all you want, but don't you ever, *ever* dis Melody. Not behind her back and not to her face. Do you read what I'm saying?"

"But she doesn't want you around."

"Tell me something I don't know."

"So why are you even bothering?" Andy asked. "You should be grateful and leave while you've got the chance. That's what *my* father did. He left before I was born even. I've never met him, you know. The closest I've ever gotten to him is this stupid watch."

Andy's watch. Melody remembered how carefully he'd checked it after fighting with Alex Parks in the playground. That had been his father's watch. She had guessed it was important to him in some way.

Jones's voice was quiet. "I'm sorry."

"Yeah, well, you know, he probably had things to do. My mother told me he was stationed overseas and she didn't want to go. He didn't have a choice, though. When you're in the Army, you've got to go where you're sent.

You don't have a lot of extra time to spend on having kids." His words were almost recited—as if this was something he'd said over and over in an attempt to justify his father's actions.

Jones was silent, and Melody knew that he didn't want to say anything that would contradict Andy.

But then Andy himself laughed—a scornful expulsion of air. "Yeah, right. I don't know why I'm sticking up for him. Like he didn't *run* to get away from us."

Melody's heart broke for the boy. He was at the age where he was starting to doubt the fairy tales his mother had told him. He still knew all the words, but he was starting to see through them to the truth beneath the surface.

It was a moment before either Jones or Andy spoke again.

"Melody's home, you know," Andy finally said. "Her car's in the garage."

"I know."

Melody closed her eyes. Jones knew.

"I figure sooner or later she'll get tired of hiding and she'll come out and talk to me."

"She'll have to come out tomorrow morning," Andy pointed out. "She's got to go to work."

"Well, there you go," Jones said. "Of course, by Monday morning, I'll be AWOL. Unless I can arrange more leave. Hell, with the amount of vacation time coming to me, I figure I could sit out here on this porch until Thanksgiving."

More leave? Melody closed her eyes. Oh, God, no…

"That would be a stupid way to spend your vacation."

"Yeah, it would be," Jones agreed. "But if that's what I've got to do…"

"But you don't," Andy argued. "She doesn't want you to stay. She doesn't want to marry you. If I were you, I'd've been out of here a long time ago. 'Cause, like, what do you get out of this anyway? I mean, seven months ago, yeah, she was probably pretty hot. But now she's all... well, no disrespect intended, but she's all fat and funny-looking."

Melody grimaced in despair. Andy was only a kid— what should she care what he thought of her physical attractiveness? But she *did* care. She cared what Jones thought and she braced herself, waiting for his response.

"She's 'fat and funny-looking,' as you so tactlessly put it, because *I* made her that way," Jones countered. "I did this, I got her pregnant, and *I've* got to make it right. I don't deal with my problems by running and hiding like some kind of frightened girl."

Melody couldn't stand it any longer. Not only was she some awful fat and funny-looking *problem,* but she was cowardly, as well.

She headed downstairs and threw open the front door before she gave herself a chance to think.

"I am *not* hiding," she announced as she stepped out onto the porch.

Andy looked startled at her sudden appearance, but Jones just smiled as if he'd been expecting her.

"I knew that one would get you out here," he drawled.

He was sitting back in one of the lounge chairs, legs crossed at the ankles, hands behind his head, elbows out, just the way she'd pictured him.

"You were listening?" Andy actually had the sense to look embarrassed.

"Yes," Melody told him tartly. "I was listening. With

my fat and funny-looking ears. I was practicing the age-old Appleton skill of eavesdropping."

"I didn't mean—"

"For me to overhear. Yeah, no kidding, Einstein. And you still owe me an apology for making me chase you across the world yesterday."

"I'm sorry," Andy said.

His quick and seemingly sincere apology caught her off guard. "Well, good," she said. "You should be."

Jones smiled at Andy. "Thanks for keeping me company, but I think you'll probably understand when I say *scat*."

Andy was gone before Melody could blink.

Jones sat up, putting one leg on either side of the lounge chair, leaving space on the cushion in front of him. He patted the cushion. "Sit down. You look like you could use a back rub."

He was right. The tension of the past few hours had turned her shoulders into knots. But there was no way she was going to let him touch her. That would be sheer insanity.

"Come on," he whispered, holding out his hand for her. His impossibly sexy smile almost did her in.

But she sat down on the other lounge chair instead. "You know darn well where we'd end up if I let you give me a back rub."

His smile didn't falter. "I was hoping we'd end up having dinner."

"Right. And we've never had dinner without it leading directly back to my bed," she said bluntly. "Jones, what possible good could come of our sleeping together?"

The warmth in his eyes got hotter. "I can think of one hell of a reason—to remind you how really good we were together."

"When we had sex," she clarified.

"The rest of the time, too."

Melody had to laugh. "There was no rest of the time. We were either having sex or unconscious."

"We spent two days together behind enemy lines and I hardly even touched you the entire time."

"That was foreplay," she told him. "For you, anyway."

His smile was gone and his eyes were nearly neon green in their intensity. "You don't really believe that."

She shook her head. "I don't know *what* to believe—I don't know you well enough to do more than guess. But it sure seemed to me that while I was scared to death, *you* were having fun."

"I was doing my job. And part of that job was to keep you from losing faith."

"You did it well," she told him. "I had total faith in you. God, I would have followed you into hell if you'd told me to."

"So where's your faith in me now?" he asked quietly.

Without his smile to light him up, Jones looked tired. He looked as if he'd slept about as well as she had last night—which was not well at all.

"The faith I have in you is still as strong," Melody said just as softly. "I believe—absolutely—that you think you're doing the right thing. But I also believe that getting married would be a total disaster." She sat up, her conviction making her voice louder. "You'd never be happy married to someone like me. Jones, I work with the local Brownie troop, going around picking up trash on the side of the road for excitement. And when I'm feeling *really* adventurous, I volunteer down at the Audubon Bird Refuge. Believe me, I'm *really boring*."

"I'm not looking to recruit you to join the Alpha

Squad," he argued. "I have six teammates—I don't need to be married to a SEAL."

"And I don't need to be married to a SEAL, either," she countered. She leaned forward. "Don't you see, Jones? I don't want to be married to someone like you. I want to find a boring, regular, average, *normal* man."

"I'm as average and normal as the next guy—"

She cut him off. "Oh, *please!*"

"I am."

"Yeah, I can just picture you in the yard with an edge trimmer or cleaning out the gutters. Or helping me shop for baby furniture—oh, that's *right* up your alley! You can 'take the point' when we go to the mall," she said, using some of the military terminology he'd taught her during their brief time together.

Jones shook his head, trying to hide his smile. "Come on, Mel. You said yourself you don't know me well enough to—"

"I know enough to be convinced that you're the polar opposite of average."

"How can you be so sure?" He threw her own words back at her. "We were either having sex or unconscious."

Jones stood up, and she knew she was in trouble. She held up one hand before he could move any closer. "Please don't touch me."

He sat down next to her anyway, invading her personal space, invading her senses. God, he smelled so good. "Please don't tell me not to touch you," he countered in that slight Western drawl that melted her insides and weakened her resolve.

He lightly trailed his fingers through her hair, not quite touching her. "We can make this work," he whispered. His eyes were a very persuasive shade of green, but there was something in his face that told her he was trying to persuade himself as well. "I know we can. Come on, Mel, say you'll marry me, and let's go upstairs and make love."

"No." Melody pushed herself up and off the chair, desperate to get away from the hypnotizing warmth in his eyes. God, he made her dizzy. She pulled open the screen door and reached for the knob....

Locked.

The door was locked.

She tried it again, praying it was only temporarily stuck. But it didn't budge. Somehow it had swung shut behind her and now was tightly locked.

She and Brittany kept a spare key hidden beneath a loose board under the front welcome mat, but when she lifted it up, there was no key to be found. Of course not. She'd used that key the *last* time she'd locked herself out. And it was sitting where she'd left it—on the foyer sideboard. She could see it through the window, gleaming mockingly at her from among the piles of junk mail.

She could feel Jones watching as she fought the waves of nausea that hit her one after another.

She was locked out.

None of the downstairs windows was open—Brittany had just finished reading a heart-stoppingly scary serial-killer suspense novel and had been making a point to lock the windows at night. Even the mudroom windows were tightly shut. The only open window in the house was the one in the baby's nursery—the tower room, way up on the third floor.

She was going to have to ask for Jones's help.

She turned toward him, taking a deep, steadying breath. "Will you help me, please? I need a ride to the hospital."

He was up out of the chair and next to her in a fraction of a second. "Are you all right?"

Melody felt a twinge of regret. For the span of a heartbeat, she allowed herself to wish that the concern darkening his eyes was the result of love rather than responsibility. But she wasn't into playing make-believe, so she quickly pushed those errant thoughts aside and forced a smile.

"I'm locked out. I need to go get Brittany's key. I think she's probably still at work." Please God, let her be there...

"As long as we're going downtown, why don't we stop and have some lunch?"

"Because I don't *want* to have lunch with you, thank you very much."

He inched a little closer, reaching out to play with the edge of her sleeve. Touching, but not touching. "So, okay, we'll skip lunch, drive into Boston and catch the next flight to Vegas instead. We can get married before sundown at the Wayne Newton Wedding Chapel or someplace equally thrilling. No, don't answer right away, honey. I know the thought overwhelms you and leaves you all choked up with emotion."

Melody laughed despite herself. "God, you're never going to give up, are you?"

"No, ma'am."

The tips of his fingers brushed her arm, and she pulled away, straightening her back. "I can be as stubborn as you can."

"No, you can't. You dull, boring types are never as stubborn as us wild adventurers."

Another wave of dizziness hit, and she reached behind her, suddenly needing to sit.

Jones held her elbow, helping her down into one of the chairs. "Is this normal?"

She pulled her hand free from his grasp. "It's normal for me."

"As long as we're going to the hospital, maybe we should get you checked out. You know, make sure everything's okay…?"

She sat back in the chair, closing her eyes. "Everything's okay."

"You're looking a little green."

She felt him sit down next to her, felt the warmth of his leg against her thigh, felt his hand press against the clamminess of her forehead. But she didn't have the strength to move. "I *feel* a little green. But that's normal—for me, or so my doctor tells me. Every now and then, I throw up. It's part of my particular pregnancy package. I just sip some ginger ale and nibble on a cracker and then—if I'm lucky—I feel a little better."

"And the ginger ale and crackers are…?"

"Conveniently stored in the kitchen," she finished for him. "Inside the locked house."

"Hang on—I'll get 'em."

She felt him stand up and she opened her eyes to see him step off the porch.

"Jones…"

He flashed her a smile. "There's no such thing as locked," he told her and disappeared from sight.

COWBOY UNFASTENED THE screen and pushed the window up even higher. He slipped into the house and looked around as he slid the screen back into place.

This room had recently been painted. The walls were white and the window frames were bright primary colors.

There was a band of dancing animals stenciled across the walls in those same brilliant hues.

He was standing in a nursery.

Some kind of baby dresser thing was against the wall and a gleaming white crib was set up in one corner of the room. Several silly-looking teddy bears were already waiting in the crib, their mouths set in expressions of blissful happiness.

Cowboy picked one of them up. It was as soft and furry as it looked, and he held it as he took in the rest of the room.

A rocking chair sat near the open window. It, too, had been painted white, with several of the same dancing animals carefully stenciled on the back. A package of what looked to be brightly patterned curtains and several curtain rods had been set on the dresser—a project yet to be completed.

It was obvious that Melody had already spent a great deal of time getting this room ready for her baby.

Their baby.

What had she been thinking about as she painted those yellow, red and blue animals on the walls? Had she thought of him at all? Had she wondered where he was, what he was doing?

He gazed into the teddy bear's plastic eyes, unable to keep from smiling back at its loopy grin. But then his smile faded. If Melody had her way, his son was going to know this bear's face better than Cowboy's. This bear was going to be the kid's constant companion while Cowboy would be a stranger.

He felt a rush of anger and frustration that quickly turned to despair. He couldn't blame Melody for her mistrust. Everything she'd said was based in truth.

They didn't know each other very well at all. And

marriage *did* need more than sex and physical attraction to make it work. Growing up in a household filled with arguments, anger and tension could well be worse than growing up in a household without a father.

And it wasn't as if he was any kind of major prize. Sure, he'd made the maverick jump from enlisted seaman to officer, but it wasn't as if he had any great aspirations to follow in his own father's footsteps and become an admiral.

He had a little money saved, but not a lot. In fact, it was barely enough to pay for that ring he'd bought at the local jeweler's. He'd spent most of his disposable income on his car and that sweet little powerboat that was docked down in Virginia Beach right this minute. He liked things that went fast and he'd spent his money accordingly.

He hadn't even considered saving up. The need for financial security hadn't crossed his mind. He'd had no intention of settling down and starting a family for a good, long time.

But now here he was. Standing in his soon-to-be-born son's nursery, his insides tied in a knot because there was no way out, no easy solution.

There was only the obvious solution—the grit-your-teeth and shoulder-your-responsibility solution that involved marriage vows and a shockingly abrupt change in lifestyle.

But hell, he'd made this baby; now he was going to have to live with it. Literally.

Cowboy gently set the bear back in the crib.

Right now, he had to go downstairs and fetch Melody some ginger ale and crackers from the kitchen. And then, despite his own doubts, he had to go out on that porch and convince her to do right by this baby and marry him.

Except every time he sat down next to her, every time

he gazed into her heaven-blue eyes, every time he as much as *thought* about her, he wanted to skip the negotiations. He wanted nothing more than to swing her up into his arms and carry her into the house. He wanted to take her into her bedroom and show her exactly how well they could get along. He wanted to bury himself inside her, to lose himself in the sweetness he'd only known in his dreams for the past seven months.

Despite the fact that her near-perfect body was swollen with child, he wanted her so much he could barely breathe. He'd never even glanced twice at a pregnant woman before—in fact, he'd considered the lack of an hourglass figure to be something of a major turnoff. But now he found himself fascinated by the changes in Melody's body. And he couldn't deny the extremely primitive rush of masculine pride he felt every time he saw her.

He had done that. He had possessed her and made her his own.

In everything but name.

Of course, that insane sense of pride was accompanied by a healthy dollop of toe-curling fear. How on earth was he going to be a good father when he didn't have a clue as to how a good father acted? And how the *hell* was that enormous, destined-to-be-six-feet-three-inches, Harlan Jones-sized baby going to be delivered from petite little Melody Evans without putting her at risk and endangering her life?

And how was he going to react on his next counter-terrorist mission with Alpha Squad, knowing he had a wife and son waiting for him—depending on him—at home?

He went down a few steps and pushed the nursery

door open, then found himself in what had to be Melody's bedroom.

It smelled like the perfume he'd caught a whiff of both yesterday and today. It smelled like Melody—sweet and fresh. The room was a little messy, with clothes flung over the back of a chair, and the bed less than perfectly made.

Her sheets had a floral print that matched the bedspread. Throw pillows spilled over onto the hardwood floor. Her bedside table was cluttered with all kinds of things—books, a tape player, CDs, bottles of lotion and nail polish.

It was a nice room, pretty and comfortable and welcoming—a lot like Melody herself.

Cowboy caught sight of his reflection in the full-length mirror attached to the closet door. The starkness of his dress uniform accentuated his height and the width of his shoulders, and surrounded by the tiny rose-colored flowers and the lacy curtains, he looked undeniably out of place.

He tried to picture himself dressed down in civilian clothes, in jeans and a T-shirt, with his hair loosened from its rather austere-looking ponytail, but even then he didn't seem to fit into the pretty picture this room made. He was too big. Too muscular. Too male.

Cowboy squared his shoulders. That was just too damn bad. Melody was going to have to get used to him. Or redecorate. Because neither of them had any choice. He was here to stay.

He went down the stairs and found the kitchen.

The entire house was decorated in a pleasant mixture of both antiques and more modern furnishings. It was neat, but not obsessively so.

He searched the cabinets for some crackers and found

a box that boasted unsalted tops. He grabbed the package and a can of ginger ale from a refrigerator that was nearly filled with fresh vegetables and went down the hall to the front door. He opened it, making sure it was unlocked before he stepped out onto the porch.

Melody was sitting, bent practically in half, her head between her knees. The position was awkward—her belly made it difficult to execute.

"Sometimes this helps if I feel as if I'm going to faint," she told him without even looking up.

Cowboy crouched next to her. "Do you feel like you're gonna faint?"

"I think it was the thought of you climbing all the way up to that third-floor window," she admitted. "I figured that's how you got into the house." She turned to look at him through a veil of golden hair, her eyes wide and her lips questioningly pursed. "Am I right?"

"It was no big deal." Cowboy wanted to kiss her, but he opened the can of soda instead.

She sat up, pulling her hair back from her face. "Except if you slipped and fell. Then it would be a *very* big deal."

He had to laugh, handing her the can. "There's no way I would slip. It just wasn't that tough a climb."

Her eyebrow went up into a delicate, quizzical arch as she took a sip of the ginger ale. "No? What exactly *is* a tough climb?"

Cowboy found himself looking at the freckles that were sprinkled liberally across her cheeks and nose. Her skin looked so soft and smooth, and he could smell the sweet freshness of her clean hair. Great big God, he wanted to kiss her. But she'd asked him a question.

"Let's see…." He cleared his throat. "Tough is going up the side of an oil rig in freezing weather, coming out of a forty-five degree ocean, carrying more than a hundred pounds of wet gear on my back. Compared to that, this was nothing. Piece a cake." He looked down at his uniform. "I didn't even get dirty."

She took another sip of her soda, gazing at him pensively. "Well, you've certainly proved *my* point."

Cowboy didn't follow. "Your point…?"

"Climbing three stories up the outside of a house *isn't* a 'piece a cake.' It's dangerous. And it's on the absolute opposite end of the spectrum from average and normal."

He laughed. "Oh, come on. Are you saying I should have just let you lie here and feel sick even though I knew it wouldn't take me more than three minutes tops to get inside the house and get you the ginger ale and crackers?"

Melody pressed the cold can against the side of her face. "Yes. No. I don't know!"

"So what? So I can do some things that other guys can't do," he countered.

She stood up. "That's like Superman saying, 'So what—I can leap tall buildings in a single bound.'"

She was preparing to go inside. He should have locked the door behind him when he came outside. "Melody, please. You've got to give me a chance—"

"A chance?" Her laughter was tinged with hysteria. "Asking someone to fly to Vegas to marry you isn't exactly what *I'd* call a *chance!*"

He straightened up. "I can't believe you don't even want to try."

"What's to try? Your leave is up tomorrow morning. God only knows where you'll be going and for how long! If I marry you tonight, I could be a…" She stopped herself, closing her eyes and shaking her head. "No," she said, "forget it. Forget I said that. That doesn't matter, because I'm *not* going to marry you." She opened the screen door. "Not now, not ever. It's as simple as that, Jones. And there's nothing you can do to make me change my mind, short of mutating into a nearsighted accountant or a balding computer programmer."

Cowboy stopped himself from taking a step toward her, afraid to push her farther into the house. "I'll make arrangements to get more leave."

"No," she said, and she actually had tears in her eyes. "Don't. I'm sorry, Jones, but please don't. The next time I need rescuing, I'll call you, all right? But until then, do us both a favor and stay away."

"Mel, wait—"

She closed the door firmly in his face and he resisted the urge to swear and kick it down.

Now what?

Short of going inside after her, Cowboy was stuck waiting for her to come back out. And something told him that she wasn't likely to do that again today.

He needed more time. *Lots* more time.

And he knew exactly the man who could help him.

CHAPTER SEVEN

"WILL *SOME*BODY SPEND the damn hundred bucks to get me more memory for this thing? It's like trying to surf the net on one of those kiddie kickboards. I swear to my sweet Lord above, if this takes much longer, I'm not going to be responsible for my actions!" Wes was giving the computer screen his best psychotic-killer glare when Cowboy tapped him on the shoulder.

"Have you seen the senior chief?"

Wes didn't even look up. "Yo, Bobby—is H. here?" he shouted across the busy Quonset hut before muttering to the computer, "Don't you hang on me. Don't you dare."

"Nope," Bobby shouted back.

"Nope." Wes finally glanced up. "Oh, hey, Cowman! You're back. Feeling better?" His smile turned knowing. "Finally get some?"

Cowboy swatted the smaller man on the back of the head. "None of your damned business, gutterbrain. And by the way, I could see with my own eyes that Harvard isn't here. I was wondering if you knew where I could find him."

"Cowboy didn't get any," Wes announced in a mega-phone voice that belied his compact size as Cowboy moved farther into the Quonset hut, searching for a free desk and a telephone. *Some*body on this base had to know where Harvard was. "Look out, guys. It's like the groundhog seeing his shadow. Cowboy goes on leave and doesn't score and we're in for another six months of winter."

"It's October," Blue McCoy pointed out in his slow Southern drawl. "Winter's coming anyway."

"Good thing *some*thing's coming." Lucky cracked himself up.

Cowboy pretended not to hear as he picked up the phone and dialed Joe Cat's home number.

"Maybe it's the hair," Wes suggested. "Maybe she'd go for you if you got it cut."

"Maybe you need a distraction," Bobby chimed in. "Wes and I hooked up with some really amazing-looking girls who hang out at the Western Bar. Problem is, there's *three* of 'em, so you'd actually be doing us a favor if—"

"No, thanks," Cowboy said, listening to the phone ring. "I'm not interested."

"Yeah, that's what I said, too." Lucky put his feet up on his desk. "I figured since it was Bobby and Wes, they didn't mean amazing-looking like a *Sports Illustrated* swimsuit model, but amazing-looking like someone from the bar scene in *Star Wars*."

Bobby shook his head. "You're wrong about this one, O'Donlon. I'm talking potential supermodels."

"*Potential.* That means either they're twelve or in need of plastic surgery." Lucky rolled his eyes.

"One of these days, O'Donlon," Blue said in his soft voice, "you're going to come face-to-face with the one woman on this earth who alone has the ability to make your sorry life complete, and you're going to walk away from her because she's not an eleven on a scale from one to ten."

"Yeah, yeah, I know. Poor, pitiful me." Lucky pretended to wipe tears from his eyes. "I'm going to die alone—an old and broken man."

Over at Joe Cat's house, an answering machine picked up. "Capt. Joe Catalanotto," Cat's New Yawk–accented voice growled into Cowboy's ear. "I'm not available. Leave a message at the beep."

"Yeah, Skipper, this is Jones. If you see the senior chief, tell him I'm looking to find him ASAP."

"This ol' bar we go to is right up your alley, Texas boy," Wesley said with an exaggerated Western drawl when Cowboy hung up the phone. "There's line dancin' and boot scootin' and everything short of a rodeo bull."

"Including Staci, Tiffani and pretty little Savannah Lee," Bobby said with a sigh. "Course with our luck, Wes, Jones'll hit the dance floor and walk out with all three of 'em on his arm."

"I'm not interested," Cowboy said again. *"Really."*

On the other side of the Quonset hut, the door burst open.

Joe Cat entered with Harvard right behind him. Neither of the two men looked very happy. "Pack it all up, guys, we've been reassigned. We're getting the hell out of here."

Reassigned. Cowboy felt his heart sink. Damn, the last thing he wanted to do was be forced to ask for a transfer away from the Alpha Squad. But if they were being sent overseas…

He had responsibilities now. Responsibilities and different priorities.

Two days ago, his number-one goal would've been to stay with Alpha Squad for as long as he possibly could, no matter where they went, no matter what they did.

Today, his number-one goal was very different.

"What the hell, Cat?" Bobby spoke up. "I thought this FinCOM agent training gig was our silver bullet."

"Yeah, this was the perfect cushy assignment," Lucky

added. "Lots of R & R with the added bonus of a chance to really mess with some Finks' minds."

Joe Cat was steamed. "Yes, pulling this assignment was supposed to be a reward," he told them. "But silver bullet or not, our job was to train a team of FinCOM agents in counterterrorist techniques. We can't possibly train these people effectively if our hands are completely tied—which is the only way the top brass will let us do it."

"Aw, come on, Cat. So we let the Finks sleep in their fancy hotel and we let them do their twenty-mile run from the backseat of a limo," Wes urged. "It's no skin off our noses."

"Yeah, Captain, we can cope with their rule book." Lucky pulled his feet down off his desk. "It's no big deal."

"It'll probably make the job that much easier for us," Bobby argued.

"These agents we were supposed to train," Harvard countered in his rich bass voice, "are going to be used in the field to back up or work with SEAL units. *I* sure as hell wouldn't want to go up against a crazy-assed pack of 'Brothers of the Light' terrorists with some badly trained FinCOM team of fools as the only thing preventing Alpha Squad from being shipped home in body bags."

There was no argument anyone could make against *that.*

"So where's Alpha Squad going, Cat?" Cowboy broke the gloomy silence.

The dark-haired captain looked up at his men and exhaled a single burst of extremely nonhumorous laughter. "Barrow," he enunciated with extra clarity.

"Alaska?" Wesley's voice cracked. "In the *winter?*"

"You got it," Cat said, smiling grimly. "The pencil

pushers upstairs are not happy with me right now, and they're making sure I know it—and you poor bastards pay."

Alaska. Cowboy closed his eyes and swore.

"Not planning to come with us, Junior?" Harvard never missed a thing, no matter how subtle the comment. And Cowboy had said "Alpha Squad," not "we."

Cowboy lowered his voice. "I have a situation, Senior Chief. I was hoping to talk to you privately. I need to take an extended leave. A full thirty days if possible."

Wesley overheard. "Leave? Hell, yeah, H., I need to take some, too. Anything to get out of going to *Alaska.*"

"Let's get this gear packed and stored," Joe Cat ordered. "Our new assignment has us going wheels up in less than two hours."

Harvard shook his head. "Sorry, Jones. There's no time. We'll have to deal with it after we get to Barrow."

"Senior Chief, wait." Cowboy stopped him short. Suddenly, the answer to this top-brass-induced snafu seemed obvious. "Don't you see? That's the solution. Leave. For *everyone.*"

Understanding sparked in Harvard's dark brown eyes and then he laughed. "Harlan Jones Jr., you have the devious soul of a master chief. Cat, guess what Junior here thought up all by himself? The Answer, with a capital *A.*"

"We've probably all got lots of time coming to us. Hell, I've got a full 120 days on the books," Cowboy continued. "And if we stall long enough, say maybe two or three weeks, they won't want to ship us up to northern Alaska because of the risk of bad weather. There's no way they'd send Alpha Squad someplace we could be snowed in—I've heard of people going up there and not able to get back until spring. No matter how ticked off they are at the skipper, they won't do that to SEAL Team Ten's top counterterrorist squad."

Everyone else in the room was listening now, too, including Joe Cat.

Blue McCoy laughed softly, shaking his head. "What do you think, Joe?" he said to the captain. "A vacation in the Virgin Islands with your wife and kid, or cold-water exercises for the squad in Barrow, Alaska?"

Joe Cat looked at Cowboy and smiled. "I'm gonna get hammered for this, but...who wants leave?"

THE CURTAINS WERE up and hanging in the nursery windows.

Melody had meant to do that project before she got too large to stand on a chair. She'd put it off for too long, of course, and had been meaning to ask Brittany to help.

It looked as if Britt had beaten her to the punch.

Melody went back into her bedroom and quickly dialed her sister's number at the hospital. As she waited for Brittany to come to the phone, she sat on her bed and wriggled out of her panty hose. Even with the stretch panel in the front, they were hellish to wear for more than an hour or two.

"Brittany Evans."

"Hi, it's me," Melody said. "I wanted to let you know that I'm home from Ted's photo op."

"It took longer than you thought."

"It was late getting started."

"You weren't standing up that entire time, were you?" Brittany asked.

"No, I wasn't," Melody said. She hadn't been standing, she'd been running. She lay back on the bed, exhausted. "Thank you for hanging the curtains."

"You're purposely changing the subject," Brittany accused her. "It was awful, wasn't it?" she guessed. "You spent half the time with your ankles swelling and the other half of the time in the ladies' room, throwing up."

"Not *half* the time."

"Sweetie, you've got to give Ted Shepherd your notice. This is crazy."

"I told him I'd work up to the election. I *promised* him." Melody *liked* the hectic busyness of her job. All day today, she'd only thought about Harlan Jones a few dozen times rather than the few million times she'd caught herself thinking about him yesterday.

She closed her eyes, feeling a familiar surge of regret. Jones had left. He'd actually gotten into his car and driven away. But that was what she'd wanted, she reminded herself. It was for the best.

"Look, I'm bringing home Chinese for dinner tonight," Brittany told her, "so don't even *think* about cooking. I want you to be in bed, napping, when I get home."

"Believe me, I'm not going anywhere."

"I'll be home around six. I've got some errands to run."

"Britt, wait. Thanks—really—for hanging those curtains."

There was a pause on the other end of the phone. "Yeah, you said that before, didn't you? *What* curtains?"

"The ones in the nursery."

"Mel, I haven't had the time or energy to even go *into* the nursery over the past few days, let alone hang up any curtains."

"But…" Melody sat up. From her vantage point on the bed, she could see up the stairs into the tower room she'd made into a nursery. The bright colored curtains she'd bought to match the animals she'd stenciled on the nursery walls were moving gently in a breeze from an open window.

An open window…?

Melody stood up. "Brittany, my God, I think he's back!"

"*Who's* back?"

"Jones."

"Oh, thank you, Almighty Father!"

"Hey, whose side are you on here?" Melody asked her sister indignantly.

"*Yours.* The man is to die for, Mel. He's clearly got his priorities straight when it comes to his responsibilities, he's impossibly polite, he seems *very* sweet, he's got excellent taste in jewelry and he's built like a Greek statue. And oh, yeah. As if that wasn't enough, he just happens to look like Kevin Costner on a *good* hair day! Marry him. The rest will sort itself out."

"I'm *not* marrying him. He doesn't love me. And *I* don't love *him*."

"Why not? I'm half in love with him myself already."

Melody crossed to her bedroom window and looked down into the yard. "Oh, God, Britt, I've got to go! There's a tent in the backyard!"

"A *what?*"

"A *tent*."

"Like a circus tent—?"

"No," Melody said. "Like a camping tent. Like…"

Jones pushed his way out of the tent and into the yard. The sun glistened off his bare chest and shoulders. He wore only faded jeans, a pair of worn-out cowboy boots and a beat-up baseball cap. His hair was down loose around his tanned shoulders.

"Like an army tent," she finished weakly.

Melody knew that the Dockers and polo shirt Jones had worn the day he'd arrived in Appleton had been similar to his gleaming white dress uniform. He'd worn both outfits in an attempt to be more formal, more conservative. But these clothes he was wearing now—this was the real Jones.

His message was clear. He was done playing games.

As Melody watched, he bent and made an adjustment to the tent, and the muscles in his back and arms stood out in sharp relief. He looked dangerous and hard and incredibly, mind-blowingly sexy.

Despite his long hair, he looked much more like the man she'd first come face-to-face with in the middle of a terrorist-controlled embassy all those months ago.

"A *tent?*" Brittany was saying. "In our yard?"

"Brittany, look, I have to go. He's definitely here." As she watched, Jones straightened up and said something. Said something to whom? But then, Andy Marshall scrambled out from inside the tent, laughing—apparently at whatever Jones had said.

"Sweetie, don't be too quick to—"

"Goodbye, Britt!"

Melody cut the connection, and taking a deep breath she headed downstairs.

She went out the kitchen door and stood on the back porch, just watching until Jones looked up. He glanced at Andy but didn't have to say a word. The kid disappeared.

Jones wiped his hands on the thighs of his jeans as he came toward her. He was smiling, but his eyes were guarded—as if he wasn't quite certain of his welcome.

He was correct to be uncertain. "What do you think you're doing?" Melody asked.

He turned to glance back at the tent as if double-checking exactly what he'd erected there. "The inn's a bit pricey," he told her. "I figured since I'm going to stay awhile, it'd be more economical to—"

"How long, exactly, are you planning to stay?" Melody couldn't keep her voice from shaking. How *dare* he just set up camp in her backyard where she would be forced to look at him, to notice him, to *talk* to him if she wanted to tend to her gardening?

Jones propped a foot up on one of the back steps and rested his arms on his knees as he gave her his best smile. "As long as it takes for you to agree to marry me."

She sat down on the top step. "Gonna get pretty cold in a couple of months, living in a tent. But after a few years, you'll probably get used to it."

He laughed. "Honey, there's no way you and I could live this close to each other for even a few weeks, let alone a few years, without one or both of us spontaneously combusting."

Melody snorted. "Get real, Jones. Have you looked at me lately? Unless you have a fetish involving beach balls, I'm not likely to set your world on fire any time soon."

"Are you kidding? You're *gorgeous*. It's very sexy…."

Melody closed her eyes. "Jones, *please* don't do this."

She never should have closed her eyes. She didn't see him settle on the step next to her, and by the time she felt him put his arms around her, it was too late. She was trapped.

She hadn't forgotten how strong his arms felt, how safe she felt inside his embrace. And when she looked up at him, she found she hadn't forgotten the little flecks of brown and gold floating in the always changing green ocean of his eyes either. And she hadn't forgotten the way the mysterious darkness of his pupils widened, seemingly enough to swallow her whole, right before he bent to kiss her.

He tasted like coffee, two sugars, no cream. He tasted like Paris in the moonlight, like the rough feel of bricks as he covered her mouth with his and pressed her up against a house that had been built four hundred years before Columbus had sailed west to reach the Far East and discovered America instead.

He tasted like chocolate, like expensive wine, like a second helping of dessert. He tasted like everything she'd ever wanted but had taught herself to refuse for her own sake.

He kissed her so gently, so sweetly, almost reverently as if he had missed her as much as she'd pretended not to miss him. And, God, she *had* missed him. There was a place in her chest that had felt hollow and cold for all these months—until now. Now she felt infused by warmth, both inside and out.

She felt him touch her, the warmth of his palm lightly pressing against her extended belly.

"My God," he breathed. "It's really all you, isn't it?"

Melody saw it then. Jones made an effort to smile as she looked up at him, but he couldn't hide the fact that he was thoroughly unnerved. She was having his baby, and as long as he was with her, there was no way he was going to forget that. She could see from his eyes how disconcerted he was, how unsettled he felt.

And just like that, the hollowness was back, making her feel emptier than ever.

She knew with a dead certainty that if Jones were granted only one wish, it would be that he'd had a condom on that flight to Paris. She knew that being tied down with a wife and a child was the last thing on earth that this man wanted. She knew that the last place in the world that he wanted to be was here, sitting on her porch, talking her into doing something he himself didn't want to do.

And yet here he was. She had to admire him for that.

She could see the determination in his eyes as he leaned toward her one more time. His lips were so soft as he kissed her again. She was reminded just how very astute he was when it came to reading her needs. He somehow knew that these gentle, almost delicate kisses would get him much further than the intensely passionate, soul-sucking inhalations of desire they'd shared time and again in Paris.

Of course, it was entirely possible that he was kissing her without that explosion of passion because he no longer felt passion for her.

And why should he? She was a constant reminder of his obligations and responsibilities. And on top of that, she was about as sexy as a double-wide trailer.

Still, he kissed her so sweetly, she felt like melting.

Melody was in deep trouble here. Lt. Cowboy Jones was a warrior and a psych expert. While other men might well have been put off by her constant rejections, he was unswervable. And it was more than obvious that he had a battle plan as far as she was concerned. He'd figured out that she wasn't immune to him. He'd realized that he was still firmly entrenched under her skin and he'd dug in to wait her out. Time and her traitorous hormones were on his side. She was going to have to be even stronger.

She was going to have to start by pulling away from this delicious kiss that was making her knees feel even more rubbery than usual. She was going to have to unlock her fingers from the thick softness of his hair. She was going to have to be tougher than this.

Melody stood up, slipping free from his embrace. "Excuse me," she said. It was amazing how she could sound so calm when inside she was experiencing an emotional tornado. "I have to go inside." He stood up, too. "Alone," she added.

He tried to hide his frustration by taking a deep breath and smiling. "Mel, honey, what do I have to do to convince you—"

"I think the presence of your tent on my property constitutes trespassing. I'll thank you very much to remove it."

He laughed at that. "I figured this way it was hidden behind the house. I thought the fewer people who knew about it, the better. But if you insist, I'll move the tent over into the Romanellas' yard. Vince said that would be okay. Of course, then everyone in town will be able to see it from the street."

"I don't care," Melody said. "Odds are everyone in town knows it's there already."

He took a step toward her and she took a step back. "Mel." He held out his hands, palms facing down as if he were calming a wild animal. "Think about this for a minute. We're both on the same side here. We're both trying to find the best solution for this situation."

"Jones, I *know* you don't really want to marry me," she said. "What I don't know is how you'd be able to make yourself say those wedding vows. It would all be a lie. 'Til death us do part. Yeah, right. Until divorce us do part is more like it. You know it as well as I do."

He leaned back against the porch rail, folding his arms across his chest. "You're right about the fact that I don't want to get married," he admitted. "But if I've got to marry *some*one, I'd just as soon have it be you."

"And *I'd* just as soon have it be someone normal—" She cut herself off. "God, haven't we had this conversation already?"

"Yes," he said. "And I'm going to say it again. I'm no different from any other man."

"Except for the fact that when you get in a knife fight with four-to-one odds against you, you win." Melody shook her head. "Jones, don't you see how incredibly out of place you are here?"

"I'm a SEAL," he said. "I've been trained to adapt to any environment or culture. Appleton, Massachusetts, shouldn't be that big a deal." He straightened up. "Where's the edge trimmer? In the garage?"

She blinked. "What? Why?"

He adjusted his baseball cap as he went down the steps and started walking backward along the path toward the garage as he talked. "You said you couldn't picture me using an edge trimmer. I'm going to help you out by actually letting you watch me use one."

Melody's laughter was on the verge of being hysterical. "You're not going to leave, are you? You're just going to stay here forever and torment me."

He stopped walking. With the sun shining down on him, glistening off his tanned skin, gleaming off his gold-streaked hair, he looked invincible. "That depends on your definition of 'torment.'"

Melody sat down on the steps, fighting the urge to burst into tears. She was *so* tired. She had all that she could handle working three-quarters time during these past few months of a difficult pregnancy. There was no way she could do that *and* go one-on-one in a battle of wills with a man who didn't know what it meant to quit.

Jones came back toward the porch, his eyes darkening with concern. "Honey, you look a little tuckered out." His voice was soft. "Maybe we should skip the lawn-care demonstration so you can go on upstairs and catch a nap before dinner, huh?"

She knew what he was doing. He was trying to show her that he knew the words and music to the middle-class, suburban song. He was trying to be normal. His words sounded as if they'd been married for years.

But all he'd proved was that he'd watched a few dozen reruns of *The Cosby Show* or *Family Ties*. It was one thing to mimic and play pretend games. It was another thing entirely to keep up the pretense of being happily married for the rest of his life.

Melody hauled herself to her feet. "You are not normal," she told him. "You'll *never* be normal. And don't kiss me," she added. "Ever again."

Another of his smiles slipped out as he reached for her again, but she escaped into the house, locking the screen door behind her.

"Thank you for hanging the curtains in the nursery," she told him stiffly through the protection of the screen. "But the next time you come into my house uninvited, I *will* have you arrested."

If Jones's smile faltered at all, she didn't see it.

CHAPTER EIGHT

"YOU DID *WHAT?*"

"I gave him a key," Brittany repeated calmly as she checked the rice and turned on the burner underneath the wok, bending over to adjust the gas flame.

Melody's knees were so weak she had to sit down. "To the *house?*"

"Of course to the house." Brittany added some oil to the pan and went back to cutting up the vegetables for the stir-fry. "What good would an open invitation to use the bathroom and the shower be without a key to the house?"

Melody put her head in her hands. "Brittany, what are you doing to me?"

"Sweetie, your SEAL's been living in the backyard for almost a week now—"

"Thanks to your *first* asinine invitation!" Melody proceeded to give a ridiculously unflattering imitation of her sister's voice: "No, Lieutenant, of *course* we don't mind your tent in our backyard. Of *course,* Lieutenant, you're welcome to stay as long as you like.' I was waiting for you to offer to do his laundry and lay a chocolate out on his pillow each night. Jeez Louise, Britt, didn't you even consider the fact that I might not want him underfoot twenty-four hours a day?"

Her sister was not fazed. "I'm not convinced you know what you want."

"Whereas you do?"

The oil was hot enough, and Brittany tossed thin slices of celery into the wok. "No."

"Yet you insist on encouraging him to stay."

"My encouragement hardly makes up for your *dis*couragement. But since he hasn't gone away yet," Brittany said, "I think it's a pretty strong indication that he intends to stay until you give in."

"I'm not going to give in."

Brittany turned to face her, knife in hand. "That's right. You're *not* going to give in—if you keep doing what you're doing. When you leave for work in the morning, you make a beeline for your car. When you come home, you make a beeline for your room. You haven't let the poor man say more than three sentences to you in the past four days."

Melody lifted her head. "The 'poor man'?"

Brittany returned some of her attention to her cooking, adding broccoli and thinly cut strips of zucchini squash to the wok. "I'm with Estelle and Peggy on this one, Mel. I know that's hard to believe—those two seeing eye to eye with me—but it's true. We think you should stop thinking only of yourself and marry the man."

Melody sat up even straighter. "You swore when I first told you that I was pregnant that you wouldn't lecture me. You said you'd support me whatever I decided to do."

"What I just told you wasn't a lecture," Brittany said firmly, stirring the vegetables. "It was an opinion. And I *am* supporting you, the best way I know how."

"By giving Jones a key to the house and an open invitation to just walk in whenever the mood strikes him?"

"The man is a gem, Mel. This yard has never looked so good!"

Of course the yard looked good. Every time Melody

turned around, Jones was outside her window, raking the leaves or tinkering under the hood of Brittany's car or lifting enormous amounts of weights. Every time she turned around, she caught a flash of sunlight reflecting off smooth, deeply tanned muscles.

Whether it was sunny and sixty degrees or drizzling and barely fifty, Jones went outside without a shirt on. Whether he was working in the yard or sitting and reading a book, he was naked from the waist up. You'd think that after a while she'd get used to the sight of all those muscles rippling enticingly in the sunshine or gleaming wet from the rain.

Yeah, right. Maybe in her next lifetime…

"And I don't know what your lieutenant's done to my car, but it hasn't run this well in years," Brittany added. "You really should let him look at yours."

"He's not *my* lieutenant. And if a smoothly running car is what you're after," Melody said hotly, "maybe I should marry Joe Hewlitt from the Sunoco station instead."

"You're impossibly stubborn," Brittany complained.

"Can we talk about something else?" Melody pleaded. "Isn't there something going on in the world that's more interesting than my nonrelationship with Harlan Jones?"

Brittany made room at the bottom of the sizzling wok for the cubes of tofu she'd cut. "Well, there's always the latest installment in the Andy Marshall adventure."

Melody braced herself. "Oh, no. What did he do this time?"

The stove timer buzzed, and Brittany turned off both it and the heat beneath the rice. "Tom Beatrice caught him outside the liquor store on Summer Street. He'd just given Kevin Thorpe ten bucks to buy him a six-pack of beer and a pack of cigarettes."

"Oh, Andy, you didn't..." Melody sighed, resting her chin in the palm of one hand. "Damn, I thought he was finally adjusting to Appleton."

She'd seen Andy out in the yard, hanging around Jones while he worked. Jones always had time to talk. Sometimes he even stopped to toss a ball around with the kid. She'd been secretly impressed with his patience and hoped that Andy had finally latched on to a man who was, indeed, a worthy role model.

There was no doubt about it. The boy was starved for affection and attention. Melody had run into him a few times downtown over the past week.

The first time they talked, he'd hesitantly reached out to touch her belly again, smiling almost shyly when the baby kicked.

The second time, she'd bumped into him—literally. His cheek was scraped and his lip was swollen, and although he'd insisted he'd fallen off his bicycle, she knew Alex Parks and his friends had been giving the younger boy trouble again. The third time, he'd actually greeted Melody with a hug. He'd said hello to the baby by pressing his face against Mel's stomach—and got kicked in the nose for his trouble. That sent him rolling on the ground with giddy laughter.

He was a good kid. Melody was convinced that deep inside he had a sweet, caring soul. He shouldn't be trying to grow up so fast, drinking beer and smoking cigarettes. "He's only twelve. He probably doesn't even like the *taste* of beer."

"He's twelve going on thirty," Brittany said grimly, "which, at the rate he's going, is how old he'll be when he finally gets out of jail. It's a wonder Tom didn't lock the little jerk up."

"Who's Tom and which little jerk didn't he lock up?"

Melody's shoulders tensed. Just like that, merely at the sound of Jones's voice, she was an instant bundle of screaming nerves.

He was standing on the other side of the screen door, looking into the kitchen.

"Tom Beatrice is the Appleton chief of police. And the little jerk is the kid who's running for Troublemaker of the Year—Andy Marshall. Come on in," Brittany called from the stove. "Dinner's almost ready."

Melody stood up, crossing to stand next to her sister. "You invited him to dinner?" she whispered through clenched teeth.

"Yes, I invited him to dinner," Brittany said evenly. "There's beer in the fridge," she told Jones. "Help yourself. And if you don't mind, would you grab one for me and pour a glass of milk for Mel?"

"It'd be my pleasure. Hey, Mel." Jones had dressed for the occasion. He was actually wearing a T-shirt with his jeans, and his hair was pulled back from his face in a single neat braid. "How're you feeling?"

Betrayed. Melody sat down at the kitchen table and forced a smile. "Fine, thanks."

"Really?" He sat down directly across from her, of course, where she wouldn't be able to keep from looking at him while they ate. *Why* did he have to be so utterly good-looking? And why did he have to smile at her that way all the time, as if they were constantly sharing a secret or a very personal private joke?

"Mel's been having trouble with backaches again," Brittany announced as she set the wok on a hot pad in the middle of the table.

Jones took a sip of his beer directly from the bottle as

he gazed at Melody. "I'm available any time you want a
back rub."

She remembered his back rubs. She remembered
them too well. She looked everywhere but into his eyes.
"Thanks, but a soak in the tub'll take care of it."

Jones took the serving bowl filled with steaming rice
that Brittany handed to him. "Thanks. This looks delicious. What's up with Andy Marshall?"

"The little fool was caught trying to get his hands on
beer and cigarettes," Melody told him.

Jones paused as he dished out the rice onto his plate,
stopping to look up at her. "Shoplifting?"

She shook her head. "No. He paid Kevin Thorpe to
buy them for him."

Jones nodded, passing her the heavy bowl. "At least
he wasn't stealing."

Their fingers touched, and Melody knew damn well it
wasn't an accident. Still, she ignored it. Her heart could
not leap when he touched her. She simply would not let
it. Still, she had to work to keep her voice even. "He
shouldn't be drinking or smoking. Whether or not he
stole the beer and cigarettes is a moot point."

"No, it's not. It's—"

The phone rang, interrupting him.

Brittany excused herself and stood up to answer it.
"Hello?"

Jones lowered his voice. "I think the fact that Andy
didn't simply go into the store and walk out with a stolen
can of beer in his pocket says a lot about him."

"Yeah, it says that he wanted more than one can of
beer. He wanted an entire six-pack."

"It says he's not a thief."

"I'm sorry," Brittany interrupted. "That was Edie
Myerson up at the hospital. Both Brenda and Sharon

called in sick with the flu. I'm going to have to go over and cover for at least two hours—until Betty McCreedy can come in."

Melody looked up at her sister in shock. She was leaving her alone with Jones? "But—"

"I'm sorry. I've got to run." Brittany grabbed her bag and was already out the door.

"Where's Andy now? Do you know?" Jones asked, barely missing a beat in their conversation, as if the situation hadn't just moved from embarrassingly awkward to downright impossible to deal with. He took a mouthful of the stir-fry. "Man, this is good. After a week of Burger King and KFC, my body is craving vegetables."

Melody set down her fork. "Did you and Brittany plan this?"

He washed down his mouthful of food with a sip directly from his bottle of beer. "You really think I'd stoop to lying and subterfuge just for a chance to talk to you?"

"Yes."

Jones grinned. "Yeah, you're right. I would. But that's not what this is. I swear. Your sister invited me for dinner. That's all."

The stupid thing was, she believed him. Brittany, on the other hand, had probably planned to leave right from the start.

Melody picked up her fork but couldn't seem to do more than push the food around on her plate as Jones had a second helping. Her appetite had vanished, replaced by a nervous flock of butterflies that took up every available inch of space in her rolling stomach.

"So how's work?" he asked. "Are you always this busy?"

"It's going to get frantic as the election gets closer."

"Are you going to be able to keep up?" He gazed at her steadily. "I got some books about pregnancy and prenatal care out of the library, and they all seem to agree that you should take care not to push yourself too hard these last few months. You know, you look tired."

Melody took a sip of her milk, wishing he would stop looking at her so closely, feeling as if she were under a microscope. She *knew* she looked tired. She *was* tired and bedraggled, and this dress she had on made her resemble a circus tent. How had Andy described her? Fat and funny-looking. "I'll be fine."

"Maybe I could come to work with you—act as your assistant or gofer."

Melody nearly sprayed him with milk. Come to work with her? God, wouldn't *that* be perfect? "That's really not a very good idea." It was the understatement of the century.

"Maybe we should compromise," he suggested. "I won't come to work with you, if you stop ignoring me."

He was smiling, but there was a certain something in his eyes that told her he wasn't quite kidding.

"I haven't been ignoring you," she protested. "I've been practicing self-restraint."

He leaned forward, eyebrows rising. "Self-restraint?"

She backed off, aware that she'd already slipped and told him too much. She had to get out of here before she did something really stupid—like throw herself into his arms. "Excuse me." She pushed her chair back from the table and stood up, then carried her plate to the kitchen sink.

Cowboy took another long sip of his beer, hiding the relief that was streaming through him. He could do this. He could actually succeed in this mission.

He'd been starting to doubt his ability to get through to her, starting to think she just plain disliked him, but in fact the opposite was true. Self-restraint, she'd said.

Hell, she liked him so much she couldn't stand to be in the same room with him, for fear she wouldn't be able to resist his attempts to seduce her.

Yes, he could win this war. He could—and he would—convince her to marry him before his leave was up.

His relief was edged with something else. Something sharp and pointed. Something an awful lot like fear. Yeah, he could take his time and make her see that marrying him was the only option. But then where would he be?

Saddled with a wife and a baby. Shackled with a ball and chain. Tied down, tied up, out of circulation, out of the action. A husband and a father. Two roles he'd never thought he would ever be ready to play.

But he had no choice. Not if he wanted to live with himself for the rest of his life.

Cowboy took a deep breath. "Mel, wait."

She turned to look warily back at him.

Cowboy didn't stand up, knowing that if he so much as moved, she'd run for the stairs. Damn, she was that afraid of him—and that afraid of the spark that was always ready to ignite between them.

Still, he'd made her trust him before, under even more difficult circumstances. He could do it again. He *had* to do it again, no matter how hard, no matter how much fear of his own he felt. This was too important to him.

He took a deep breath. "What if I promised—" What? That he wouldn't pull her into his arms? Wouldn't try to kiss her? He needed to do both of those things as much as he needed to keep breathing. Keeping his distance from this woman was going to be hard to do. Nevertheless, he had no choice. It was gonna hurt, but he'd done hard and painful things before. "What if I swore I wouldn't touch you? You pick a distance. Two feet, three feet, six feet, whatever, and I promise I won't cross that line."

She wasn't convinced. He could see her about to turn him down, but he didn't give her a chance to speak.

"I also promise that I won't say a single word tonight about weddings or obligations or responsibilities or anything heavy. We'll talk about something entirely different. We'll talk about—" he was grasping at straws here, but she hadn't left the room yet "—Andy Marshall, all right? We'll figure out what we're going to do about him."

She turned to face him. "What *can* we do?"

Cowboy already knew the best way to deal with Andy—directly, ruthlessly and mercilessly. He'd been intending to call on Vince Romanella later tonight and ask his permission to spend part of tomorrow with the kid.

But why not teach Andy his lesson tonight?

"There's a place in the woods, up by the old quarry," he told Melody, willing her to sit back down at the table, "that's always littered with beer bottles and cigarette butts. My guess is that's where Andy was going to go with his six-pack."

Melody actually sat down, and Cowboy used all of his self-control to keep from reacting. He had to play it really cool or she'd run.

"I know the place you mean," she said. "It was a popular hangout spot back when I was in high school, too. But Andy's only twelve. He wouldn't exactly be welcome there."

"He would if he showed up with a six-pack of brew under his arm."

"Why on earth would Andy want to make friends with high school seniors?" Melody wondered.

"That kid he's always fighting with," Cowboy said. "What's his name? Parks?"

"Alex Parks."

"He's only a freshman or a sophomore, right?"

Melody nodded. She was actually looking into his eyes. She was actually sitting there and talking to him. He knew it was only a small victory, but he'd take 'em where he found 'em.

"Well, there you go," he concluded. "It seems like a pretty sound strategy to me. Make friends with people who can crush—or at least control—your enemy. Andy's not stupid."

"Then the six-pack was really just an offering to the gods, so to speak. Andy wasn't really going to drink it."

Her eyes begged him to tell her she was right. He wished he could agree so that she would smile at him, but he couldn't.

"I'd bet he wasn't planning to drink all of it," he told her, "but he was certainly intending to drink some. Probably enough to give him a good buzz. And to come out of it thinking the entire evening was a positive experience. Which would leave him wanting to go back and do it again."

Melody nodded, her face so serious, her eyes still glued to his as if he held all the wisdom and knowledge in the universe.

"So what we've got to do," Cowboy continued, "is make sure his first experience with a six-pack of beer is a nightmare."

She blinked. And then she leaned forward. "I'm not sure I understand."

"Remember Crash?" Cowboy asked. "William Hawk? My swim buddy?"

"Of course."

"To this day, he doesn't drink. At least I assume he still doesn't. He didn't during the time we were going through BUD/S training. Anyway, he told me he wasn't much older than Andy when his uncle caught him sneaking a beer from the downstairs refrigerator." It was one of the few stories about his childhood that Crash had told Cowboy. And he'd told it only to convince Cowboy that no, he didn't want a beer, thank you very much. "Crash's uncle taught him a thing or two that day, and we, in turn, are going to run the same drill with Andy." He smiled ruefully. "It's a lesson I could've used myself, but the admiral wasn't around enough to know what kind of trouble I was getting myself into."

She was watching him. "I thought you told me your father was really strict."

"He was—when he was home. But after we moved to Texas, he was hardly ever home. There were a few years he even missed Christmas."

He had her full attention and he kept going. She claimed they didn't know each other. And as hard as it was to talk about his less-than-perfect childhood, it was important that she understood where he came from—and why walking away from her and this baby was not an option for him.

"You know, I used to be like Andy," he continued, "always making excuses for my old man. He had to go where he was needed. He was very important. He had to be where the action was. Even though—during the Vietnam conflict—he'd more than earned the chance to sit back and relax, he wouldn't ask to be assigned to a cushy post like Hawaii. Hawaii wasn't exactly what my mother wanted, but she would have settled for it. But old Harlan wanted to keep moving forward in his career.

"I always used to think he had such a tough job—going out to sea for all those months, being in charge of all those men, knowing that if an aggressive action started, he'd be right in the middle of it. But the fact is, that stuff was easy for him. *We* were the hard stuff. A wife who honestly didn't understand why he didn't retire from the Navy and take a job selling cars with her uncle Harold. A kid who needed more than constantly being told that B's and B-pluses weren't good enough. You know, I could work my butt off, cleaning my room for him, making it shipshape, and he would focus on the one spot of dust I'd missed. Yeah," he repeated softly, "we were the hard stuff, and he ran away from us."

She didn't say anything, but he knew she read his message loud and clear. *He* wasn't going to run away.

Cowboy pushed back his chair, still careful to move slowly. "Mind if I use your phone?"

She shook her head, distracted, as if she were still absorbing all that he'd told her. But then she looked up. "Wait. You haven't told me exactly what Crash's uncle did that day."

"Do you have Vince Romanella's number?" Cowboy scanned the list of neighbors' and friends' numbers posted on a corkboard near the kitchen phone. "Here it is. And as for Crash's uncle..." He smiled at her. "You're just going to have to wait and see." He dialed Vince's number.

She laughed in disbelief. "Jones. Just tell me."

"Hey, Vince," he said into the phone, "it's Jones—you know, from the Evanses next door? I heard about the trouble Andy got into this evening. Is he there?"

"He's probably in his room, grounded for a week and writing a twenty-page paper on why he shouldn't drink beer," Melody said, rolling her eyes. "Vince's heart is in the right place, but something tells me all the essay writing in the world isn't going to have any impact on a kid like Andy Marshall."

Across the room, Jones smiled again. "You're right," he mouthed to her, shaking his head as he listened to Vince recount the evening's excitement—and the subsequent ineffective punishment.

"Yeah," Jones said into the phone, "I know he's grounded, Vince, but I think I know a way to make sure he doesn't drink again—at least not until he's old enough to handle it." He laughed. "You heard of that method, too? Well, a friend of mine told me that when he was a kid… Yeah, I can understand that. As his official foster parents, the state might not approve of… But I'm not his foster parent, so…" He laughed again.

The way he was standing, leaning against the kitchen counter, phone receiver held easily under his chin, reminded Melody of Paris. He'd stood the same way in the hotel lobby, leaning back against the concierge's desk as he took a call. Except back then, he'd been wearing a U.S. Navy uniform, he'd been speaking flawless French and he'd been looking at her with heat simmering in his eyes.

There was still heat there now, but it was tempered by a great deal of reserve and caution. In Paris, the idea of an unwanted, unplanned pregnancy had been the furthest thing from either of their minds. But here in Appleton, the fact that they'd made an error in judgment was kind of hard to avoid. She carried an extremely obvious and constant reminder with her everywhere she went.

And as much as he was pretending otherwise, Melody knew that Jones didn't really want to marry her.

"Okay," he said into the telephone now. His slightly

twangy Western drawl still had the power to send chills down her spine. "That'd be great. There's no time like the present, so send him over." He hung up the phone. "Andy's on his way."

Melody forced the chills away. "What are you planning to do?"

Jones smiled. "I'm going to wait and tell you at the same time I tell Andy. That way, we can get a good-cop, bad-cop thing going that'll sound really sincere."

"Jones, for crying out loud..."

His smile turned to a grin. "I thought pregnant women were supposed to be really patient."

"Oh, yeah? Guess again. With all these extra hormones flying around in my system, I sometimes feel like Lizzie Borden's crazier sister."

"One of the books I was reading said that during pregnancy most women feel infused with a sense of calm."

"Someone forgot to give me my infusion," Melody told him.

Jones opened the door to the pantry. "I'm ready with a back rub at any time. Just say the word."

She narrowed her eyes at him. "Hey, you promised—"

"I did, and I'm sorry. Please accept my apology." He pulled the string and the pantry light went on. "Do you have any beer that's not in the fridge?"

"Brittany keeps it in there, on the bottom shelf," Melody directed him. "Why?"

"Yup, here it is." He emerged from the pantry with a six-pack of tallboys. "Nice and warm, so the flavor is... especially enhanced. Tell your sister I'll replace these. But right now, Andy needs it more than she does."

"Andy needs...? Jones, what are you—"

"We better go out on the patio." He flipped the light

switches next to the kitchen door until he found the one that lit the old-fashioned stone patio out back. "This *will* get messy. It's better to be outside."

"*Please* just tell me—"

Melody broke off as she saw Andy standing defiantly at the bottom of the porch stairs. "Vince said you want to see me."

"Yes, we certainly do." Jones held open the back door for Melody.

"He said to give you this." The boy spoke in a near monotone as he held out a half-empty pack of cigarettes. "He said they're from three months ago, when his brother came to visit. He said to tell you that they're probably stale but that he didn't think you'd mind."

Andy tossed the pack into the air, and Jones caught it effortlessly in his left hand. "Thanks. Heard you were hoping to do some partying tonight."

Melody grabbed her jacket from the hook by the door and slipped it on as she went out into the cool evening air. "Hello, Andy." The boy wouldn't meet her gaze. He wouldn't even glance up at her.

"So what? It's not that big a deal," Andy sullenly told Jones.

"Yeah, that's what I figured you'd say." Jones set the beer down on the picnic table that sat in the center of the patio. He brushed a few stray leaves from one of the chairs for Melody. "You just wanted to have some fun. And it was only beer. What's the fuss, right?"

There was a flash of surprise in Andy's eyes before he caught himself and settled back into sullen mode. "Well, yeah," he said. "Right. It's only beer."

Melody didn't sit. "Jones, what are you doing?" she whispered. "Are you actually *agreeing* with him?"

"All I'm saying is that people get uptight about the

littlest things. Sit down, Andy," Jones commanded. "So you're a beer drinker, huh?"

Andy slouched into a chair, a picture of feigned nonchalance. His nervousness was betrayed by the way he kept fiddling with the wide leather band of his beloved wristwatch. "It's all right. I've had it a few times. Like I said, it's no big deal."

Jones took one of the cans off the plastic loop that held the six-pack together. "Drinking some brew and having a few smokes. Just a regular old, no-big-deal Saturday night. You were planning to go up to the quarry, huh?"

Andy gave Jones a perfect poker face. "Up where?"

"To the quarry." Jones exaggerated his enunciation.

Andy shrugged. "Never heard of it."

"Don't try to con a con artist. I know you know where the quarry is. You've been up there while I was doing laps. You don't really think I didn't notice you—sneaking up on me like a herd of stampeding elephants."

"I was quiet!" Andy was insulted.

"You were thunderous."

"I was *not!*"

"Well, okay, so you were relatively quiet," Jones conceded, "but not quiet enough. There's no SEAL on earth who would've missed hearing you."

Melody couldn't stay silent a moment longer. "You swim *laps* in the *quarry?*"

"First he runs five miles," Andy told her. "I know, because I clocked it on my bike. Then he swims—sometimes for half an hour without stopping, sometimes with all of his clothes on."

It was Jones's turn to shrug. "Every so often in the units, you take an unplanned swim and end up in the water, weighed down with all your clothes and gear. It's good to stay in practice for any situation."

"But the water up there's cold in August," Melody argued. "It's October, and lately we've had frost at night. It must be *freezing*."

Jones grinned. "Yeah, well, lately I've been swimming a little faster."

"And then after you swim, you run another five miles back here," Andy said, "where you work out with your weights."

Melody knew about the weights. She'd been getting dressed each morning for the past week to the sound of clinking as Jones bench-pressed and lifted enormous-looking weights. But she'd had no idea that he ran and swam before that. He must've been up every morning at the very first light of dawn.

"Even though I'm on vacation, it's important to me that I stay in shape," he explained.

She nearly laughed out loud. This was the man who was going to prove to her how average and normal he truly was?

"But we're getting sidetracked here," Jones continued. "We were talking about beer, right?" He held one of the cans out to Andy. "You want one?"

Andy sat straight up in surprise.

Melody nearly fell over. "Jones! You can't offer him that—he's twelve years old."

"He's clearly been around the block a few times," Jones answered, his eyes never leaving Andy. "Do you want it, Andy? It's not particularly a great brand, but it's not bad, either—at least as far as American beers go. But you probably already know that, right? Being a beer drinker."

"Well, yeah. Sure." Andy reached for the can, but Jones wouldn't let go.

"There's a catch," the SEAL told the boy. "You can't

have just one. You have to drink the entire six-pack right now. In the next hour."

Melody couldn't believe what she was hearing. "There's no way Andy could *possibly* drink an entire six-pack by himself in an hour."

Andy bristled. "Could, too."

Cowboy leaned forward. "Is that a yes?"

"Damn straight!" the boy replied.

Cowboy popped the top open and handed him the can. "Then chug it on down, my friend."

"Jones," Melody hissed, "there's no way Andy could drink that much without getting…" She stopped herself, and Cowboy knew that she'd finally caught on.

She was right. There *was* no way this kid could drink two cans of warm beer, let alone an entire six-pack, in an hour without getting totally, miserably, horrifically sick.

And that was the point.

Cowboy was going to make damn sure that Andy would associate the overpoweringly bitter taste of beer with one of the most unpleasant side effects of drunkenness.

He watched as Andy took a tentative sip from the can, then as the kid wrinkled his nose at the strong beer taste.

"Gross. It's warm!"

"That's how they serve beer in England," Cowboy told him. "Chilling it hides the taste. Only sissies drink beer cold." He glanced at Mel. She was giving him an "Oh, yeah?" look, complete with raised eyebrow. He'd had a chilled beer with dinner tonight himself. He shot her a quick wink. "Come on, Andrew. Bottoms up. Time's a-wasting, and you've got five more cans to drink."

Andy looked a little less certain as he took a deep breath and a long slug of beer, and then another, and another. The kid was tougher than Cowboy had thought—he was actively fighting his urge to gag and spit out the harsh-tasting, room-temperature, totally unappealing beverage.

But Andy wasn't tough enough. He set the empty can on the table, burping loudly, looking as if he was about to protest as Cowboy opened another can and pushed it in front of him.

"You don't have time to talk," Cowboy said. "You only have time to drink."

Andy looked even more uncertain, but he picked up the can and started to drink.

"Are you sure this is going to work?" Melody asked softly, sliding into the seat next to him.

It was already working far better than he'd hoped. Melody was sitting beside him, talking to him, watching him, interacting with him. He was aware of her presence, aware of the heavenly blue of her eyes, aware of her sweet perfume—and more than well aware that he still had a hell of a long way to go before he gained her total trust.

But that wasn't what she'd meant. She'd been talking about Andy.

"Yes," he told her with complete confidence. It would work. Especially with the cigarette factor.

Taking a lighter from the pocket of his jeans, he picked up the half-empty pack Vince had sent over. They were old and stale, Andy had said. Yes, this was definitely going to work.

Cowboy held out the pack to Andy, shaking it slightly so that one cigarette appeared invitingly.

Andy thankfully set down the can of beer and reached for the smoke. He may or may not have wanted it—but Cowboy knew what he was thinking. Anything, *any*thing to take a break from having to drink that god-awful beer.

Cowboy could hear Melody's disbelieving laughter as he leaned across the table to give Andy a light. "Good Lord," she said, "I can't believe I'm sitting here giving beer and cigarettes to a child."

Andy couldn't argue with her use of the word *child*. He'd taken a drag of tobacco smoke and was now coughing as if he was on the verge of asphyxiation.

Cowboy handed him his can of beer. "Here, maybe this'll help."

He knew damn well it wouldn't. It only served to turn Andy a darker shade of green.

"I can't...drink any more," he gasped when he finally found some air.

"Are you kidding?" Cowboy said. "You've got to finish that one and drink four more. We had a deal, remember?"

"Four more?" Now Andy looked as if he was on the verge of tears.

Cowboy opened another can. "Four more."

Melody put her hand on his arm. "Jones, he's just a kid...."

"That's the whole point." He lowered his voice, leaning closer to her so Andy couldn't hear. "He's a kid—who wants to hang out with high school seniors who are too young to drink themselves. It's dangerous in those woods, the way that quarry's flooded. If those kids are going to be walking around up there in the dark, they should be doing it sober, not drunk." He turned to Andy. "You're not even a third done. Get busy, Marshall."

Melody's grip on his arm tightened. "But he's—"

"On the verge of learning an important lesson," Cowboy interrupted. "I don't want him to stop until he's *got* to stop. Believe me, it won't be long now." She was about to protest and he covered her hand with his. "Honey, I know this seems harsh to you, but the alternative is far harsher. Imagine how awful you'll feel if some Sunday morning we've got to go and drag that quarry because the boy genius over there was out staggering around drunk and stupid the night before and fell in and drowned."

She hadn't considered such dire possibilities, and he could see the shock in her eyes. She was close enough for him to count the freckles on her nose, close enough to kiss....

Her thoughts must've been moving in the same direction because she quickly straightened up, pulling her hand out from underneath his.

She'd touched *him.* He saw her realize that as a flush of pink tinged her cheeks. All that talk about keeping his distance—and she was the one who couldn't keep her hands off him.

"I'm sorry," she murmured.

"I know that wasn't about you and me," he quickly reassured her. "That was about your concern for Andy. I didn't read it the wrong way, so don't worry, all right?"

But before she could reply, Andy bolted from the table and lunged for the bushes.

Cowboy stood up. "Go on inside, Mel. I'll take care of him from here on in. I think it's probably best not to have an audience—you know, save the last shreds of his manly pride."

The sound of Andy throwing up a second time seemed to echo in the stillness of the night. Melody winced as she got up and moved toward the kitchen door. "I guess I should go in before I join him in sympathy."

"Oh, hell, I'm sorry—I didn't even think of that possibility."

"I was making a joke. Granted it was a bad one, but…" She smiled at him. It was just a little smile, but it was a smile just the same. His heart leaped crazily at the sight of it. "Are you sure I can't get you anything? A towel or maybe some wet washcloths?"

"No. Thanks. I've got a spare towel in my tent. No sense making you do extra laundry." A joke. She made a joke. He managed to make her feel comfortable enough to make a joke. "Go on, Andy'll be fine. I'll see you later."

Still, she hesitated, looking down at him from the back porch of the house. Cowboy would've liked to believe it was because she was loathe to leave his sparkling good company. But he knew better, and when he looked again, she was gone.

"Hey, Andy," he said as he gently picked the boy up from the dirt under the shrubbery. "Are we having fun yet, kid?"

Andy turned his head and, with a groan, emptied the rest of his stomach down the front of Cowboy's shirt and jeans.

It was the perfect topper to a week that had already gone outrageously wrong.

But Cowboy didn't care. He didn't give a damn. All he could think about was Melody's smile.

CHAPTER NINE

THE BABY WAS working hard on his tap-dancing routine.

Melody looked at the clock for the four millionth time that night. It read 1:24.

Her back was aching, her breasts were tender, she had to pee *again,* and every now and then the baby would twist a certain way and trigger sciatic nerve pain that would shoot a lightning bolt all the way down her right leg from her buttocks to her calf.

Melody swung her legs out of bed. The only way she was going to get some sleep was if she got up and walked around. With any luck, the rocking movement would lull the baby to sleep.

She shrugged her arms into her robe and slipped her feet into her slippers and, after a brief stop in the bathroom, headed downstairs. She actually had a craving for a corned beef sandwich *and* she knew there was half a pound of sliced corned beef in the fridge. If she was really lucky, she'd manage to make herself a sandwich and eat half of it before the craving disappeared.

But the light was already on in the kitchen, and she stopped in the doorway, squinting against the brightness. "Brittany?"

"No, it's me." Jones. He was sitting at the kitchen table, shirtless, of course. "I'm sorry, I was trying to be quiet—did I wake you?"

"No, I was just…I couldn't sleep and…" Melody tried

to close her robe to hide the revealingly thin cotton of her nightgown, but it was useless. The robe barely even met in the front.

Her urge to flee was tempered by the fact that she no longer was merely hungry—she was starving. Her craving for that sandwich had grown out of control. She eyed the refrigerator and gauged the distance between it and Jones.

It was too close for comfort. Heck, anything that put her within a mile of this man was too close for comfort. She turned to go back upstairs, aware of the irony of the situation. The baby had been quieted simply by her walk down the stairs, but now she wouldn't be able to sleep because *she* was restless.

But Jones stood up. "I can clear out if you want. I was just waiting for my laundry to dry."

She realized that he was wearing only a towel. It was fastened loosely around his lean hips, and as she watched nearly hypnotized, it began to slip free.

"Andy did the psychedelic yawn on my last clean pair of jeans," Jones continued, catching the towel at the last split second and attaching it again around his waist.

Melody had to laugh, both relieved and oddly, stupidly disappointed that he wasn't now standing naked in front of her. "I've never heard it called that before. As far as euphemisms go, it sounds almost pleasant."

He smiled as if he could read her mind. "Believe me, it wasn't even *close* to pleasant. In fact, it was about four hundred yards beneath *un*pleasant, way down in the category of awful. But it was necessary."

She was lingering in the doorway. She knew she was, but she couldn't seem to walk away. The towel was slipping again, and he finally gave up and just held it on with one hand.

"How *is* Andy?" she asked.

"Feeling pretty bad, but finally asleep. He had the added bonus of the dry heaves after Vince and I got him cleaned off and into bed."

His hair was still wet from his own shower. If she moved closer, she knew exactly how he would smell. Deliciously clean and dangerously sweet. Jones had the power to make even the everyday smell of cheap soap seem exotic and mysterious.

"Why don't you come sit down?" he said quietly. "If you're hungry, I could make you something to eat. Same rules apply as during dinner. We talk, that's all."

Melody could remember staying up far later into the night with this man, feeding each other room-service food and talking about anything that popped into their heads. Books, movies, music. She knew he liked Stephen King, Harrison Ford action flicks and the country sounds of Diamond Rio. But she didn't know why. Their conversations had never been that serious. He'd often interrupted himself midsentence to kiss her until the room spun and to bury himself deeply inside her so that all talk was soon forgotten.

He'd told her more about himself this evening than he'd had the entire time they'd been in Paris. She could picture him as a boy, looking a lot like Andy Marshall, desperate for his father's approval. She could imagine him, too, getting into the kind of trouble that Andy attracted like a high-powered magnet. She was dying to find out how he'd turned himself around. How had he gone from near juvenile delinquent to this confident, well-adjusted man?

Melody stepped into the room. "Why don't you sit down?" she told him. "I'm just going to make myself a sandwich."

"Are you sure I can't help?"

"I'd rather you sat down. That way, I know your towel won't fall off."

He laughed. "I'm sorry about this. I honestly didn't have anything clean to put on."

"Just sit, Jones," she ordered him. She could feel him watching her as she got the cold cuts and mustard from the refrigerator. She set them on the table. "What I really want is a Reuben—you know, a grilled sandwich with corned beef, sauerkraut and Swiss cheese on rye? Thousand Island dressing dripping out the sides. Except we don't have any Swiss cheese or Thousand Island dressing."

"Salt," he said. "What you crave is salt. But I read that you're not supposed to have a lot of salt while you're pregnant."

"Every now and then, you've just got to break the rules," Melody told him as she took two plates from the cabinet.

"If you want, I'll run out to the store," he volunteered. "There's got to be a supermarket around here that's open twenty-four hours."

She glanced at him as she got the bread from the cupboard. "I can picture you at the Stop and Shop wearing only your towel."

He stood up. "I'll put my jeans on wet. It doesn't bother me. Believe me, I've worn far worse."

"No," Melody said. "Thanks, but no. By the time you got back, the craving would be gone."

"Are you sure?"

"Yeah. It's weird. I get these cravings, and then as soon as I'm face-to-face with the food, I get queasy—particularly if it's something that takes me awhile to prepare. Suddenly, the food I was craving becomes absolutely the last thing I want to get anywhere near my mouth. I stand a better chance if I can make it and start eating it quickly." She sat across from him at the table to do just that. "Help yourself."

"Thanks." Jones sat back down. He pulled one of the plates in his direction and took several slices of bread from the bag.

"So what happens next with Andy?" Melody asked.

"I'm going to get him up early," Jones told her, reaching for the mustard. "Let him experience the joys of a hangover. And then we're going to go over to the library and get some statistics on the correlation between starting to drink at age twelve and alcoholism." He glanced up at her, licking his fingers. "I think it would be a really good idea if you came along."

"What possible good can I do for Andy by coming with you?"

"Oh, it's not for Andy. It's for me. I want you to come because I enjoy your company." He smiled as he took a bite of his sandwich.

Melody tried not to feel pleased. She knew his words were just part of his effort to charm her.

"I don't know," she said. "Saturday's really the only morning I have to sleep late."

"Andy and I'll be at the library for a while," he told her. "You could meet us over there."

"I don't know…"

"You don't have to tell me now. Just think about it. See how you feel in the morning." He watched as she took a tentative bite of her own sandwich. "How is it?"

It tasted…delicious. "It's good," she admitted. "At least that bite was good."

"It must be so bizarre to be pregnant," Jones mused. "I

can't even imagine what it would feel like to have another person inside me."

"It was really strange at first, back when I first felt the baby move," Melody said between bites. "I wasn't even really showing that much, but I could feel this fluttering inside me—kind of as if the grilled cheese sandwich I had for lunch had come alive and was doing a little dance."

Jones laughed. "I've felt that. It's called indigestion."

"No, this is different. This doesn't hurt. It just feels *really* strange—and kind of miraculous." She couldn't keep from smiling as she rested her hand on her belly—on the baby. "Definitely miraculous."

"The entire concept is pretty damn amazing," Jones agreed. "*And* terrifying. I mean, you've still got a month and a half to go before that baby decides he wants to get shaken loose. But by then, he's going to be three inches taller than you. I swear, I look at you, Melody, and I get scared to death. You're so tiny and that baby's so huge. How exactly is this going to work?"

"It's natural, Jones. Women have been having babies since the beginning of time."

He was silent for a moment. "I'm sorry," he finally said. "I promised we wouldn't talk about this. It's just…I don't like it when things are out of my control."

Melody put her half-eaten sandwich back down on her plate. Her appetite was gone. "I know how hard this must be for you," she told him. "I know it must seem as if—in just one split second—your entire life's been derailed."

"But it happened," Jones pointed out, "and now there's no turning back. There's only moving ahead."

"That's right," Melody agreed. "And what lies ahead for you and what lies ahead for me are two entirely different paths."

He laughed, breaking the somber mood they'd somehow fallen into. "Yeah, yeah, different paths, yada, yada, yada. We've talked about this before, honey. What I want to know is, who's going to be your labor coach? You *are* planning to use Lamaze, aren't you?"

Melody blinked. "You know so much about this...."

"I've been reading up. I'd like to be considered for position of coach. That is, if you're still accepting applications."

"Brittany's already agreed to do it," she told him, adding a silent *thank God*. She could just imagine having Cowboy Jones present in the delivery room when she was giving birth. Talking about double torture.

"Yeah, I figured. I was just hoping..." He looked down at her unfinished food. "I guess you hit the wall with your sandwich, huh?"

Melody nodded as she stood up. "I better get to bed."

"You go on up. I'll take care of the mess." Jones smiled. "This was nice. Let's do it again sometime—like every night for the rest of our lives." He smacked himself on the top of his head. "Damn, there I go again. Of course, as you pointed out yourself—every now and then you've got to break the rules."

"Good night, Jones." She let her voice drip with exaggerated exasperation.

He chuckled. "Good night, honey."

As Melody went up the stairs, she didn't look back. She knew if she looked, she'd see Jones smiling at her, watching as she walked away.

But she knew that his smile would be a mask, covering his frustration and despair. This was hard enough for him, considering that marrying her was not truly what he wanted to do. It would've been hard enough to set the wheels in motion and simply follow through. But for him to sit there night after night, day after day, and try to convince her that marriage was for the best when he didn't quite believe it himself...

She felt sorry for him.

Almost as sorry as she felt for herself.

"Hey, guys. Find out anything good?"

Cowboy glanced up from the library computer to see Brittany Evans standing behind Andy's chair. He turned, looking past her, making a quick sweep of the library, searching for her sister. But if Melody was there, she was out of sight, hiding among the stacks.

"She's outside," Brittany answered his unspoken question. "She was feeling a little faint, so she's taking a minute, sitting on one of the benches out front."

"You left her alone?"

"Only for a minute. But I figured, instead of me sitting with her... Well, I thought you might want to switch babysitting jobs."

"Yeah," Cowboy said as he stood up. "Thanks."

Andy glared. "Hey. I don't need no *baby*sitter."

"That's right," Brittany said tartly to him as she slid into the seat Cowboy had left empty. "You don't. You need a *warden*. And a grammar instructor, apparently. So what are you researching here? The statistics of alcohol overdoses among minors, resulting in fatalities? Kids who've died from drinking too much. Fascinating subject, huh? How's your stomach feeling this morning, by the way?"

Cowboy didn't wait to hear Andy's retort as he crossed the library foyer, pushed open the heavy wooden door and stepped outside.

Mel was sitting on a bench, just as Brittany had said. The sight of her still had the power to make him pause.

She was beautiful. Her golden hair cascaded down around her shoulders, reflecting the bright autumn sun. And although the air was cool, she'd taken off her sweater and wore only a sleeveless dress. Her arms were lightly tanned and as slender as they'd ever been. In fact, he was certain he could encircle both of her wrists with the thumb and forefinger of one hand. That is, if she would let him get close enough to touch her.

As he moved toward the bench, he was surprised that she didn't leap up and back away—until he realized that behind her sunglasses, her eyes were closed.

Her face was pale, too.

"Honey, are you all right?" He sat down beside her.

She didn't open her eyes. "I get so dizzy," she admitted. "Even just the walk from the car…" She opened her eyes and looked at him. "It's totally not fair. My mother was one of those ridiculously healthy people who played tennis the day before I was born. Two kids, and she didn't throw up once."

"But you have more than just your mother's genes," Cowboy pointed out. "You're half your father, too."

She smiled wanly. "Yeah, well, he never had morning sickness, either."

The breeze ruffled her hair, blowing a strand across her cheek. He wanted to touch her hair, to brush it back and run his fingers through its silk.

"You don't talk about him much." Cowboy reached down and picked up a perfect red maple leaf that the wind had brought right to their feet. "I remember when we were in Paris, you told me about your mother getting remarried and moving to Florida, but you never even mentioned your father."

"He died the summer I was sixteen." Melody paused. "I never really knew him. I mean, I lived in the same house with him for sixteen years, but we weren't very close. He worked seven days a week, eighteen hours a day. He was an investment broker. If you want to know the awful truth, I don't know what my mother saw in him."

"Maybe he was dynamite in bed."

Melody nearly choked. "God, what a thought!"

"Hey, you and Brittany came from somewhere, right? Parents are people, too." He smiled. "Although I have to admit that the idea of my mom and the admiral together is one very scary concept."

Melody was chewing on her lower lip speculatively as she gazed at him. "How come we always end up talking about sex?"

"Maybe because it's been more than seven months now since I've had some," he admitted. "It's kind of on my mind a lot."

"You can't be serious." She was shocked.

Cowboy shrugged. He hadn't meant for it to be such a big deal. "You want me to get you a soda or something to help settle your stomach?"

Melody wouldn't let herself be distracted. "You're telling me honestly that since we were together in Paris, you haven't…? Not even once?"

"No." He was starting to get embarrassed. He stood up. "Why don't I run down the street and get us a couple ginger ales?"

"Jones, *why?*" Her eyes were wide. "I can't believe you didn't have plenty of opportunities to… I mean…" She laughed nervously. "Well, I've seen the way women look at you."

Cowboy sighed as he sat down again. He should have known she wouldn't simply let this go. "Yeah, you're right. Over the past months, I've been in bars where I've known for a fact that I could've gone home with some girl." He held her gaze. "But I didn't want just some girl. I wanted *you*." He twisted his mouth into a crooked smile, aware that he'd revealed far more than he'd intended. "Pretty powerful for a feeling based only on lust and relief, don't you think?"

He saw the confusion in her eyes as she tried to process all that he'd just told her. He willed her to reach for him, to surrender to the truth, to admit that he was right—that there *was* more between them than pure physical attraction. He wanted her to whisper that she, too, hadn't taken another lover since they'd last been together. He couldn't believe that she had, but he didn't know for certain, and he wanted to hear her say it.

But most of all, he wanted her to kiss him.

She didn't.

So Cowboy did the next best thing. He leaned forward and kissed her.

She didn't pull away, so he kissed her again, coaxing her mouth open, pulling her closer, pressing the palm of his hand against the sensual fullness of her belly. She was so sweet, her lips so soft. He felt himself melt inside, felt his muscles turn liquid with desire, felt his soul became infused with new hope.

He *was* going to have another chance to make love to her. Maybe soon. Maybe even—please, God—today.

"I've dreamed about kissing you like this." He lifted his head to whisper, hoping to see a mirror image of his own breathless passion in her eyes.

She was breathless all right, but when he lowered his head to kiss her again, she stopped him. "God, you're good, aren't you?"

"I'm what…?" But he understood what she meant the moment the words left his lips. Melody thought that everything he'd said, everything he'd done, was all just part of his elaborate plan to seduce her.

In a way, she was right. But she was wrong, too. It was more than that. It was much more.

But before he could open his mouth to argue, he felt it. Beneath his hand, Melody's baby—his baby—moved.

"Oh, my God," he said, his mouth dropping open as he gazed into Mel's eyes, all other thoughts leaving his head. "Mel, I felt him move."

She laughed at his expression of amazement, her accusations forgotten, too. She slid his hand around to the side of her belly. "Here, feel this," she told him. "That's one of his knees."

It was amazing. There was a hard little knob protruding slightly out from the otherwise round smoothness of her abdomen. It was his knee. It was their baby's knee.

"He's got a knee," Cowboy breathed. "Oh, my God."

He hadn't thought about this baby in terms of knees and elbows and arms and legs. But this kid definitely had a knee.

"Here." Melody brought his other hand up to press against her other side. "This is his head, over here."

But just like that, the baby shifted, and Cowboy felt a flurry of motion beneath his hands. That was not Melody doing that. That was…someone else. Someone who hadn't existed before he and Melody had made love on that plane to Paris. He felt out of breath and tremendously off balance as the enormity of the situation once again nearly knocked him over.

"Scary, huh?" Melody whispered.

He met her eyes and nodded. "Yeah."

"Finally," she said, smiling slightly, sadly. "Real honesty."

"I've never even really *seen* a baby before, you know,

except in pictures," Cowboy admitted. He wet his suddenly dry lips. "And you're right, the idea of there being one that belongs to me scares me to death." But the baby moved again and he couldn't keep from smiling. "But God, that is so cool." He laughed with amazement. "He's swimming around in there, isn't he?"

She nodded.

He was still touching her, but she didn't seem to mind. He wished they were alone in the privacy of her kitchen rather than here on a bench outside the very public library.

She closed her eyes again, and he knew she liked the sensation of his hands on her body.

"I know you think you're winning, but you're not," she said suddenly, opening her eyes and looking at him. "I'm as stubborn as you are, Jones."

He smiled. "Yeah, well, as a rule, I don't quit and I don't lose. So that leaves really only one other option. And that's winning."

"Maybe there's a way we can both win."

He tightened his grip on her, leaning closer to nuzzle the softness of her neck. "I know there is. And it involves going back to your house and locking ourselves in your bedroom for another six days straight."

Melody pulled away from him. "I'm serious."

"I am, too."

She shook her head impatiently. "Jones, what if I acknowledge you as the father and grant you visitation rights?"

"Visits?" he said in disbelief. "You're going to give me permission to *visit* the kid two or three times a year, and I'm supposed to think that means I've *won?*"

"It's a compromise," she told him, her eyes a very earnest shade of blue. "It wouldn't be a whole lot of fun for me, either. So much for the clean end to our relationship I'd hoped for. And imagine how awful it's going to be for the man I finally do marry—you showing up, flashing all your big muscles around two or three times each year."

Cowboy shook his head. "No deal. I'm the baby's father. And a baby's father should be married to that baby's mother."

Melody's eyes sparked. "Too bad you weren't feeling quite so moral on that flight to Paris. If I remember correctly, there was no talk of marriage then. If I remember, just about all that you had to say concerned how and where I should touch you, and the most efficient way to rid ourselves of our clothing in that tiny bathroom."

He couldn't hide a laugh. "Don't forget our three-point-five-seconds discussion about our lack of condoms."

She frowned at him. "This *isn't* funny."

"I'm sorry. And you're right. I've picked a hell of a time to join the moral majority." He picked up her hand and gently laced their fingers together. "But, honey, I can't help the way I feel. And I feel—particularly after spending the morning with Andy—that it's our responsibility, for the sake of that baby, at least to give marriage a try."

"Why?" She turned slightly to face him as she gently pulled her hand free from his grasp. "Why is this so important to you?"

"I don't want this kid to grow up like Andy," Cowboy told her soberly. "Or me. Honey, I don't want him growing up the way I did, thinking my old man simply didn't give a damn." He gave in to the urge to touch her hair, pulling a strand free from where it had caught on her eyelashes and wrapping it around one finger. "You know, I honestly think this morning is the first time Andy's ever been inside a library. He didn't know what a library card was—I'm not sure he can read half of what we pulled up on that computer screen. And I know for a fact that boy has never held a book in his hands outside of school. *Tom Sawyer,* Mel. The kid's never read it, never even heard of it. 'Mark Twain, who's he?' Andy said. *Damn.* And I'm not saying that if his father was around, it'd be any different, but fact is, it's hard to like yourself when one of the two most important people in your life deserts you. And it's hard as hell to get ahead when you don't like yourself very much."

Cowboy took a deep breath and continued. "I want that baby you're carrying to like himself. I want him to know without a shadow of a doubt that his daddy likes him, too—enough to insist upon marrying his mom and giving him a legitimate name."

Melody met his gaze as she pulled herself to her feet, and he hoped his plea had made an impact.

"Think about it," he told her. "Please."

She nodded. And changed the subject as he followed her into the library. "We better go rescue Andy. Britt's not one of his all-time favorite people."

But as Cowboy looked, he saw Andy and Mel's sister sitting where he'd left them, in front of the computer, heads close together.

The two of them barely glanced up as Cowboy and Melody approached. They were playing some kind of bloodthirsty-looking computer game they'd no doubt found while surfing the Net.

"This would be *so* much better on my computer at home," Britt was telling Andy as she skillfully used the computer keyboard to engage a pack of trolls in mortal combat. "The graphics would be much clearer. You should drop by some time—I'll show it to you if you want."

"Can your computer do an Internet search like this one did?" Andy asked.

Brittany snorted. "Yeah, in about one-sixteenth the time, too. Wait'll you see the difference. I swear, this library computer is from the Stone Age."

Melody looked at Cowboy, her eyebrows slightly raised.

He had to smile. If Brittany and Andy could form a tentative alliance, there was definite hope that he and Melody could do the same.

As Melody moved off to glance at a shelf filled with new books, Cowboy watched her.

She had no idea how beautiful she was.

She had no idea how badly he wanted her.

She also had no idea how patient he could be.

He'd once gone on a sneak and peek—an information-gathering expedition—with Blue McCoy, Alpha Squad's XO. They'd been assigned to scope out a vacation *Haus* in Germany's Schwarzwald that was, according to FinCOM sources, to be inhabited at the end of the week by a terrorist wanted in connection with a number of fatal bombings in London.

The Fink sources had been wrong—the tango showed up five days early, leaving McCoy and Cowboy pinned down in the bushes next to the front door and directly beneath the living-room window. They'd been trapped between the house and the brightly lit driveway, hidden by the shadow of the foliage but unable to move without immediate detection from the teams of security guards and professional soldiers that constantly patrolled the premises.

They'd lain on their bellies for three and a half days, counting soldiers and guards and listening to conversations *auf deutsch* and in various Arabic dialects from the living room. They'd relayed all the information to Joe Cat over their radio headsets and they'd waited—and waited and waited—for Alpha Squad to be given permission to apprehend the terrorists and to liberate McCoy's and Cowboy's butts.

He'd come away from that little exercise smelling really bad and hungry beyond belief, but knowing that he could outwait damn near anything.

Melody Evans didn't know it, but she didn't stand a chance.

CHAPTER TEN

MELODY WOKE UP, aware that her afternoon nap had stretched on far past the late afternoon. It was dark in her room and dark outside, as well. Her alarm clock read 11:14 p.m.

Someone had come into her room while she was asleep and covered her with a blanket. But that someone couldn't have been her sister, who had been called away to the hospital before Melody had gone up for a nap, and who, from the obvious emptiness of Britt's room and the quietness of the house, had not yet returned home.

Melody glanced out the window at the tent in the backyard. It was dark. No doubt Jones had gone to sleep himself after he'd tucked her in.

Either that, or it had been Andy. The boy had been spending a great deal of time over at their house, working—or playing—with Britt on her computer. In the week since Jones had done his "tough love" Intro to Drinking 101 session, Andy had been acting less like a twenty-three-year-old ex-con and more like a twelve-year-old boy.

He and Brittany had really hit it off—which was good for both of them. Ever since Britt's divorce, she'd been more likely to focus on the negative instead of the positive. But when Andy was around, Melody heard far more of her sister's musical laughter.

Oh, Britt complained about him. Crumbs around the

computer. Dishes left out on the kitchen table. But she gave the kid his own screen name on her computer account and let him use it even while she was doing the evening or night shift at work.

He *was* a nice kid, despite his bad reputation. He had a natural charm and a genuine sense of humor. But there was no way he would've left Britt's computer long enough to come upstairs and throw a blanket over her. It had to have been Jones who'd done that.

In the past week, he'd been up every morning, sitting in the kitchen while she'd had her breakfast before going to work. After watching her halfheartedly eat dry toast for several days in a row, he'd actually cooked her bacon, eggs, pancakes and oatmeal in the hopes that one of those foods would be something that she would want.

He'd been waiting when she'd returned home from work, as well. She'd gotten into the habit of sitting on the front porch with him, talking quietly and watching the setting sun turn the brilliant autumn leaves even more vivid shades of red and orange.

Jones was always around for dinner, too. Just like Andy, he'd managed to totally charm Brittany. And as for Melody, well, she was getting used to him smiling at her from across the kitchen table.

She was waiting for him to kiss her again—the way he'd done out in front of the library. But as if he sensed her trepidation, he was keeping his distance, giving her plenty of space.

But more often than not, when their eyes met, there was a heart-stoppingly hot spark, and Jones's gaze would linger on her mouth. His message was very clear. He wanted to kiss her again and he wanted to make sure that she knew it.

The thought of Jones up in her room, covering her

with a blanket and watching her as she slept was a disconcerting one, and she tried to push it far away. She didn't want to think about that. She didn't want to think about Jones at all. She focused instead on her hunger as she went downstairs to the kitchen. She was, as they said in Boston, *wicked* hungry.

Melody nibbled on a soda cracker as she searched the refrigerator, then the pantry, for something, *any*thing to eat. With the flu still running rampant through the nursing staff at the hospital, Brittany hadn't had time to pick up groceries. There was nothing in the house to eat. Correction—nothing Melody *wanted* to eat.

She would've gone shopping herself, but Britt had made her promise under pain of death that she wouldn't try to wrestle both the shopping cart and the crowds at the Stop and Shop until after the baby was born.

Of course, if Britt had her way, Melody would spend the next few months in bed. And from the way he'd been talking last week outside the library, Jones was of the same mind-set. But *he* wanted her to stay in bed for an entirely different reason.

Melody couldn't quite believe that his motive was pure passion. She wasn't exactly looking her sexiest these days—unless, of course, one was turned on by a pumpkin. Andy's words, "fat and funny-looking," sprang immediately and quite accurately to mind. No, she had to believe that Jones wanted her in bed only because he knew that once he got her there, he'd be that much closer to his goal of marrying her.

For the baby's sake.

With a sigh, she took her jacket from the hook by the door, checking to make sure her car keys and her wallet were in the pockets. Brittany may have made the supermarket off-limits, but the convenience store up by the highway was fair game.

Maybe if Melody wandered through the aisles she'd see something she actually wanted to eat—something besides an entire sleeve of chocolate chip cookies, that is.

She unlocked the door and stepped out onto the porch, nearly colliding with Jones. He caught her with both arms, holding her tightly against him to keep them both from falling down the stairs.

His body was warm and his hair was disheveled as if he, too, had just woken up. She'd seen him look exactly like this in Paris. She couldn't remember how many times she'd slowly awakened underneath warm covers, opening her eyes to see his lazy smile and sleepy green eyes.

Time had lost all meaning back then. They'd slept when they were tired, eaten when they were hungry and made love the rest of the time. Sometimes when they woke, it was in the dark hours of the early morning. Sometimes the warm light of the afternoon sun slipped in beneath the curtains.

But it never mattered. The rest of the world had ceased to exist. What was important was right there, in that room, in that bed.

"I saw the light go on," he said, his voice still husky from sleep, his drawl more pronounced. "I thought I'd come over, make sure you were okay."

"I'm okay." Melody stepped back, and he let her go. The night air had a crisp chill to it, and she missed his warmth almost immediately. "I'm hungry, though. I'm making a run to the criminal."

He blinked. "You're...what?"

She started down the steps. "Going to the Honey Farms—the convenience store on Connecticut Road."

Jones followed her. "Yeah. But...what did you call it?"

"The criminal. You know, because the prices they charge are criminal."

He laughed, genuine amusement in his voice. "Cool. I like that. The criminal."

Melody couldn't help but smile. "Boy, it doesn't take much to make you happy, does it, Jones?"

"No, ma'am. And right now it would make me downright ecstatic to go to the criminal for you. Just hand me the keys to your car, tell me what you want and I'll have it back here for you inside ten minutes."

Melody looked around. "Where's *your* car?"

"It was, um, getting costly to keep a rental car for all this time." He fished a ponytail holder out of the front pocket of his jeans. Raking his hair into some semblance of order with his fingers, he tied it back at the nape of his neck. "I returned it about a week and a half ago."

"God, and I didn't even notice."

Jones held out his hand. "Come on. Give me the keys and your dinner order."

She stepped past him, heading toward her car. "Thanks, but no thanks. I don't know what I want. I was intending to go and browse."

"Do you mind if I come along?"

"No," Melody said, surprised that it was true. "I don't mind."

She opened the front door of her car, but he moved to block her way. "How about I drive?"

"Do you know how to drive a stick shift?"

Jones just looked at her.

"Right," she said, handing him the keys. "Navy SEAL. God, can you believe I almost forgot? If you can fly a plane, you can certainly handle my car, as particular as it is."

It was much easier getting in the passenger side without the steering wheel in her way. Jones waited to start the engine until after she closed the door behind her and fastened her seat belt.

"The clutch can be really temperamental," she started to say, but stopped when he gave her another pointed look.

But he smiled then, and she found herself smiling, too. She always found herself smiling when he was around.

Jones managed to get the car down the driveway and onto the main road without stalling, without even hiccuping. He drove easily, comfortably, with one hand on the wheel and the other resting lightly on the gearshift. He had nice hands. They were strong and capable-looking, just like the man himself.

"I was thinking," he said, finally breaking the silence as they approached the store, "that tomorrow might be a good day to put your garden to bed for the winter. It's supposed to be in the high fifties and sunny." He glanced at her. "I could help you do it after church, if you want."

Melody didn't know what to say.

"I'm afraid I've never been much of a gardener. I'm not really sure what needs to be done." He cleared his throat. "I figure the best way to do the job is for me to act as your hands and back. You tell me what to do, what to lift, what to carry, and I'll do it for you."

There was only one other car in the convenience-store parking lot and it was idling over by the telephones. Jones slid Melody's car neatly into one of the spots near the doors and turned off the engine. But he shifted slightly to face her rather than climb out.

"What do you think?" he asked.

Melody looked into his eyes and smiled. "I think you heard about the charity apple picking that's going on up at Hetterman's Orchards tomorrow after church, and you want to make sure you have a really good reason not to go."

Jones laughed. "No, I haven't heard anything about anything. What's the deal? Apple picking?"

"Hetterman's has always had a problem hiring temporary help to pick the last of the apples. It's a self-service farm, and people come out from the city all season long to pick their own apples, but there's always a lot left over. About seven years ago, they made a deal with one of the local Girl Scout troops. If the girls could get twenty people to come out and pick apples for a day, Hetterman's promised to award one of the high school kids a five-hundred-dollar scholarship. Well, the girls outdid themselves. They got a hundred people to come and got the job done in about three hours instead of an entire day. And in the seven years since then, it's become a town tradition. Last year, four hundred people turned out for the event, and they finished in less than two hours. And the five hundred dollars from Hetterman's has been matched by Glenzen Brothers Hardware, the Congregational Church, The First City Bank and a handful of private benefactors, making the scholarship a full five *thousand* dollars."

She laughed at herself. "Listen to me. I sound like such a Pollyanna. I can't help it, though. The thought of all those people working together like that for such a good cause just makes me all goose bumpy and shivery. I know, I know, I'm a sap."

"No, you're not." Jones was smiling at her very slightly. "I think it's cool, too. It's real teamwork in action." He was watching her closely, paying careful attention, as if what she had told him was the most important piece of news in the universe. Being the center of the tight focus of all his intensity was somewhat overwhelming, though.

The yellowish parking-lot lamps shone dimly through the car windows, creating intricate patterns of shadow and light on the dashboard. It was quiet and far too intimate. She should get out of the car. She knew she should.

"This year, they're trying to get six hundred people to participate and do the whole thing in under an hour. They want to try to set a record."

He reached forward to play with one of her curls. Touching but not touching. "Then we better plan to show up, huh?"

Melody laughed, gently pulling her hair free from his grasp, trying to break the mood, knowing that she *had* to. She had no choice. If she didn't do *some*thing, it wasn't going to be long before he leaned over and kissed her. "Somehow I just can't see you spending even half an hour picking apples." She unfastened her seat belt, but Jones still made no move to get out of the car.

"Why not?"

"Get serious, Jones."

"I *am* serious. It sounds like fun. Serious fun."

"Apple picking isn't exactly your speed."

"Yeah, well, maybe I don't know anything about that," he drawled, "but I *do* know all about working in a team, and it sounds as if this is one team I'd be proud to be a part of."

Melody got out of the car, fast. She had to, or else she was going to do something really stupid—like kiss *him*.

But he must've been able to read her mind because he followed and caught her hand before she even reached the convenience-store door.

"Come on," he said, his eyes daring her to take a

chance. "Let's make this a plan. We'll do the apple-picking thing, have lunch, then come home and tackle the garden." He smiled. "And then in the evening, if you're feeling really adventurous, we can take a walk down at the Audubon Bird Refuge."

Melody laughed, and Jones leaned forward and kissed her.

She knew exactly what he was doing, what he had been doing over the past week. He was wearing her down little by little, piece by piece. He was actively trying to make her fall in love with him. He was taking everything really slowly. He was making a point to be extraordinarily gentle.

Except this was no languorous, gentle kiss. This time, he took her by storm, claiming her mouth with a hunger that stole her breath away. She could taste his passion along with the sweet mint toothpaste he must've used right before he came out of his tent to meet her.

She could feel his hands in her hair, on her back, sliding down to cup the soft fullness of her rear end. He'd held her that way in Paris, pressing her tightly against him so that she would be sure to feel the evidence of his arousal, nestled tightly between them.

But the only thing nestled between them now was her watermelon-sized stomach.

She heard him half growl, half laugh with frustration. "Making love to you is going to be *really* interesting. We're going to have to get kind of creative, aren't we?"

Melody could feel her heart pounding. She was breathing hard as she looked up into his eyes, but she couldn't seem to pull away. She didn't *want* to pull away. She actually *wanted* him to take her home and kiss her that way again. She wanted to make love to him. God, she was weak. He'd broken down her defenses in just a little over fourteen days. But maybe she had been crazy ever to think she could resist this man.

But instead of pulling her back toward the car, Jones reached for the criminal door. "Let's get what we came for."

He stood back to let her go through first.

Melody reached up to touch her lips as she went into the store. That kiss had been so scalding it should, by all rights, have marked her. But as far as she could tell, her lips were still attached.

The overhead lights were glaring compared to the dim parking lot, and she squinted slightly as she looked around the depressingly bleak little store.

Isaac Forte was clerking tonight. He always handled the night shift—which seemed appropriate. With his pale, gaunt face and painfully thin, almost skeletal frame, he reminded her of a vampire. If daylight ever actually came in contact with him, no doubt he would crumble into dust. But she, too, had become a creature of the night over the past few months. And her odd cravings had made her a frequent customer of the Honey Farms, so she'd come to know Isaac rather well. He had his problems, but having to drink human blood to stay alive *wasn't* one of them, thank goodness.

"Hi, Isaac," she said.

Two men in black jackets were at the checkout counter. Isaac was waiting on them and—

Jones moved so fast he was almost a total blur.

He kicked, and something went flying to the other side of the room.

A *gun*. One of these men had had a gun, and Jones had disarmed him, knocking it out of reach before Melody had barely even noticed it.

"Get out of here!" he shouted as he slammed one of

the men down onto the floor, forcing the one to trip up the other.

The first man was dazed, but the second scrambled away, trying to reach the fallen gun. Melody could see it, gleaming and deadly, on the floor in front of the popcorn and corn chips.

"Melody, dammit, *go!*" Jones bellowed even as he grabbed for the second man, his hand closing around the leather of the thug's jacket.

He was talking to *her.* He wanted her to get to safety.

A rack of paperback books crashed to the floor as the man furiously fought to get free, to reach the gun. Melody watched, hypnotized with icy fear, as Jones fought just as hard to hang on, not even stopping for a second as he placed a well-aimed kick behind him that dropped the first man, the dazed man, to the floor with a final-sounding thud.

There was nothing even remotely fair about this wrestling match. No rules were being followed, no courtesies allowed, no time-outs granted. Jones slammed the gunman's head against the floor even as the man continued his own barrage of blows. Elbows, knees, hands, feet—it was meant to drive Jones back, but the SEAL was unstoppable. He just kept on coming.

The look on Jones's face transformed him, and his eyes sparked with an unholy light. He looked more like beast than man, his lips pulled back in a terrifying snarl of rage.

He kicked the gun even farther away as he flung the man violently in the opposite direction. Cheerios boxes exploded everywhere as he followed, pounding the man, hitting him hard again and again until there was no doubt in anyone's mind that the robber wasn't going to get up. At least not right away.

Outside in the parking lot, the car that had been idling sped away with a squeal of tires.

Even though both men were down and still, Jones moved quickly, going for the gun. Melody nearly collapsed with relief as his hands closed around it. He was safe. She wasn't going to have to stand there and watch him get pumped full of bullets.

She could hear police sirens in the distance. Isaac, no doubt, had triggered the alarm when the fight had started. He now peered warily over the top of the counter, his eyes wide as he gazed at Jones.

Jones checked the gun, removing the clip and releasing the chambered round. And then he looked at her, his eyes still lit from within with the devil's own anger.

"The next time I give you an order, dammit, you *do* it!" He was breathing hard, his chest still heaving as he fought to suck in enough air. His nose was bleeding and the front of his T-shirt was stained bright red with blood, but he didn't even notice.

"An order? But—"

"No buts." He slammed the empty gun down on the checkout counter. Melody had never seen him like this. Not even during the hostage rescue. He was furious. With *her.* "These scumbags had a weapon, Melody. If that dirt-wad over there—" he gestured toward the man who'd put up a fight "—had managed to get his hands on it, he damn well would've used it! And these days, honey, you aren't exactly the tiniest of targets!"

Stung, Melody turned and walked out of the criminal.

"*Now* you leave," he said, pulling the door open to follow her. "*Perfect.*"

She spun back to face him. "I don't take orders from *you*. I'm not one of your SEAL buddies—I don't know *how* to take orders!"

"You managed just fine in the Middle East."

"Yeah, well, look around you, Lieutenant. This *isn't* the Middle East. This is Appleton, Massachusetts. And *I* haven't trained myself to react instantly when I walk into the middle of a convenience-store stickup." Her voice caught on something that was half laughter, half sob. "God, and I was just starting to think that maybe you *were* just a normal guy. Yeah, you're normal—and I stand a shot at winning the Miss America swimsuit competition. What a joke!"

The night was getting downright frosty. Or maybe it wasn't the chill in the air that was making her start to shake.

"I'd like my car keys," she said, lifting her chin, determined to keep from crumbling in front of him. "I want to go home now."

He ran his hands back through his rumpled hair, closing his eyes and pressing the heels of his hands against his temples, visibly trying to bring himself out of combat mode. And when he spoke, his voice was more even. "I don't think I can just leave. They're going to want a statement—"

"I'm not asking you to leave. I'm sure one of the police officers can give you a lift when you're done."

Jones reached for her. "Melody…"

She stiffened, closing her eyes and refusing to feel anything as he put his arms around her. "I don't want you to touch me," she told him through clenched teeth.

He backed off, but only a little. He took a deep breath, forcing even more of his anger to dissipate. "Honey, you gotta understand. I saw that revolver and—"

"You did what you had to do," she finished for him. "What you've been trained to do. You attacked. You're very good at that, I'll give you that much." She stepped out of his embrace. "Please tell Chief Beatrice that I'll stop by the station tomorrow to give my statement. But right now, I have to go home."

He held the car keys in his hand. "Why don't you let me drive you?" He glanced up as the first of the police cars pulled into the lot, and he raised his voice to be heard over the wailing siren. "I'll just tell these guys that I'll be back in a second." The siren cut off, leaving him shouting in the stillness, "I don't want you to have to drive."

She took the keys from him. "I'm fine. I can drive myself."

Isaac Forte came out to meet the policemen and all three men approached Jones. Melody used the opportunity to get into her car. But she should have known Jones wasn't going to let her just drive away. He came to the side of the car and waited until she opened her window.

"I won't be too long," he told her. He looked down as if noticing the blood on his shirt for the first time. He had an angry-looking scratch on his arm, as well, and he was gingerly touching the inside of his lips with his tongue as if he'd cut himself on his own teeth. "Can we talk when I get back?"

She looked out the windshield, afraid to meet his eyes. "I don't think that's a good idea."

"Mel, please? I know I had no right to speak to you that way, but I was scared to death you were gonna get hurt—"

"I'm tired, Jones," she lied. "I'm going to grab a bowl of soup and go back to sleep." He was leaning with both hands braced on the top of her car, so she couldn't just drive away. She did put the car into gear, though. She knew he could see that the reverse lights had come on. But when he still didn't step back, she finally looked up at him. "I want to go now," she said, fighting to keep her voice from shaking.

All of his earlier anger was gone, and he looked worn-out and beaten—as if he'd lost the fight instead of won.

"I'm sorry," he told her, straightening up. If she didn't know better, she might've thought those were tears in his eyes. "Mel, I'm deeply sorry."

"I am, too," she whispered.

Melody released the clutch and backed out of the parking lot. She only stalled once as she pulled onto the road that took her home.

"WHAT'S UP?"

Cowboy glanced up from his book to smile at Andy. "Hey, kid. I'm getting Mel's garden ready for winter."

"No, you're not," Andy scoffed. "You're sitting there reading a book."

Andy had a swollen lip and a nasty-looking scrape on his jawline. He'd been in another fight, probably with that older kid—Alex Parks—who took such pleasure in tormenting him. Andy's brown eyes dared him to comment on his injuries.

"Well, yeah, I'm reading a book," Cowboy said, purposely saying nothing. "That's the first step. See, first I have to learn how to do it—you know, figure out what kind of tools and supplies I need."

"That book tells you all that?"

"It does. Believe it or not, all the information I need to do damn near anything is two miles down that road in the town library. Need your refrigerator fixed? Piece a cake. Just get me a book. I can learn another language, build a house from the foundation up, shoe a horse—you name it, the knowledge I need to get the job done is in the library, guaranteed. Especially now that they're plugged into the Internet."

Andy looked at the garden bed, at the plants that had shriveled and turned brown in the cool night air, then at the last of the beans that were still clinging stubbornly to life. He looked back at Cowboy, clearly unimpressed. "So what's there to do? Everything's dead. You can't plant anything new until spring anyway."

"Ever hear of mulching?" Cowboy asked.

"No."

"Me, neither. At least not more than really vaguely before I picked up this book. But apparently, it's good to do. I haven't quite reached the part that tells me why, but I'm getting there."

Andy rolled his eyes. "You know, there's a much easier way to do all this."

"Oh yeah?"

"Yeah. Just ask Melody what she wants done."

Ask Melody. That was a damned fine idea. But unfortunately, Cowboy couldn't ask Melody anything until she stopped hiding from him again.

It had been nearly three days since the incident at the Honey Farms convenience store. The criminal, she'd called the place. And the name fit. They'd certainly run into some criminal activity, that was for sure.

God, he'd never known fear like that hot-and-cold streak of terror that had shot through him when he'd seen that revolver. He'd had about one-tenth of a second to decide what to do, and in that fraction of a moment, for the first time in his life, he'd actually considered backing down. He'd actually thought about surrendering.

But he couldn't tell in that heartbeat of time if the men were using or not. He didn't know for sure from that one quick glance if they were out of their minds, high on some chemical substance, or strung out, desperate and ready to eliminate anyone who so much as looked at them crooked.

All he knew was that in his experience, when he carried a weapon, *he* was always prepared to use it. He had to assume the same was true for these clowns. So he'd attacked in that one split second when the revolver was pointing away from the clerk, catching the assailants off guard.

The entire fight had lasted all of eighty-five seconds.

But it had been eighty-five seconds of sheer hell.

Melody had just stood there, staring at him. She hadn't even ducked for cover. She just *stood* there, a target, ready to be knocked over or shot full of lead if that bastard had gotten hold of his revolver.

It had taken Cowboy twice as long as it should have to subdue the enemy and gain control of the weapon. His fear that Melody would be hurt or killed had gotten in the way. And he'd lashed out at her afterward because of it. He'd shouted at her when all he really wanted to do was drag her into his arms and hold her until the end of time.

But she'd been less than thrilled with his performance—in more ways than one. And she'd run away again.

Before they'd gone into that store, Melody had been ready to invite him up to her bedroom to spend the night—he'd been almost certain of that. He'd been so close to relief from this hellish frustration.

Of course, now the frustration was ten times as bad. He hadn't even *seen* her in three days. The hell with the lack of sex. Just not seeing her was driving him damn near crazy.

"You want me to ask Melody for you?" Andy asked. "I'm going inside—Britt said it was okay if I used her computer to do an Internet search."

"What are you searching for?"

Andy shrugged. "Just some stuff about the Army."

"Oh, yeah? What kind of stuff?"

Another shrug. "I dunno."

Cowboy gazed at the boy. "You thinking about enlisting?"

"Maybe."

"Only way to become a SEAL is to join the U.S. Navy, not the Army."

"Yeah," Andy said, "I know. You running again tonight?"

Cowboy had taken to working out both in the evening as well as the early morning in an attempt to run some of his frustration into the ground. "Why? You want to try again?" Andy had run along with him yesterday evening. The kid had only made it about two miles before he'd dropped out.

"Yeah, I do."

"You know, if you start getting in shape now, you'll be a monster by the time you graduate high school."

Andy kicked at a clump of grass. "I wish I could be a monster now."

Cowboy acknowledged the boy's scraped face. "Alex Parks again, huh?"

"He's such a *jerk*."

"If you want, I can help you out with your PT," Cowboy volunteered. "You know, physical training. And, if you want, I can also help you learn to fight."

Andy nodded slowly. "Maybe," he said. "What's the catch?"

Cowboy grinned. This boy was a fast learner. "You're right. There *is* a condition."

The kid groaned. "I'm going to hate this, aren't I?"

"You have to promise that after I teach you to beat the crap out of Alex Parks, you use what you've learned only to defend yourself. And after he figures out that you're ready and able to kick his butt, you turn and walk away."

Andy looked incredulous. "What good is *that?*"

"That's my deal. Take it or leave it."

"How do you know I'll even keep my promise?"

"Because if you don't, I'll break you in half," Cowboy said with a smile. "Oh, and there is one other catch. You need to learn a little self-discipline. You need to learn to follow *orders*. My orders. When I say jump, you jump. When I say chill, you cool it. You give me any attitude, any garbage, any whining, any moaning of *any* kind, and the deal's off."

"Gee, you're making this sound too good to pass up," Andy said, rolling his eyes.

"Oh, yeah. One other thing. If I ask you a question, you answer me straight. You say, 'Yes, sir,' or 'No, sir.'"

"You want me to call you *sir?*"

"Yes, I do." God knows Andy could learn a thing or two about showing respect.

Andy was silent.

"So do we have a deal?" Cowboy asked.

Andy swore. "Yeah, all right."

"Yes, *sir*," Cowboy corrected him.

"Yes, sir. *Jeez.*" Andy turned toward the house. "I'll tell Melody you could use her help with the garden."

"Thanks, kid, but that's not going to get her out here. She's been hiding from me for days."

"I'll tell her you're sorry, too. Sir. God."

"Sir is good enough, Marshall. You don't have to call me God, too," Cowboy teased.

"Sheesh." Andy rolled his eyes again as he headed toward the kitchen door.

In truth, Cowboy *was* sorry. He was sorry about a lot of things. He was sorry that he hadn't gone into the house and hammered on Melody's bedroom door after he'd gotten home that night. He was sorry he still hadn't found a way to force the issue, to make her sit down and talk to him.

He wasn't quite sure what he would tell her, though. Cowboy wasn't sure he was ready to share the fact that after she'd left the Honey Farms, right as he was giving his statement to Tom Beatrice, the Appleton chief of police, he'd had to excuse himself. He'd gone into the men's room and gotten horribly, violently sick.

At first, he'd thought it might've been the flu—people all over town were falling victim to a virulent strain of the bug. But as the night wore on and he didn't get sick again, he'd been forced to confront the truth.

It was the residual of his fear that had made him bow to the porcelain god. His fear for Melody's safety had squeezed him tight and hadn't let go, making his gut churn and his blood pressure rise until he'd forcefully emptied his stomach.

It was weird. His career as a SEAL involved a huge amount of risk taking. And he was fine about that. He knew he would survive damn near anything if surviving entailed fighting. But if his survival depended on something outside his control—like the intrinsic danger they all faced every time they jumped out of a plane, knowing that if their chute failed, if the lines got tangled or the cells didn't open right, they would end up as a mostly unrecognizable stain on the ground—if his survival depended on a twist of fate like that, Cowboy knew he would either live or die as the gods saw fit. No amount of fear or worry would change that, so he rarely bothered with either.

But he found he couldn't be quite so blasé when it came to Melody's safety. Whenever he thought about that revolver aimed in her direction, even now, three days later, he *still* felt sick to his stomach.

It was similar to the sensation he felt when he thought about her having to give birth to that baby she was carrying.

As was his usual method of operation when forced to deal with something he knew nothing about, he'd taken a pile of books about pregnancy out of the library. He'd read nearly every one from cover to cover, and frankly, the list of possible life-threatening complications resulting from pregnancy or childbirth made his blood run cold.

Women went into shock from pregnancy-related diabetes. Or they had strokes caused by the strain on their system. Some women simply bled to death. The mortality rates reported in the books shocked Cowboy. It seemed impossible that even in this day and age of enlightened modern medicine, women died simply as a result of bearing children.

He'd wanted to go into the hospital and donate blood to be set aside and used specifically for Melody in case she needed it. He was a universal donor, but he knew that all of the inoculations he'd had as he'd traveled around the world would make him ineligible.

He'd just approached Brittany to find out if her blood type matched her sister's—to see if she might be willing to donate blood and help soothe some of his fear. She'd looked at him as if he was crazy, but she'd agreed to do it.

Cowboy looked toward the house, up at the window he knew was Melody's room. He willed the curtain to shift. He hoped to see a shadowy form backing away or a hint of moving light, but he saw nothing.

Melody was staying far from the window.

And his patience was running out.

CHAPTER ELEVEN

MELODY HEARD THE doorbell ring from up in her bedroom.

She focused all of her attention on her book, determined to keep reading. It was Jones. It had to be Jones.

It had been five days since she'd driven away from him at the Honey Farms, and she'd been bracing herself, waiting for him to run out of patience and come confront her.

Andy was downstairs, using Britt's computer. Melody had told him she was going to take a nap. She closed her eyes for a moment, praying that he would send Jones away.

But then she heard voices—a deep voice that didn't sound very much like Jones, and then Andy's, higher-pitched and loud. She couldn't hear the words, but he sounded as if he was angry or upset.

The lower voice rumbled again, and she heard what sounded like a chair being knocked over. No, that was definitely not Jones down there with Andy.

Melody unlocked her bedroom door and hurried down the stairs to the kitchen.

"It *wasn't* me," Andy was shouting. "I didn't do *nothin'*."

Tom Beatrice, the police chief, stood between Andy and the door, ready to catch the boy if he ran. "It'll go easier on you, son, if you just tell the truth."

Andy was shaking with anger. "I *am* telling the truth."

"You're going to have to come with me, son."

"Stop calling me that! I'm *not* your son!"

Neither of them had noticed that Melody stood in the doorway. She raised her voice to be heard. "What's going on here?"

"That's what I was wondering, too." Jones opened the screen door and stepped into the kitchen.

The police chief glanced at them both apologetically. "Vince Romanella said I'd find the boy over here. I'm afraid I need to bring him down to the station for questioning."

"What?" Melody looked at Andy, but he was silent and stony-faced. She tried not to look at Jones at all, but she could feel his eyes on her from across the room. "Why?"

"House up on Looking Glass Road was broken into and vandalized several nights ago," Tom explained. "Andy here was seen up in that area at about nine—about the time the break-in occurred."

"That's pretty circumstantial, don't you think, Chief?" Jones voiced Melody's own disbelief.

"Oh, there's other evidence, too, that points in his direction." Tom shook his head. "The place is trashed. It's a real mess. Windows and mirrors broken. Spray paint everywhere."

Jones briefly met Melody's gaze, then he turned to the boy. "Marshall, did you do it?" His voice was soft, almost matter-of-fact.

Andy straightened his shoulders. "No, sir."

Jones turned back to Tom. "Chief, he didn't do it."

Tom scratched the back of his head. "Well, Lieutenant, I appreciate your faith in the boy, but his fingerprints are all over the place. He's going to have to come down to the station with me."

"*Finger*prints?" Jones echoed.

"Inside and out."

Jones's eyes pinned the boy in place. This time when he spoke, his voice was harder, more demanding. "Marshall, I'm going to ask you that question again. Did you have anything to do with vandalizing that house?"

Andy's eyes had filled with tears. "I should've known you wouldn't believe me," he whispered. "You're really no different from the rest of them."

"Answer my question."

Andy answered with a blisteringly foul suggestion. Like an afterthought, he added, "sir." He turned to Tom Beatrice. "Let's get this over with."

"Andy, I'm on your side…" Jones started to say, but Andy just pushed past him, Tom's hand on his arm.

Melody stepped forward. "Go with him," she urged Jones. "He's going to need you."

Jones nodded, taking in her tentlike dress, her unbrushed hair, the blue nail polish on her toes, before looking in her eyes. "I was scared I'd lose you, Mel," he said. "That night—I shouted at you because I was more scared than I've ever been in my life. It was wrong, but so's not letting me apologize."

He turned and went out the door.

"JONES."

Cowboy sat up in his tent, suddenly wide-awake, wondering if his mind was finally starting to snap. He could've sworn he'd heard Melody's voice calling his name. Of course, he *had* been dreaming a particularly satisfying and sinfully erotic dream about her….

"Jones?"

It *was* her. He could see her unmistakable silhouette outside of the tent. He reached up to unzip the flap. "Mel, are you all right?"

"I'm fine." She was wearing only a nightgown and a robe and she shivered slightly in the chill night air. "But we just got a phone call from Vince Romanella." She peered into the darkness of his tent. He was glad for the darkness, and glad for the sleeping bag that still covered most of him—including an extremely healthy arousal, the direct by-product of that dream. "Jones, Andy's not in here with you, is he?"

"No." He opened the flap a little wider. "Honey, it's freezing outside. Come on in."

"It feels like it's freezing in there, too," she pointed out, not moving any closer. He couldn't quite see her eyes in the darkness. "I don't know how you stand it."

"It's not that bad." His sleeping bag was nice and warm. And the dream he'd been having about Melody had been hot enough to heat the entire state of Massachusetts.

"Jones, Andy's missing. Vince said he heard a noise, and when he got up to check it out, he looked in on Andy, and his bed was empty."

Cowboy reached for his jeans, swiftly slipping them on, wrestling with the zipper, willing his arousal away. "What time is it?"

"Nearly four. Vince thinks Andy's been gone since around midnight, when he and Kirsty went to bed. Tom Beatrice is organizing a search party."

He pulled on his boots and grabbed a T-shirt and a jacket. "Can I use your phone?"

"Of course." She moved aside to let him come out of the tent. "Do you know where he might've gone?"

He sealed the flap to keep any stray animals out, then straightened up, pulling on his T-shirt as they walked toward the house. "No. He wouldn't talk to me down at the police station. And all he said to the chief was that he'd been set up and framed." With impatient fingers, he tried to untangle a knot that was in his hair. "I might've believed it if his fingerprints had only been found on, you know, something like a single can of soda, or a few things here and there." He gave up on his hair as he opened the door for Melody, then followed her into the brightly lit warmth of the kitchen. Brittany was awake, too, and talking on the phone. "But according to the police report, his prints were on the furniture, on the walls, in every single room. He was in that house, there's no denying it."

"But he *is* denying it," Melody said, her blue eyes wide. "And rather vehemently, I've heard." She lowered herself into one of the kitchen chairs, shifting uncomfortably, as if her back was hurting again. What else was new? Never mind the fact that he knew how to give a killer back rub—she wouldn't let him near enough to give her one.

But despite her obvious discomfort, she looked particularly lovely tonight. She'd put her hair in a single braid down her back, but while she'd slept, several tendrils had escaped. They floated gracefully, delicately, around her face. Without any makeup on at all, she looked fresh and sweet—barely old enough to babysit, let alone have a baby of her own.

As he watched, she chewed on her lower lip. She had gorgeous lips—so full and red even without the help of cosmetics. In his dream, she'd smiled at him almost wickedly before she'd lowered her head and…

Don't go there, Cowboy admonished himself. As much as he would've liked to, he couldn't let his thoughts continue in that direction right now. He had to think about

Andy Marshall instead. Damn fool kid. What the hell was he trying to prove?

"Running away like this is a pretty strong admission of guilt," Cowboy pointed out.

"Sometimes people run because they're afraid." Melody was talking about more than Andy—he knew because she suddenly wouldn't meet his gaze.

"Sometimes people don't realize that everyone in the world is afraid of *some*thing," he countered. "Best thing to do is face your fear. Learn all you can about it. Then learn to live with it. Knowledge goes a long way when it comes to declawing even the scariest monsters."

"Is that what you've been doing here with me?" she asked, no longer even pretending to talk about Andy. "Learning to live with your fear? Facing the terrors of a lifetime commitment? And don't try to pretend that the thought of marrying me doesn't scare you to death—I *know* it does."

He went for the truth. Why not? He had nothing to lose. "You're right," he said. "It *does* frighten me. But I've done frightening things before and come out a better man because of them."

Before Melody could respond, Brittany grimly hung up the phone. "They're starting the search up by the quarry," she announced. "Alex Parks just told his father that Andy had called him and told him to meet him in the woods up there just after midnight. Alex is claiming he never went, but my gut feeling is that we haven't gotten the full story from this kid yet. Anyone who's willing and able is supposed to meet out at the end of Quarry Road."

Melody stood up. "I'm going to go change."

"Willing and able, sweetie," Brittany said. "Not willing and seven and a half months pregnant."

"But I *want* to help!"

"Help by giving the lieutenant your car keys and waving goodbye," Brittany told her sister. "You don't really think Cowboy'll be able to give the search for Andy his full attention if you're there for him to worry about, do you?"

Melody looked directly at him. "So…just don't worry about me."

Cowboy smiled ruefully. "Honey, that's kind of like telling me don't breathe."

She looked as if she was going to cry. "My keys are by the door," she told him. "Take my car. But call as soon as you hear *any*thing."

BY SEVEN FORTY-FIVE, Melody had gotten tired of waiting. Jones hadn't called. He *still* hadn't called. Fortunately, Brittany had gotten tired of waiting, too.

By eight, Britt was driving her down to the end of Quarry Road. The narrow road was lined on both sides with parked cars for about a good half mile.

"You get out here," Britt told her. "I'll park and walk back."

"Are you sure?" Melody asked.

Brittany raised her eyebrows. "Do you honestly believe that I would bring you up here in the cold, and then make you walk an *extra* half mile? I should have my head examined for driving you over here in the first place—and all for the sake of some stupid kid."

"He's not stupid." Melody opened the door.

"He's incredibly stupid," Britt argued. "He didn't call *me* before he ran away. I know he didn't vandalize that house."

Melody stared at her sister. "You *do?*"

"Yeah, and I realized as we were driving here that I can prove it, too. The kid's been on-line, using my computer every night this week, right? I was working the night of the break-in, and you were probably already in bed, but Andy *was* at our house, at my computer. I just realized I got email from him at work that night. Unless he scheduled a flash session, I can give him a solid alibi. And whether or not there was a flash session scheduled should be easy enough to prove. I just have to access my account information. It'll prove he was logged on and actively using the net that night."

"You seriously believe Andy's innocent?"

Brittany shrugged. "Well, yeah. He said he didn't do it. The kid may be a royal pain the butt, but I've gotten to know him pretty well over the past few weeks, and he's *not* a liar."

"But all those fingerprints..."

"I know. I haven't figured that out yet, but if Andy says he didn't do it, he didn't do it."

"I think you should tell this to Tom Beatrice right now," Melody said. She had to smile. "Of all people, I wouldn't have thought *you'd* be Andy's champion."

"Yeah, well, I was wrong about him. He's an okay kid." Worry flickered across her face. "I hope he's okay."

"Jones'll find him," Melody told her sister as she hauled herself out of the car. She had total faith in the SEAL. This was what he was good at. Rescuing hostages and disarming gunmen and finding missing little boys would all fall under the category labeled "piece a cake."

"Don't go any farther than the quarry," Brittany said threateningly, leaning across the seat to look up at her. "If I get back here and find out that you've done something insane, like join a search party, I swear I'll never let you leave the house again."

"I won't join a search party. I promise." It was then that Melody saw them. "Oh, God!"

"You all right?"

"Boats, Britt." There were two trucks parked at haphazard angles, both of which had boat trailers behind them. They were empty, which meant the boats were in use. "They're dragging the quarry."

Brittany put the car in Park and shut off the engine. She opened the door, then stood looking across the roof of the car at the telltale trailers. Her face was pale, but she shook her head in denial. "It doesn't mean that. Not necessarily."

Melody blinked back tears. "Yes, it does. You know it."

Brittany slammed the car door, leaving the vehicle right there, blocking in at least four other cars. "No, it doesn't." Her voice rang with determination.

Mel followed her sister down the trail that led to the flooded quarry.

A crowd had gathered. She could see Estelle Warner and Peggy Rogers, surrounded by other members of the Ladies' Club decked out in their hiking boots and jeans. Tom Beatrice and nearly all of Appleton's police force were talking to several state troopers as Vince and Kirsty Romanella hovered nearby. Even Alex Parks was there, sitting on a rock, looking as if he'd been crying. And standing off to the sides were all the people who had volunteered to help search the woods for Andy. The turnout was nearly bigger than last weekend's apple picking at Hetterman's. They were talking in hushed voices, somberly watching the boats.

"They're not dragging the water." Brittany shielded her eyes with her hand, trying to see past the glare of the early-morning sun. "What *are* they doing?"

Jones was out on one of the boats. Although he was too far away to see clearly, Melody recognized him from his easygoing posture. That, the baseball cap he wore on his head and the fact that, even though it was only forty chilly degrees out, he wore his jacket unbuttoned more than tipped her off.

The man was totally immune to the cold.

"The water's too deep to drag in many places." Melody turned to see Estelle Warner standing behind them. "They're using some kind of sonar contraption to try to get a reading on anything that might be a body down at the bottom of the pit," the elderly woman said. "This old quarry's three hundred feet deep in some places. Maybe even deeper in others."

"They can't be sure he's in there." Melody's heart was in her throat. "Aren't they searching anywhere else?"

"Considering the fact that an eyewitness saw the boy go into the water, and that the searchers found his clothes exactly where that witness said they'd be..."

"Oh, no..." Brittany reached for Melody's hand.

Estelle looked even more dour than usual. "I'm afraid so. It seems the Parks boy met Andy Marshall up here late last night. From what he says, Andy was always trying to pick a fight, and this time was no different. Andy dared the Parks boy to swim across the quarry, and when the Parks boy backed down, Andy took of his own clothes and dove into the water. Had to have been close to freezing, but that wild kid just dove right in."

Both boats were heading to shore. Jones took off his baseball cap and raked his hair back out of his face, refastening his ponytail. As Melody watched, he put his hat back on, making sure it was securely on his head. As he got closer, she could see that his face was decidedly grim.

"Apparently, the Parks boy didn't see young Andy come back up," Estelle told them. "He says he searched for a while, calling to Andy, but there was no reply. Of course, it was dark and hard to see much of anything. It's likely the boy dove in the wrong spot, hit his head on a rock. Or maybe the cold just got to him."

Brittany was squeezing Melody's fingers. "Please don't let them have found something," she whispered.

"That lieutenant of yours," Estelle told Melody. "He took one look at Andy's clothes—left right where the Parks boy had said they were—and he made a few phone calls to Boston. And this other man, the tall black fellow, he was out here within a few hours with this sonar whatever. Brought diving gear with him, too."

Harvard. Harvard was on that boat with Jones. Melody could see him now, towering over everyone—even Jones. His shaved head gleamed exotically in the sunlight. His expression, like Jones's, was less than pleased.

Melody saw Jones spot her as he climbed out of the boat. She saw him hesitate, glancing quickly back at Harvard, and she knew. He hadn't told his friend that she was pregnant.

It would have been funny if the situation weren't so deadly serious.

Still, he came toward her, and Melody knew when she looked into his eyes that Harvard's reaction to her pregnancy was the least of his worries.

He didn't say hello, didn't mince his words. "Honey, we think he's down there."

Brittany sank to the ground. Estelle knelt next to her, holding her tightly—two mortal enemies allied once again, this time through the death of a child.

"No," Melody whispered. But she could see the truth written clearly in the stormy green of Jones's eyes. He was stony-faced, sternly angry.

"It's my fault." His voice was raspy and as dry as his

eyes. "I thought he was ready to learn some discipline. I'd been taking him out, running him through some PT. I told him that SEALs had to condition themselves against cold water. I told him about Hell Week—about having to sit in that freezing surf and just hang on. He wanted to try it—try swimming in the quarry, so I let him do it. We just jumped in and jumped out. I thought I'd let him get a taste of what cold *really* was."

He stopped, taking a deep breath before he continued. "That was my mistake. I didn't let him stay in. I just pulled him back out. I didn't let him cramp up or find out how hard it is to swim when every muscle in your body is cold and stiff. I think I must've given him the false confidence to try it again."

"That still doesn't make this your fault." Melody wanted to reach for him, to put her arms around him, but he seemed so distant, so unanimated and still, so grim and hard and unreachable.

Harvard had come to stand beside them, and she could feel his curious eyes on her, but she didn't look away from Jones. She *couldn't* look away. He truly blamed himself for this tragedy.

"It *is* my fault. I told him about swim buddies—about how SEALs never swim or dive without another team member, but I know he saw me breaking the rules by swimming alone in the quarry."

"Junior, we should probably make that dive," Harvard said quietly. "If we've got to go down to 175 feet, it's going to take awhile." When Melody finally glanced at him, he nodded. "How are you, Melody? You're looking very…healthy."

"Will you tell him, please, that this is not his fault?"

"The lady says it's not your fault, Jones."

Jones's expression didn't change as he turned away. "Yeah, right. Let's get this over with."

Melody couldn't stand it a second longer. She reached for him, catching his hand in hers. "Harlan—"

There was a flash of surprise in his eyes, surprise that she'd actually used his given name, surprise that she'd actually touched him, but that emotion was quickly turned into stone, along with everything else he was feeling. Even his fingers felt cold.

She knew this stony anger was his defense against having to go down into that water and possibly—probably—bring up the lifeless body of the boy they'd all come to love over the past few weeks. But she knew just as well that everything he felt—all the blame and the fear and the awful, paralyzing grief—was there inside him. His anger didn't cancel his feelings out; it merely covered them.

She knew him quite well, she realized. Over the past few weeks, despite her attempts to keep her distance, she'd come to know this man's vast repertoire of minutely different smiles—what they meant, how they broadcast exactly how and what he was feeling. She'd come to know his silences, too. And she'd had a firsthand look at his method of dealing with fear.

He hid it behind icy cold anger.

"Be careful," she whispered. A local diving club had frequented the quarry several years ago—until someone had gotten killed and it had been deemed too dangerous a place to dive.

His eyes told her nothing—nothing but the fact that underneath all that chill, he was hurting. He nodded and even tried to force a smile. "Piece a cake."

"We'll be down for a while," Harvard told her. "Diving at this depth requires regular stops both on the way down and coming back up. It's time-consuming, and for you, waiting up here on the surface, it'll seem as if it takes forever. You might want to go home and wait for a phone call."

"Jones has forgotten how to use the phone," Melody said, still gazing into his eyes.

"I'm sorry I didn't call you," he said quietly, "but all I kept getting was bad news." Emotion shifted across his face, and for a heartbeat, Melody thought he was about to give in to all of his pain and crumple to the ground just as Brittany had. But he didn't. "It seemed senseless to make you worry until I knew for sure Andy was dead." He said the word flatly, bluntly, using it to bring back his anger and put his other emotions in check.

"We still don't know that for sure." Melody squeezed his hand. But her words were pure bravado. She could see Jones's certainty in his eyes.

"Go home," he told her.

"No," she said. If he did find Andy down there, he was going to need her to be here—as badly as she was going to need him. "I'll wait for you to come back up. We can go home together."

She couldn't believe the words that were coming out of her mouth. *Go home together...*

His expression didn't change. For a moment, he didn't even move. But then, in one swift movement, he pulled her into his arms and kissed her hard on the mouth. She clung to him, kissing him back just as ferociously, wanting him, needing him—and needing him to know it.

He pulled away, breathing hard. He didn't say a word about that incredible kiss. He just took off his jacket and handed it to her. "Spread this on the ground so you'll have something dry to sit on." His voice was harsh, and his eyes were still so angry, but he gently touched the side of her face with one finger. "I don't want you catching cold."

It was almost as if he loved her. It was almost as if they were lovers who had been together for years.

"Be careful," Melody said again.

As he gazed at her, his eyes suddenly looked bleak. "It's too late," he told her quietly. "When it came to dealing with Andy, I wasn't careful enough, and now it's too damn late."

Melody tried not to cry as he turned and walked away.

CHAPTER TWELVE

COWBOY USUALLY LOVED to dive, but this was sheer hell. He and H. were heading nearly straight down, using a marked rope to gauge their distance, stopping at regular intervals to let their bodies adjust to the increasing pressure of the water.

The time spent stopping and waiting dragged on interminably.

It was necessary, though. If they moved too quickly from the surface to a depth below a hundred feet, and then back, they could—and would—get the bends.

Cowboy had seen a guy who hadn't believed how crippling the bends could actually be. The stupid SOB had gotten brain damage from bubbles of nitrogen expanding in his system. He still couldn't walk to this day.

Despite the fact that SEALs were known for breaking the rules, this was one rule they never even bent. Even when they were in as big a hurry as he was.

Contrary to what he'd told Melody, this dive was anything but a piece of cake. At this depth, he and Harvard had to breathe from special tanks of mixed gas to prevent nitrogen narcosis—also known as the rapture of the deep. As if that wasn't dangerous enough, there was a definite time limit to how long they could remain at that depth. And the number and lengths of decompression stops they would have to make on the way back to the surface were intensely complicated.

With the scuba gear on, he and Harvard couldn't talk. And at this depth beneath the surface, it was very, very cold and very, very dark. He couldn't even see Harvard next to him. He could only sense his presence.

Out of all the men in Alpha Squad, Cowboy was glad it was the senior chief who'd been just a short drive away, visiting his family in his hometown just outside Boston. Unlike some of the guys, Harvard knew when *not* to talk.

As they'd pulled on their cold-water diving suits, Harvard had had only a brief comment to make about Melody's pregnancy. He'd said, "When you told me you had a situation to deal with, you weren't kidding. You don't do anything halfway, do you, Junior?"

"No," Cowboy had replied.

"I assume you're going to do right by the girl?"

"Yeah," Cowboy had answered automatically. For so long now, his single-most goal had been to marry Melody and be a real father to their baby. But that was before he'd failed so utterly with Andy. Who was he trying to fool here anyway? He knew less than nothing about parenting. The fact that he was diving in this quarry in hopes of recovering Andy's drowned body was proof of that.

Cowboy floated in the darkness, uncertain of what to wish for. He hoped they weren't going to find Andy's body, but at the same time, if the kid *had* drowned in this quarry, he hoped that they'd find him right away. It would end the waiting and wondering. And it would be far better than never finding him, never quite knowing for sure.

He shone his flashlight straight down, knowing that the light couldn't possibly cut through the murky depths to that place where the sonar camera had found an object the approximate size and density of a human body.

Cowboy turned off the light, sending both Harvard and himself back into the deprivation-tanklike darkness. They had to save their flashlight batteries for when they were really needed.

He closed his eyes. He knew he could do anything if he had to. But watching the beam from his light reflect off Andy Marshall's pale, water-swollen face was going to be one of the hardest things he would ever have to do.

It was going to be almost as hard as admitting that maybe Melody had been right all along, almost as hard as it would be to walk away from her sweet smile.

Cowboy *was* going to do right by her. Only now that he knew better, he was going to do it by leaving her alone.

"IT WAS ONLY a bundle of trash," Melody heard Jones report to Tom Beatrice as she inched closer to the group of men. "There *was* an outcropping of rocks. We searched that area as extensively as possible, given our time limit at that depth." His mouth was still a grim, straight line. "However, that was only one part of the quarry."

She had nearly fainted with relief when she'd seen Jones's and Harvard's heads break the surface of the water.

Jones must've known she'd be watching, worried out of her mind, because he'd turned to search for her, picking her out in the crowd on the shore. As he'd treaded the icy quarry water, he'd looked at her, touching the top of his head with the tips of his fingers, giving her the diver's signal for okay. He was okay, thank God. And the blip they'd picked up on the sonar wasn't Andy's body. It was only a bag of trash.

"How long do you have to wait before you can make another dive?" Tom Beatrice asked.

"The earliest we could do it would be late tonight," Jones told the police chief.

"But it would be smarter and safer to wait until morning," Harvard added. He met the other SEAL's eyes. "You know as well as I do, Jones—a four- or five-hour delay isn't going to matter one bit to that boy if he's down there."

Jones glanced around the somber crowd, at the Romanellas, at Estelle Warner and Brittany. His gaze lingered on Melody before he turned back to the police chief. "I'm sorry, Tom," he said. "Senior Chief Becker's right. We'd better wait and continue the search in the morning."

"That's fine, son," Tom told him. "It's risky enough diving down there in daylight." He looked around at the men who'd brought the boats. "We'll meet back here at 8:00 a.m. Let's get those boats up and out of the water!"

Brittany touched Melody's arm, pulling her aside. "I'm leaving."

"I'm waiting for Jones," Mel told her sister.

"I know," Brittany said. Her eyes were rimmed with red, but she managed a watery smile. "It's nice to know that something good will come of this."

Melody shook her head. "Britt, don't get the wrong idea here. Just because I care about Jones doesn't mean I intend to marry him. Because I don't. This isn't about that. We're friends."

She wasn't certain herself what it *was* about. Friendship, maybe. Or comfort. Comfort and friendship with a healthy dose of attraction. Yeah, when it came to Cowboy Jones, her intense attraction to him was always a part of the equation.

Brittany was looking at her with one eyebrow elevated skeptically. *"Friends?"*

Melody blushed, remembering how he'd kissed her, right there in front of everyone, remembering the way she'd clung to him—returning all of his passion and then some. But whatever she'd been thinking, whatever she'd been feeling, the moment had passed. Her sanity has returned.

She hoped. "I'd like Jones to be my friend. Of course, based on our history, it's bound to be a little confusing as we iron things out…."

Brittany didn't look convinced. "Whatever. I'm going in to work—try to keep my mind off Andy. I have the afternoon shift. You and your 'friend' will have the house to yourselves."

Melody sighed. "Britt, I'm not going to…"

But her sister was already gone.

The crowd had moved off, too, leaving Jones and Harvard to stow their diving gear and strip out of their bulky dry suits.

For the first time since Melody had met him, Jones actually looked cold. The water had been icy, and he'd been submerged in it an endlessly long time. He was shivering despite a blanket someone had put around him.

His fingers fumbled on the zipper, and she moved toward him. "Do you want me to get that?"

He smiled tightly. "The irony here is incredible. It's only *after* I screw up beyond belief that you want to undress me."

"I was…I thought…" She blushed. The truth was that she'd wanted to undress him from the moment she saw him again. But God help her if he ever realized that.

His smile faded with the last of his anger, and he looked dreadfully tired and impossibly unhappy. "I'm not sure exactly what's happening here between us, honey, but I've got to tell you—I sure as hell don't deserve any kind of consolation prize today."

"I didn't hear any of that," Harvard singsonged, peeling his own dry suit off his well-muscled body and nearly jumping into his jeans, pulling them on directly over the long woolen underwear he'd worn underneath. "I am so not listening. Got water in my ears, can't hear a damn thing." In his haste, he didn't bother with his shirt. He just yanked his winter coat over his undershirt. "In fact, I'm so outta here, I've already been gone for ten minutes. I've got all the gear except for your suit, Junior. You get that dried out, and I'll get the tanks filled for tomorrow."

"Thanks, H."

"Melody, girl, you don't need my admonishment to be careful around this man. Clearly, you two have already taken the concept of being careful, packed it in a box and tied a big red ribbon around it." Harvard took one look at Jones's face and backed away. "Like I said, though, I'm gone. I'll be back in the morning."

And then he *was* gone, leaving Jones and Melody alone.

"Jones, I didn't mean to imply…" she started lamely. She took a deep breath. "When I said that about us going home, I'm not sure I really meant to make it sound as if—"

"Okay," he said. "That's okay. I misinterpreted. I'm sorry. That kiss was my mistake."

No, it wasn't. And he *hadn't* misinterpreted. At the time, Melody *had* meant what she'd said. She was just too cowardly to admit it now. Obviously, she'd been swept along by the rush of high emotions. Now that she was thinking clearly again, the thought of taking him home and bringing him up to her room scared her to death.

She could not let herself fall in love with him. She absolutely couldn't.

"One step forward, two steps back," Jones added softly, almost as if he was talking to himself, almost as if he was able to read her mind. "This is your game, honey. You make up the rules and I'll follow them."

He had managed to unzip his diving suit and he pushed it off his body. Like Harvard, he had long underwear on underneath. He pulled that off, too, covering himself rather halfheartedly with the blanket, uncaring of who might be watching.

Melody quickly turned away and picked up his jeans from the rock he'd left them on. But when she started to hold them out to him, still carefully averting her eyes, she realized that they were at least six sizes too small.

She knew what must have happened even before Jones spoke. She was holding Andy's jeans.

"Someone must've put those over here by mistake," he said.

Andy's jeans and Andy's sweatshirt. The clothes Andy had been wearing before he'd jumped into the quarry. The clothes he had taken off just moments before he'd drowned.

Jones found his own jeans and pulled them on as Melody slowly sat down on the rock.

The woods around the quarry had been searched for quite some distance. If Andy *had* managed somehow to crawl out of the quarry and collapse in the bushes, he would have been found. And if he'd crawled out of the quarry and *hadn't* collapsed—well, it was hard to imagine him running around the woods in only his underwear.

Andy *had* drowned. He'd gone into the water and he hadn't come back out. As she sat holding his clothes, the reality hit her hard. Andy Marshall was dead.

Melody had been hanging pretty tough all day, but now the realization hit her, and she couldn't hold back her tears. Try as she might, she couldn't keep them from escaping. One after another, they rolled down her face.

Jones sat down next to her, close but not quite touching. He'd put on his T-shirt and pulled on his cowboy boots. He still had that blanket wrapped around his shoulders for warmth, and without a word, he drew it around her shoulders, too.

They sat for a moment, watching the noonday sun reflecting off the surface of the flooded quarry.

"I feel like I'm never going to be warm again," he admitted.

Melody wiped ineffectively at her tears. She couldn't stop them—they just kept on coming. "We should go home, get you something warm to drink."

It was as if he hadn't heard her. "Melody, I'm so sorry." He turned to her, and she saw that he had tears in his eyes, too. "If I hadn't come to town, this never would've happened."

She took his hand underneath the blanket. His fingers were icy. "You don't know that for certain."

"I thought I could help him," Jones told her. His eyes were luminous as he held her hand tightly. "I thought all he really needed was someone who cared enough to help get him in line. Someone to set some limits, and at the same time, make some demands that were above and beyond what he'd been asked to do in the past." He stared back out at the water, his jaw muscles jumping. "I remembered what joining the Navy—joining the SEALs—had done for me, and I thought I could give him a taste of that. I thought…"

He trailed off, and Melody finished for him. "Piece of cake?"

Jones looked at her and laughed, half in disbelief, half in despair. He wiped at his eyes with the back of his free hand. "Sweet Lord, was I ever wrong about that." He shook his head. "I can't believe he lied to me about breaking into that house on Looking Glass Road."

"He wasn't lying," Melody told him. "At least Britt doesn't think so. She thinks she can prove that he was using her computer that night. She claims he was at our house, surfing the Net on the night the vandalism took place."

"If he didn't do it, how did his fingerprints get all over the place?"

Melody shook her head. "I don't know. But I *do* know that he stuck to his story. He insisted he didn't do it. What *I'd* like to know is why he called Alex Parks. And why would Alex agree to meet Andy out here after midnight?"

"I should've believed the kid. Why didn't I?" The muscles in Jones's jaw were clenching again. "He said he didn't do it. I asked, and he answered me. I should've stuck by him. I should have trusted him unconditionally."

Now it was Melody's turn to gaze out at the water. "It's hard to trust someone unconditionally," she told him. "Even the most powerful trust has its limits. I should know." She forced herself to look at him, to meet his eyes. "I would—and I did—trust you with my life. But I found myself unable to trust you with my heart. I expected you to hurt me and I couldn't get past that."

His eyes were so green in the early-afternoon light. "You really expected me to hurt you?"

Melody nodded. "Not intentionally, but yeah."

"That's why you didn't want to see me again. That's why you didn't give what we had going a chance."

"Yes," she admitted.

"I probably would've," he admitted, too. "Hurt you, I mean. Like you said, not intentionally, but…"

She didn't want to talk about this. Nodding again, she pushed on, hoping he would follow. "In the same way, you expected Andy to mess up. So when it seemed as if he was lying, you went with your expectations."

"God, I really blew it." The tears were back in Jones's eyes. "I thought I knew what I was doing, but the truth is, I was really unprepared to deal with this kid. I did *every*thing wrong."

"That's just not true."

But he wasn't listening. "When we hit 175 feet, we weren't quite on target and had to search for the object that the sonar picked up." He was talking about the dive he'd made in the quarry with Harvard. "It took us so long to get down there with all the stopping and waiting, but once we were there, I was scared to death. I just wanted to close my eyes and sink to the bottom myself. I didn't want to look, I didn't want to know. And then my light hit something, and it reflected back at me, and for one split second, Mel, I saw him. My eyes played a nasty trick on me, and I saw Andy's face down there."

Melody didn't know what to say, so she said nothing. She just kept holding his hand.

"Tomorrow, I'm going to have to go back down there," he continued. "And tomorrow, I probably *am* going to find him."

He was shaking. Whether it was from the wintery chill of the air or the darkness of his thoughts, Melody wasn't sure. She *did* know it was time to bring him home, though.

She stood up, tugging him gently to his feet, escaping from the confines of his blanket. "Let's go, Jones." She paused. "Do you still have my car keys?"

"Yeah." He gathered up his diving suit. "They're in my pocket."

Melody folded Andy's jeans, putting them back on the rock. "I wonder if we should try to contact Andy's father. Andy was running some searches on the Internet—he told me he thought he might've located his father at an Army base up in New Hampshire and—"

She realized what she was saying at the exact same moment Jones did.

"What did you just say?" he asked, turning to face her.

"He was looking for his father on the Net."

"And he thought he found him in *New Hampshire*."

Transfixed, Melody stared into the sudden glaring intensity of Jones's eyes. "Do you think…?" she breathed.

Jones grabbed Andy's jeans, searching quickly through the pockets. "Honey, did you see his watch? Was his watch here with the rest of his clothes?"

"No." Melody was afraid to get too excited. Although Andy never went anywhere without that watch, he certainly wouldn't have worn it into the water. So why wasn't it here? "It's possible Alex Parks took it. I wouldn't trust that kid any farther than I could throw him."

"Yeah, you're right. It's possible Alex has it. But…" Jones ran his hands through his damp hair. "Last week at the library, I talked Andy into checking out a copy of *Tom Sawyer*. He told me that he liked it—so he must've been reading it."

"Oh, my God." Melody turned to look at the quarry. "He might've set this whole thing up to make it look as if he'd drowned."

Jones grabbed her hand. "Come on."

"Where are we going?"

"You're going home. *I'm* going to New Hampshire."

MELODY'S BACK WAS killing her.

Cowboy shook his head in disgust, amazed that he'd let her talk him into coming along with him. It was an hour-and-a-half drive up to New Hampshire—each way.

She was careful not to mention her discomfort. Of course not. This was the woman who had walked for eight hours across the desert, the back of her heels raw from blisters, without complaining even once. No, she didn't say a word, but her constant shifting in her seat gave her away.

"We're almost there," she said, looking up from the map into the midafternoon glare.

The town was small, clearly built as an afterthought to the neighboring U.S. Army base. There were a series of bars and pool halls along the main strip, along with a tired-looking supermarket, a cheap motel, a tattoo parlor, a liquor store and a bus station with a sputtering neon sign.

Cowboy did a U-turn, right there in the middle of town.

"What are you doing? The base is in the other direction."

"Just following a hunch."

"But—"

"This whole thing—driving all the way up here without even being able to talk to Private Marshall on the phone—is a long shot, right?" He'd used a contact he had at the Pentagon to locate Andy's father, Pvt. David Marshall, here at the Plainfield, New Hampshire, Army Base.

Plainfield wasn't any kind of cushy silver-bullet

assignment. In fact, it was the opposite. Men were assigned to Plainfield as a punishment just short of a jail sentence. And according to Cowboy's Pentagon friend, David Marshall had had plenty of reasons to be reprimanded. He had a rap sheet a mile long, filled with unsavory charges including sexual harassment and use of excessive violence in dealing with civilians.

When Cowboy had called Plainfield, he was told that Private Marshall was not available. He couldn't even get the unfriendly voice on the other end of the line to verify if the man was still stationed at the base. From the tone of the phone call, though, he suspected the elder Marshall was currently in the middle of a severe dressing-down—or maybe even in the lockup.

If Private Marshall *was* at Plainfield, assuming Andy had even been able to see him, it wasn't too hard to imagine his reaction as he came face-to-face with the son he'd abandoned twelve years earlier. There weren't going to be many kisses and hugs, that much was for sure.

Cowboy pulled into the potholed parking lot next to the bus station.

"You think Andy's father won't want anything to do with him," Melody guessed correctly. "But do you really think Andy would have enough money to buy a bus ticket out of here? He probably spent everything he had getting here from Appleton."

"I think he probably doesn't even have enough to buy himself dinner, but the bus station's warm and dry. He can stay here all night if he needs to. He can even sleep on one of the benches if he pretends he's waiting for an arriving bus."

She was watching him closely in the shadowy dusk as he pulled up the parking brake and turned off the engine. "You sound as if you're speaking from experience."

Cowboy gazed into her eyes. It felt as if it had been a million years since they shared a smile. The trip from Massachusetts had been a quiet one. In fact, this entire day had been the furthest thing from a laughfest he'd ever known. "I think maybe you know me a little too well."

"How many times exactly did you run away when you were a kid?"

"I don't know—I lost count. The dumb thing was, no one ever really missed me. So I finally stopped running. I figured I could tick my parents off more by being around."

Melody shifted in her seat. "But you ran away again when you were sixteen, right? You told me you went to see a rodeo and just never went home."

"That wasn't running away. That was growing up and leaving home." He managed a wan smile. "Well, maybe not growing up. I'm still not sure I've managed to do that yet."

"I think you've done just fine." Her eyes were soft in the rapidly fading light, and Cowboy knew with a sudden certainty that all he had to do was lean forward and she would let him kiss her. Despite everything that she'd said about misinterpretation and mistakes, with very little effort on his part, she would belong to him.

He couldn't figure it out. Certainly if Andy was dead, but even if the kid was alive, Cowboy had proven himself to be irresponsible and incapable of dealing with a child. It didn't make sense. He screws up and *now* he gets the girl? What he'd done should've made her want to put even more distance between them. He just didn't get it.

Maybe it *was* only based on comfort, on shared grief—or hope. Or hell, maybe it was only his imagination. He'd find out soon enough by kissing her again, by lowering his mouth to hers and…

It was funny. All this time, he would've risked damn near anything for a chance to take this woman into his arms and lose himself in her sweet kisses. But now, as badly as he wanted to feel her arms around him, he was going to have to deny himself the pleasure. They'd come here hoping to find Andy. He should be looking for the kid, not kissing Melody.

But God, he wanted to kiss her. He was drowning in the ocean blue of her eyes, wondering just how much comfort she'd be willing to give him, how much comfort she'd be willing to take in return….

"We're stalling," she told him, breaking the spell. "We should go inside."

Cowboy nodded, realizing he was gripping the steering wheel so hard his knuckles had turned white. He pried his fingers free. "I know." He *was* stalling. Truth was, he was afraid of going into that bus station and finding out his hunch was wrong. He was afraid this entire trip was just the result of wishful thinking and that Andy really *was* down at the bottom of that quarry.

Melody unfastened her seat belt. "I'll go. You stay here."

Cowboy snorted at that. "I don't think so."

He helped her out of the car, and as he closed the door behind her, she held on to his hand. He'd been on quite a few difficult missions since he'd become a SEAL, but this was the first time he'd had a hand to hold as he took the point. And odd as it was, he was glad for it, glad she was there.

"Please, God, let him be here," she murmured as they started toward the door.

"If he *is* here," Cowboy told her, "do me a favor. Don't let me kill him."

She squeezed his hand. "I won't."

He took a deep breath, pushed open the door and together they went inside.

It was vintage run-down bus station. The odor of cigarette smoke and urine wasn't completely masked by the cloyingly sweet chemical scent of air freshener. The bleak walls were a hopeless shade of beige, and the industrial-bland floor tiles were cracked and chipped in some places, revealing triangles of the dirty gray concrete beneath. The men's room had a sign on the door saying Out Of Order—Use Facilities Near Ticket Agents. The snack bar had been permanently shut down, replaced by vending machines. The cheery orange and yellow of the hard plastic chairs had long since been dulled by thousands of grimy fingers.

And Andy Marshall, a picture of dejection, sat in one of them, shoulders slumped, elbows on knees, forehead resting in the palms of his hands.

Relief roared in Cowboy's ears. It made the bus station, and the entire world with it, seem to shift and tilt on its axis.

The relief was followed by an icy surge of anger. How could Andy have done this? The little bastard! He'd had them all worried damned sick!

"Jones." He turned and looked down into Melody's eyes. They were brimming with tears. But she blinked, pushing them back as she smiled up at him. "I think he's already been punished enough," she said as if she could read his mind, as if everything he was feeling was written on his face.

Cowboy nodded. It was obvious that the kid's last hope had been ripped from him without any anesthetic. It wasn't going to do either Andy *or* Cowboy the slightest bit of good to foam at the mouth and rage at him.

"I'm going to go call Tom Beatrice," he told Melody,

knowing that he had to attempt to regain his equilibrium
before he confronted the boy. "I want to give Harvard a
call, too. Tell him we found Andy alive."

She held on to his hand until the last possible moment.
"Call Brittany, will you? Please?"

"I will." He went to a row of beat-up pay phones,
punching in his calling-card number and watching as
Melody approached Andy.

She sat down next to him, and even then the kid didn't
look up until she spoke. Cowboy was too far away to hear
what she said, but Andy didn't seem surprised by her
presence.

He watched them talk as he made his calls. Tom was
quietly thankful. Harvard was out, and Cowboy left a
message for him with his father. Brittany cried and then
cursed the boy for his stupidity in the same breath in
which she thanked God for keeping him safe.

As Cowboy hung up the phone, Andy glanced warily
in his direction. The flash of his pale face called to mind
that other ghastly image he'd thought he'd seen 175 feet
beneath the surface of the flooded quarry.

Andy's face looked much better with life glistening in
his eyes.

And just like that, Cowboy's anger faded. The kid was
alive. Yeah, he'd made a pile of very huge mistakes, but
who was Cowboy to talk? He'd made some whopping
mistakes here himself.

Starting seven and a half months ago in that 747 bathroom with Melody. With barely a thought, he'd gambled
with fate and lost—and changed her life irrevocably.

She looked up at him as he approached, and he could
see trepidation in her eyes. He tried to smile to reassure
her, but it came out little better than a grimace. Great big
God, he was tired, but he couldn't even consider slowing

down. He had a ninety-minute drive back to Appleton that he had to make before he could even *think* about climbing into bed.

Climbing into Melody's bed.

If she let him. Hell, if he let himself, knowing what he now knew for certain—that he had no right to be anyone's father.

He laughed silently and scornfully at himself. Yeah, right. Like he'd *ever* turn Melody down. Whether it was comfort, true love or sheer lust that drove her into his arms, he wasn't going to push her away. Not in *this* lifetime.

"I'm sorry," Andy said before Cowboy even sat down.

"Yeah," Cowboy told him, "I know. I'm glad you're okay, kid."

"I thought maybe my father would be like you." Andy kicked once at the metal leg of the chair. "He wasn't."

"I wish you had told me what you were planning to do." Cowboy was glad he'd made those phone calls first. His voice came out even and matter-of-fact rather than harsh and shaking with anger. "I would've come up here with you."

"No, you wouldn't've." The boy's words were spoken without his usual cheeky attitude or resentment. They were flat, expressionlessly hopeless. "You didn't believe me when I said I didn't mess up that house."

"Yeah," Cowboy said. He cleared his throat. "Lookit, Andy, I owe you a major apology on that one. I know now that you didn't do it. Of course, now is a little bit late. Still, I hope you can forgive me."

There was a tiny flare of surprise in Andy's eyes. "You know I didn't…?"

"Brittany believed you," Melody told him. "And she

figured out a way to prove you were telling the truth. The account information from her computer is going to show that someone—you—were on-line that night. And although that probably wouldn't hold up as an alibi in a court of law, it'll go far in convincing Tom Beatrice he's caught the wrong kid."

"Brittany believed me, huh?" Andy looked bemused. "Man, there was a time when she would've been organizing a lynch mob." He looked up at Cowboy and squared his narrow shoulders. "Maybe I *am* at least partly guilty, though. I *did* go into that house about two weeks ago. One of the upstairs windows was open a crack. I knew the place was empty, so I climbed up and went inside. I didn't break anything, though, and I didn't steal anything. I just looked."

"And touched," Cowboy added.

Andy rolled his eyes. "Yeah. I left my fingerprints everywhere. What a fool. Someone must've seen me go in and told Alex Parks. He did the spray painting and broke the windows and mirrors and stuff. He told me last night up by the quarry. He told me he'd made sure I was going to leave town. He told me he'd reserved a room for me at juvy hall." He smiled grimly. "I scared the hell out of him when I jumped into the quarry."

"You scared the hell out of *all* of us."

"It was a stupid, *dangerous* thing to do," Melody admonished him hotly. "You might have really drowned."

Andy slouched in his seat. "Yeah, like anyone would've missed me. Like anyone in the world gives a damn. My father doesn't—that's for sure. You know, he didn't even know my name? He kept calling me Anthony. *Anthony.* And he stood and talked with me for five lousy minutes. That's all he could spare me in all of twelve years."

"Forget about your father," Melody said fiercely. "He's

an idiot, Andy. You don't need him because you have us. You've got me and Brittany and Jones—"

"Yeah, for how long?" There were actually tears in Andy's eyes. He couldn't keep up the expressionless act any longer. His voice shook. "Because after this mess, Social Services is going to pull me out of the Romanellas' house so fast I won't even have time to wave goodbye."

"We won't let them," Melody said. "I'll talk to Vince Romanella and—"

"What are you going tell him to do?" Andy sneered. "*Adopt* me? That's about the only thing I can think of that would keep me around. And I'm *so* sure that would go over *really* well." He shook his head, swearing softly. "I bet Vince already has my stuff packed in boxes."

"Someone at Social Services must have the authority to give you a second chance," Cowboy said. "Alex Parks is the one who should be thrown into the brig for this, not you."

Andy wiped savagely at his tears. "What do *you* care? You're going to leave town yourself in a few weeks!"

Cowboy didn't know what to say. The kid was right. He *wasn't* going to stay. He was a SEAL. His job pulled him all over the world. Even under the best of circumstances, he'd often be gone for weeks at a time. He glanced up, and Melody made a point of not meeting his gaze.

"I don't know why you're so hot to marry her," Andy continued, gesturing with a thumb toward Melody, "when you're only going to see her and the kid a few times a year. My father might've been a real jerk, but at least he didn't pretend he was doing anything besides giving me his name when he married my mother."

Melody stood up. "I think we'd better get going," she said. "It's getting late."

"You know, Ted Shepherd's got a thing for you," Andy said to Melody.

"Andy, I changed the subject." Melody's voice sounded strained. "We need to go, and we need to stop talking about this now."

Andy turned to Cowboy. "The guy she works for has the hots for her. You didn't know that, did you? The guy's got money, too. He could take care of her and the kid, no problem. Brittany told me he's going to be governor some day. But as long as you're around, she doesn't stand a chance of getting anything started with him. And if *you* marry her—"

"Home, Andrew," Melody said in that tone that she used when she had reached the absolute end of her rope. *"Now."*

CHAPTER THIRTEEN

"YOUR LAMAZE CLASS starts tonight." Brittany was in the dining room, rifling through the sideboard drawers, searching for something. "Seven o'clock. At the hospital. In the West Lounge."

Melody sank into a chair at the kitchen table, aware of Jones watching her from the other side of the room. Lamaze class. God. It was nearly six. She would barely have enough time to take a shower. "Britt, I'm beat. I'm just going to stay home."

Brittany stopped her search long enough to poke her head through the door. "Abigail Cloutier has a waiting list a mile long for this class. If you don't show up, she'll fill your slot, and then you'll be stuck waiting for the next session, which doesn't start until next month. You'll probably end up having your baby before you're halfway through." She disappeared again. "I made some pea soup—it's on the stove. And there's bread warming in the oven."

"Wait a minute," Melody said, sitting up straight. "Aren't you coming with me?"

"*Here's* my passport," Brittany said triumphantly. She slammed the drawer shut and came into the kitchen, adjusting her hair. "I need it as a second form of ID."

"You *aren't* coming with me, are you?" Melody looked at her sister, fighting her panic. If Brittany didn't come as her coach, then that left Melody going solo, or… She didn't look at Jones. She refused to look at Jones.

But Britt was all dressed up, and it was obvious it wasn't for Abigail Cloutier's benefit. She was wearing a dark suit, complete with panty hose and her black heels that meant business. Her blond hair was pulled up into a French braid and she actually wore makeup.

"Sweetie, Social Services is intending to take Andy back to Boston tonight. I've been on the phone with Vince Romanella and at least twelve different social workers since Cowboy called this afternoon. There's a meeting at six at the Romanellas'," she told them, turning to look at Jones, who was silently leaning against the kitchen counter. "I expect it to drag on until quite late, so no, Mel, I can't go to the Lamaze class with you tonight."

"I'll go," Jones said. Melody closed her eyes.

Britt laughed. "I figured you'd be willing to volunteer as temporary coach."

God, the last thing Melody wanted to do was sit with Jones in a room with a dozen other expectant, *married* couples. But that wasn't the worst of it. She'd seen childbirth classes portrayed on TV, and all of them had demanded a certain amount of physical intimacy—touching at the very least—between the mother-to-be and her coach.

It was obviously all she could do to keep from throwing herself at Jones even under normal circumstances. Add any strong emotions into the churning pot of passion, and she would be on the verge of meltdown. Add a situation in which Jones would be *forced* to touch her, and she would be lost.

"Jones, you look even more exhausted than I feel," Melody countered, knowing that no matter what she said, he wouldn't quit. He didn't know how to quit. He'd never quit before in his entire life.

He gave her a crooked smile. "Honey, is it going to be harder than diving to 175 feet?"

"No." Melody realized that for the first time since he'd arrived in Appleton all those weeks ago, he was wearing a sweatshirt. She'd honestly thought he didn't have one. Before today, she'd thought he wasn't capable of feeling the cold.

"Well, there you go. As long as it doesn't involve breathing a tank of mixed gas, it'll be a—"

"Piece of cake," Melody finished for him with a sigh. "Speak for yourself," she muttered.

He straightened up, concern darkening his eyes. "Mel, if you're really feeling too tired to go, I'll go for you. I can take notes and tomorrow I can tell you everything you missed."

He was serious. He looked a total mess, but he stood ready to help her however he could, and the effect was touching. She tried to look away. When it came to Jones, she shouldn't be thinking words like "touching."

But his chin glinted with golden brown stubble, and although he looked exhausted to the bone, and as if by all rights he should be sitting rather than standing, he looked...undeniably touchingly adorable. Melody couldn't help but glance at him, and he mustered a tired smile. She knew him well enough to believe he would be ready and willing to run ten miles if it was asked of him. Twenty if *she* asked him.

Brittany pulled on her overcoat. Her purse was by the door, and she gathered it up. "If you're not going to go, call Abby now," her sister told her.

Melody closed her eyes. "I'm going to go." With Jones. Oh, God. The feeling that gripped her was more than pure dread. In fact, the dread was laced with stomach-flipping, roller-coaster-style excitement.

Brittany opened the door, but as a seeming after-thought, she turned back. "Oh, just so you know, I'm planning to begin the preliminary paperwork tonight to adopt Andy."

Melody nearly fell out of her chair. *"What?"*

"You heard me."

"I can't believe you're serious."

Britt bristled. "If you can be a single mother, then I can, too. And it's not as if we don't have four empty bedrooms in this house."

Melody shook her head. "I'm not criticizing you," she told her sister. "I'm just…amazed. A few weeks ago, Andy's name was interchangeable with Satan's."

"Well, yes, but that was before I got to know him."

"Britt, you don't really know Andy Marshall," Melody countered. "I mean, you might *think* you do, but—"

"I know all that I need to know," Brittany said quietly. "I know that right now the one thing that boy needs more than anything in the world is someone who loves him and wants him, *truly* wants him. I know he's not perfect. I know he's going to give me headaches over things I can't even imagine, but I don't care. I don't care! Because you know what? The thought of my life without that kid around…well, it just feels cold—like spring will never come again. I've thought about it long and hard. I honestly want him, Mel."

"It's not going to be that easy to cut through the red tape," Melody cautioned. "A single woman trying to adopt a kid who's a known troublemaker… I can imagine Social Services deciding that he's going to need a strong father figure and turning you down."

"Even if it doesn't work out," Brittany told her, "at least Andy will know that *some*one wanted him. At least I can give him *that* much."

Melody stood up and gave her sister a hug. "You go and fight for him," she whispered, blinking back tears.

And then Brittany was gone, leaving her alone in the kitchen with Jones. Jones and his stormy green eyes...

"I better shower and change if we're going out," he said.

She nodded. "I have to, too."

"Are you certain you just don't want to let me go?" he asked.

Melody was certain of nothing anymore. "The class is only an hour and a half," she told him. "It'll be over before we know it."

She hoped.

JONES WAS HELPING himself to a cup of coffee as Melody returned from the ladies' room. Abby Cloutier, the Lamaze instructor, had called a ten-minute washroom break—a definite necessity for a class filled with hugely pregnant women.

So far, they'd sat on folding chairs in a darkened room and watched a movie that focused on giving birth. She'd barely been able to pay attention with Jones sitting so close to her. Having him here was a thorough distraction. He smelled good and looked even better.

But he hadn't had to touch her.

Not yet.

Jones was smiling as he listened to another man talk. He was standing in a group of about five men, most of whom were helping themselves to cookies from the snack table. He'd broken out his Dockers and polo shirt for the occasion, and with his hair neatly pulled back into a ponytail at the nape of his neck, and his chin freshly shaven, he looked impossibly handsome. But even though he was dressed nearly the same as the other men, he stood out in the crowd. He might as well have been wearing his dress whites.

"Is that your Navy SEAL?" a voice behind Melody asked. She turned to see Janette Dennison, one of Brittany's high school friends who was pregnant with her fourth child. Janette peered across the room at Jones. "Dear Lord, he's bigger than Hank Forsythe!"

Hank owned the local gym. His wife, Sandy, was pregnant with their first. "Jones *is* taller," Melody pointed out.

"Your Lieutenant Jones is more than taller," Janette countered. "Your Lieutenant Jones is…beyond description, Mel. Haven't you noticed every single woman in this place looking at you as if you've won the lottery?"

Melody *had* noticed. But she was well aware that everyone's envy would fade rapidly as soon they were told exactly what a U.S. Navy SEAL did for a living. She'd heard several women complaining in the ladies' room about husbands who had to fly to Boulder or Los Angeles or Seattle on business and were gone for days, sometimes even weeks, at a time.

They didn't know how lucky they were. Their husbands weren't going to be parachuting out of airplanes or helocasting—jumping from low-flying helicopters into the ocean below—as they inserted into enemy territory. Their husbands carried briefcases, not submachine guns. Their work didn't expose them to physical dangers. Their husbands would always be returning safe and sound. There was no chance of their being brought back home strapped to some medic's stretcher, bleeding from gunshot wounds, or—worse yet—zipped inside a body bag.

"Did he really rescue you from that embassy where

you were being held hostage?" Janette asked. "That is *so* romantic."

Melody smiled. But Janette was wrong. Yes, Jones had saved her life. But he'd saved Chris Sterling's and Kurt Matthews's lives, as well. He would've saved anyone's life. It wasn't personal—it was his job. And because of that, the fact that he'd saved her wasn't particularly romantic.

What *Melody* found truly romantic was the image of Jones, up on a step stool in the baby's nursery, hanging curtains patterned with brightly colored bunnies and teddy bears.

Romantic was the wondrous look in his eyes that she'd seen when he'd touched her and felt their baby move.

Romantic was Jones, driving home from New Hampshire after they'd found Andy, furtively wiping tears of relief from his eyes when he thought she wasn't looking.

Romantic was the way he could gaze at her from across the room—the way he was gazing at her right now—as if she were the most beautiful, most desirable woman on the entire planet. His eyelids were slightly lowered, and the intensity of the expression on his face would be a little frightening if not for the small smile playing around the corners of his lips.

She'd seen that smile before. In Paris. And she knew for a fact that Jones had the ability and the wherewithal to make everything that little smile promised come true.

She turned away, her cheeks heating with a blush. She didn't want this man, she reminded herself. She didn't love him. God help her, she didn't *want* to love him….

"Gentlemen," Abby Cloutier announced, "grab a floor mat and some pillows and find your ladies. We're going to do some simple breathing and relaxation exercises to get you started."

Across the room, Jones waited patiently for a chance to take a mat from the pile. As if he felt Melody watching him, he looked up at her again and smiled. It was a tentative, apologetic smile, as if he knew what was coming and how much the thought of his touching her scared her.

Scared her and exhilarated her.

"Gentlemen, sit down on the mat and use your bodies and the pillows to make as comfortable a nest as you possibly can for your ladies," Abby continued.

Jones set the mat and the pillows toward the back of the room, giving them what little privacy he could. No doubt he was well aware of the curious glances they'd been receiving all evening long. Appleton was a fairly conservative community, and they were the only unmarried pair in the group—although a few of the younger couples looked as if there had been a shotgun present at their nuptials.

He sat down, imitating their classmates as he spread his long legs for her to sit nestled against him, as if they were riding a toboggan.

Knowing it would be far worse if she hesitated and stood there gaping at him like some landed fish, Melody lowered herself to the mat. At least this way, she would keep her back to him. At least this way, he wouldn't see the blush that was heating her cheeks. At least this way, she wouldn't have to gaze into his eyes or watch his lips curve up into one of his smiles. At least this way, she wouldn't be tempted to do something foolish, such as kiss him.

She gingerly inched her way back, bumping against the inside of his knee. "Oh, I'm sorry!"

"That's all right, honey. Keep coming on back."

She didn't dare look at him. "Are you sure? It's a little warm in here, and I'm not exactly a lightweight these days."

"Mel. You're *supposed* to lean against me. How're you going to relax if you're not leaning back?"

How was she supposed to relax, leaning back against this outrageously sexy man's solid chest, her legs against the inside of his thighs?

"Come on," he whispered. "I promise it won't be that bad."

Bad wasn't what she was afraid of. She was afraid it was going to be irresistibly *good*.

"Get comfortable, ladies," Abby ordered.

Melody inched farther back, closing her eyes as Jones took control and pulled her in close. Too close. He put his arms around her, the palms of his hands against her belly, and she felt both impossibly safe and in terrible peril. She felt his breath, soft against her ear. She felt his heart beating against her back. She didn't want to move, didn't want to talk. She just wanted to sit there with him like this. Forever.

And that was absolutely the wrong thing to be thinking.

"This makes me really uncomfortable," she whispered. It was both a lie *and* the understatement of the year.

"Sorry—I'm sorry." He removed his hands but then didn't know quite where to put them.

God, now she'd gone and made *him* tense, too.

Abby's voice was just a drone in the background. She was saying something about breathing, about the importance of taking a deep cleansing breath before and after contractions. Melody inhaled deeply through her nose, releasing her breath through her mouth, along with the rest of the class.

She tried her best to follow the breathing exercises but knew without a doubt that she was retaining absolutely nothing. Come tomorrow morning, she would remember none of this—except for the way Jones smelled, and the warmth of his body pressed against her, and...

"...back rub while she's doing this." Abby's voice cut into her thoughts. "Come on, guys, make her feel good."

"At last," Jones said, trying to make light of it. "I'm finally going to get a chance to give you a back rub."

Melody closed her eyes. There was nothing even remotely funny here. She remembered his back rubs far too well. They had involved a great deal more of both of their anatomies than simply her back and his hands.

She felt him move aside the mass of her long hair, felt his hands touch her shoulders, his fingers gently massaging the too tense muscles in her upper back and neck. She tried to focus on her breathing, but with him touching her that way, she could barely get a breath in, let alone push one out.

"Tell her how wonderfully she's doing, gentlemen," Abby urged. "Tell her how beautiful she is. Tell her how much you love her. Don't hold back. Practice letting her know. When she's in labor, she's going to need to hear all these little things you take for granted."

"Don't you dare say anything," Melody said from between clenched teeth.

His husky laughter moved the hair next to her ear. "Are you kidding?" he asked. "I wouldn't dream of it. I'm supposed to be relaxing you, not getting you more tense. I know you pretty well by now, Mel—enough to know that when you look into a mirror, you don't see what I see. I happen to think you're crazy, but this is not the time to debate the issue."

"...called *effleurage*," Abby was saying. "It's a French word, meaning to stroke or lightly massage. Gentlemen, when your lady is in labor, it may comfort her to stroke her abdomen very lightly in a circular motion. Ladies, let him know the right amount of pressure. Tell him what feels good. Don't be shy."

Melody closed her eyes tightly as Jones's long fingers caressed the mountain that was her belly. Somehow he knew exactly how to touch her. Watching those powerful-looking hands touch her so exquisitely gently was enough to make her dizzy.

"Is this all right?" he asked. "Am I doing this right?"

She managed to nod. *Right* was not quite the word for what he was doing.

"How's your lower back?" he asked, using his other hand to reach between them and massage her. "This is where you're always hurting the most, isn't it?"

She nodded again, unable to speak.

"Are you focusing on the breathing?" he asked, his voice soft and soothing in her ear. "If I know you, you're not. You're thinking about something else entirely—about Brittany and Andy, about what's going on over at the Romanellas'. You're always thinking and worrying about someone else, but right now, you've got to clear your mind and think only about yourself. Relax and breathe and just shut everything else out." He laughed softly. "I know that's hard because I'm probably the one problem you'd like to shut out the most, right?"

Wrong. Jones was wrong. He was incredibly, impossibly, amazingly, *totally* wrong. Melody realized with a sudden startling clarity that she didn't want to shut him out. She'd tried, but he'd been doggedly persistent, and somehow, someway, over the past few weeks, he'd gone from former lover and near stranger to dear friend.

He'd been patient and he'd let her see that although he would never be called average or normal, there *was* a part of him that could be content just sitting on the porch, talking and watching the sunset. He'd taken his time and told her stories about himself as a boy, about growing up, so she felt she had a good sense of him, of why he did the things he did. And his dealings with Andy had told her even more about the kind of man he'd become.

He was the kind of man she could fall in love with.

The kind of man she *had* fallen in love with.

I know you pretty well by now, he'd said. *If I know you...* He *did* know her. And she knew him.

Oh, she didn't know him completely. Even if she spent the rest of her life with him, there'd still be secrets she knew he'd never share with her. And even the parts of him she *did* know, she'd never totally understand. His need to risk his life, to be a SEAL. But even though she didn't understand it, she could appreciate it. And God knows he was good at what he did.

She was starting to believe that if he *did* marry her, he *would* stick by her—for the rest of his life, if need be. If he made a vow, he wouldn't break it. He had the strength and the willpower to keep to his word, no matter how hard.

But would that be enough for her? Knowing that he was with her not out of love, but out of duty? Was it possible that her own feelings for him were strong enough to sustain them both?

She didn't think so.

She knew he liked her. And although she couldn't quite believe it, he seemed to desire her. But unless he loved her, *truly* loved her, she couldn't *marry* him. Could she?

"Mel, you're tightening up again," Jones whispered. "Just let it go. Whatever you're wrestling with, just give it up, throw it away."

"We're out of time," Abby announced. "The next class is about to break down the doors, so just leave your mats and pillows where they are. Next week, we're going to work on Modified-Paced Breathing and the Progressive Relaxation Exercise, so read over those sections in your books—it'll save us a little time. Ladies, remember to do your stretches and your Kegels!"

Jones helped Melody to her feet. He would've held on to her hand, but she pulled away, afraid he would somehow know the awful truth just from touching her. She'd done what she'd sworn she wouldn't do. She'd fallen in love with him. She was doomed.

A shadow flickered in his eyes, and all at once he looked about as tired as she felt. "You're never going be able to relax around me, are you?" It was a rhetorical question, and he didn't wait for her to answer. "It was stupid to think I could be your labor coach. Come on, let's get you home. You look beat."

He was careful not to touch her again as he opened the door for her. And he was noticeably silent in the car on the way home. And it wasn't until they pulled into the driveway that Melody gathered up the nerve to speak.

"Jones, I'm sorry...I, um..." What could she possibly say? I love you? She wasn't sure she'd ever be able to tell him that. Not with words anyway. Not in *this* lifetime.

He pulled up the parking brake and turned to face her.

"Mel, look, I've been thinking about…a lot of things. Andy. Our baby. You and me. You—what you want and what you don't want." The muscle in his jaw was jumping. "As in *me*."

"Jones—"

He stopped her by holding up one hand. "I need to say this, so please let me talk. I think it's kind of obvious that my parenting skills need a lot of work. I'm not sure anymore that I should help you raise our child.

"But I keep coming back to the fact that I don't want this kid growing up thinking I don't give a damn. Because I do. I do." His voice broke, and he took a deep breath, steadying himself. "I care about him, but I care about you, too. And what Andy said is right. If you marry me, you'll never find someone that you can really love, someone who can be a real father to our baby."

"Jones—"

"Hush and let me finish. I'm giving you your deal, Melody. You acknowledge that the baby's mine, put my name on his birth certificate, let me come and visit a couple times a year. I'll want to pay child support, too, but we can have our lawyers work that out."

He cleared his throat. "My only other condition is that I'd like to be there when the baby's born. I know there's no real way to be certain when that's going to take place, but it's not likely to happen within the next three weeks. So I figure what I'll do is pack up and head back to base as soon as possible. I'll apply for additional leave at the start of December, and then we'll just cross our fingers and hope it happens sooner rather than later."

Melody was speechless. He was accepting her deal. He had it all figured out, down to being there when the baby

was born. He was capitulating, backing down, giving in.
She could barely believe it.

Didn't he realize that she was on the verge of surrender
herself?

But there was no need to worry anymore. She'd
won.

So why did she feel as if she'd lost?

CHAPTER FOURTEEN

COWBOY STOOD ON the steps of the porch, waiting while Melody unlocked the front door. He was making sure she got safely inside before he returned to his tent. He'd grab a combat nap—just enough to refresh him—and then he'd pack up and walk over to the gas station by the highway, bum a ride off someone heading into Boston. Once in town, he'd take the T to Logan Airport. By sunup, he'd be wheels up, heading back to base.

Harvard had told him most of Alpha Squad had long since returned to Virginia. After a great deal of bitching and moaning, FinCOM was ready to negotiate with Joe Cat about the counterterrorist training session. It looked as if FinCOM would keep its rule book with the understanding that the program was going to happen on a trial basis only. Although latest word was that the combined SEAL/FinCOM training program wouldn't happen until spring—May or June at the earliest.

Which left Alpha Squad with a *looong* time to prepare. But as they waited, of course, they were ready to go wherever they were needed at a moment's notice.

The moon had risen above the trees, and its silvery light made Melody's face seem exquisitely otherworldly as she pushed open the door and then turned to face him. "Good night."

"You *are* beautiful, you know."

She closed her eyes. "Jones, we're done. We've come to an agreement. There's no need for you to—"

"Yeah, I know," he interrupted. "I figure that's why I can say it. I don't have to worry anymore about you freaking out and running away. Hell, I don't have to stop there. I can tell you that despite what you think, you're the sexiest lady I've ever known."

She tried to make a joke of it. "Well, sure, you're a SEAL. After spending all that time in the ocean, it's no wonder you'd be attracted to someone who reminds you of a whale."

Cowboy didn't laugh. "You know what you remind me of?"

"A circus tent?"

He refused to acknowledge her attempts at humor. He continued as if she hadn't spoken. "You remind me of the hottest, most powerful sex I've ever had in my life. Every time I see you, I think about what we did to make you look that way. I think about locking myself in that bathroom with you on board that 747. I think about the way you made me feel, about the fact that for the first time in my entire life, I honest to God didn't care that I didn't have a condom."

He lowered his voice. "I think about the way you kissed me when you climaxed so you wouldn't cry out. I look at you, Melody, and I remember every stroke, every touch, every kiss. I look at you, and all I can think about is how badly I want another chance to make love to you like that again."

Melody was silent, just staring at him, her eyes wide.

"So," Cowboy said, "now you know."

She still didn't say a word. But she didn't run away, either.

He took a step toward her, and then another step, and she still didn't move. "I may be way out of line here—no, I *know* I'm way out of line, but I figure as long as I'm being brutally honest, I have to tell you that I've spent these past few weeks damn near tied in knots from wanting you so badly. I wanted you and I thought I needed you, but I found out today that wanting and needing aren't the same thing. Need's not about sex, is it? Not really. Because today I needed you more than I've ever needed anyone, and you were there for me." He forced a smile. "And what do you know? We had our clothes on the entire time."

He touched her hair, touched the softness of her cheek. "Look at me," he said. "Still putting the moves on you. We've reached an understanding, made an agreement. We've achieved a friendship of sorts, and I still can't seem to back away. I still want you more than I've ever wanted any woman."

She was trembling. He knew damn well that kissing her wasn't the gallant, gentlemanly thing to do, but he couldn't keep himself from lowering his mouth to hers.

She tasted so sweet, so perfect. Her lips were deliciously soft, exquisitely inviting. He pulled her closer, and the tautness of her belly pressed against him. He loved the way she felt beneath his hands, loved the way she seemed to sigh and melt against him as he kissed her again, deeper, longer, but just as slowly and gently.

"Come inside," she whispered. Her eyes were soft and dreamy as she gazed up at him. "Please?" Her fingers were laced through his hair, and she tugged his head down toward her to kiss him again.

She kissed *him.*

Cowboy knew he should turn and walk away. He knew nothing had changed. He was still going to have to leave tomorrow. But hell, it was entirely possible that she was doing this *because* he was leaving.

He broke free from her kiss. "Mel, are you sure?"

"Yes."

Yes. It wasn't something he needed to hear twice.

She took his hand and drew him into the house. She didn't say another word as she led him toward the stairs and up to her bedroom.

Cowboy felt compelled to speak. "Honey, I don't have any condoms. Again."

She glanced back at him. "Jones, it's not as if you're going to get me pregnant," she said. "Again."

"Still, I was reading this whole huge debate about whether or not women should have sexual relations in the eighth and ninth months of their pregnancies," he told her. "The consensus was unless the pregnancy was high risk, anything goes. Except there was a minority who seemed to think unprotected sex increased the risk of potential infection to the baby."

She'd gone into her room without turning the light on and now stood there in the moonlight, gazing at him. "Sometimes I think you go a teeny bit overboard with your research. My garden, for instance. It looks as if it's ready for a Siberian winter. All I really needed was someone to clear out the dead plants and throw down a little mulch." A smile softened her words. "Thank you for taking care of it, by the way."

"You're welcome. But yeah," he agreed, "I've definitely read far more than I should have about the potential dangers of pregnancy. Eclampsia. God. Just the thought of it scares me to death."

Damn, he was nervous. He'd wanted her for so long, but now all he could do was stand here and talk. Yada, yada, yada. He couldn't seem to make himself shut up.

He cleared his throat, fighting the urge to ask her about her blood pressure. She was fine. He knew she was fine. With the exception of the relentless morning sickness she suffered, she was healthy. Melody's was *not* a high-risk pregnancy. He'd already discussed it with Brittany, and she'd reassured him. She was a nurse; she should know.

He cleared his throat again. "May I lock your door?"

Melody nodded. "Please."

The door had an old-fashioned hook-and-eye lock, and he fastened it. It wouldn't do much against an invading horde, but for privacy, it would work just fine. When he turned around, she was closing the curtains. Without the moonlight, the room was very, very dark. He switched on the light.

"Oh," she said, "please don't."

He turned it off. She must've had some kind of room-darkening shades because it was nearly as dark in there as it had been down at 175 feet in the quarry. "Mel, I'm going to need night-vision glasses to see you."

She was a disembodied voice, lost in the shadows on the other side of the room. "That's the idea."

"Oh, come on. Weren't you paying attention to *any*-thing I said downstairs on the porch?"

"Yes," she said. "And it got you this far. It was...very nice. But... You know that cover Demi Moore did for *Vanity Fair* when she was pregnant?"

"You mean the one where she was naked?"

"Yeah. Pregnant and naked. She looked amazingly beautiful." She paused. "I don't look anything like that."

Cowboy had to laugh. "How will I ever know?"

She laughed, too. She had a musical laugh that

brushed over him like velvet in the darkness. "My point exactly."

"How about we turn on the light in the bathroom? Nothing *too* bright?"

"How about you come over here?"

It was an invitation he couldn't refuse. He moved toward her, sensing more than seeing that she'd climbed into bed. He reached for her, and with an explosion of pleasure, discovered that in the darkness she'd rid herself of her clothes. Every last little stitch was gone.

It was a total surprise, and as he touched her, he realized that with the lights off and the room so very dark, his other senses were heightened. Making love in the dark this way might not have been exactly what he'd wanted, but it was going to be very, very, *very* good.

He kissed her, her skin smooth beneath his still-exploring fingers. Her breasts were so full, they rested on the enormous bulge of her belly—the bulge that held their baby.

She moaned as he kissed her harder, deeper, filling her mouth with his tongue and his hands with the softness of her breasts. Her nipples were hard peaks pressed against the palms of his hands, a sensation that was impossibly delicious.

And apparently, it felt as good from Melody's end.

She pulled his shirt free from the waist of his pants, slipping her hands underneath and sliding her fingers up along the muscles of his chest as they knelt there together on her bed.

"You have no idea how long I've wanted to touch you like this," she whispered. "All those weeks of watching you run around with hardly any clothes on..."

Cowboy had to laugh. All this time, he'd thought she'd

become immune to damn near everything he'd thought he had working in his favor.

He ran his hands lightly down her stomach, marveling at the way it seemed to bloom from her body. The rest of her was still slender. It was true, she'd put on a few extra pounds since Paris, but he'd thought she was a bit too skinny before. She felt good beneath his hands—so soft and utterly, thoroughly feminine. He strained to see her in the darkness, but though his eyes had tried to adjust, he still couldn't see a damn thing.

She kissed him as she tugged at his shirt, breaking off to say, "I'm feeling very much as if I'm the only one naked here."

"That's because you are. And, to be honest, I like it. There's a real hint of a master-slave thing to it," he teased. He lowered his head to draw one hard bud of a nipple into his mouth as his hand explored lower, sweeping beneath the taut curve of her stomach, his fingers encountering her soft nest of curls. Talk about a turn-on. She was ready for him, slick with heat and desire, and as he touched her, first lightly, then harder, deeper, she clung to him.

"Master and slave, huh?" Her voice was breathless. "In that case—slave, take off your clothes."

Cowboy cracked up. Damn, he couldn't get enough of this girl. He yanked his shirt over his head, then kissed her, pulling her back with him onto the bed, careful, so careful to be gentle.

He felt her fingers fumble with the buckle of his belt, and he tortured himself for a moment, just letting her knuckles brush against him as she worked to get him free. There was no way she'd ever figure out how to unfasten that belt—certainly not in this blanket of darkness, and probably not even in the light.

"Jones…"

He reached down with one hand and released the catch.

"Thank you," she murmured.

It took her next to forever to unfasten the button. And he was so aroused, it took her another eon to work the zipper down, and then...

She didn't touch him. Damn, she didn't touch him! She dragged his pants and his shorts down his legs instead, leaving him screaming with need, aching for her touch, and loving every minute of the way she always kept him guessing.

Melody pulled off his boots one by one, and he wished for the zillionth time that it wasn't so damned dark. He would've loved to have watched.

He propped himself up on his elbows as he helped her pull his legs free from his pants. "Honey, do you have a condom?"

She froze. "You're not kidding, are you?"

"No. I...just want to protect you and the baby."

He felt her sit down next to him on the bed, felt her touch his leg, her fingers trailing up from his calf to his knee to his thigh. "Most guys wouldn't think past the fact that they couldn't get me more pregnant than I already am."

Her fingers did slow figure eights on his thigh. He reached for her, but she heard him start to move and backed away. He felt her fingers again, this time down near his ankle. He'd never realized that being touched on the ankle could be such a mind-blowing turn-on. He tried to moisten his dry lips. "Most guys wouldn't have gotten totally paranoid by reading every book in the library on pregnancy."

"Most guys wouldn't have bothered." She kissed him

on the inside of his knee, her mouth soft and moist and cool against the fiery heat of his skin.

Cowboy reached for her again, but again, she wasn't there. He had to move slowly, searching for her carefully in the pitch black. He didn't want to knock her over with quick moves and flailing arms. Besides, he liked this game she was playing too damn much to want it to end.

But it was going to end. In just a handful of hours, the sun was going to creep above the horizon, and this night *was* going to end. And he was going to crawl out of Melody's soft bed and walk out of her room, out of this house. He was going to pack up his tent and be gone. Game over.

It was ironic. The fact that there was an end in sight was quite possibly the only reason Melody was making love to him tonight. It was possible that it was only because he'd already told her that he wouldn't stay that she could let herself have this time with him.

But with each kiss, each touch, each caress, *he* was wishing that he could keep this crazy game alive forever.

Forever.

She touched him again, and this time he was ready for her. His fingers closed around her arm and he gently pulled her up, finding her mouth with his, her body with his fingers, entangling their legs, the heaviness of his arousal against the roundness of her belly.

She moved languidly, lazily, kissing his neck, his ear, that delicate spot beneath his jaw that drove him crazy and made him want nothing more than to bury himself inside her forever.

Forever.

In the past, the word had scared him to death. It meant a deadly sameness, a permanent lack of change. It meant stagnation, boredom, a life of endless reruns, a slow fade from the brilliant colors of fresh new experiences to the washed-out gray of tired and old.

But Cowboy could be a SEAL forever without ever fearing he'd fall victim to that fate. Even if he ever got tired of parachuting out of jet planes, Joe Cat would have Alpha Squad doing HALO jumps—jumping out of planes at outrageously high altitudes, yet not opening the chute until they reached a ridiculously *low* altitude. And if he got tired of that—and he'd have to do one whole hell of a lot of 'em ever to be blasé about the adrenaline-inducing sensation of the ground rushing up to meet him—there was always Alpha Squad's refresher courses in underwater demolition, or Arctic, desert and jungle survival, or...

The truth was, he could be a SEAL forever because he never knew what was coming next.

Cowboy had always thought he'd feel the same about women. How could he possibly agree to spend the rest of his life with only one, when he never knew for certain who might be walking into his life at any given moment? How could he survive the endless stagnation of commitment even as temptation walked toward him every time he turned a corner?

But as he lost himself in the sweetness of Melody's kisses, he found himself wondering instead how he could possibly survive the constant disappointment of searching for her face in a crowd—despite the fact that he knew damn well she was two thousand miles away. How could he survive turning corner after corner, coming face-to-face with beautiful women, women who wanted to be with him—women he wanted nothing to do with, women whose only real faults were that they weren't Melody?

She pulled away from him slightly, opening herself to

his hand, lifting her hips to push his fingers more deeply inside her. Her own fingers trailed down his side, moving across his stomach, almost but not quite touching him.

"You're driving me insane," he breathed.

"I know." He could hear the smile in her voice.

"I want you so badly, honey, but I'm terrified I'll hurt you." His own voice was hoarse.

She pulled back. "Do you mind if I get on top of you?"

Mind? Did she actually think he would *mind?* But then he realized that she was laughing at his stunned silence.

"But first…" She touched him, and his mind exploded with white-hot pleasure as she kissed him most intimately. "Do you think if I keep doing this while calling you Harlan," she wondered, "you'll learn to associate positive emotions with the use of your first name?"

Cowboy didn't know whether to laugh or cry.

"Harlan," she said. "Harlan. Harlan. Harlan. You know, I never really thought about it before, but I *like* that name."

He could barely speak. "I like it, too."

Melody laughed. "Wow, that was easy. I think I may have just developed a powerful brainwashing technique. Better not let any enemies of the U.S.A. get their hands— so to speak—on this, or we'll all be in trouble."

"Yeah, but it wouldn't work with anyone else but you."

Melody was quiet for a moment. "Well, that was really sweet," she said. He could tell from her voice that she didn't believe him.

He pushed himself up on one elbow. "Melody, I'm serious."

She pushed him back down, straddling his thighs.

"Let's not argue about this now," she told him, reaching for something. He heard the sound of a drawer opening, and then she moved back. "Let's just…pretend that we might've been able to make this thing between us work."

"But—"

"Please?" He felt her touch him, covering him with a condom.

"Mel, dammit, if you could look into my eyes—"

"Hush up and kiss me, Jones."

It was an order he couldn't refuse. And when she shifted herself forward, and in one smooth, languorous motion, surrounded him with her tight heat, he couldn't do more than groan her name.

He wanted more. He wanted to thrust deeply inside her. He wanted to flip her onto her back and rock her, hard and fast, the way he knew she liked it. He wanted to turn on the light and gaze into her eyes. He wanted to watch her release, see the incredibly sexy look on her beautiful face as he took her higher than she'd ever been before.

Instead, he lay on his back. "Mel, I'm afraid to move." His voice was a paper-dry whisper in the darkness.

"Then I'll move," she whispered back, doing just that.

The sensation was off the charts. Cowboy clenched his teeth to keep from raising his hips to meet her. It was possible that he'd never been more turned on in his entire life. Not in the bathroom of the 747. Not in Paris. Not anywhere.

"But I want—"

She pushed herself a little bit farther onto him, and he heard himself groan. "Come on," she urged him, "I promise I won't let you hurt me. I promise there are pregnant women everywhere around the world, making love just like this, right this very minute...."

Her long, slow movements brought him almost entirely out of her before he glided deeply back in.

And it was then, as Cowboy pushed himself up to meet her in this, the sweetest of dances, that he knew the truth at last.

He wanted to come home to this woman every night for the rest of his life.

He wanted forever, and he knew that that forever with Melody would be as fascinating and endlessly exciting as his future with the SEALs, because, bottom line—he loved her.

He *loved* her.

And he knew right at that moment that in Paris, when Melody had kissed him goodbye and told him not to write, not to call, not to see her anymore, she'd been both very, very wrong *and* very, very right. She had been wrong in not giving them a chance to be together. She had been wrong not to let their passion deepen. But she had been right when she'd told him that real love was so much more than the hot flood of lust and relief. Because while his feelings for her had been born of danger and attraction and the powerful rush of being trusted and needed so desperately, it wasn't until he was here, in everyday, average Appleton, U.S.A., that those feelings had truly started to grow.

He loved her, but not because she needed him. In fact, one of the reasons he loved her so very much was because she refused to need him.

He loved her laughter, her point-blank honesty, her gentle kindness. He loved the faraway look she would get in her eyes when she felt their baby kick. He loved the fierceness with which she supported her sister. He loved the sheer courage it must have taken for her to stand up in front of the conservative Ladies' Club of Appleton to announce her pregnancy. He loved sitting on her back porch and talking to her.

He loved the heavenly blue of her eyes and the sweetness of her smile.

And he especially loved making love to her.

"Oh, Harlan," she breathed as he felt her release, and he knew without a single doubt that he would indeed forever associate sheer pleasure with his name.

He'd been clinging rather desperately to the edge of the cliff that controlled his own release, and as Melody gripped him tighter, as he filled his hands with her breasts, he felt himself go into free fall, felt the dizzying, weightless drop.

And then he exploded in slow motion. Fireballs of pleasure rocketed through him, scorching him, making him cry out.

Melody kissed him, and the sweetness of her mouth took him even further.

And then, with Melody's hands in his hair, with her head on his shoulder, with their unborn child resting between them, Cowboy began his ascent back to the surface of reality.

He was leaving in the morning. She didn't want to marry him, didn't need him, didn't love him. There were no decompression stops, although he wasn't sure it would have mattered either way. There wasn't anything he could have done to protect himself from the painful truth.

As much as he wanted her, she'd be happier without him.

Melody rolled off him, then snuggled next to him, drawing up the covers. "Please hold me," she murmured.

Lt. Harlan Jones pulled her in close, fitting their bodies together like spoons.

He would hold her tonight. But tomorrow, he would let her go. He knew he could do it. He'd done impossibly difficult things before.

He was a U.S. Navy SEAL.

CHAPTER FIFTEEN

ALPHA SQUAD WAS back in Virginia. Someone at the base apparently disapproved of the SEALs' disagreement with FinCOM, because the Quonset hut to which they'd been reassigned was several very healthy steps down from the first one they'd been given. And *that* had been no palace.

As Cowboy went inside, the door creaked on rusty hinges and a spider damn near landed on his head. He could see daylight through part of the corrugated-metal roof.

Whatever top brass had placed them here hadn't simply disapproved of their disagreement with FinCOM—he no doubt disapproved of SEALs in general. But that was no big surprise. This wasn't the first time they'd run into narrow-minded thinking.

Wes was on the phone. "Computers and rain don't mix, sir," he was saying. His tone implied that *sir* was merely a substitution for another, far less flattering word. "We have close to half a dozen computers we need up and running, plus a series of holes in the roof that will not only make it very chilly, *but,* when it starts to rain—which according to the forecast will happen within the next few hours—will make it very wet in here. As a matter of fact, there are already several permanent-looking puddles on the floor. Sir."

Built during World War II, this place looked as if it hadn't been used since the Vietnam conflict.

"We've been waiting on that request for a week, sir. Meanwhile, our computers are still in their boxes and we're sitting here with our thumbs up our—"

Joe Cat and Blue were on the other side of the gloomy room, deep in discussion.

"Well, *yippee-yi-oh-kai-ay!* Look who's back!" Cowboy looked up to see Lucky O'Donlon grinning down at him through the biggest hole in the roof.

Harvard was up there, too. "Get your butt up here, Junior. Aren't you some kind of expert when it comes to fixing roofs?"

"No—"

"Well, you are now. You're always claiming that with a little time and a library, you can learn to do anything. Here's your chance to prove it. And if that's not a compelling enough reason, how about this? As last man back from leave, you've won yourself the honor."

"Jones. Welcome back."

Cowboy turned to see Joe Cat coming toward him. He shook his captain's hand. "Thank you, sir."

Wes hung up the phone with a crash. "No go, Skipper. Apparently, there's no other location for us on the entire base."

Bobby joined them, bristling. "This place is huge. That's a load of—"

"Hey, I'm just saying what they told me." Wes shrugged. "We can request repairs, but it's got to go through channels and you know what that means. We'll still be able to stargaze from our desks three weeks from now."

"I say we forget about channels and fix this place ourselves," Lucky called down from his perch on the roof.

"I'm for that, too, Cat," Harvard chimed in. "We can get the job done better in a fraction of the time."

Cowboy squinted up at the roof. "Can we patch it, or will we have to replace the whole damn thing?" This was good. He could get into the distraction of creative problem solving. It would take his mind off the woman he'd left behind in Appleton, Massachusetts.

Melody hadn't thrown herself at his feet and begged him not to go. She'd only taken a few minutes away from the frantic housecleaning she was helping Brittany do in anticipation of a visit from Social Services. Britt's request to adopt Andy Marshall was actually being considered. Melody had been so focused on Britt's need to make everything as perfect as possible, she'd barely noticed when he left.

She'd kissed him goodbye and told him to be careful. And then she'd gone back to work.

Cowboy had passed a billboard advertising Ted Shepherd's candidacy for state representative on his way out of town. The man's pasty face, enlarged to a giant size, made him feel sick with jealousy. He'd had to look away, unable to gaze into the man's average brown eyes, unable to deal with the thought that this could well be the man Melody would spend her life with. This could be the man who would raise Cowboy's child as his own.

If he'd had a grenade launcher in his luggage, he would have blown the damn billboard to bits.

"Jones, I understand congratulations are in order." Joe Cat slapped Cowboy's back, bringing him abruptly back to the present. "When's the big day?"

The big...?

"Yeah, you gonna invite us to the wedding?" Lucky asked. "Damn, I feel like singing a verse of 'Sunrise,

Sunset.' I can't believe our little Cowboy is actually old enough to tie the knot."

"You want us to wear dress whites, or should we cammy up?" Wes asked. "Dress whites are more traditional, but the camouflage gear would probably go better with the shotgun accessories."

Beside him, Bobby broke into a chorus of "Love Child."

Cowboy shook his head. "You guys are wrong—"

"Yeah, you know, that's probably the only way *I'm* going to go," Lucky said. "Trapped in the corner with no way out."

"Yo, Diana Ross," Harvard called from the roof. "S-squared."

Bobby obediently sat down and shut up.

"The rest of you guys back off," Harvard continued. "Junior's doing the right thing here. Maybe if you pay attention, you might actually learn something from his fine example."

Cowboy looked up at Harvard through the hole in the roof. "But I'm not marrying her, H." He looked around at the other guys. "I'm going to be a father in a few weeks, but I'm not getting married."

Blue McCoy, a man of few words, was the first to break the silence. He looked around at the rest of Alpha Squad. "This just goes to show we should learn to mind our own business." He turned to Cowboy. "I'm sorry, Jones," he said quietly.

But Wes couldn't keep his mouth shut. "Sorry?" he squeaked. "How could you be sorry? Jones's luck is rocketing off the scale. In fact, the way I see it, O'Donlon's just lost the right to his nickname. From now on, I'm calling *Jones* Lucky."

Cowboy shook his head, unable to respond, unable

even to force a smile. By all rights, he should have been agreeing with them and celebrating his freedom, but instead he felt as if part of him would never feel like celebrating again. "I'm gonna go check out this roof," he told Joe Cat.

The captain had a way of looking at a man that made him feel as if he could see clear through all the bull and camouflage to the heart and soul that lay beneath. He was looking at Cowboy that way right now.

"I'm sorry, too, kid," he said before nodding and dismissing him.

Cowboy escaped out the door, searching for the easiest way up to the curving metal roof. There was a drainpipe on the southwest corner of the building that looked pretty solid. In fact, as he approached, Lucky was using it to climb down.

"Kudos to you, Jones," he said, wiping the remnants of rust from his hands onto his pants. "How about getting together tonight over a cold beer? You could share the secrets of your success." His smile turned knowing. "I remember that girl, Melody. She was something else. And she was on top of you like a dog in heat right from the word go, wasn't she?"

Something inside Cowboy snapped, and snapped hard. He knocked Lucky down into the dust. "Just shut the hell up!"

Lucky was instantly on his feet, crouched and ready in a combat stance. "What the—"

Cowboy rushed him again, and this time Lucky was ready for his attack. They landed together, hard, in the dirt. Cowboy's elbow hit a rock and he welcomed the pain that shot through him. It was sharp and sweet, and it masked the pain in his heart.

But Lucky didn't want to fight. He kneed Cowboy hard

in the stomach. While Cowboy was struggling to regain his breath, Lucky scrambled free. "You crazy bastard! What the hell's wrong with you?"

Cowboy pulled himself to his feet, breathing hard, moving menacingly toward the other SEAL. "I warned you if you bad-mouthed her again, I'd kill you."

Wes had stuck his head out the door to see what was causing the commotion. "Senior Chief!" he bellowed after taking one quick look.

Harvard was across the roof and down that drainpipe in a flash. "Back off," he shouted to Cowboy, stepping directly between the two men. "Just back off! Do you hear me, Jones? You hit him again, and your butt is going to be in deep trouble!"

Cowboy stood, bent over, hands on his knees, still catching his breath.

Harvard turned and glared at Wesley and Bobby, who both stood watching by the door. "This doesn't concern you!"

They disappeared back inside.

"What the *hell* is this about?" Harvard asked, looking from Cowboy to Lucky.

"Beats me, H." Lucky brushed dirt from his shoulder. "The psycho here jumped me."

Harvard fixed his obsidian glare on Cowboy. "Junior, you have something to say?"

Cowboy lifted his head. "Only that if O'Donlon so much as breathes Melody's name again, I'll put him in the hospital."

"Damn, I feel like a kindergarten teacher," Harvard muttered, turning back to Lucky. "O'Donlon, were you really stupid enough to be dissing his woman?"

"His *woman...?*" Lucky was genuinely confused and not entirely unamused. "Jones, you just got through telling us that you're not going to marry…the one who shall remain nameless because I don't want to have to put *you* in the hospital."

Harvard swore pungently. "It's obvious that right here we've got a live showing of *Dumb and Dumber, Part Two.*"

"I don't get it," Lucky said to Cowboy. "If you're so hot for this girl, why the hell aren't you marrying her?"

Cowboy straightened up. "Because she doesn't want me," he said quietly, all of his anger and frustration stripped away, leaving only the hurt behind. God, it hurt. He looked at Harvard. "H., I tried, but…she doesn't want me." To his absolute horror, tears filled his eyes.

And for maybe the first time in his entire life, Lucky was silent. He didn't try to make a joke. Harvard looked at the blond-haired SEAL. "Jones and I are going take a walk. That okay with you, O'Donlon?"

Lucky nodded. "Yeah, that's uh… Yeah, Senior Chief."

Harvard didn't say another word until they'd walked halfway across the exercise field. By then, thank God, Cowboy had regained his composure.

"Jones, I have to start by apologizing to you," Harvard told him. "This whole snafu's my fault. I told the guys you were going to marry this girl. I guess I just assumed you'd do whatever you had to, to convince her that marrying you is the right thing. Which leads me to my main point. I'm honestly surprised at you, Junior. I've never known you to quit."

Cowboy stopped walking. "Bottom line, what do I really have to offer her? Thirty days of leave a year." He swore. "I grew up with a father who was never there. With only thirty days each year, there's no use pretending I could be any kind of a real father to my kid—or a real husband to Melody. This way, we're all being honest. I'll be the guy who comes to visit a few times a year. And Mel will hook up with someone else. Someone who'll be there for her *all* the time."

Harvard was shaking his head. "You've talked yourself into believing this is a lose-lose situation, haven't you? Open your eyes and look around you, boy. Your captain's in the exact same boat. It's true Veronica and his kid miss him when he's gone, but with a little effort, they're making the situation work."

"Yeah, but Veronica is willing to travel. I couldn't ask Melody to leave Appleton. It's her home. She loves it there."

"Junior, you can't afford *not* to ask."

Cowboy shook his head. "She doesn't want me," he said again. "She wants an average guy, not a SEAL."

"Well, there I can't help you," Harvard said. "Because even if you quit the units tomorrow, you're never going to be mistaken for an average guy."

Quit the units tomorrow...

He could do that. He could quit. He could move to Massachusetts, set up permanent residence in that tent outside Melody's house....

But he didn't want to quit. Except that was exactly what he'd done. Harvard was right. In what could possibly be the most important fight of his life—the fight to win Melody—he'd surrendered far too easily.

He should have told her he loved her before he left. He should be there right now, down on his knees, still telling her that he loved her, telling her that this time it was real. No matter what she said, he knew it was real. And she loved him, too. He'd seen it in her eyes, tasted it in her kisses, heard it in her laughter.

Yeah, she might not know it yet, but she definitely

loved him. He should have realized it a full day ago, from the way she'd held him so tightly up at the quarry.

Cowboy looked at Harvard. "I've got to go back to Massachusetts right away. A weekend. That's all I need. Just two and a half days."

Harvard laughed. "Come on. I'll go with you. We'll go talk to Joe."

"Thank you, Senior Chief."

"Don't thank me yet, Junior."

JOE CATALANOTTO SIGHED. "I can't do it, Jones. It's going to have to wait a week or so." He gestured to the television in the corner of his office. "I've been monitoring a situation in South America for the past day and a half. A plane's been hijacked. Two hundred forty-seven people on board." Sure enough, the TV was tuned to CNN. "Any minute now, this phone's gonna ring, and Alpha Squad's going to be ordered over to Venezuela to help create order out of chaos." He shook his head. "I'm sorry, kid. I need you with the team. Best I can tell you is to let your fingers do the walking. Make a phone visit, but do it now. Get your gear ready to go, too. Because once we get the word to move, there won't be time."

Cowboy nodded. "And if you're wrong, sir?"

Cat laughed. "If I'm wrong, I'll give you an entire week. But I'm not wrong."

As if to prove his point, the telephone rang.

Cowboy scrambled for the door. He threw it open and made a dash for the nearest telephone. He punched in his calling-card number and then Melody's number. Please, God, let her be home. Please, God...

The phone rang once, twice, three times. All around him, he could hear the sounds of Alpha Squad getting

ready to move. On the fourth ring, the answering machine
picked up.

"Come on, Cowboy!" Wes shouted. "You don't even
have your gear together yet!"

Brittany's recorded voice came on, followed by the
beep.

"Melody, it's me, Jones." God, he had no clue what to
say. "I just wanted to tell you—"

Beep. Damn, he paused too long and the answering
machine, mistaking his silence for a disconnected line,
had cut him off.

"Come on, Cowboy! Move!"

"I love you!" he shouted into the receiver. *That* was
what he should have said. KISS. Keep it simple. Bottom
line. But it was too late to call her back.

Cowboy hung up the phone with a curse.

MELODY WAS DREAMING. She knew she was dreaming
because Jones was with her, and they were back in the
Middle East, hiding from the soldiers who were patrolling the city.

"Close your eyes," Jones told her. "Keep breathing,
shallowly, softly. They won't see us. I promise."

Her heart was pounding, but his arm was around her,
and she knew at the very least, if she died, she wouldn't
die alone.

"I love you," she whispered, afraid if she didn't say it
now, she'd never get the chance.

He motioned for her to be silent, but it was too late.
One of the soldiers had heard her, then turned and fired
his gun. The bullet slammed into her with wrenching
force. Pain exploded in her abdomen.

The baby! Dear God, she'd been shot, and they'd hit
the baby.

Her legs felt wet with blood, but Jones was fighting the enemy soldiers. He was firing his own gun, driving them away.

Another knife blade of pain seared through her, and she cried out.

Jones turned toward her, touching her, and his hands came away red with her blood.

He looked at her and his eyes were so green, even in the darkness. "Wake up," he said. "Honey, you've got to wake up."

Melody opened her eyes to see the first dim light of dawn creeping in through her windows. She'd been so tired last night, she hadn't even taken the time to draw the curtains.

Pain knifed through her, real pain, the same pain she'd dreamed. She gasped, turning to reach for the lamp on her bedside table. She switched it on, and with shock realized that her hands had left behind a smear of blood.

She was bleeding.

She pulled back the covers to see that her nightgown and the sheets below were stained bright red.

Brittany was still at work. She wouldn't be home until after seven.

Pain made the room spin.

"Jones!"

But Jones wasn't there to help her, either. Melody didn't know *where* Jones was. He'd called and left a message on the machine over two weeks ago. She'd tried to call him back, but was told he was unavailable and would remain that way for an undetermined amount of time.

He was out of touch on some mission, risking his life doing God knows what. She'd spent the past two weeks scared to death and kicking herself for not being honest with him. She should have told him that she loved him while she had the chance.

Please, God, keep him safe. Every time Melody thought about him, she said that silent prayer.

The pain gripped her again, and she cried out. God, what was happening? This wasn't labor. She wasn't supposed to *bleed* when she went into labor....

Her door was pushed open. "Mel?"

Brittany. Thank God, she'd gotten home from work early.

"Oh, dear Lord!" Brittany saw the blood on the sheets. She picked up the phone, dialed 911, smoothed back Melody's hair, feeling her forehead, checking her eyes. "Sweetie, when did the bleeding start?"

"I don't know. I was sleeping...God!" The pain made her see stars. "Britt, the baby! What's happening with the baby?"

But Brittany spoke into the phone, rattling off their address. "We need an ambulance here stat. I've got a twenty-five-year-old woman in the ninth month of her first pregnancy, experiencing severe abdominal pain and hemorrhaging."

Melody closed her eyes. Please, God, keep both Jones and her baby safe and alive...

"Yes, I'm a nurse," Brittany responded. "I suspect placental abruption. We'll need fetal monitors and an ultrasound ready and waiting at the hospital. Yes. I'll have the door open. Just get here!"

"JONES, YOU BETTER get down here." Harvard's voice sounded tight and grim over the telephone line. "There's a stack of messages for you that's four inches high."

Cowboy's heart leaped. "From Melody?"

"Junior, just get *down* here."

Fear flickered inside him. "H., what's the deal? Is Mel all right? Did she have the baby?"

"I don't know for sure. It looks as if the first few messages are from Melody, but the rest... Jones, Mel's sister has been calling nearly every hour for the past two days. I recommend you get down here and call her back ASAP. She's left a number at the hospital."

A number at the hospital. Cowboy didn't even say goodbye. He hung up the phone and ran.

The temporary barracks he was sharing with the other unmarried members of the team were a good half mile from the leaky-roofed Quonset hut that housed Alpha Squad's office. Cowboy was still wearing his clunky leather boots and his heavy camouflage gear, but he covered the distance in a small handful of minutes.

As he burst through the door, Harvard handed him both the pile of messages and a telephone. The sheer number of message slips was enough to terrify him. Brittany had, literally, called every hour on the hour since early Monday morning.

Cowboy's hands were shaking so badly, he had to dial the number twice. Harvard had backed away, giving him privacy. He sat down at the desk, shuffling through the pile of messages as, up in the County Hospital in Appleton, Massachusetts, the phone was ringing.

"Hello?"

It was Brittany's voice. She sounded hoarse and worn-out.

"Britt, it's Jones."

"Thank God."

"Please tell me she's safe." Cowboy closed his eyes.

"She's safe." Brittany's voice broke. "For now. Jones, you've got to come up here and talk her into having a C-section. I think one of the reasons she's refusing to do it is because she promised you that you could be here when the baby was born."

"But she's not due for another two and a half weeks."

"She had a partial placental abruption," Brittany told him. "That's when the placenta becomes partially separated from the uterus—"

"I know what it is," he said, cutting her off. "Did she hemorrhage?"

"Yes. Early Monday morning. It wasn't as bad as I first thought, though. She was taken by ambulance to the hospital and her doctor managed to get her stabilized. Both she and the baby are being monitored. If there's the slightest change in either of their conditions, they're going to *have* to do a C-section. She *knows* that. But right now, the doctor has told her that the baby's in no real danger, and she's determined to hold on as long as possible."

Cowboy drew in a deep breath. "May I talk to her?"

"She's sleeping right now. Please, Lieutenant, I don't think she's going to agree to have this baby until you get up here. But if she starts hemorrhaging again, there's no guarantee that this time they'll be able to get her to stop. They'll be able to save the baby, but they'll lose the mother."

Cowboy looked down at the phone messages in his hand. There were four from Melody, all dated close to the day he'd left for South America. The first three were just notices that said she'd called. The last actually had a message. It was written in quotes, and the receptionist who answered the phone had put a smiley face next to the words, "I love you."

Cowboy stood up. "Tell her our deal's off," he told Britanny. "Tell her not to wait for me to have the baby. Tell her I'll be mad as hell if I get up there and that baby's not hanging out in the hospital nursery. Tell her I'm on my way."

He hung up the phone, and Harvard silently appeared. The senior chief handed him papers signed by the captain, granting him as much personal emergency leave as he needed.

"There's an air force transport heading up to Boston in twenty minutes," Harvard told him. "I've called in some favors from some people I know—they're holding the flight for you. Bobby's out front with a jeep to drive you to the airfield."

Cowboy held up the message that Melody had left. "She loves me, H."

"This is news to you, Junior?" Harvard laughed. "Damn, I knew that last year in the Middle East." He followed Cowboy to the door. "Godspeed, Jones. My prayers are with you."

Cowboy swung himself up and into the jeep, and with a squeal of tires, he was away.

"SHE WAS GIVEN an amniocentesis so we could assess the baby's lung development." Brittany was talking in a whisper as she came into the room. Melody kept her eyes closed. "All of the tests have indicated that this baby is ready for delivery. His estimated weight clocked in at over eight pounds. But Melody insists that unless the baby is in danger, she's not going to deliver him any earlier than December 1st. You've got to convince her that her stubbornness is putting her life in danger."

"The worst part about being in the hospital is that everybody always talks about you as if you weren't in the room." Melody opened her eyes, expecting to glare up at her sister and some new doctor she'd enlisted. Instead, she found herself looking directly at Harlan

Jones. He was wearing camouflage pants and a matching shirt, and he looked as if he'd come directly from the jungle.

"Hey," he said, smiling at her, "heard you've been raising a little too much hell around here."

She recognized that smile he was giving her. It was his "I'm going to pretend everything's all right" smile. In truth, he was scared to death.

"I'm fine," she told him. As she watched, Brittany quietly left the room.

He sat down next to her. "That's not what I hear."

She forced a smile of her own. "Yeah, well, you've been talking to Nurse Doom."

He laughed. She realized he was carrying a clipboard in his hands, and he held it out to her now. "Sign these forms," he told her. "Have the C-section. It's time to stop playing games with your life."

Melody lifted her chin. "You think that's what this is? Some game? Everything I've ever read stressed the importance of carrying a baby to term. Or at least carrying for as long as possible. The baby's not in danger. I'm not in danger. I see no reason to do this."

Jones took her hand. "Do this now because until this baby is born, there *is* a risk that you will bleed to death," he said. "Do this because although the chances of that happening are very slim, so were the chances of your having a placental separation in the first place. You don't have high blood pressure. You aren't a smoker. There's no real reason why this should have happened. Do this because if you die, a very large part of me will die, too. Do this because I love you."

Melody was caught in the hypnotizing intensity of his gaze. "I guess you got my message."

"Yeah," he said. "But you only got part of mine. I had

literally ten seconds before I had to leave and I blew it. What I meant to say on your answering machine was that I want you to marry me, not for the baby's sake, but for *my* sake. Purely selfish reasons, Mel. Like, because I love you and I want to spend my life with you."

He cleared his throat. "And I was going to tell you that I knew there was a part of you that could love me, and that I was going to keep coming back to Appleton, that I was going to court you until you *did* fall in love with me. I was going to tell you that I wasn't going to quit, and that sooner or later, I'd wear you down—even if you only married me to shut me up." He handed her the clipboard. "So sign these release forms, have this baby and marry me."

Melody's heart was in her throat. "Do you really understand what you're asking me to do?"

He looked out the window at the dreary late-afternoon light. "Yeah," he said, "I do. I'm asking you to leave your home and come live with me near naval bases, moving around God only knows how many times in the course of a year. I'm asking you to give up your job, and your garden, and your sister and Andy, just to be with me, even though some of the time—hell, most of the time—I'll be gone. It's a bad deal. I don't recommend you take it. But at the same time, honey, I'm praying that you'll say yes."

Melody looked at the man sitting beside her bed. His hair was long and dirty, as if he hadn't showered in days. He smelled of gasoline and sweat and sunblock. He looked spent, as if he'd run all the way from Virginia just to be here with her.

"Trust me," he whispered, leaning close to kiss her softly. "Trust me with your heart. I'll keep it safe, I swear."

Mel closed her eyes and kissed him. Harlan Jones wasn't the average, run-of-the-mill, home-every-day-at-five-thirty type she would have chosen if the choice could be made with pure intellect. But love wasn't rational. Love didn't stick to a plan. And truth was, she loved him. She had to take the chance.

"You are going to get *so* sick of me telling you to be careful," she whispered.

"No, I'm not."

Melody signed the medical procedure consent forms. "Do you think Harvard would agree to be our best man?"

Jones took the clipboard from her hands. "I want to hear you say yes."

She gazed up at him. "Yes. I love you," she told him.

Tears filled his eyes, but his smile was pure Jones as he leaned forward and kissed her.

EPILOGUE

MELODY JONES SAT in her new backyard, watching her neighbors, her friends and her new family gather to celebrate her wedding.

It was only February, but the South was having a mild winter, and the daffodils in her garden were already in bloom.

The growing season in Virginia was at least three months longer than in Massachusetts. She loved that. She loved everything about her new life. She loved this little rented house outside the naval base where Alpha Squad was temporarily stationed. She loved waking up each morning with Jones in her bed. She loved holding their son, Tyler, in her arms as she rocked him to sleep. She even loved the late-night feedings.

Brittany sat down next to her. "The papers came through," she said. "Day before yesterday. Andy's my kid now." She laughed. "God help me."

Melody embraced her sister. "I'm so happy for you."

"And I'm so happy for you." Brittany laughed again. "I'm not sure I've ever been to a party before with so many incredible-looking men. And all those dress uniforms! I nearly fainted when I went into the church. I suppose you get used to it."

Melody grinned. "No," she said, "you don't."

Across the yard, Jones had Tyler on one shoulder. He swayed slightly to keep the baby happy as he stood talking to Harvard and his father, the admiral. As Melody watched, he laughed at something Harvard said and the baby started. Jones gently kissed the baby's head, soothing him back to sleep.

As Melody looked around her yard, she realized that Brittany was right. Nearly all of the men there were SEALs, and they were, indeed, an unusual-looking group.

Jones looked across the yard and met her eyes. The smile he gave her made her heart somersault in her chest. It was his "I love you" smile—the smile he saved for her and her alone. She smiled back at him, knowing he could read her love for him as clearly in her eyes.

Despite her best intentions, she had gone and married the least everyday, ordinary, average man that she'd ever known. No indeed, there was absolutely nothing normal about a man called "Cowboy" Jones. He was one hundred percent out of the ordinary—and so was his incredible love for her.

And she wouldn't have it any other way.

* * * * *

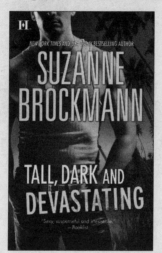

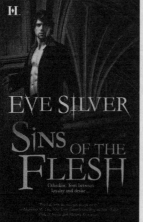

REQUEST YOUR
FREE BOOKS!
2 FREE NOVELS PLUS 2 FREE GIFTS!

HARLEQUIN®

nocturne™

Dramatic and Sensual Tales of Paranormal Romance.

YES! Please send me 2 FREE Harlequin® Nocturne™ novels and my 2 FREE gifts (gifts are worth about $10). After receiving them, if I don't wish to receive any more books, I can return the shipping statement marked "cancel." If I don't cancel, I will receive 4 brand-new novels every other month and be billed just $4.47 per book in the U.S. or $4.99 per book in Canada. That's a saving of at least 15% off the cover price! It's quite a bargain! Shipping and handling is just 50¢ per book.* I understand that accepting the 2 free books and gifts places me under no obligation to buy anything. I can always return a shipment and cancel at any time. Even if I never buy another book from Harlequin, the two free books and gifts are mine to keep forever.

238/338 HDN E9M2

Name   (PLEASE PRINT)

Address   Apt. #

City   State/Prov.   Zip/Postal Code

Signature (if under 18, a parent or guardian must sign)

Mail to the **Reader Service:**
IN U.S.A.: P.O. Box 1867, Buffalo, NY 14240-1867
IN CANADA: P.O. Box 609, Fort Erie, Ontario L2A 5X3
Not valid for current subscribers to Harlequin Nocturne books.

Want to try two free books from another line?
Call 1-800-873-8635 or visit www.ReaderService.com.

* Terms and prices subject to change without notice. Prices do not include applicable taxes. N.Y. residents add applicable sales tax. Canadian residents will be charged applicable provincial taxes and GST. Offer not valid in Quebec. This offer is limited to one order per household. All orders subject to approval. Credit or debit balances in a customer's account(s) may be offset by any other outstanding balance owed by or to the customer. Please allow 4 to 6 weeks for delivery. Offer available while quantities last.

Your Privacy: Harlequin Books is committed to protecting your privacy. Our Privacy Policy is available online at www.ReaderService.com or upon request from the Reader Service. From time to time we make our lists of customers available to reputable third parties who may have a product or service of interest to you. If you would prefer we not share your name and address, please check here. ☐

Help us get it right—We strive for accurate, respectful and relevant communications. To clarify or modify your communication preferences, visit us at www.ReaderService.com/consumerschoice.

HN10

SUZANNE BROCKMANN

77516	TALL, DARK AND DANGEROUS	___ $7.99 U.S.	___ $9.99 CAN.
77471	NOWHERE TO RUN	___ $7.99 U.S.	___ $9.99 CAN.
77336	HERO UNDER COVER	___ $7.99 U.S.	___ $7.99 CAN.

(limited quantities available)

TOTAL AMOUNT	$ _____
POSTAGE & HANDLING	$ _____
($1.00 FOR 1 BOOK, 50¢ for each additional)	
APPLICABLE TAXES*	$ _____
TOTAL PAYABLE	$ _____

(check or money order—please do not send cash)

To order, complete this form and send it, along with a check or money order for the total above, payable to HQN Books, to: **In the U.S.:** 3010 Walden Avenue, P.O. Box 9077, Buffalo, NY 14269-9077; **In Canada:** P.O. Box 636, Fort Erie, Ontario, L2A 5X3.

Name: _____

Address: _____ City: _____

State/Prov.: _____ Zip/Postal Code: _____

Account Number (if applicable): _____

075 CSAS

*New York residents remit applicable sales taxes.
*Canadian residents remit applicable GST and provincial taxes.

HQN™

We *are* romance™

www.HQNBooks.com